House of Orphans

House of Orphans

HELEN DUNMORE

FIG TREE
an imprint of
PENGUIN BOOKS

FIG TREE

Published by the Penguin Group
Penguin Books Ltd, 80 Strand, London WC2R ORL, England
Penguin Group (USA) Inc., 375 Hudson Street, New York, New York 10014, USA
Penguin Group (Canada), 90 Eglinton Avenue East, Suite 700, Toronto, Ontario, Canada M4P 3YZ
(a division of Pearson Penguin Canada Inc.)
Penguin Ireland, 25 St Stephen's Green, Dublin 2, Ireland (a division of Penguin Books Ltd)
Penguin Group (Australia), 250 Camberwell Road,
Camberwell, Victoria 3124, Australia (a division of Pearson Australia Group Pty Ltd)
Penguin Books India Pvt Ltd, 11 Community Centre,
Panchsheel Park, New Delhi – 110 017, India
Penguin Group (NZ), cnr Airborne and Rosedale Roads, Albany, Auckland 1310, New Zealand
(a division of Pearson New Zealand Ltd)
Penguin Books (South Africa) (Pty) Ltd, 24 Sturdee Avenue,
Rosebank, Johannesburg 2196, South Africa

Penguin Books Ltd, Registered Offices: 80 Strand, London WC2R ORL, England

www.penguin.com

First published 2006
3

Copyright © Helen Dunmore, 2006

The moral right of the author has been asserted

Set in 12/14.75pt Monotype Dante
Typeset by Palimpsest Book Production Limited
Polmont, Stirlingshire
Printed in Great Britain by Clays Ltd, St Ives plc

A CIP catalogue record for this book is available from the British Library

ISBN Hardback 0-670-91451-7
Trade paperback 0-670-91452-5

for Frank

I

Finland, 1902

Each winter there was an outbreak of fever at the House of Orphans. Each year Anna-Liisa took fright as the number of cases increased, and sent for Dr Eklund. He knew she had a terror of typhus, from living through an epidemic as a child. No matter how often he reassured her, she fired off notes with URGENT sprawled over them in a flourish of capitals.

So he came. Some matrons wouldn't trouble to write those notes, or get a doctor to the children. Let sickness flourish, if it was God's will. They'd rather balance the books than pay for medicine. He didn't charge for his attendance; never had. It wasn't charity, but plain good sense. A crowd of children, packed together, poorly fed even though Anna-Liisa did her best: of course they were wide open to infection.

He knew of orphanages where part of the children's food was kept back to sell for profit, but Anna-Liisa was honest. The children had what belonged to them. They had porridge and black bread, skimmed milk and a bit of cheese, soup . . . In summer they foraged for berries and mushrooms, like everyone else.

It wasn't enough to nourish them. The food was scant, and the weakest didn't even get their share. A toddler with mouth ulcers needed his hard bread softened in hot water, but that wasn't going to happen unless one of the big girls took a fancy to him. He'd be left to moan and cry and spit his bread away, and get a slap for waste. The big ones stole porridge from the little ones' plates and got away with it. Anna-Liisa was decent enough but she wasn't sharp. Or maybe she didn't want to antagonize the big ones, who did most of the household work.

They had no one to look out for them, these kids with their flat, tired faces. Inheritors of TB and syphilis and God knows what else. The House of Orphans was as potent a site for infection as he could imagine, and set slap-bang in the middle of town too. They hadn't hidden their orphanage away, like a dirty secret. Maybe they were proud of it. He was glad that he lived six miles outside town, in the forest. He didn't have to pass the House of Orphans every day.

The children came in from miles around, off farms which had broken their parents' health, from villages where you still had a chance of marrying off a girl as long as you could get rid of the product of her shame, and even from as far away as Helsingfors these days. The new theory was that if you removed a child from the tainted atmosphere of city life to the purity of the country-side, there was a better chance of that child turning out a well-trained, biddable domestic servant or farm worker, rather than a prostitute or a criminal.

And with so much emigration going on, families were in con-fusion as never before. A child might get left behind in Helsingfors with its grandmother. The plan might be to bring it over to America once the family was settled. But then the grandmother died, or things in America went wrong, or there was illness that couldn't be paid for . . .

It was always a long story that brought a child here. The House of Orphans was a stone block of a building, gaunt, but solid and well maintained. He couldn't stop himself looking it over apprais-ingly every time he visited, as if he were somehow responsible for a leaking roof or warped window frame.

The crust of snow was a foot thick, but it was softening and it had a greyish tinge. The first melt was ticking off the eaves, drop by drop. It would freeze again tonight, but the process had begun. The long thaw that's half feared and half desired. All it would reveal at first was scoured brown grass and mud, but then every-thing would begin. Lilac buds would fatten and birds would shriek and squabble in the bushes, tumbling over and over in the tumult of mating. Sharp, sparse threads of green would push through the brown. You had to face it every year, and then you got used to it.

The sight of everything that the snow hides; everything that's flawed or damaged and needs work.

Well, it's got to happen, he thought. Tick, tick, tick went the meltwater into the snow. Its surface was pitted all over where the drops had sunk in. He raised his hand to the bellpull.

It would be the first time he saw the girl, without even noticing her much. This is the way it happened.

He went upstairs to the long low attic room where Anna-Liisa had put the sick children together, away from the rest, for fear of contagion. There were eight beds in a row. Anna-Liisa swished into the room before him. 'Hush now! Stop that crying! The doctor's come to see you. He'll make you better, if you're good.'

But the crying didn't stop. It came from a very young child who lay on her back, knees drawn up to her chest. Her eyes were shut. He went over to her, drew down the sheet, gently moved her knees. She cried harder as he examined the swollen stomach, the rash, the quick, low pulse in her wrist. Her skin was hot and dry and she had defecated onto the pad of flannel beneath her. Her faeces were no more than thin, evil-smelling liquid. Her eyes were set in shadowy hollows. Gently, he pinched her cheek.

'She needs water,' he said. 'Will she drink?'

'No,' said Anna-Liisa. 'She can't hold her cup and there's nobody to sit with her. I try when I've a moment.'

'Bring me a spoon. A small one. A salt spoon is big enough.'

He lifted the child's head. Her hair was matted and it smelled of mice. It ought to have been cut, but Anna-Liisa didn't follow the practice of shearing orphans' hair. He pushed the child's hair back from her face and brought the salt spoon to her cracked lips. A little water went in, then rolled away from the corner of her mouth. Anna-Liisa was right, the child needed someone to sit with her. Without such help, she would probably die. But it wasn't necessary for her to die.

He became aware of movement at the far end of the long room. He turned. A girl of twelve or thirteen was sweeping with a broom that was too long for her. She brushed energetically, in and out of the little beds.

3

'What is that girl doing in here?'

'You know, Dr Eklund, you told me it was important to keep everything clean –'

'Yes, but that girl should not be here. She'll fall sick herself.'

'But she has already had the sickness. She was one of the first. She recovered in a couple of days. She doesn't look it, but she's strong.'

He looked at the girl more closely, and, as if she were aware of his interest, she began to brush even more vigorously. She stooped to a dish of water, took a handful and scattered drops onto the boards to settle the dust. She seized her broom again and thrust it under one of the beds. A thin child, but she seemed unusually energetic for an orphan.

'I haven't seen her before, have I?'

'Surely you have. She's been with us a year or more, since they sent her to us from Helsinki,' added Anna-Liisa in her significant manner, which often turned out to mean nothing.

An idea struck him.

'Come here,' he called to the girl. 'Yes, you. Put down that broom.'

She propped her broom against the wall, glancing at Anna-Liisa first to be sure she was doing the right thing. She came towards him, wiping her hands on her apron. Grey skirt, rough calico apron and cap, the heavy boots that Anna-Liisa got in bulk at a special price and which never fitted properly. The orphans wrapped rags around their feet like Russian soldiers. She looked just like the rest of them, but he'd known immediately that he hadn't seen her before. It was the way she moved, which was quick and free, as if she hadn't learned to walk like an orphan yet.

'That's right. Come closer. Don't be afraid.'

But she didn't look afraid at all. Her skin was pale, her nose and cheekbones sharp. She looked straight at him. Her eyes were pale green and without expression, as if she already knew how to mask herself against intrusion.

'She can sit here, by the bed, and give water to this child,' he said to Anna-Liisa. 'Look,' he told the girl, 'this is what you must do.' He lifted the sick child's head again. 'Hold the spoon like this. Touch her lips gently, just here. She will open her mouth. Give her a very small amount of water each time, or she'll vomit. Can you do that? Are you patient enough?'

The girl nodded.

'And she's dirty. Can you change the flannel, and wash her?'

'They're all dirty,' commented the girl. 'All of them. They all need changing.'

He couldn't tell if she meant that since all were dirty, there was no point cleaning just one, or if she was telling him that since one was to be cared for, then all should be. But he felt a power in her, as if he had to answer her.

'I know,' he said. 'We'll do what we can.'

'They all had their flannels changed this morning,' said Anna-Liisa defensively. 'Sirkka is down there boiling them up in the copper. As fast as you wash their bedding, it's dirty again.'

He nodded, pleased. He had told her last winter to boil the flannels and bedding, and she'd remembered.

'She's crying because it hurts,' observed the girl suddenly, watching the sick child. 'It's her stomach, that's where the pain grips her. I know what to do.' And she bent down and began to rub the swollen stomach with a light, circular motion. 'You rub like this, see, and it warms her. It doesn't hurt so much then.'

'Yes, do that too,' he said. It was true, the child was growing calmer. Her cries sank to a thin moan. It wasn't the warmth that soothed her, but the girl's touch.

'Give her water as often as you can. Keep her clean and rub her like that if it helps. Tomorrow we'll try a little sugar-water.'

The girl nodded. She knelt beside the little bed, with the salt spoon in her hand.

'Is there a stool that could be brought here?' he asked Anna-Liisa. 'If she's going to nurse that child, she'll need to sit by the bed.'

He went around the room, from one bed to the next. The rest of them would do, he thought. They were sick and wretched, but they would survive it. All of them were taking water. They seemed indifferent to each other, staring at the ceiling or curled up in a

5

stupor. The same matted hair, the same crusts of yellow around the eyes, the same yellowish pallor.

'They've had their porridge this morning, those that would take it,' said Anna-Liisa.

'Good. I'll get a nurse sent in. There's more work than you can manage here. The Board will cover the cost.'

She looked at him gratefully. Maybe she guessed that he would pay for the nurse out of his own pocket, but it was better if nothing was said. Anna-Liisa preferred the idea of the Board's approval. She liked things to be done in a proper manner. And if you started to think of where your personal duty to these children might lie, where would it end?

It would end in my not visiting them, he thought. It would end in not seeing them at all, to save my fine feelings. Anna-Liisa works with them, eats with them, sleeps with them. She does what she can.

'And how is Mrs Eklund?' asked Anna-Liisa respectfully, as she saw him out.

'She's perfectly well, thank you,' he said mechanically, but the words scratched in his mind as he said them, because he knew they were not true. In her angry way his wife was a brave woman. She said nothing to him, but sometimes he knew she was in pain. She wrote long letters to her daughter, their daughter; and she stared at him with challenging eyes if he came into the room while she was writing.

If they'd still slept in the same bed he would have known everything. He'd have smelled the nature of her sickness on her skin and in her sweat as she slept. He'd have seen the signs and changes that he knew she was keeping from him. She'd sent her clothes to be altered, he knew that. She had lost weight, these past months. Tendons stood out on her neck, and her wrists looked big and clumsy as her flesh shrank away.

She slept in the bedroom along the corridor now, in Minna's old room. Sometimes at night he woke and went to his bedroom door and opened it silently, to stare down the corridor towards the room where Johanna now slept. He thought he heard her walking to and fro, to and fro. But the door of Minna's old room stayed shut.

'Did you sleep well, my dear?' he'd asked her in the morning.

'Of course. Haven't I always slept well?'

'You'd tell me if there was anything wrong?'

'Of course. Why ever shouldn't I? You're a doctor, after all,' she said with cold emphasis on the word 'doctor'.

Why had he called her 'my dear'? No wonder she looked at him like that. She was a brave woman. She had never cried out when Minna was born. He'd wanted her to cry out, to ease her suffering, but she wouldn't. He'd never forgotten the way she glared at him when he came to stand at the bedside, impotent.

'Yes, she's well,' he said to Anna-Liisa. 'I'll call again tomorrow morning. That girl you've got – the girl who was sweeping – what's her name?'

'Eeva.'

'Give her a cup of coffee tonight, with plenty of sugar. She'll need to keep awake. If that little one lasts the night, then she has a chance.'

'They have no stamina,' said Anna-Liisa.

'They have no mothers,' he said. 'Excuse me, Anna-Liisa, that isn't a criticism of you.'

'We do what we can.'

'I know. And if you're worried tonight, send for me again.'

2

'You'll take a house in town. Of course you will.'

Lotta sounded utterly confident. This was something he'd noticed since Johanna's death. His friends seemed to know more about how he should live his life than he did. To him the future hung like one of those white sheets soaked in disinfectant over the doorway of a room where there is infectious disease. But Lotta saw a map with clear directions.

'Will I?'

'If you have any sense, you will. You'll give up this barn of a place. Let it out, if anyone will take it, and find yourself a house in town.'

'My dear Lotta, my house serves me perfectly well.'

She looked at him. 'No, it doesn't. You're wretched here. Prowling from room to room, not knowing what to do with yourself. And no wonder.'

'Well.' He spread his hands on the table. 'Lotta, Lotta.' Sometimes it was good to say her name like that. His oldest friend, almost.

'Yes, you're wretched,' she went on firmly. 'And the question is, how many years of misery have you got planned for yourself? You might last twenty years, Thomas.'

'It's true, I might. Twenty years – or even forty. My heart's perfect. My digestion's good. What a prospect.'

She tapped her fingers on the wood. 'You shouldn't talk like that.' She really was angry now, he could see that. She stood very upright, always the same Lotta, her shoulders back, her spine as straight as she could make it. Every morning, when she got out of bed, her pain began. The fire in her joints that he couldn't do anything about, any more than any other doctor. It would go on and on like this and no matter how many spas she visited, no matter what medicines she took, it would keep on getting worse. She knew it. And here I am, he thought, with my perfect heart and my perfect digestion, and I can still walk twenty miles if I want to.

'You ought to get out of this climate, Lotta. You've got the money. You could go to the south of France each winter. Take a house and sit in the sun, under the almond trees.'

She shook her head, as she always did.

'No. My life is here, in Finland. Nobody can have two lives. What would I do in the south of France? Besides, this is where God has placed me.'

She really believed it, he knew that. It wasn't lip service with Lotta, a bit of holy polish on a sleek life. Nor was religion, for Lotta, simply the most efficient way of stopping others from doing what they wished to do, and living the lives they might have wanted to live . . .

No. Don't think of that.

'Why do you think God has placed you here, Lotta?' He'd never asked her that before, but after a sharp look she seemed to realize it was a genuine question.

'To look after you,' she said. 'No, don't start preening yourself. You're not the only one. To look after you, and Erika, and Simon, and to make the house pleasant for the servants, and to raise money for charity, and to be bored, and to think that I can paint landscapes when I can't, and to sit with people when they're dying, and be tedious on the subject of where people choose to live and how they choose to waste their lives. And to be married to Karl.'

'How is Erika?' he asked, to divert her. Erika was her sister's child, not very happily married, but very happily the mother of Simon.

'Erika and Simon are going to St Petersburg. Frans has business there. He is being very lavish about Erika's summer wardrobe, so all's well for the time being.'

Lotta's gift is to love people while knowing what they are like, he thought. Also, he'd never seen her plump up with pleasure at anyone's misfortune.

'But we were talking about you,' said Lotta firmly. Her small, dark eyes were steady. Yes, she'd looked like that when she rose from Johanna's bedside, after Johanna died. She'd folded Johanna's hands over her breast. Minna had fallen to her knees at the bedside, her hands knotted into the sheets. She wouldn't look, she wouldn't see that her mother had died.

Thank God, Johanna's eyes had been shut. There was no need to close them. He should have gone round to the other side of the bed, raised Minna up, put his arm around her shoulders, led her away. But the space between them had been as hard as iron.

'Thomas. We were talking about you and this house. Why stay here? It's too big for you, it's in the middle of nowhere. Your friends can't call round and take you out of yourself. It will make such a difference if you move into town. One of those houses by the church would suit you perfectly. So much better than being out here on your own.'

'I like it here.'

'I know you do. But it's not good for you. You'll become –'

'What?'

'Strange. Wrapped up in yourself. *Who lives in that big old house in the forest? Oh, that's Dr Eklund's house. Nobody ever sees him. He wanders about when it's dark sometimes.*'

He laughed. 'That's not going to happen, Lotta. I've got my work. But you're right that the house is too big for me. I'm going to shut up the top floor, and move my bedroom and study downstairs. Jenny doesn't want to stay, and Kirstin'll go with her. One girl can do all the work that's necessary for a single man. The laundry will be sent out, and Matti will take care of the garden and stables as usual. There's no need for anything more.'

'It doesn't sound very cheerful.'

'I'm a widower, Lotta. It doesn't have to sound very cheerful.'

'What about Minna?'

He looked away. The catch on the window frame still hadn't been mended. Johanna had asked him about it months ago, in her cool, crisp voice that expected results. He'd forgotten. Minna and Johanna didn't forget such things.

'I don't imagine she'll be here very often, now that her mother's dead.'

Lotta was silent. She knew as well as he did that it was true.

Why has God placed you here, Lotta?

To look after you.

Lotta sat by Johanna until she died. She folded Johanna's hands. I couldn't do it. Couldn't take her hands while they were still warm and soft, and feel them unresisting as I placed them on her breast. It was too final. I felt ashamed, that Johanna lay there while I could stand up and walk away.

Johanna's breasts were beautiful. That day I came into the dining room of her father's house, and she was placed beside me. She looked down. She was wearing a dark dress, with a high round neck. Every so often she caught her breath, and her breasts rose.

I didn't know then that she caught her breath because she'd been crying upstairs for hours before dinner. She loved a little shit who'd made a fool of her, drawing her on, letting her show him her love, enjoying the excitement that not even Johanna could completely hide. He wanted her to show her love so that he could reject it. There are men like that, and women too. So she sat there with that catch in her breath, full of grief and fury that I didn't understand until months later. As often as I dared, I would glance at the fullness of her breasts under that dark material that was a little bit shiny, not very, but just enough for the light to change on it as her breasts rose and fell.

And that's why we married, Lotta, and is it any wonder that we were unhappy? I came along, and Johanna knew from the first day that I was completely crazy about those breasts and wouldn't be happy until I'd got to them. Not that she would have put it to herself as crudely as that. She married me as fast as she could, so that he would never guess – that other one – he would never know how much he'd wounded her. No one would ever, ever know and Johanna would be smiling and beautiful in her wedding dress. She would have won her victory, even if the only person who suffered from it was herself. That was the guiding principle of Johanna's life. To win, or if she couldn't win, to refuse to let her losses be known.

No, I couldn't have folded those hands on Johanna's breast. I didn't have the right, anyway. You think God has placed you here to look after me, Lotta, but you wouldn't be so confident if you knew what kind of man I am.

'So you're going to keep this house on,' said Lotta. 'All right. And you need a girl to cook and clean. One girl's going to do all that?'

'I told you. Most of the house will be shut up. I won't dine at home more than three or four times a week.'

'How depressing . . . Well, never mind. Let's think of the practicalities. Where's this girl to come from?'

'I haven't thought that far ahead, Lotta.'

'Hmm – what about the orphanage? They give them a good training there, and she won't be homesick.'

'That's a good idea,' he said slowly. That girl: Eeva. He heard the whisking of her broom on the boards. The sick child had lived. Anna-Liisa was surprised at the tenacity Eeva had shown. Not one night, but three she'd spent sitting on that little stool, spooning water into the child.

'And do you know, Dr Eklund, you'll scarcely believe it but that sick little girl has been adopted! Yes! By a good family – farmers. The wife has no children, although they've been married ten years, and she happened to see our little Annika in church one Sunday. Once the child recovered she turned out to be pretty, really very pretty. It's always the way. The pretty little girls get taken, and the boys are left behind until they're old enough to work.'

Anna-Liisa spoke with broad good humour, as if there were no questioning the ways of the world.

'So Eeva doesn't see the child any more?' he asked.

'Oh no! Bless you, why ever should she? Little Annika's got her new life now and we don't want to hold her back. They don't like to think of the child as it was *before*, you see, Doctor, living in an orphanage and all that. They like to think of it as their own, and that's fair enough, especially when it's a pretty little thing like Annika turned out to be, that any mother would be proud of.'

'I suppose you're right.'

But the girl with the broom had gone, in all likelihood. She'd have been found a place. It must be a year ago or more now; yes, Johanna was just beginning to be ill.

'There's a girl who might be suitable,' he said to Lotta. 'She would be about the right age. She seemed to have plenty of energy, and to be teachable.'

'That's all you want,' agreed Lotta. 'Better to take a girl who hasn't any experience, and shape her to your ways, than get some little madam who thinks she knows everything and won't do what she's told –'

He nodded, to stop Lotta launching into one of her favourite topics.

'I'll call on Anna-Liisa, and find out if the girl is available,' he said.

'What's her name? The girl? I might have heard of her.'

'Not very likely. She was sent up from Helsingfors under some new scheme they've got. Her first name is Eeva, but I didn't hear the surname.'

'Eeva?' Lotta tasted the name. 'Wouldn't you rather have a Swedish-speaking girl?'

He thought back, surprised. Anna-Liisa had been speaking Swedish, out of courtesy to him. And the girl had spoken Swedish too, he was sure of it.

'She speaks Swedish, and understands it too,' he said. 'Besides, I like to speak Finnish. It's in keeping with the spirit of the times,' he added, smiling. Lotta, he knew, spoke Finnish badly and was irritated by talk of fennicization. *We are Swedish Finns, as we have always been, and that's good enough for me,* she would say.

Not quite always, he wanted to say. *Didn't our ancestors come over here from Sweden sometime?* But if he joked on that subject, Lotta would flush with annoyance and retort, *Everyone came from some-where else at some time, if you go back far enough, Thomas, as you very well know. Didn't the Finnish language itself originate in India? We belong here, as much as they do.*

'Anyway, the girl has probably got a place already,' he said aloud.

But she had not, even though she was older than he'd thought. Sixteen past, said Anna-Liisa, as they sat drinking coffee. She'd turned sixteen in January. So that skinny child he'd seen sweeping the floor must have been at least fifteen. Strange that a place hadn't been found for her already.

'Yes, it *is* unusual,' said Anna-Liisa, looking fat and comfortable with secrets. 'Another cup of coffee, Dr Eklund? There are particular reasons why it was felt best for her to work for us, past the usual age. She's a hard-working girl, on the whole.' Anna-Liisa's voice trailed off dubiously, and he wondered what the parts of that whole might be. 'Yes, she's hard-working and she's quick,' went on Anna-Liisa, more definitely now, surer of her ground. 'You don't have to explain things to her twice. This past year I've been teaching her to cook and put up preserves. She can dry and pickle mushrooms, pickle cucumbers, and make jam.'

'Excellent.'

'You'll find sometimes . . . Well, Eeva likes to do things her own way. It's not that she argues, but she has a way of looking back at you which isn't right, and I've told her so many times.'

Obviously without result, he thought.

'She likes the little ones. She helps them wash and dress and make their beds. It's part of her duties.'

'I hope she won't find it too quiet. There's only Matti for the garden and the stables, and old Agneta comes up from the village to char. But they don't live in.'

'Oh no, no. Too quiet, no, that won't be a problem at all. It's a great advantage for her, Doctor – a real opportunity. There aren't many of our girls who can find a place like this, working for a doctor's household. I sent off one of our girls this morning, younger than Eeva she was, to a farm with five children under six and mud traipsed in from dawn to dusk, as you know, and there's no other servant kept. Well, it's right and proper and it's what has to be, but I'm glad to give Eeva her chance.'

'Those "particular reasons",' he said carefully. 'Is there anything I should know?'

Anna-Liisa picked out a cardamon biscuit. Her colour was high.

'There was a question of her moral welfare, back where she was in Helsinki. Helsingfors, that is,' she added hastily, deferring to his Swedishness. 'You take my meaning. There were *special considerations*. It was thought best for her to leave the city and go right away from any influences there might be. When she was put here with us I was told she wasn't to be sent out to a place until she was sixteen.'

'She's turned sixteen, you say.'

'Oh, there'll be no difficulty. Not with her going to you. It's if they go off to a farm or even a town house where there are young men hanging about. They get taken advantage of and before you know it they're bringing a baby back to mother.' Anna-Liisa gave an unexpectedly loud laugh. 'Or, since they've got no mothers, back they come to us, and the whole thing starts all over again. They say they want to keep the baby, they beg and promise all manner of things, but of course they can't. And then you've a hard job to get them fixed up in a decent place a second time. And so they drift – and like as not it happens again. You don't know whether to laugh or cry.'

'No,' he said. He looked at Anna-Liisa thoughtfully. Whatever did she really make of all this? She wasn't married. Presumably she was a virgin. And yet that laugh – as if everything that led to the making of those babies was an enormous joke in which she assumed he'd share.

'You'll be glad to know that Matti is close to fifty and has bow legs,' he said.

'She won't try anything on under *your* roof. She's an intelligent girl, I'll say that for her, she won't foul her own nest. I'll ring for her now.'

'Wait a moment,' he said sharply. He wasn't ready to see Eeva yet. Their talk of her hung in the room like dirty laundry. 'Let's get the practicalities out of the way. When she'll come. Her wages. Does she need clothes? You'll have to forgive me, I'm not used to all this. Johanna dealt with everything concerning the servants.'

'Of course. I always say, it's more difficult for the man when he finds himself alone. He's like a babe unborn.'

He leaned back, wishing he could shut his eyes. Why did he still have that feeling – soiled, uneasy – as if he'd done something wrong and that if people knew the truth they would shun him? Anna-Liisa's large, worn face was full of sympathy. She had spread a cloth on the table and offered him biscuits she'd baked herself. He knew that these half-hours taking coffee with him in the clean pallor of her little sitting room were precious to her.

Her life was work. The care of the children was only a part of it. She had to keep the Board happy, flatter her visitors, show herself loudly grateful to anyone in the town who sent a free load of wood or a bag of potatoes to the House of Orphans, make a fat farmer's wife feel like a benefactress when she took on a child to slave from dawn to dusk for half-nothing, and carry her crew of souls to the Lutheran Church twice every Sunday so that the town could judge her by their clothing, cleanliness and behaviour.

But he understood her difficulties; or at least, for some reason she thought that he did. She could confide in him about ringworm and measles outbreaks, about a child who wouldn't speak and looked away even when you framed her face with your hands, about a girl who knew every obscenity under the sun, about bereaved children who put up their arms to be carried every time they saw Anna-Liisa, when they first came. But she didn't pick them up, and soon they abandoned the habit for ever. *They have to learn, but it's hard sometimes.*

The wintry light fell on the polished wooden floor, the deep red rug, the tiled stove. Next month would be April, and spring would come. Already it was a year since he'd first known that Johanna would die. The year turns around and it can't be stopped. This year, the thought of spring's power was a relief. It would happen in spite of him. He could no more resist it than he could resist death. Its desire for new life would brush him aside, if it couldn't sweep him up with it.

But maybe it could. He could begin again. He was not so guilty that he had to lock himself away. Johanna was dead. He would make a new life. He wouldn't expect Minna to come and visit him.

He wanted to get up and walk about the room. Such a revelation, such a discovery. After death, there was life. What could be more obvious, more stupidly obvious? And yet he hadn't seen it until now, until this very minute sitting in the House of Orphans.

He would travel more, take his part in life. He would write up his cases more systematically, read the medical journals, make his contribution. Why had he fallen into believing that all the fruits of life were for other people, who were somehow more active or more suitable to receive them?

He would work in the big back sitting room, with his desk in front of the window. That would be his new study. It had the best view in the house, over a slope of lilac and birch and cherry trees, down to the deep cleft where the stream ran in summer. Soon the stream would unfreeze. He'd be startled one morning to hear the sound of water running. The first rush of water sounded so loud, then you got used to it. And beyond the stream, the forest, rising again up towards the ridge where it made a shaggy horizon. Dark now, dusty with winter, but even the spruce and larch would push out sparks of brilliant green before long. And beyond the forest, the forest. Nothing but forest eastward, whether you walked for a day or a week or a year. How happy that made him.

Johanna didn't like it. She wanted him to cut back the birches and cherry trees. They spoiled the view, she said. All these trees crowding up to the house made her feel closed in. Oppressed.

He'd taken Matti's axe and made a notch in the skin of a young birch. He was twenty years younger and stronger then. The tree was full of sap, slippery with it. He swung at it badly, hacking the trunk. The mess of it stirred his temper and he lifted the axe again, too fast, not really seeing what he was doing. It missed the notch and skidded down the trunk. Pure luck that it didn't embed itself in his foot.

'Let me do that, Doctor,' said Matti behind him. 'You aren't hardly dressed for it.'

'I'll finish it,' said Thomas. He swung again and again, bludgeoning the thing open. He'd made a mess of it. A wet, splintered mess of unripe wood. No good to anyone, but he was almost through the trunk. The branches swished and crashed and it was done. The tree fell, staggering into the branches of another birch, smashing twigs as it settled. You couldn't see where one tree ended and the other began.

'Get some men up from the village,' he said to Matti. 'All this lot has to come down. They can have the wood and I'll pay them well for the work. I'll mark the trees which are to be cleared.'

He had taken a pail of whitewash and a brush, and gone from tree to tree, marking their trunks. When he'd finished the trees stood with their white slashes, their leaves fresh and shivering. They didn't have the first idea what those white marks meant. He touched the dry bark of a cherry. Its sap was rising, it was pushing out growth with all its might, pouring energy into flower and leaf and fruit.

The raw stumps were dug up and the ground turfed over. Johanna had her vista.

He would work at his desk by the window. It would be quiet. He'd hear the scratch of his own pen, moving over the paper, making observations and striking them out again. There'd be Matti in the garden, calling to old Agneta. And maybe footsteps in the hallway, quick and light on the wooden floor. He would look up. He'd see the forest and his heart would grow calm again, because the forest went on for ever.

She'd find it quiet, but she might grow to like it.

Agneta had closed up the bedroom floor of the house, on his orders. The room that had once been his and Johanna's; Minna's room where Johanna had died; the 'nursery' next to their old bedroom, which had only ever had one inhabitant; the spare bedroom and his old study-dressing-room. Everything on that floor was sheeted and shut, apart from the bathroom he'd had made from a fourth bedroom. The best bathroom in the district, with its big, royal, claw-footed bath, its elegant little sofa where Johanna liked to sit after her bath. He preferred the sauna, but the bathroom was useful when he wanted to come home and strip and wash away the smell of a day of sickrooms from his skin.

The girl would sleep up in the attics, in what had been Kirstin's room. He'd asked Agneta to clean and prepare it. It was a small room, but not cramped. He'd ordered a new mattress for the iron bedstead after Agneta told him Kirstin had left the old one soiled. There was a washstand, a rag rug, a table and chair, and a picture of St John the Baptist on the wall.

He walked upstairs to check that everything had been done, the day before the girl arrived. Yes, Agneta had done the job well. The bedding was clean, the boards scrubbed. The room looked east, like the downstairs sitting room. He hadn't been up here for years. Strange how much closer the forest looked from up here. Johanna's garden looked insignificant.

As long as she wasn't one of those girls who takes fright at the sound of a mouse running in the attic. She wouldn't have to mind being alone in the house at night, when he was called out.

He lifted the bedding to check the mattress. Yes, it was as he had ordered. Good quality. He'd told Agneta to make sure of that.

She would be living here. She would have her life here, this orphan who could have ended up more or less anywhere. She would look out of this window, and feel these boards under her bare feet. It was a long way from growing up in a city which was expanding so fast that now it bulged with more than eighty thousand souls.

3

It was hot and stuffy in the room where Brigitta Nordström lay. Thomas stood by her bed, taking her pulse. The room smelled of birth. The smell of blood was already staling.

He never noticed such things while he was with a patient. He'd only realized the smell because he'd been outside and then come back in. After the baby was born and the placenta delivered, he'd become aware of pressure in his bladder. It had been safe to leave her for a few minutes.

The air was cold and pure as he crossed the yard to the privy. He snuffed the sharp scent of pine, blown from the timber yard. At the mill, the saw squealed and whined. That sound had been there all through her labour. He'd become aware of it from time to time, a mechanical chorus to her grunts and moans.

He came in from outdoors and the smell of the bedroom hit him, almost making him gag. The iron of her spilled blood, the sweat of her effort, a smothered smell of the excrement that had been forced out of her with the child. She had still to be stitched. He drew in his breath. The reality of the birth room folded around him again.

There was no baby by the bed. It had been taken downstairs, out of the way. It was another boy, now deeply asleep after the battering it had taken. The face was bruised, and the skull pointed. He'd been worried and had examined the child carefully, but there were no signs of serious harm. The baby flung out his arms and flexed and shrieked as he should. A big-boned child, like his father. What they call a fine boy. Those big bones had cost the mother a hard, dangerous labour, and she was too exhausted even to look at him.

Her husband stood behind Thomas now. He hadn't changed position while the doctor was out of the room. His feet were planted apart, and he gaped at his wife as if wondering why she didn't get up and make herself useful. She'd been working in the sawmill office when it started. A couple of days earlier she'd had a cough and a cold. She kept going, because the work had to be done.

It wasn't as if she did heavy work these days. She kept house, minded the children, and looked after the figures. She even had Silja to help her with the scrubbing and laundry. She never had to lift anything heavier than a sack of flour for her baking. Those days were past. He was making money, yes, really making money at last after all the lean years of borrowing and building up the business and Brigitta lugging timber like a man when he was short-handed.

Their children were coming to them late. He'd been getting worried, starting to ask what was wrong with her. But now she'd had the three boys, pop pop pop, one after another. This year, last year and the year before. Three fine boys. Well, once you've got that settled, you can start fancying a girl.

'Keep still, Mrs Nordström. Don't try to move just yet.'

The woman's eyelids remained shut. She was completely exhausted. A long, difficult delivery followed by a haemorrhage, fortunately not too serious and now safely contained. The baby had been breech. He could maybe have turned it if he'd been called earlier, but this was the first time he'd seen his patient since the previous birth. The man obviously wanted to save his money. It was going to take months for her to get her strength back. Thomas glanced behind him, at the husband. He would send him out of the room in a minute, while the stitching was done, but first there was something to be said, and in his wife's hearing.

'She mustn't have another. She was lucky to get through it this time.'

The man looked at him as if he was crazy. 'What do you mean, Doctor?'

'Look at her.'

'But she'll be all right, won't she, in a week or two?'

'Not if she has another child.'

'I don't know what you're saying to me.'

Oh yes you do, Thomas thought. Ten months between this boy and the last. You were in there even before she'd stopped bleeding. Rutting in her like a boar with a sow.

She was sunk back flat on the bed, her feet raised with pillows and the end of the bed raised too as he'd directed. She was grey-yellow in the face. But very likely she could hear them. He wanted her to hear. He wanted her to know.

'Three fine healthy boys, that's enough for anyone,' he said, in a bluff manner that felt false.

'But you need a girl to look after you when you grow old,' said Nordström, as if pointing out that you needed a table to eat off.

'You've got a wife,' Thomas said. 'If you carry on like this, you won't have her, and then who's going to look after those boys?'

The point sunk home. He saw it register, then the man's selfishness elbowed it away. 'Yes, but, Doctor, a man's got his needs, hasn't he?'

'We can have a talk about that,' said Thomas. 'But not now. Get your girl – what's her name, Silja? I'll need her to help me. When I've gone, I want her to sit with your wife, and fetch the child to her when it wants feeding. Mrs Nordström is not to move off that bed until I say so, and you're to send for me if there's any change at all. If by some outside chance she starts bleeding again –' Nordström's face wrinkled as if asking why he was being forced to hear this – 'then raise the foot of the bed higher, pack clean ice in a clean flannel as quick as you can and get Silja to hold it tight against the bleeding until I come. Send for me any time of night if that should happen.

'I'll be back tomorrow and I'll know at once if your wife has so much as put a foot on the floor. Ask Silja to come up here now, and I'll give her directions.'

It was the only way with a man like Nordström. You had to be firm. If his wife said she would go downstairs now and make his supper, he'd let her. Thomas felt a familiar helplessness and weariness. It would seize hold of him, if he let it. He could only do so much, and maybe it didn't improve matters anyway. After he'd gone, what would happen? Nordström, angry and frustrated, would take it out on someone. And who better to bear the brunt than his wife, who'd been the cause of the doctor speaking to him like that?

'Have you some brandy?'

'What for?'

'For your wife.'

'She won't take anything like that,' said Nordström with satisfaction. 'She's Temperance.'

'It's for medicinal purposes. She's very weak.'

'She won't touch it,' said Nordström, shaking his head.

'Ask your Silja to bring it up, all the same.'

'Have a drop yourself, Doctor, if you like. You had heavy work with that boy of mine.' Nordström spoke largely, as if the blood and pain of his wife's labour was a credit to his own manhood. Another fine big boy, never mind if it had nearly killed his wife.

No, thought Thomas. He would not lose his temper with this man.

Thomas stitched the tear while Silja held the lamp close, as he directed. She was a blockish girl, stubborn-looking in the same way the man was stubborn-looking. She could have been his daughter.

'Hold that lamp still,' he said sharply. The girl was gaping at her mistress as if she were a cow in a field. But no doubt they worked her hard enough, these Nordströms. Silja's hands were red and raw.

He finished the stitching. The husband was right, Mrs Nordström wouldn't take the brandy even when he called it medicine. She turned her head aside mutely as he brought the glass to her lips. He wasn't going to force her.

Thomas went downstairs. 'I'll call again tomorrow,' he said to the husband. The man looked at him with his shrewd money-making eyes, and nodded. 'All the same, Doctor,' he said, 'you don't know my wife.'

Thomas knuckled his forehead to get rid of the tension there. His eyes closed briefly, wiping out the room and the man. Red sparks crowded into thick, velvety darkness. He wanted to stay there inside that darkness, but he must open them.

'She won't flinch, when it comes to it,' said Nordström. 'Remember what the Good Book says: "In sorrow shalt thou bring forth children."'

Don't send for me, then, when she's in labour with the fourth, Thomas thought, but he would not say it. He could vent his anger, but once the words had passed this man would stick to them. Nordström would nurse the grudge. He would let his wife die in her bed without relief, and then say that the doctor wouldn't come.

Outside the house, Thomas breathed in the smell of pine resin again.

I won't take his money, he thought. I'll tell him to make an offering of it to the church, to give thanks for his wife's survival. That'll make him angry. He walked fast, relishing the crunch of his boots on the shrivelling crusts of ice.

'You ought not to walk when you visit patients,' Johanna used to tell him. 'It lessens their respect for you. You should always ride, or take the carriage.'

'By the time the horse is saddled and out of the stable I could be halfway there.'

'That's not the point, Thomas. A doctor shouldn't arrive with mud on his boots.'

But a patient had said to him once, 'I can smell the spring, Doctor. It's come in with you.' No wonder, in those tightly sealed sickrooms that smelled of urine, sweat and medicine.

The sawmill was less than a mile from his house. He'd be home in quarter of an hour, if he walked fast. And he wanted to walk fast. Walking between patients was the only time he seemed to get to himself, when Johanna . . .

No. He was not going to think about Johanna.

The sun was dropping; it lay big and red between the trees. He kicked at a crust of ice and it splintered like glass. Beneath it, the snow was open and porous in texture. Late-winter snow. Soon it would be gone. Spring was coming, and this year he felt less afraid of it.

He'd repair Johanna's garden swing-seat. It only needed new canvas webbing. He could do the job himself. He could sit out on summer evenings, reading, smoking to keep the midges away.

Suddenly an image assaulted him. He stood still. It was Johanna again, frowning with concentration as she smeared Minna's plump wrists with citronella oil, so that the midges wouldn't bite her. As her mother screwed back the top of the citronella bottle, Minna twisted free from where Johanna had been holding her firmly between her knees. The child ran to the swing-seat and plunged herself into it, head down, frilled underwear flapping, the plumpness of her calves bulging above her tight little boots.

'I'm hiding!' she screamed.

'She thinks that because she can't see us, we can't see her,' said Johanna. Her face was soft with pleasure. For a moment that pleasure bound them: their shared child, their shared life.

He shivered all over at the memory, like a dog, and began to walk home quickly, through the snow.

4

Eeva in the kitchen. Eeva learning to be alone after the packed rooms of the House of Orphans.

The tap dripped. She watched the next drip gather, bulging at the tap's mouth. It became full and it hung for a few seconds, as if it could hang there for as long as it chose. But of course it stretched itself out, and fell. Eeva picked up a ring of dried apple and ate it. Nobody saw, nobody knew.

She'd been stripped of her privacy for over two years. It was deliberate, part of changing her from what she was into an orphan, ready for service. No one was ever alone. Even their clothes were communal. When they came back from the wash there was always a scramble to find something that fitted.

When she'd first stood in the doctor's kitchen she almost couldn't remember what it was like to walk around a room and hear only the sounds of her own body, her own movement and voice. She raised her arms above her head, and let them fall. She stretched them as wide as she could, pointing her fingers until they ached. Nobody saw. Nobody asked what she was doing.

'It's quiet here,' the doctor had said. 'You may find it strange at first.'

She couldn't tell from his voice if he was apologizing for the quietness or telling her that was the way things were and she must get used to it. So she hadn't said anything.

Eeva lit the lamps. She loved to do this. Warm goldenness spilled around the room from the globes of the lamps. Light was plentiful here, she already knew that. She didn't need to be careful of oil. He'd told her she mustn't be afraid of lighting the lamps. She could take candles out of the store cupboard whenever she needed them. Anna-Liisa had said she'd be allowed to burn the stubs of candles in her room, but the doctor told her to take whole candles for her own use She had her own candlestick, made of pewter, and she burned the candles in it until they were halfway down, and then she hid them in her drawer, and took a fresh candle from the store cupboard. This way she would always have light to read by, even if the doctor changed his mind.

She held her candlestick high as she went upstairs, and made the wide corridors shine. Eeva wasn't afraid of the quiet, or of the closed, sheeted rooms on the bedroom floor, below her attic. She liked to think of their emptiness beneath her as she slept. Nobody could interfere with her.

He has money, she thought. If you have money as he's got money, you don't even need to think of it. It's there, like light, like heat. Like something natural. It's been there since before he was born and it'll be there after he dies. She could see it in the way he walked around. You could tell that he always felt private and independent, wherever he was.

She didn't think he had ever been cold, unless he'd chosen to be outdoors in the frost for his own reasons. His skin had a close, fine texture that told her he'd always eaten well and always been warm. His eyes weren't clouded and he didn't peer at the newspaper. He could read perfectly well without glasses.

She knew exactly how old he was. He didn't know she knew that. Anna-Liisa had told Eeva that she and the doctor were born in the same year.

'But of course I didn't know him then. We didn't meet that sort of family. But I've come to know him quite well . . .' She smoothed her apron, satisfied. Anna-Liisa, Eeva knew, was forty-seven. So the doctor was old, many years older than her father had been. But he wouldn't die yet. He'd live for a long time, and when he died he'd be put in the Eklund family grave, with his wife. He would never be alone, or unknown.

Dr Eklund had a wife who was dead and a daughter who lived in Turku, which Dr Eklund called Åbo because he was a Swedish Finn. Swedish Finns were the top layer, and owned most of everything. The Russians hadn't done anything to change that, even though they ruled Finland. Her father had explained to her the place of the Swedish Finns under Russian rule.

All the things her father had told her were like jewels which she kept in a box where no one could see them. His remembered anger flashed in her memory.

'The Russians want to make serfs of us, Eevi, like they made of the peasants in Estonia. And those Swedes'll help them to do it, just as long as it doesn't hurt their own position. They've no loyalty to us, even though they're supposed to be our fellow countrymen. You must understand, Eevi, that working people mean nothing to those high-up ones. We exist for their use.'

He was the only one who called her Eevi.

'What's a serf, Dad?'

'Someone who doesn't belong to himself. You should know that. That's how they live in Russia, like slaves tied to the land. Serfdom's been done away with, so they say, but I can tell you there's not much change. The Russians said they wouldn't bring their systems here, but now they've changed their minds, and the Swedes couldn't stop them even if they wanted. Which they don't. *Russification*, they call it.

'Listen, Eevi, because this is important. The high-up ones, the ruling classes as we call them, they'll even help a foreign power against their own nation, if it protects their personal interests. Or their class interests. You know what I mean by that?'

She nodded.

'Good,' he said. 'The things I tell you, don't forget them. Keep them inside yourself.'

He began to cough. He was huddled up by the stove, too close to it. She couldn't have borne to be so close to the heat, but he was always cold. There was cold in his bones, he said, but as if it was a fact and not as a complaint. His bones were sharp under his shirt. If it hadn't been for his TB they would have emigrated, the two of them. They would have gone away to America and had a different life. There were thousands of Finns in America now, whole towns full of them keeping their own language and customs.

They had farmland such as they could never dream of here. Her father told her all about it when she was little, six or seven maybe, before his illness began, when he still thought they'd be able to leave.

'You'll learn English, Eevi. I don't want you to live in a ghetto like the Jews. If Finns want to live in Finnish towns, why leave Finland? We'll go to New York. You'll learn English. You'll get a proper education. Some people will tell you that America's easy, you only have to stoop down to pick gold off the pavement. But that's foolishness. Nowhere's like that. There are systems everywhere. But in America, you belong to yourself. There's no Tsar over there, no Grand Duchies.'

He'd paused, she remembered that. He'd laid his hand on her hair and gone on as if speaking to himself, not to her any more: 'Even if it doesn't happen for you, it can happen for your children.'

But there's no use thinking of America, once you've got TB. They have doctors who examine everyone when the ships dock. They sound your chest and make you cough. You'll be sent back if you have a communicable disease, they won't even let you through Immigration. Back you go on the long journey home, with all your money gone and nothing to show for it. Her father knew all about it. He explained everything to her – that was his way. He'd brought her up like that, not hiding what life was like.

Her mother had died when Eeva couldn't remember, and her aunt lived with them until she married. Eeva was seven then, and could manage the cooking. Her father worked in the shipbuilding yard. Casual work, most of the time. Sometimes there was money and sometimes there wasn't. He'd had a permanent job, but the bosses didn't like him.

Her father knew everyone. He was respected. There were meetings in their apartment, and people came and went and sometimes they paused as they came in, to look over Eeva's shoulder where she sat studying. They would stare at the page of figures her father had set her, or the passage of Swedish she was learning. Her father told her that languages would set her free, allowing her to cross the boundaries which divided working people. These boundaries served the interests of the ruling classes. She must learn Swedish, and Russian, and later on he'd find a way for her to learn English, which he couldn't teach her himself. Education would set her free.

He spoke Russian well, because he had worked in Petersburg for several years long ago, before he married. Like so many Finns, he'd gone where the work was. He hadn't lived with Finns in Petersburg, even though there was a big Finnish community there. He'd lived with Russians, and learned the language. He had friends there, good friends he still saw. Some of the people who came to the apartment were his Russian friends, and he spoke in Russian with them, translating it into Finnish if there were Finnish comrades there.

Some days their Russian was a thick fog. She couldn't find hard words in it, let alone understand them. Other days the fog cleared, and she caught a snatch of meaning. Almost without her noticing it, more and more of the hidden landscape came clear. Her father recited Pushkin to her as often as he recited the Kalevala. Pushkin had been punished by the Tsar, exiled, trapped into the duel that killed him. Nothing was as it seemed on the surface.

They sat by the stove, her father in his wooden chair, Eeva on her stool at his knee. He stared at the stove without seeming to see it, his face in shadow.

> My talisman, preserve me,
> Preserve me through the days of persecution,
> Through the days of remorse and distress:
> Thou wast given to me on a day of sorrow.

He repeated the last line, dreamily, reaching out his hand to stroke Eeva's hair. "'Thou wast given to me on a day of sorrow . . .'"

'Am I your talisman?' Eeva asked him. He started, and looked down at her.

'Why do you say that?'

'Because of Mum dying when I was born.'

'No,' he said. 'The poem's not about that.'

Some of her father's friends couldn't read. She knew it from the way they would stare respectfully at the pages she was studying and then say, 'Well, that's good. That's the way. You'll be like your father, you'll know what's what.'

She would sit in the corner while they held their meetings. Her father would put the candle close to her while she studied, even though it left the men in a dimmer light. Sometimes there were women comrades too, but not as often. Their voices rose and sank in the shadows outside Eeva's pool of light. Sometimes a man who was new to the meetings would pause in what he was saying, and glance at Eeva, and her father would say, 'It's all right. She understands. She says nothing.'

She knew, before she was aware of how she knew it, that what happened in the apartment was never to be mentioned outside it. The knowledge was as vivid in her as the knowledge that fire would burn her. When she was little she didn't even listen to what was being said. Some of it must have gone into her mind, however, because later she found that she knew the words, they were familiar, and the ideas too. They were like clothes she'd worn before she knew how to put them on herself.

> *Preserve me, my talisman,*
> *Preserve me through the days of persecution.*

He repeated the words over in Russian, then in Finnish. She followed after him, shaping the words in her mouth.

The doctor would be home soon, she thought. The baby at the sawmill had been born, old Agneta had burst in to tell her so. Agneta liked the excitement of birth.

'Her sheets were soaked in blood!' she told Eeva happily. 'Lucky they'd put the old ones on. That's what to do when the sheets are worn through: keep them for when you have a baby.' Agneta had no children nor was likely to. She lived with her brother and went from house to house, charring, with her sleeves rolled up to show the muscles in her arms. She was called 'old Agneta', although she wasn't so very old, because her brother's child had the same name.

Eeva turned to the stove, where the soup was simmering. He'd told her when she first came that he liked plain food. He was quite happy with a supper of soup and pickled herrings. Afterwards he would eat preserved fruit.

In summer, he told her, they grew their own vegetables and salads. Matti showed her the sheltered, southerly part of the garden where the fruit bushes crouched under snow, packed in straw. Matti told her that Dr Eklund sent abroad for seeds that you couldn't get here. Sometimes they grew, sometimes they didn't. Matti would rather stick with what he knew, but he had to admit it was interesting when a lettuce came up red or a radish was black-skinned. The doctor was a great one for cloches and cold frames, and he liked to be the first in the season to have his salads on the table. He would send a triumphant bunch of lettuce into town, to Mrs Eriksson. It was a race between them each year, who would be first with the salads, and the doctor liked to win.

Plain food. A supper of soup and pickled herring with preserved red cabbage, and she'd stewed some of the dried apple rings from the storeroom. The soup seemed to be asleep in its pot. She stirred it and a bubble broke the surface. Ham and barley soup, rich and glistening. There'd been plenty of meat on the ham bone. People who lived in houses like this might consider it plain food.

She knew there'd been fancy cooking here once, from the range of kitchen equipment on shelves and hooks. Ranks of thick-bottomed copper pans in all sizes, sieves and colanders and slotted spoons and steamers and fish kettles and baking tins. There were things she didn't even know the use of, spiked implements that looked as if you could brain a man with them, probes and tweezers that resembled the medical instruments in the doctor's bag. There were measuring cups and jugs, rolling-pins and spoons. Row after row of knives, some of them big and wicked, some of them so slender they looked as if they could cut out your heart without you noticing it. And serving dishes. Some wide enough for a roast swan, others which wouldn't hold more than two spoonfuls of caviar.

The silver was in the dresser's deep oak drawers. It wasn't fancy but it was heavy. The knives were wrapped in felt rolls which smelled of knife powder. A knife man would come in to polish them, the doctor said. She was to leave them alone.

There were shelves of beautiful china in glass-fronted cabinets, but he said not to bother with any of it. She was to use the everyday china.

One day, Eeva had taken down a plate from one of the cabinets. She held it up to the light and the light showed through it, because the china was so fine and hard. Not like the everyday china, and even that was quite different from the clumsy pots they used at the House of Orphans.

She examined the plate closely. Figures painted in pure, deep blue gestured at each other. One seemed to be a shepherdess, because a fat lamb lay at her feet. A man in tight stockings was bowed over in front of her, one arm around his stomach and the other stuck out behind him to one side, the fingers stretched and exposed. Trees waved above them, and a stream looped across the plate.

She brought it closer. More detail appeared. A knot of ribbon on the shepherdess's straw bonnet. A similar knot – but not quite the same – on the man's shoes. The shoe-ribbon was coming undone, and one end trailed on the grass. He would fall over, when he straightened up from his bow and began to walk.

If the plate dropped to the bare kitchen floor it would shatter. She balanced it between her index fingers. Only their bare pressure prevented it. She stared at the plate, trying to make it choose. Would it slip, or would it stay?

No, she thought. It was her choice. She could make things happen. She nodded at the tiny, gesticulating painted figures, and then she laid the plate on the table, wiped it with a clean cloth, and replaced it in the glass cabinet. The painted man stayed as he was, bowed over, fingers flourishing. He would never trip over the loose ribbon of his shoe.

'You'll never go anywhere,' Eeva said to him. Maybe he would rather be smashed. Maybe he'd rather fly into a thousand pieces, and be free.

*

The doctor was home. She heard the front door open, and then his tread. She lifted the lid of the soup pot and a cloud of steam blew in her face, making her eyes water. Ham, split peas, onions, barley, carrots and a flavouring of dried sage. She stirred the soup.

Here I am in the middle of nowhere, she thought. Trees every-where, moving their branches and murmuring day and night, or thrashing when the wind caught them. Beyond the town there was the lake, frozen over, stretching out white until it met the white sky. The lake went on for miles and where the ice was cleared of snow people were skating like spiders. It made her dizzy to think of the miles between her and Helsinki. But if she had to, she could walk home. It would take many days, maybe a month or more, but in the end she would get there. And she wasn't without friends in Helsinki. No, her life was there, her real life that stirred her and wouldn't leave her alone.

Anna-Liisa said you had to forget your old life. Start again, away from bad influences. Eeva knew what Anna-Liisa meant. She was talking about the company they'd taken Eeva away from. Anna-Liisa knew nothing about it but lies that people from Helsinki had told her when they brought Eeva to the House of Orphans. Eeva didn't think Anna-Liisa even knew Lauri's name. But she'd been told the story. Doughy, snobbish Anna-Liisa had swallowed it whole.

Those little talks she liked to have with the older girls, on Sundays after the little ones had gone to bed. All about tempta-tion, and purity, and the way men couldn't help themselves, they were made like that, but it was up to the girl to put a stop to it. She leaned forward and told them solemnly that they had to be on their guard. Men had urges which couldn't be controlled, once they were roused.

Anna-Liisa was in the Guild of Temperance. She would tell them of families kept together by a woman who banished strong drink from the house. Women who had poured vodka on the grass, even though their husbands had knocked them to the ground for it. But these same men had come to repentance.

The girls stared back, their eyes flat with knowledge which Anna-Liisa would never possess. They said nothing.

'Some of you may marry, if this is God's plan for you. But whatever happens, your duty is to work hard in the place to which God
has called you. To show your gratitude to God and to those who
have given you a home here, and your training. We send you out
to good places, girls, and we expect you to do us credit.'

She looked around at their faces. She believes it, thought Eeva.
She really thinks she's doing Kirsti a favour by sending her off to
a farm where they'll have her out in the fields picking potatoes,
as well as taking care of three kids and scrubbing the house from
top to bottom. And all for the lowest wages they can get away
with, with a third paid direct to the House of Orphans in return
for her training. She really is stupid enough to think such slavery
will stop Kirsti going the way of her mother. But Kirsti's bound
to run off the first chance she gets, back to Turku, down to the
harbour, and that'll be that. When Anna-Liisa gets to hear of it
she'll apologize to the farm people and say that sometimes you
can't overcome these 'inherited tendencies'.

When the little talk was over, Anna-Liisa read to them from the
Bible. She read slowly, with breathy pauses, and her voice droned
until you felt yourself folding on your stool, your head jagging
with tiredness. Anna-Liisa liked to read them the story of Martha
and Mary. They were Marthas, beavering away behind the scenes,
keeping the house clean for Our Lord and making sure he had a
hot meal to keep his strength up.

Eeva's fingers tightened on the handles of the soup pot. It was too
hot but she still held on. The handles were no hotter than the stove
where her father had sat. She wouldn't let go. They'd taken her
away and tried to make her into an orphan, but it hadn't worked.
She was still Eeva. Inside her, where the jewel of her father's anger
burned, she was Eevi.

5

She was shocked out of her sleep. A sound somewhere. A footstep. She listened, taut and strained, for the sound to come again. Darkness and silence tiptoed around her bed, coming closer, closer . . .

Eeva sat upright, soaked with sweat, her hands braced on the pillow behind her. The acrid smell of her own skin clung to her. She pushed back clumps of damp, tangled hair.

She'd had a dream, that was all. It happened sometimes. Kirsti would thump her for it. Their beds were close and Kirsti could lunge over and thump her. 'Shut up yelling, Eeva!' Eeva didn't mind, even when Kirsti bruised her. She was glad to be woken.

But she was at the doctor's. There was no Kirsti. She huddled her nightdress close, shivering. Someone had been walking in her dream, to and fro. Every house makes its own sounds, she thought, it's just that I don't know all the sounds this house can make. It's fine in daytime but at night I forget where I am.

Eeva hugged her knees. She was cold, clammy cold with sweat. She hugged herself tighter. Suddenly she pulled up her nightdress and licked the bare skin of her knees. It tasted salty and comforting. She was the same as ever. She hadn't gone away from herself and she never would. She belonged to herself.

No, she wouldn't stay here in the dark, even though she wasn't frightened of it. She would get up. If she went downstairs very quietly she could find something to eat in the kitchen. She ought to keep a crust of bread and a lump of cheese in her room, along with the candle stubs, but she was afraid of rats. With food in her stomach she'd be able to settle.

Eeva lit her candle, and picked up yesterday's underwear from the floor. It was good to drop things and crumple them, kick them aside if you needed to. No one came up here, not even Agneta.

In the House of Orphans, boots had to be side by side under the chair. On the chair clothes had to be folded precisely, with underwear hidden at the bottom of the pile, out of sight.

Eeva pulled on her skirt, calico blouse and grey woollen house-jacket. She was thirsty, so she scooped water out of the jug she kept for her morning wash, and drank it out of her hands. She bundled her hair into a knot. She wouldn't go back to bed once she'd had something to eat, in case the dream came back. She would read in the warmth of the kitchen. You mustn't sleep again after a dream like that, she thought.

She moved slowly, because the dream had soaked to the heart of her and was nesting there, sad and heavy. It was waiting to return as soon as she closed her eyes. What had she dreamed of? Footsteps. What was there to be afraid of in that, when people were walking around the world all their lives long? Down in the kitchen she'd warm a cup of milk, soak pieces of black bread in it, and sprinkle sugar on top. He never noticed what she took. She'd heard of houses where they marked the place where the bread was cut, and marked the milk jug to be sure none was drunk, and locked sugar in a cupboard.

When she was dressed she knelt by the bed, lifted her mattress, and swept her hand beneath it, over the wooden slats of the bedstead. Her hand knew the three books that lay there. It touched all the covers before it chose one.

Three books, out of all *his* books. Her father had had fifty at least. He'd sold some to pay for medicine. These three were all she'd been able to bring when they took her away from Lauri's house. She'd hidden them in her clothes and then under her mattress in the House of Orphans, the same way as now. Kirsti knew, because she saw Eeva reading in secret. She would have given her away except that she had her own secrets. Sometimes Eeva gave Kirsti pieces of bread to keep her happy. She never said why she did it, but Kirsti kept the bargain. Kirsti had a way of holding bread with her fingers wrapped round so you could hardly see it. Even at table she did that. And if you went too close she would glare.

Eeva's finger touched the worn, soft cover of the book she wanted. It was bound in dark blue leather, with the title in gold on the spine, although the gold had been fingered away. It was her father's Pushkin, the one he had bought in Petersburg when he was young. He had brought it back to Finland and kept it with him wherever he went. He had taught Eeva from this book. Every page of it they had turned together at some time.

She let the mattress drop. The dream was sweeping over her again, and she couldn't push it back. She clutched the book tight, holding it in front of her body like a shield, but the dream surged through it.

Yes, it was her father she'd been dreaming of. He lay in bed, his nose a sharp prow, his brown eyes sunk. His hair straggled on the pillow. His voice had changed. It creaked and rasped and she had to bend low to hear it. A foul smell came from his lips.

'I'm no good to you,' he said. 'I'm a failure.'

'What d'you mean, Dad?' she asked in terror. Her father never talked like this.

'Everything I've done.'

He paused to get breath. His hand struck feebly on the blanket in frustration.

'My life's gone. That's it. Over.' He looked at her coldly, in a way he'd never looked at her before, almost as if he disliked her.

'I've wasted my life,' he said.

'No, Dad, no!'

She couldn't look at him any more. She fell forward and pressed her face into the grey blanket, sobbing. After a while she heard his voice again.

'Eeva, my girl. Eevi, look at me.'

She lifted her head just a little, as if the full sight of him hurt her.

'I'm leaving you. You know that.'

But the way he was looking at her was as if he was on a train and the train wouldn't leave, and she was on the platform waving and waving with a bright fixed smile on her face, both of them wishing that the train would leave and put an end to it.

'A few more days of this, and it'll be all over for me.'

He said it with strange satisfaction. He had no pity for himself, and none for her. He had never talked to her like this before.

'Don't cry,' he said, and she realized that tears were running down the sides of her face and trickling into her ears.

'I've got nothing to leave you,' he went on in a detached voice that cut her like a knife. 'The landlord will be round the same day they carry me out. He'll give you your marching orders. You'll go to Mika's – you've always got on well with his boy, Lauri. It's all arranged. Mika's been very good to me,' he added, with the same cold, fixed smile.

'But he's your friend, Dad!' she protested. 'They're our friends.'

She wanted to bring it all back: what he'd lived his life by. That they all belonged to each other, that they were linked by ties deeper than blood. Solidarity, unity, comradeship: she wanted to throw the words at him, the words that had got into her head almost before she was born.

'Yes,' he murmured, humouring her wearily. 'You'll go to Mika's. I should have looked out for you better. But it's too late for that now.'

It wasn't a dream. Or only partly a dream. Some of those things had happened. At night they came back to her and walked around her mind. Lauri knew. He heard her crying at night, and he came padding across the floor to her.

She couldn't tell Lauri all of it. She couldn't risk Mika ever coming to know that her father, whom Mika looked up to, had talked like that. Mika would have said she was throwing dirt on the memory of her father. He would have kicked her out, maybe. She was there in his apartment, not because she was Eeva, but because of those other things. Solidarity, unity, comradeship.

Lauri put his arm around Eeva's shoulders, in respect for her grief. He didn't try to offer words of comfort. Just his arm, quite heavy around her, making her feel that whatever happened she wouldn't fly off alone into the dark nowhere that had swallowed her father.

'Lauri.'
'What?'
'Nothing.'

The footsteps in her dream were her own. After her father died it was silent. Mika had stayed by his bedside. Eeva had got up and begun to walk, from the window to the door, from the door to the window. The tap of her boots on the boards was all she let herself hear. All she had to do was turn and walk, and turn and walk again, and that way she'd been able to think of nothing.

Eeva went down the attic stairs with her boots in her hand, and stopped to listen. Nothing. No one slept on the bedroom floor. Imagine a whole layer of a house kept empty. That one floor of the doctor's house was three times bigger than the apartment she'd shared with her father.

'It's not a big place,' the doctor had said when she arrived. 'I live quite simply.'

'Yes,' she'd said.

Down again, down the back staircase to the kitchen. The narrow wooden stairs were friendly. The warmth of the kitchen was coming up to meet her, and the faint smells of yesterday's food.

In the kitchen she put on her boots, and lit another candle. Why not, she thought, defying herself. Why not have light. Why not scoop the creamy top of the milk into her own cup.

She sipped the milk and it tasted rich and thick in her mouth. She crumbled her black bread into pieces, dropped them in the milk, let them soak and swell. Then the sugar, and a dusting of cinnamon from the spice rack. She snuffed the scent rising from her bowl, and began to eat, quicker than she wanted to but she couldn't help herself. Soon it was gone, but she still wasn't full.

No, better take no more. He seemed not to notice, but maybe he was taking note of everything, and had counted each one of the jars of preserves ranged in the larder. Or if he hadn't, that woman who came round poking into everything would have. He called her Lotta, but her name was Mrs Eriksson. She came into the kitchen as if she lived here, looking around with bright sharp eyes, watching Eeva without comment. But there was plenty of comment in her head, Eeva knew. She read those looks which said, 'The doctor is only a man, he doesn't know what's what. But you won't put anything past me.'

Eeva imagined Mrs Eriksson naked. When she was little, Lauri had told her this was a good thing to do when someone was telling her off, and he was right, it always worked. There would be deep marks in her flesh, from her corsets. She had the blue-white skin that bruises easily, and sandy Swedish hair.

As she thought of naked Lotta, malice curled inside Eeva and licked her heart like a cat. The dream was distant now. How good it would be to make coffee, but the scent of it might rouse him. There are people who can smell coffee through their sleep.

She sat at the table, drew her candle close and opened her book.

Something woke Thomas, he didn't know what. He reached over, lit his bedside candle, and fumbled his watch towards him. Four in the morning. No good trying to go back to sleep now.

He rolled over on his back, thinking about the Nordström birth. In the final stages of labour she had kept trying to roll over and get up on all fours, grunting and panting. It had shocked Silja.

It had shocked him, too. Between them they had returned her to a safer position, lying on her back. But she had shrieked with pain and arched away from the mattress.

Maybe – yes, maybe it had been better for her, the position she had chosen. It would have taken the pressure off her spine. But how could he attend a woman on all fours, like a dog?

He shifted in his bed, going through the stages of the labour again in his mind.

Later, on his way back from the bathroom, he crossed to the window and opened the shutters. It was still dark. Darkness everywhere, a whole winterful of it at his back. He longed for it to end. Well, at least he could end this night now, and make the day begin. He'd go down to the kitchen and make coffee, and then go to his desk.

As he went down the kitchen passage, he saw a line of light under the door. He stopped still, shielding his own candle to be sure. Yes, someone was awake. It could be no one but Eeva. But why had she got up this early? Surely she didn't think he expected her to rise at four, as if they were living on a farm?

No. Eeva's no country girl. She's from Helsingfors, remember? There must be something wrong. Maybe she's ill, or homesick. She seemed so used to the house already that it was difficult to remember how short a time she'd been there.

He felt a surge of fellow-feeling. She woke in the night, like him, and couldn't sleep again. What thoughts were crowding in her head? She was so light and quick you wouldn't think that anything weighed on her. He had never seen her look distressed.

He reached for the kitchen door handle, but stopped. He would frighten her. And besides, he was dressed in an old woollen dressing gown that Johanna said was a disgrace and ought to be thrown away. No, he wouldn't open the door.

But he ought to make sure that she was all right. She was under his roof, after all. And not much more than a child. Years younger than Minna. At the thought of Minna his eyes screwed shut in pain.

He would just walk around the outside of the house to the kitchen window, and check. The shutters would be closed, but there was a knot-hole in the wood that he used to spy through on winter evenings when he was a boy, standing on tiptoe to peep in at old Gudrun making ginger cake. If she was singing hymns to herself he'd know it was worth going in to beg a spoonful of the cake mixture. The old knot-hole would still be there. He made sure the shutters were painted regularly, so they didn't need to be replaced.

Yes, he would just check that she was all right.

Thomas slid back the bolts of his house like a thief. They moved easily in their oiled sockets, and made no sound. He stepped out into the cold, tying the cord of his dressing gown more tightly around his waist. The leather soles of his slippers slid on the new frost. Lightly, setting his feet so the snow would not crunch, he made his way around the side of the house. There was enough starlight to see the outlines of trees, the white ground and the bulk of the house. The kitchen window was beside the back entrance. There was a small wooden porch, and a stoop where Gudrun sat in summer to shell her peas.

He came alongside the window, and moved stealthily forward, as if the girl could see him. But that was impossible. He was in the dark and she was in the light. Even if the shutters were open she'd be unlikely to see him, and they were closed.

The ground-floor shutters of his house were always closed at night. Why it was he couldn't be sure. He only followed the pattern set he didn't know how many generations back. Perhaps his grandfather had decided that it was good to close the shutters. Even on summer nights it was done, last thing before they went to bed, when the garden was still light. The hooks that held the shutters back against the outside walls would be unfastened, someone would lean out from inside and pull the shutters together, and the iron bar that closed them would slide into place. The embrasures were deep, so it was possible to leave the windows open for the air to circulate even when the shutters were fixed. That was the way the house had been planned, long ago, by men who looked like him.

In the old days it was said that a starving wolf might hurl itself through a glass window after food. And there were robbers in the forest then. And so Thomas kept to the old way, whether there was need for it or not.

He was thinking all these thoughts to put off the moment when he looked through the knot-hole. Frost wrapped itself around his legs. He was a fool to be out like this. He would make sure that she was all right, and then he would go back to bed and get warm.

Thomas leaned forward. At first he could see nothing, but then he moved and his eye found the bright sliver of light. He pressed right up against the shutter, to widen his field of vision. And there she was. Sitting opposite him at the kitchen table, with her back to the stove. Her chin was propped on her fists. She was looking down, frowning in concentration. What was she doing? He craned but he could not quite see what lay on the table before her. And then her hand moved, and he caught the blur of a turning page, and he knew. She was reading. Eeva was quietly reading, in his kitchen, in the middle of the night.

It shocked him. So studious, she was. He had never seen such a look on Minna's face, not in all those years of tutors. What was she reading?

As if she'd heard his thought, Eeva looked up. He flinched, but she wasn't looking at him. A moment of intense thought had roused her to look up, that was all. It passed, and her gaze dropped to the page.

Probably it was some pulpy servants' novel. He half wanted to believe it. Why should she look up like that, as if seized by her own inner life? This was Eeva, who made his soup and whisked his floors with her broom.

But if it were servants' trash, why should she look like that?

No, he was too cold. He could not watch her any more.

6

Lotta was coming to wash the china. Well, Thomas couldn't stop her. She had declared her intention.

'Your mother's china, Thomas. It must be washed at least once a year. And Johanna's beautiful china too, of course,' she added. By this, she meant the English porcelain that Johanna had bought, and preferred. Poor Lotta, she could never hide her opinions.

'I'll come on Thursday,' she decided. 'I'll bring my own special liquid soap. I'll need three large bowls, and muslin to line them, and plenty of hot water. You might tell your girl.'

'Yes.'

'Eeva, isn't it?' Lotta went on, as if she didn't know perfectly well.

'Yes, Eeva. Perhaps, Lotta, if she watches you, she'll be able to wash the china herself next time.'

'I very much doubt it,' said Lotta briskly. 'My mother would never have dreamed of letting a servant wash her china, and nor should I. I'll be here at ten o'clock on Thursday morning.'

'Eeva.'

'Yes?'

'Mrs Eriksson will be coming on Thursday morning, at ten o'clock, to wash the china.'

'Wash the china? But I do that.'

'The stuff in the cupboards,' he explained, nodding towards them.

'Oh.'

'She has a special system, apparently. She's bringing her own soap, but she'll need plenty of hot water, Eeva, and three large bowls, and muslin to line them.'

'There's always plenty of hot water here.'

'I know.'

'I could wash the china easily. She doesn't have to come here.'

Eeva looked measuringly at the painted figures on the fine plates. She hadn't smashed them, had she? She'd chosen not to.

'It's the way it's always been done,' said Thomas.

'Did your wife used to come down here and wash it?'

He thought back. 'No, I don't believe she did. I think Mrs Eriksson came, even then.'

'Oh well, in that case –' Eeva shrugged, picked up another potato, and started to gouge out its eyes. 'I suppose it's a tradition.'

He almost smiled at her cleverness. She had turned it all around, so it was longer a question of Lotta washing the china because she couldn't trust the girl to do it, but of Eeva respecting a tradition, as she might have respected those of a Trobriand Islander. She was very quick at peeling those potatoes. Her face was rounding out, he thought. The line of her jaw was softer, and her nose was less sharp.

Mrs Eriksson washed the china like the priest at his altar, Eeva thought. She stood up straight behind the table, still wearing her grey velvet hat with its grey velvet rose. Her ruffled collar was tight under her chin. Eeva had asked if she'd like an apron, but Mrs Eriksson declined. 'It won't be necessary, Eeva.'

No, it wasn't necessary. There was no haste, no splashing of soapy water, no drips. Each piece of china was lifted carefully into the water, washed with a soft brush that Mrs Eriksson had brought along with the soap, dipped in one rinsing bowl and then the second. After that, Mrs Eriksson placed the china on more clean muslin cloths to drain.

Her hands were big. She could have done any kind of work, with hands like those, Eeva thought. But they were also pale and soft-looking, because of always wearing gloves. Eeva watched as the hands dealt with a cup, a saucer, a small fragile plate. Mrs Eriksson didn't seem to mind her just standing there. Maybe she thought it would do Eeva good to watch.

'Shall I dry those?' asked Eeva meekly, knowing what the answer would be.

'No, that's all right, Eeva,' said Mrs Eriksson kindly. 'But I'll need fresh hot water soon.'

Eeva took the bowl of warm soapy water from her, and emptied it in the sink. The water was still almost clean. Why trouble to wash the china, she wondered. No one had eaten off those plates. She replaced the bowl on the table. Mrs Eriksson measured in liquid soap with a spoon, and then Eeva poured in a jugful of hot water followed by half a jugful of cold. Mrs Eriksson tested the temperature.

'Put your hand in, Eeva,' she said generously. 'This is how hot it should be.'

Eeva dipped her hand in the soapy water. 'I see,' she said. 'Thank you, Mrs Eriksson. Now I'll know what temperature the water should be, when I wash my own china one day.'

Lotta glanced at her sharply. Was the girl being insolent? No, surely not. Her expression was serious, almost earnest. Poor child, did she really think it was possible that one day she should have such things of her own? That was the trouble with orphanages. The children were so much separated from the realities of life.

'This china belonged to Dr Eklund's mother,' she explained, 'and before that to *her* mother.'

'So it's quite old,' said Eeva. 'Lucky it hasn't got broken.'

'My dear child, why do you think I have come here to wash it? China like this, Eeva, is an inheritance. It has a life of its own, you might say,' and she smiled at her own fancy.

'So you don't use it? I mean, to eat off?'

'The doctor prefers not to,' said Lotta.

There was a knock at the back door, and Eeva went to open it. It was only Matti; come for his ginger tea. He preferred it to any other drink, he said. It warmed the stomach. The doctor bought ginger root specially. Eeva had learned how to peel and slice the ginger root, bruise it and steep it in hot water and sugar.

Matti had sworn off all strong drink since the night he'd fallen asleep in a snowdrift on his way home from a shebeen. If it hadn't been for the doctor chancing to find him on his way home from a call, he'd have had his fingers and toes frostbitten. And then where would he have been? It was fifteen years since Matti had tasted strong drink, and all the better for it.

He hung back at the kitchen door and nodded towards Mrs Eriksson's back. 'Why's she here?' he mouthed.

'Mrs Eriksson's here to do the washing-up,' replied Eeva distinctly. 'Aren't you coming in for a warm, Matti?' He always drank his tea by the stove.

'I don't believe I will today,' said Matti hastily. 'No, Eeva, I believe today I'll just dander down to my hut.' And he was gone.

She's still got to dry every single piece of it, thought Eeva. She'll be here for hours.

'I'd better get on,' she said aloud, 'I've got my ham to boil.'

'Of course, get on with your work, Eeva,' said Mrs Eriksson, as if Eeva belonged to her. Eeva fetched out the ham hock she'd soaked overnight to get out the salt, and began to jab it with cloves.

'Have you any sage leaves for the stock?' asked Mrs Eriksson.

'No.'

'Mrs Eklund had a wonderful recipe for boiled ham. Now, let me think. She copied her recipes into a red notebook. It was usually kept in the kitchen . . . I can't see it. Do you know where it is, Eeva?'

'I've never seen it,' said Eeva.

Dear me, the girl looked sulky. 'Well, have a look, have a look, it's bound to be here somewhere. Mrs Eklund had such a splendid collection of recipes. You could try them, Eeva.'

'Dr Eklund says he likes plain food.'

'I daresay he does. But what men say and what men like are two different things.'

The salt in her tone caught Eeva's attention. 'Why?' she asked. 'Why would he say he liked plain food if he didn't? He's got plenty of money.'

'I don't think Dr Eklund's financial circumstances are our concern, Eeva.'

Eeva looked down at the ham, bored again. Mrs Eriksson drew the last cup out of the water, and added it to the collection waiting to be dried.

'I'll just see if I can find that recipe book . . .' She prowled around the kitchen, scanning the shelves. 'Ah! I do believe – yes, there it is, behind those scales. Let me just wipe off the dust.' She took a clean cloth and wiped off the recipe book as carefully as if it were china, then opened it and began to flick through.

'I thought so. Here it is: *Boiled Spiced Ham*. I think you could manage this, Eeva. Come here and let me show you.'

Reluctantly, Eeva left the ham and came to stand by Mrs Eriksson, who pointed at the list of ingredients. '*Cloves* . . . you've got those. *Ginger root, allspice, brown sugar . . .*'

But the girl remained unresponsive, staring blankly at the page.

'Eeva,' said Lotta gently, 'can you not read, my dear?'

A flush rose through the girl's skin. 'I can a bit,' she said.

'Never mind,' said Lotta, and she replaced the book on its shelf.

Something must be done about this. She would speak to Thomas. She looked over to where the girl was studding the last few cloves into the ham. 'Ham with cloves. I'm sure the doctor will like that,' she said. 'But I must get on with drying the china.'

At last she was gone, and the china was back in the glass-fronted cabinets. The ham was simmering, and a scent of cloves rose with the steam. Eeva would drink some of the broth for her dinner, with a slice of the meat. Her mouth watered. Quickly, she reached for a jar, dug out a handful of raisins, and crammed them into her mouth. They clung stickily to her teeth, and a pang of pain shot through her jaw. She swallowed, and replaced the jar exactly where it had been. There was the china in the cabinet, just as before. There were the painted people. The shepherdess with her distant smile and her fat sheep.

'Can you not read?' Eeva asked her, going right up to the glass so that her breath clouded it. 'Can you not read, my dear?'

Lotta stood by Thomas's desk, putting on her gloves. He'd thanked her for coming, and offered coffee, but she knew he wanted to get on with his work. There was a book open on the desk. She glanced down at it, and then quickly away. Of course a doctor had to study such things.

'Your girl,' she began. 'Eeva. It's a great pity that she can't read.'

'Eeva can't read?'

'Didn't you know? I was showing her one of Johanna's recipes, and it was clear that she couldn't make out a word.'

'I always found Johanna's handwriting difficult myself,' he observed.

'Really, Thomas. You know Johanna's red recipe book. Such excellent recipes. It would be a great advantage to Eeva if she were able to read it. Even you, my dear Thomas, are going to tire of pickled herrings and plain boiled ham. We must do something about it.'

'Yes, Lotta.'

'All right, I'm going. I know you want to be alone with your books,' and she glanced at his desk with a respectful aversion that almost made him laugh. But Lotta wouldn't like it if he laughed.

When Lotta had gone, he sat back at his desk, staring out of the window. Why had Eeva lied? If he asked, would she lie to him, too? It was ridiculous. What had she to gain from pretending that she couldn't read? He would ring the bell, and when she came he would ask her flat out. *Mrs Eriksson tells me you can't read, Eeva. Is that the case?* No. *Is that true?* And then see what she said.

The image of himself peering at the knot-hole made his hands clench into fists. No, he wouldn't ask her. If she wanted secrets, let her keep them.

The smell of cloves made his mouth water. She didn't need Johanna's damned recipe book. He could see Johanna now, very erect at her writing desk, copying a recipe from a friend into her own book, in her upright, curiously unreadable handwriting. Another day, she would lend her book so that others could copy it. Her reputation grew. She was a fine manager, Johanna, and he was a fortunate man.

If Eeva had a book, what would she write in it?

7

These new corsets were comfortable, very comfortable indeed. So much more satisfactory than those she'd had to wear as a girl. Her mouth twitched, remembering Karl's look of alarm when he put his arm around her, stiffly, the day they became engaged. What had he been expecting? Heaven knows. There she was, squeezed as tightly as possible into her iron brace. Lotta was big. Big-boned, her mother called it, as she worked out clever ways to disguise exactly how much of Lotta there was.

'She gets it from your side of the family,' her mother used to say, looking at the big handsome father. But what was right for a man wouldn't do for a girl.

Those crippling dance slippers and walking boots, those carefully chosen vertical stripes which hid the bulk of bust and hips. Plain, dark, well-tailored skirts and jackets were what suited Lotta, but she was a young girl and had to look like one. Worst of all were the corsets that made her want to vomit after she'd eaten. And she could never get enough breath to run. Those noises her stomach had made, thought Lotta, remembering the acid gurgling and growling that had accompanied Karl's courtship. Fortunately he'd always been slightly deaf. It had taken her a long time to realize it. She had deeply admired his air of calm, his apparently thoughtful self-sufficiency. When she made some timid comment and Karl didn't respond, she blushed for her own triviality.

All that had changed. My God, it had certainly changed. That clumsy, eager, self-critical girl hadn't had a chance of surviving. She no longer existed. Hadn't done so for years, thought Lotta, buttoning her collar. She held her head high and drew her shoulders back. The pain was nothing today. She could almost feel nothing. She straightened her spine. A good day. Her tailored navy skirt hung well on her. She looked better now than she had looked at seventeen. Plain skirts, high-necked blouses, her seal-skin jacket or her furs, and boots that fitted perfectly. She went for cut, and quality of fabric.

They'd faded, those fair girls. She'd stared at them during her hungry years, fascinated in the same way as a man might be fascinated. But she wasn't a man, she was female, too female. Her breasts were heavy. Her thighs chafed. In summer her dress-shields were soaked in sweat. Her mother taught her to use eau-de-cologne during her monthly periods, but she was always afraid that she smelled bad. Female, she thought, but not feminine. She didn't know any of the graces which time, thank God, had now shrivelled in those glancing girls.

All that was over, and it would never return. Some women might regret it, but never Lotta. She was herself now. It felt almost like being a child again, apart from the pain. Being a child had suited her well. Long legs covered in bruises and scratches because she always hoicked up her skirts as soon as she was out of sight of the house. Racing, climbing, jumping, scrambling. Lotta was crazy, a tomboy, admired by the boys and happily unaware of the girls. She swam in the lake in summer and skated on it in winter. She split her head open, diving into shallow water. She stirred up a wasps' nest and was stung thirty-two times. She rode a shaggy four-square pony and dreamed he was a racehorse.

Until she was thirteen, she was free. Her parents didn't trouble. If you have five children, you let them go wild in summer and try to teach them some manners in the long winters. But even in winter Lotta would be out, muffled to the eyeballs, building a house of snow.

And then it had all changed. Her older sister, Astrid, had turned into a young lady. It had happened quite suddenly. Her hands grew delicate, her hair was piled and lustrous. She developed a way of running which was no more than a skitter of feet. Astrid laid her bare foot side by side to Lotta's, and Lotta's was bigger, broader, even though Astrid was three years older. Astrid smiled, and for the first time Lotta knew that to be bigger, stronger and braver was not going to be enough.

Well, Karl had married her, anyway. Karl had started coming to the house and before Lotta knew it everyone was sharing pleased smiles, as if they already knew something she did not. Astrid put her cool, scented arms around Lotta and said, 'Lotta, I'm so glad.' They had married, and then Karl had found out what was inside those carefully chosen blouses with their vertical stripes, and those crushing shoes.

Even now, standing in her own bedroom, in her own house, Lotta flinched, and her hands crept up to her face, to hide it. There she had been in her bed, in her nightdress tent of white lawn. They had managed it somehow, the thing you were meant to do, which neither of them had a word for. It was a dumb, embarrassed struggle.

'Well,' he had said afterwards, 'I think I'll go and read for a while.' And he'd gone, leaving her to get rid of the stains and stickiness.

She had washed in cold water, because she was too shy to ring for hot.

No children. No. All that is over and the pain of it has gone. Just as the lovely girls grew up and faded, so the damp, powdery babies she never dared to hold grew up and became ordinary adults, such as the world has produced since time began. Lotta saw quite enough of disappointing sons and sullen daughters.

Her own children would never turn out like that. There they went, racing away on long, fleet legs, calling to each other, or rushing to her for a quick, passionate hug before they vanished again into their play. There were always two of them, only two. Neither in any way resembled herself, or Karl.

It didn't happen, and by now the fact that it didn't happen only made those children more real. But Lotta still believed that it could have happened. These days, perhaps she might have gone to a doctor. But not then. She looked down, tapping the table with her forefinger. No, she would not have gone then. But she might have had children, all the same. There was one night when she thought she would conceive a child.

She'd been asleep, deeply asleep. And warm. It was a July night and the summer was a hot one. She'd woken. Their bed was tumbled where they'd kicked away the bedclothes in their sleep. Her nightdress was rucked up. And there was Karl, on his back, sleeping. He was naked. His face looked stern and distant and for the first time, the very first time, she felt a surge of feeling in her which was nothing personal at all. Nothing to do with the feelings she had for the 'Karl' she'd married, hedged as they were with pain and disappointment.

She realized that she had never wanted him before or even known that it was possible for this to happen. She didn't name the feeling to herself, or let herself think about the opening, aching sensations in the centre of her body, the part of her which didn't have a name and shouldn't be thought about. For a moment she wondered if she was bleeding at the wrong time, two weeks early. It ached so much. She touched a fold of her nightdress between her legs to find out. No, there was no stain. Only dampness. She rolled over, on her elbow. The warm, milky night air was lightening with July's early dawn.

'Karl,' she whispered. 'Karl.' Her breasts swung against the tucks of her nightdress bodice, and her nipples tingled. But he lay still, his face like wood.

'Karl,' she said, more loudly. She reached out and hooked her leg over him. Very gently, she slid on top of him, holding her weight off with her elbows. Her nightdress had ridden higher. It was in her way and she pulled it right up, past her waist. She couldn't take it off without getting up, because there were too many buttons at the neck. She was still too modest to look at 'that part' of Karl, but she felt it stir. She had for the first time a huge, greedy curiosity for it, for him, for Karl. It was going to happen and this time wasn't going to be like any of the other times. She was opening like a flower. She was damp like those babies other women had. Karl would know it. This is what's meant to happen, she thought with absolute sureness. Those other times, they weren't right. She moved her body, letting her breasts brush his bare skin.

Suddenly his eyes snapped open. He stared without properly seeing her, and then he focused. He looked startled, even afraid.

'What are you doing?' he asked sharply.

'Nothing,' she said. Surely, surely he would know that this was the right time. She couldn't tell him, but he would know. But his face was struggling into its daytime expression. He moved impatiently, as if he wanted to get rid of her weight. 'What time is it?'

'Dawn.'

'Why did you wake me, Lotta?'

His voice rapped out, sharp, staccato. As if he were afraid. He was pushing her away with words.

'I don't know – I woke up, and then I saw you lying there –' she said. He frowned a little, like a judge. Suddenly she knew that she was a fool, lying on top of him with her bare bum up in the air (they used to say that when they were children, *your bare bum*, and laugh) and Karl shifting away as if he wanted to escape but she was too heavy. He frowned, a critical, fully clothed frown.

'Really, my dear Lotta, you are a donkey. I sleep beside you every night of my life. Is there any reason for waking me at dawn like this?'

But that part – that part without a name – was stirring. Sideways – and now rising . . .

He glanced down with irritation, at the part of him which was hidden by her damp female flesh.

'Lotta,' he said peevishly, 'I can't move.'

She rolled off him quickly. He swung his legs over the side of the bed, stood up like a mechanical soldier and marched to the door. Out he went, with his pale, long back, and his legs opening and closing like scissors.

She pulled her nightdress down, right down, tugging it around her ankles and wrapping it there as if to keep herself safe. Now her legs were gone, her long strong legs that nobody wanted to see. Her hips were hidden, and the *bare bum* that used to make them shriek with laughter when they said it as children. 'Lotta, you donkey,' she murmured, and flushed with anger and shame.

It had never happened like that again. She'd lain still while he poked that thing into her less and less frequently, and that was all. She never betrayed herself by a movement. Karl had his workshop,

55

and she had her garden, and so much more besides: the house to run, Erika, Simon. And, of course, Thomas. She said their names in that order, even to herself, making Thomas's name come last, as was seemly.

'Oh yes, Thomas Eklund, such an old friend of the family. We try to keep an eye on him. Men are no good at living alone.'

Karl was, of course, perfectly indifferent to Thomas, as he was to almost everyone. Sometimes she'd wondered if there was something wrong with Karl; really wrong, not just unpleasant. Could anyone really have as little feeling as Karl, and still be human? He loved his wood, that had to be said. That way he had of caressing a fine piece of olive wood with his thumb, before he began to carve. He was always fondling his carvings. Even when they were finished, he couldn't leave them alone. He would wander to the shelves, as if he didn't know what he was doing, and take down one piece, and then another.

Johanna is dead. The words still sounded strange and untrue. Johanna was her friend, in the way that women can sometimes be friends without any great affection. Lotta had helped as much as she could, during Johanna's illness. For long hours she'd lain awake at night, questioning her conscience, asking if it were honest, this care of Johanna as her flesh failed. Could Lotta be sure of her own motives? Did she secretly relish Johanna's weakness, when Johanna had always been so firmly in control of her own household, her husband, her child?

But it had been honest. Lotta was sure of that now. If Johanna had changed, so had she. She and Minna together had helped Johanna to sit, to drink, to raise herself up in awkward agony so the bedpan could be slid beneath her. Thomas had procured an excellent nurse, of course, but Johanna took against her in the last few days. Johanna had always been so rational, but she whispered fiercely to Minna, 'Don't leave me alone with her. Promise you won't leave me alone with her.'

They never had. She had held Johanna's wasted hand, and Johanna had not drawn it away. She seemed to notice Thomas less than she noticed her daughter, or Lotta. He had sunk beneath the rim of her horizon, Lotta thought, as if Johanna were a boat, voyaging out.

In those few days, she loved Johanna.

Thomas. Thomas alone in that house, covering the rooms with sheets. He ought to move into town, thought Lotta again. Yes, the house in the forest is his family home, yes, he has always lived there. But it isn't good. The girl he's got – what's her name, Eeva – how can she possibly run a house like that on her own?

Eeva. Lotta knew her name perfectly well. *Dr Eklund says he likes plain food.* She was too independent. She would be unsettling everything. It didn't work, these girls from the city coming to the country. If the idea was that country life would influence them for the better, it was a mistake. Girls like Eeva hold on to what they are. On this question and no other, Lotta was with the Jesuits. *Give me a child until he is seven . . .*

What had happened to Eeva before she was seven, wondered Lotta, and dark thoughts floated in her mind. She tried to smother them in pity, but it wouldn't work. She saw only a smaller Eeva, knowing and complicit. *They bring the city wherever they go.* And the political ideas that were racing around Helsingfors now were contagious. Once those ideas were brought to the country, they spread and dug deep roots into the clean soil. *He's got plenty of money.* Imagine a child like that making such an impertinent observation.

But she's not a child. No. Thomas hasn't noticed, but she's beginning to look much older, now that she's got some good food inside her. A young woman who liked her own way, that was Miss Eeva.

But she couldn't read. Really, one should feel sorry for her. Ignorant, uneducated: no wonder she expressed herself awkwardly. *Mrs Eriksson's here to do the washing-up.*

I'll arrange a reading class, thought Lotta.

The sensation of benevolence was familiar, and safe. But it couldn't entirely damp down the unease of those hours in the kitchen with Eeva. Yes, Lotta was uneasy, it had to be admitted.

She crossed to her glass. There she stood, tall and well kept. No matter how her back burned, she would stand upright. You could call her a fine figure of a woman now. There was no trace of the clumsy, too-eager girl she'd been. They had buried that girl between them, her and Karl. So why, when she stood opposite Eeva at Thomas's table, did she feel big-boned and awkward, out of place in the kitchen of her oldest, dearest friend?

She should put Thomas on his guard. He wasn't always very practical. It might be a good deed to take in a girl like Eeva, and give her a chance, but the girl would take advantage if he let her. *He's got plenty of money.* It wasn't just the words, but something hard and free in her tone which wasn't suitable. *You have to respect social realities, my dear Thomas,* Lotta imagined herself saying. *You are doing this girl no good, if you give her ideas.* Everywhere, Lotta knew, the same spirit was rising. Restless, rebellious anger against the order of things. It comes from Russia, Lotta thought, like all extremes. We must look westward, to Sweden. To a properly ordered society which had yielded its empire without losing its character.

Long ago, rebellion might have found its echo in her. But not now. She'd learned the hard way that things are as they are. People had their natures, which couldn't be changed. Lotta the gardener had learned to bow to the sun, the wind, the rain, the late, piercing frost. She'd learned to yield. If she hadn't had love, she'd had something else.

We must adapt, thought Lotta. We must shape ourselves to reality, not expect reality to shape itself to us. Eeva's face was clear in her mind. The dropped eyelids, the lips pressed together, the sudden rush of speech. That girl was angry. Perhaps she had a right to be. But an eye must be kept on her. A description from the newspapers popped into Lotta's mind. Surely to goodness it couldn't be applied to a girl like Eeva, an orphan with no education? But her mind said yes, in spite of her common sense. Troublemaker. Agitator, said her mind with newspaper certainty. Thomas has got a little agitator in his kitchen.

8

So why did she lie? Why did she tell Lotta she couldn't read? The question troubled him even now, weeks after Lotta's china-washing.

It was spring now, real spring. The snow had washed away, the sour brown earth was prickling with fresh shoots. Everywhere water raced and gurgled, birds sang, mud oozed, sap rose. Every year the rush of spring grew more potent, more mysterious. When he was a child he'd taken it for granted. He'd pulled off his boots and squished mud through his bare toes, down by the stream.

A lie is potent, Thomas thought. He had lied to Johanna, and the lie had acted upon the whole of his life, like a drug that the bloodstream carried to every part of the body. The power of a lie was so great. And he hadn't known that. He'd lied hurriedly, guiltily, because it was the only thing he could think to do. He had never thought of himself as a man who would need to know what lies did to a life. He'd lied to Johanna, and betrayed Minna. It had taken less than twenty seconds, but the lie had spread like poison into the bloodstream of their three lives.

Boiling water bubbled around his instruments. Thomas was meticulous about sterilization, and supervised it personally. He'd seen enough of instruments dunked in hot water, then wiped and used again. And by the time infection set in, the doctor had moved on and most patients would be too ignorant to guess the cause, or blame the doctor.

Would Eeva lie to him, if he questioned her? *I never learned to read.* He could see her face as she sat reading in the kitchen, intent and absorbed. A student's face, not a servant's. He had been shocked at this other Eeva, this quite different person living unsuspected under his roof. Under his roof, where the mice ran no matter how often the yard cat was sent up to catch them. Did she read up there, too, when she'd finished her long day?

Maybe it was something in Lotta which had provoked the lie. Lotta was so upright, so sure of herself. Yes, there was something provoking about Lotta's certainties. The girl didn't want Lotta to know everything about her. She'd lied to conceal herself from Lotta, perhaps. And in a way he had a certain sympathy, a certain fellow-feeling for Eeva. Lotta was so sure. *You'll take a house in town. Of course you will. At least, Thomas, you have the comfort of knowing that you did everything you could for Johanna. No doctor, no husband could have done more.*

I did more to Johanna than you know, Lotta. I conceal myself from you, too, though you are my oldest friend. I want you to think I am better than I am. Because I'm afraid.

But it was senseless to lie about being able to read. If he asked her, and she lied to him, too, would he challenge her?

The instruments were ready. He laid them on a clean white cloth to cool. Lies, he thought, yes, they're an infection. You can die of them.

'I'll take you upstairs again, Dr Eklund,' said the servant whose name he could not remember.

He went back to the child's bedroom. Henrik was propped up on pillows, while his mother sat beside him, holding his hands with the lavishness of emotion that was slowly crushing her child. He must get her out of the room.

'All right, Henrik,' he said, 'what I'm going to do is prop your leg with these pillows, to keep it in a good position.'

The bed linen was clean, the room immaculate.

'Maybe I shouldn't have called you, Dr Eklund,' panicked the mother, sensing the moment was near. 'In a few days it'll get better on its own.'

'I don't think so,' said Thomas. 'This boil needs to be lanced. Henrik will feel better then.'

The mother's fear was getting into the child. He sat stiffly, tensing himself to be hurt. Poor child, he didn't have much luck. Asthma, eczema, bronchitis, weeks in bed each winter, and now a crop of boils which were among the worst Thomas had seen on a child. Hot fomentations had done nothing. The worst was on the left leg, angry, red, refusing to burst and release its poison. Thomas feared that the poison would go inwards, to the child's bloodstream.

Henrik was heavy-eyed, with a coated tongue. He had little resistance, after the long winter.

'Mrs Brenner, I'd like you to fetch your girl, please. I want her to hold Henrik's leg steady. You don't want your leg wobbling like a jelly, do you, Henrik? Or maybe you like jelly?'

The child offered a pale smile. He was a good boy, in spite of the mother.

'Oh no, no, I can't leave Henrik! He needs me here, don't you, sweetheart?'

'No,' said Thomas. 'I have a job of work for you, Mrs Brenner. I want you to go downstairs and make up the drink on this prescription for Henrik, with your own hands.'

He handed her the paper. 'Two dessertspoonfuls of raspberry jam, the zest of two lemons, the juice of two lemons, a teaspoonful of pepper vodka . . .'

'Pepper vodka! For a child of his age?'

'Yes. Pepper vodka, one teaspoonful. It's restorative. Mix all the ingredients thoroughly, let them stand for five minutes and then add the same quantity of boiling water and bring it to me. But send the girl up, before you begin.'

Would she leave? He watched her narrowly. She looked at the paper in her hand, then at Henrik, then at him. She didn't trust him, not quite. But she stood up slowly.

'I'll be back as soon as ever I can, my darling. Mother has to make up a drink for you.'

'That's right,' said Thomas encouragingly. Henrik said nothing, but he made no move to hold her back.

She was gone. He winked at Henrik. 'Sounds terrible, doesn't it? Lemon juice and vodka and raspberry jam . . . I bet you were getting worried there. But you're not going to drink it. It's to give your mother something to do while we get on with the job. You don't need anyone to hold your leg. Keep still now for me. It'll hurt, but not too much.'

Swiftly, he wiped the angry skin with iodine. The child flinched and made a noise in his throat. Thomas reached for his scalpel, keeping his eyes fixed on the child's face, then very quickly he bent over the leg, holding it firm with his left hand while with his right he brought up the scalpel.

'Big breath, Henrik.'

It was done. Pus spurted from the boil. He wiped again with clean cloths, gently massaging the flesh towards the boil so the pus would drain. Tears started down the child's pale cheeks.

'It's all right, Henrik, you did very well. You've had worse than this to deal with, I know.'

'I know,' echoed Henrik, with an old-man resignation that affected Thomas where the tears had not. 'I think I'm quite brave really.'

'I think you are. I shall tell your mother so.'

'One night,' said Henrik, 'when my chest was bad, I thought, *Shall I go on breathing?* And then I said to myself, *Yes, Henrik, you'd better.*'

'That was good advice you gave yourself,' said Thomas. 'We'll put a dressing on this leg now.'

He looked up, and there was the girl staring roundly at him from the door.

'Missus said I was to hold his leg.'

'It's all done. Take these dressings downstairs and burn them. No, wait a minute. Have you any cuts or scratches on your hands? Show me.'

The girl spread out her broad hands. 'That's fine. Now, before you change these dressings on Henrik's leg, you need to wash your hands in hot water, with soap. Scrub your nails and scrub your hands with a brush, rinse them and dry them with a clean towel. And do the same afterwards, every time. Don't think, because I'm not here, that I shan't know whether you've done it or not. I shall be able to tell. You'll need to apply fomentations today and tomorrow, fresh ones every four hours when the dressing is changed. I'll leave directions. Do you understand?'

'Yes,' she said. 'I'm to wash my hands and dry them. Will you tell missus? I only get my one piece of soap, and it's to do for my clothes as well. If I waste it, I won't get another.'

'I'll talk to Mrs Brenner. Don't worry about that. Use plenty of soap.'

And here was the mother, with the concoction of raspberry and pepper vodka held proudly before her. Her lower lip was caught between her teeth. He winked at Henrik again, and took the child's wrist to take his pulse. Mrs Brenner waited respectfully, glass in hand, until he had finished counting.

'Splendid pulse rate, Henrik. Do you know, Mrs Brenner, I believe he won't need that drink, after all. It may even be a little too stimulating for him.'

'What shall I do with it then, Doctor?' she asked in open disappointment.

'It looks perfect, you've followed my directions to the letter. But you might just . . . throw it away. As it turns out, the stimulation of the pepper vodka isn't necessary. He's a sensible boy, your Henrik. He'll do very well.'

Humbug, hocus-pocus, mumbo-jumbo, he told himself as he left the house. What had he come to? All those high ideas he'd once had of being in the vanguard of medical advance. And here he was, getting an overanxious mother to brew up a mess of raspberry jam and vodka while he lanced a boil. One of the hundred or so boils and carbuncles and whitlows he'd be dealing with over the next couple of months. Spring was the worst time. The body was at its lowest. A fine diet of ulcerated legs, suppurations, wounds that wouldn't heal: that's what he'd be living on. He thought of the curious expression of pride some patients wore, as they slowly unwrapped their home-made bandages to show him their weeping ulcers. He would treat them, and prescribe spring tonics, and listen to their stories of pain, and then it would be summer.

Thomas walked faster. It was getting late and his back hurt. He felt old and tired. Here he was, forty-seven. The boundless energy he hadn't even known he possessed, because he took it for granted, had suddenly dwindled. When it's gone, then you know that you had it, he thought with grim amusement. Maybe that was true of more than health. 'You're looking tired today, Doctor. You must take care of yourself. We're none of us getting any younger.'

When you're forty-seven, he thought, spring is difficult. All that uprush of sap and melting water and fresh growth. Maybe the joy of it would come back to him when he was truly old. He had seen old people, quite content, sitting on their doorsteps in the first warmth of May, doing nothing but turn up their faces to the light.

I'll tell Matti to prepare the sauna tomorrow, he thought. Yes, that was what he needed. He could almost smell the heat, the parched smell of wood and resin, the spurt of steam that made his eyes water. He could hear the sauna creak like a living thing. And he would sit there, blind with sweat, sweat trickling down his chest. He would go to the sauna and it would drive his thoughts out of him with his sweat. Let it bake to the very heart of him.

He would go from the sauna to the stream, and wash in its icy meltwater. It wasn't deep enough to bathe, but you could kneel in the current and splash the water over your head and shoulders. The cold took your breath away. The sauna was in among the birch trees, close to the stream and not visible from the house. Yes, he would do that. And then back to the steam, bathing in it to his heart's content.

Afterwards, back to the house in his dressing gown, put on clean clothes, every stitch clean, and sit at his desk with a glass of vodka and a cigarette. The delicious taste of that first cigarette after a sauna! Quite different from any other cigarette: almost spicy. He would draw in deeply and blow out supple coils of smoke. The only time he blew perfect smoke-rings was after a sauna. Then the vodka, with its faint oiliness and the fiery spread of it into every fibre of the flesh. Sauna and vodka, they do the same thing. They purify you.

He'd been born in the sauna. Yes, his mother had followed the old custom. Her mother was Finnish, after all, even though she'd assimilated so well that many people took her for a Swede. She had her fine carved bed, her grand bedroom and a doctor from Åbo to attend her, but she'd been adamant. Her child would be born in the sauna, because it was healthier.

She'd been perfectly right. By instinct or inheritance, she'd known what was now understood by most of the medical profession: that babies born in the sauna had a better chance of survival because it was clean, almost sterile, purified by years of intense heat. And their mothers had lower rates of puerperal infection. We knew that once, and then we managed to forget it, thought Thomas.

His mother had walked around the birch grove for hours on that June morning, and then she lay down on the wooden bench, in the pine-scented dimness of the sauna, and gave birth to him. Thomas's nurse, who was there, told him the story. His mother gave birth with no trouble at all; she was made for having babies. But God only gave her that one chance. No doubt He had his reasons.

His mother must have given scandal; certainly she'd raised some eyebrows by behaving 'like one of us', as his nurse said. But she'd been right. And she'd stood up with Thomas in her arms that same evening, when he was only a few hours old, and had walked back to the house. It was as if she'd known by instinct that she would only conceive once, and that she must do everything she could to ensure that baby's survival.

They had something, that generation, he thought. They didn't doubt themselves. They knew what life was, and where they belonged in it. Not like us.

Matti knocked at the back door while Eeva was pouring a kettle of boiling water over soda crystals in the sink, to clean out the pipes.

'The doctor's had his sauna,' Matti observed. He wouldn't come in, because he'd been digging and his boots were claggy.

'Does he want something?'

'No, he's gone back up to the house,' said Matti, as if they weren't in the house themselves. 'He'll be settling himself down for a drink. That's his way.'

'Does he drink, then?' asked Eeva, surprised.

'Drink? No, not to say drink, he doesn't. But he likes his glass of vodka after the sauna, like anyone. But what I mean to say is, the sauna's heated.'

'Oh. Would he mind?'

'He's not going to know, is he?' said Matti. 'And I'll be out of your way. I'm heading home now. That was good coffee bread you gave me this morning, Eeva. You're a fine cook, you are.'

'Thank you, Matti,' she said, and smiled. Matti was easy. He never pressed himself on you. If you gave him cake, he was glad. If you didn't, he wasn't bothered. He worked like a horse, that one, but never got flurried.

'We'll be getting some real spring weather now,' he said, looking up. 'You'll be glad to be out of the town, with summer coming.'

'You've never been to Helsinki, have you, Matti?'

'Me? No. Never been anywhere.'

She couldn't tell from his tone if he was glad of it, or sorry.

When Matti was gone, she walked out into the yard. Yes, he was right, the sky had a clear green tint to it, like the flesh of an unripe apple. Good weather was coming. You could feel the spring.

She wasn't sure that she wanted to feel it. She wanted the clatter and dust of Helsinki. She wanted their apartment, full of smoke and talk. Even in Mika's house it was the same familiar atmosphere. Pamphlets, meetings, reading, bashing out arguments like steak on a wooden plank, friends from Petersburg appearing and then disappearing again, bringing ideas and leaving them behind to grow or just shrivel away into nothing. Eeva hadn't come across an idea since she left Helsinki. They didn't have ideas in the House of Orphans; there'd have been trouble if they had.

She loved Helsinki in summer, when all the rich people had gone to their summer houses, and the city belonged to them, the workers. Never again those late-evening summer walks after her father got home from work. That was before he got ill. She would trot alongside him, sometimes holding his hand, sometimes darting away to explore. He would let her run, kicking up dust from the strong little boots he soled and heeled himself. Along the magnificent cobbled spaces of the harbour they'd go, past the big ships, looking out over the water which was silky with evening and filled with yellow light. He liked to pick a handful of birch twigs, to smell their sap. He held them to her nose. 'Breathe in deep, Eevi, it's good for you.' They would wander farther than they meant, and he would carry her home on his shoulders. He was strong then, solid, with his hair springing under his cap. Her father was a short man, but he seemed tall to her.

He ought to have been taller. He told her that once. 'Look at the people you see in the streets, Eevi. The well-dressed ones, the ones with money, they're taller than us. Even their children are taller. Do you know why that is?'

She'd shaken her head.

'They eat better,' he said. 'Their children have butter and meat and milk whenever they want, and so they grow taller. Never forget that, Eevi. Two winters when I was a boy, we were boiling up a dry ham bone over and over. You don't grow tall on that. Look at them, Eevi, when they go into the big shops or when they wait for their carriages. Look close. And remember it.'

She did remember it. She was growing, since she'd come to the doctor's house, where there was proper food. The ham bones in her soup had meat on them. She'd had to let down her skirt hem. Her bodice was tight.

Yes, she'd go to the sauna. Why shouldn't she? The sauna wasn't just for the master. Matti had as good as said so. She was tired, and she ached all over. She would fetch the clean underwear Mrs Eriksson had given her in a bundle, along with a blue striped skirt and blouse. They were only a little worn. Much better than the things Eeva had brought with her. After the sauna, she'd put on all her clean things.

She'd stay as long as she wanted in the steam. When the orphans were taken to the public sauna, once a week, they were always rushed because there were so many of them. Yes, she'd bathe in the steam as long as she wanted, this time, and no one was going to stop her.

9

No, the second cigarette was never as good as the first. The taste had gone. But look – he'd smoked six. There was the ashtray, brimming with cigarette ends. The room was thick with smoke. His glass was empty, too.

Thomas lifted the bottle. But how full had it been in the first place? He couldn't remember.

What he would do was, he would go outside in the fresh air. The sun was low, but there would be light for a while yet. He'd go for a walk and he'd feel better.

He wouldn't drink any more. He didn't really drink, never had. Only very occasionally, to defy Johanna, to get away into a place where she couldn't follow him. He could count the number of times he'd been drunk on the fingers of his left hand.

His sense of relaxation after the sauna had drained away. He was back in the itch of everyday frustrations. No, that last cigarette hadn't tasted good, nor had the last glass of vodka. If only he could begin again. If he walked outside, in the fresh air down in the birch grove, maybe he'd recapture that warm relaxed feeling. He had got to turn away from these bitter thoughts that tore at him like claws. He wasn't so old, surely it wasn't time to say that the struggle of life was over and he had failed. He was only forty-seven.

I might live another twenty years, he thought. He was standing, pressing hard with the heels of both hands on the leather top of his desk. And why? Why am I living? To do good, is that it? Is that what I imagine I'm doing?

He looked down at his hands. They were still strong and flexible. Doctor's hands. There were skills built into his fingers which it had taken a lifetime to learn. He had good hands for diagnosis.

She hadn't wanted them, he thought, crisping his fingers. She didn't want my hands on her. Never, never. It was always I who reached out to her, towards the scent of her skin. It's all gone now, all of it. No use thinking of it. She's dead, she's under the earth.

But it was impossible that Johanna was under the earth, part of it. Surely her distinct self wouldn't let itself dissolve like that. She stepped out so firmly and decisively. If she came across something she couldn't control she simply turned away. He'd always been too eager, that was what had put her off. And now he was old and dry and tired and none of it mattered.

He turned his head to look out of the window. There they were, his beautiful trees. The birches were full of spring sap, rising through the chalky pink flesh of the tree. His mother used to bind a handful of twigs for him.

My mother is dead, he thought. My mother is dead, and Johanna is dead. Even old Katariina is dead. This is the way it happens when you're middle-aged. The people who remembered you as a child have gone. You know more and more faces among the dead. Once you'd known only a handful of dead people – a grandfather and a couple of old servants – but now you had as many friends among the dead as among the living. And then, one by one, you realized that the dead outnumbered the living. They were all around you, possessive and strong.

Children were what held you firm in the land of the living. But Minna . . . No, he wasn't going to think about Minna. And he wasn't going to think about Johanna any more either. That bunch of birch twigs his mother had bound for him one June morning was as real as anything. Hold on to that.

He stepped out into the clean air. How quiet the house was behind him, settling into itself for the night. She'd be lighting her candle soon, to read where she thought nobody would see her. Johanna's plates were shining behind the glass doors. Johanna would never see them again, but Lotta still distinguished them. 'Johanna's plates', she said, and 'your mother's plates'. The history of possessions was like a religion to Lotta. Those plates had outlived both women, breakable though they were. They'd outlive him too. Those smirking, gesticulating painted figures. He'd never liked them. Minna ought to have them now, in her house. Next time she came, he would ask her to take them away.

Minna's next visit wouldn't be soon, he realized that, but it would be soon enough not to cause gossip about neglect of her widowed father. Minna had her mother's respect for convention. and her mother's strength. She could be iron when she wanted.

You are becoming morbid, he told himself. You must not give way to self-pity, or you'll be of no use to anyone. Why blame Minna? None of it was her fault.

It was lighter outside than he'd thought. The air was soft and wet and sweet. He snuffed it greedily. There was a faint scent of celery: yes, he was treading on herb robert. He walked slowly, bathing in the freshness of evening. Everything he smelled or saw or heard was piercingly sharp, but distant. He'd drunk too much vodka, that was it. He was wearing a coat of vodka. A nice feeling again, now that he was outdoors.

Lucky that Lotta wasn't here to see him. It was hard work living up to Lotta. The Thomas who was Lotta's friend was a stranger to Thomas, and he wasn't sure he'd care to meet him. Responsible, even distinguished, devoted to his profession and to his patients, dignified in bereavement – no, surely Lotta couldn't really believe in that Thomas either?

'Or if she does, the more fool her,' he muttered, tripping over a root.

The knees of his trousers were covered in mud. What did it matter? It would brush off. And if it didn't, there were more. Plenty more trousers, pair after pair of them hanging in that monumental wardrobe that smelled of camphor and close-packed wool. But his heart was thudding. He stood still, regaining himself.

And there, through the slender birch boles, he saw the sauna door open. He nearly yelled out, 'Hey! You there! What d'you think you're doing?' But he stopped himself, seeing who it was. It was the girl. She pushed the door wide and stepped out into the clearing. She stood still for a moment, looking up. Her skin was flushed all over from the sauna, her damp hair clung to her neck and shoulders. He could not stop looking at her.

He'd thought of her as a child. Or maybe he'd pretended to himself that she was a child. But she was not. She was too thin still: she should grow fuller. But her naked body was a woman's. He was close enough to see her nipples grow hard as the cool air touched them.

She stood still for a moment and then she walked away through the trees, to the stream. As soon as she entered the trees her white flesh was camouflaged by shadows.

She was gone. There was a bright fuzz of leaves on the underbrush, where she'd disappeared. He strained to see her, hear her. Maybe that was the sound of her splashing into the water. No cry of shock at the cold, no cry of pleasure. He pictured her where she was, where he'd been only an hour or so before. Crouched on her haunches in the shallow pool, scooping up water in her cupped hands and throwing it over herself. Bathing herself in the fast, brown, icy water, just as he'd done. He felt as if that water were prickling his own thighs, as sharp as thorns.

He wanted to move forward. He could move quietly. He wouldn't disturb her or frighten her. He must see more. He must see her.

No. He held himself back. If she caught sight of him, that would be the end. She would run back to the house in a panic, up to her attic bedroom. She'd throw her possessions into a bundle and leave tomorrow. She would tell Anna-Liisa what had happened, and Anna-Liisa would find another place for her. Anna-Liisa wouldn't say anything, because after all it would only be the girl's word against the doctor's. But she would believe the girl. She had enough experience for that.

He held himself back, pressed against the trunk of a cherry tree. The bark was dirty. It would come off on his clothes. Dusk was creeping through the trees now, thick and blue. Soon it would be dark. Surely she wouldn't stay long? He could hear nothing but the purling of the stream. Maybe something had happened to her. She'd slipped on the wet stones, and fallen. She'd struck her head. Her face lay in the water. He should help her – after all, he was a doctor . . .

No, you fool, he told himself. His coat of vodka was wearing thin. It wasn't keeping him warm any more. He hadn't realized how much he had sweated. The sweat was cold now, and his shirt clung to him. Had he really seen the girl, or not? The image of her slipping into the trees seemed barely real. Had it all been just vodka and a trick of the light?

How rough and dirty the cherry-tree bark was. Who would believe that such white flowers could grow from it, or such round glistening fruit? He had cut down his cherry trees, because of Johanna. But not all of them. Even Johanna couldn't pretend that this stand of cherries threatened her view. She'd never liked this wild part of their grounds, but it was what he loved best. The boggy patches down by the stream, the smell of water peppermint, the little yellow irises that flowered there in late spring, the wild mallow and stray forget-me-nots and croaking frogs with their slippery billows of spawn. He would bend down and peer at the threads of life wriggling in the spawn, as tadpoles began to develop.

And in summer, the tall rods of rosebay willowherb. He'd rolled in the bog as a child, over and over, crushing the vegetation, soaking himself in mud and slime. He had picked wild strawberries in the sunny clearing. He had chewed leaves of water peppermint, he had blown away the seeds of rosebay willowherb and spent hours watching the frogs. He had never known Johanna half as well as he knew the touch and smell and contour of this stream and its bogland, these cherry and birch trees.

Maybe she likes it here too, he thought. Eeva. Maybe that's why she stays so long. He pictured her squatting in the stream, head up, alert as a deer, and then dipping her hands again into the water.

Just when he'd given her up, she came. A blackbird broke through the bushes ahead of her, its wings flapping the leaves, protesting at the disturbance. The girl ran quickly across the clearing. Her arms were wrapped tight around her shivering body, hiding her belly and breasts. She pulled open the door of the sauna, and disappeared inside. She hadn't spotted him. She'd never known he was there.

Eeva was going to bathe in the sauna again. She didn't care that it was getting dark. He wouldn't care, if he were her. The dry, resinous heat of the sauna would be folding around her already, warming her cold flesh. She would sigh, and lean back on the bench, and let the heat enter her. No doubt she would go to the stream again later, when she was flushed and sweating from the sauna. Her feet would pick their way over grass and damp earth. There would be streaks of mud on the pale sides of her feet.

The sauna door was closed. It was so ordinary and so familiar, a sauna like a thousand others. But she was in there. It wasn't his sauna any more, but a mysterious, hidden space that belonged to Eeva. Even though the door was closed and she couldn't possibly see him, he stayed in the shelter of the cherry, doubly hidden by the growing dark. He would not frighten her.

He'd been born there, in that sauna which seemed to be Eeva's now. His mother had wrenched open the door in the last stage of her labour, and clambered onto the bench to give birth to him. Old Katariina had followed her inside, and closed the door on his father. He'd first opened his eyes there, to see that knotted pine wood and his mother's face, flushed with birth, the whites of her eyes stained with tiny broken blood vessels. Katariina's stories had been so real that they'd become his own memories.

'And then you slipped out, just like a fish. You didn't give your mother any trouble. She couldn't wait until you were swaddled to hold you. No, she had to have you right away, all naked.'

How embarrassed he'd been, at eight, when Katariina said 'all naked'. He'd been afraid she'd go and tell the story in front of other people. But he'd been glad, too.

At eight he'd had no idea what birth was. After years of attending childbirth he knew more. The baby would have been bloodstained and greasy with vernix. Its bluish colour would have flushed red as it took its first breaths. Probably it would have urinated in its first spasm of crying. But his mother, his firm, contained mother with her tight waist and long dragging skirts, she had not been able to wait for him. She'd grabbed hold of that wet, slippery, bloodstreaked little creature and put him naked to her breast.

But he couldn't go into the sauna now. He must stay outside.

10

If she could read, she could also write. He would test her, Thomas thought.

'Eeva, I was thinking that you may have friends. That you may want to communicate with them.'

She stood perfectly still, a bowl of dried peas in her hands. Slowly, she lowered it to the kitchen table. She said nothing.

'I mean that you may wish to write a letter.'

'Write a letter? But –'

'I will pay the postage for you,' he added quickly, to forestall her. He was afraid that she was about to say to him what she'd told Lotta. *I can't read. I don't know how to write.*

'I know you're an orphan,' he went on, 'but perhaps you have friends? Distant relations?'

'Yes,' she said, but as if she was thinking, not agreeing. 'I have a friend.'

'If you want to write, I could send the letter for you, when I am next in town.'

She wiped her hands on her apron, looking at him. 'Why?' she asked.

'Because – because I want to help you, Eeva.'

'Oh.'

He thought she wasn't going to say any more, but suddenly she looked him straight in the face and said, 'We weren't allowed to write letters, in the House of Orphans.'

'I know.'

'Nobody's heard from me for years. They probably think I'm dead.'

Had she really said that? The anger in her voice almost made him step back.

'Anna-Liisa means well. She believes it's better to sever all

74

connections,' he said hurriedly. 'Some of the girls, you know, had to be taken away from bad influences. You are too young to understand. It seems harsh, but it's for your welfare.'

Eeva's hands tightened on a fold of her apron. 'She thinks it's better to take us away from everything,' she said.

She seemed not to care what she said to him. Suddenly he felt a fool. She didn't look too young to understand anything, in fact her face was full of knowledge. But she shouldn't know such things, he thought.

'Anna-Liisa is a good woman,' he went on, feeling he must assert himself. 'She has a difficult job to do. You don't know what some of these girls have been removed from.'

Incest, he thought. Families crammed to sleep in a room. Brothers and sisters in one bed, fathers too close to daughters. The children of prostitutes being taught their trade.

He'd treated a child whose back was permanently scarred by being burned with a flat iron. 'It was done deliberately,' Anna-Liisa told him, her gossipy lips drawn tight for once, her eyes full of a knowledge he wouldn't have thought she possessed. 'There are people who take pleasure in such things.'

Eeva was looking at him with a strange expression. Impatient, and a little pitying, the look of an adult waiting for a child to catch up. He wondered, suddenly, what her experience had really been. What had Eeva been taken away from?

'Why do you want to help me?' Eeva asked. The question fell like a drop of water, and ran away into silence. He couldn't answer it. He didn't even know what she'd meant by it. Was she mocking him, telling him she knew what he was like, and what he wanted? He could only fumble.

'Because I'm responsible for you. Because you're living under my roof and I want you to be –'

She didn't fill the pause.

'Happy,' he said at last. 'Or at least, not unhappy.'

'My work's good,' she said, 'I do everything that's needed. Don't I?'

'Don't be silly, Eeva, I'm not complaining of your work. All I'm

75

saying is that I want you to feel . . . I want you to feel that this is your home.'

'Helsinki is my home.'

He wanted to shake her. 'I know. Of course that's where you come from. But you're here, now. This is where you're living your life. It's not a railway waiting room.'

'What do you think I'm waiting for?' she asked quickly.

'I don't know. For heaven's sake, Eeva, I'm not attacking you. All I'm saying is that you are living here. This isn't some other girl's life, it's yours. It belongs to you and you won't get a better one. It's a crime to let even one day disappear. So, if I can make your life better –'

'But why? Why should you? Why do you want to? I'm nothing to you.'

'No,' he said, 'that's not true.'

'I'm just a servant.'

She was angry now and she couldn't hide it. She wanted to shout at him. Words boomed in her head, powerful enough to break every plate in the kitchen: *Don't talk to me like my father. You are nothing compared to him. Nothing, do you hear me?*

'You are not my father,' she said, in a voice so low that he was not sure he'd heard her correctly. Her face was shuttered with anger and pain. He wanted to hold her as once he had held Minna.

'Your father's memory is sacred to you,' Thomas said, as gently as he could. 'We won't talk about this any more.'

Her eyes shone and he thought she was going to cry, but instead she said in a voice that was tight but not hostile any more, 'Yes.'

They looked at each other. How were they going to get back onto safe ground, where he was the doctor and she was Eeva, working in the kitchen? It was like a game of chess that had gone wrong, he thought. They were supposed to move only in certain ways. If a pawn refused to soldier forward step by step, stopping where it ought to stop, this is what happened. Boundaries broke, and the pieces lay everywhere. She was a girl, and he was a man. She was the age of his daughter – no, younger. And that made it even worse.

He was going to tell her to pack her things and go, she thought. He was going to tell Anna-Liisa what she'd said. *You are nothing. You are nothing.* Had she really said that to him? No, she can't have said those words aloud. They only boomed in her thoughts. He'd have slapped her face, kicked her out of the door.

He could kick her out of the door. If he told Anna-Liisa she was no good, Eeva would never get another place.

And then what? Out in the road with her bundle, miles from anywhere. Those trees everywhere, all around, pressing in on her. Not so much as a shop to steal from if she got desperate. Never mind. I can walk to Helsinki if I have to. It'll take days and days but I'm strong. And I'll find Lauri and he'll help me.

She saw herself at farm doors, being chased away by dogs. They would think she was a bad girl, a beggar or worse. I'll find work along the way, she thought. There'll be something I can do.

They're clever, she thought. They train you for domestic service and that's it. They won't teach anything that lets you escape. But she could read and write and she could learn fast. There were women who worked in offices now; typewriters, they were called. They sat down in warm clean offices and they had a holiday every Sunday. She had seen them hurrying to work in Helsinki.

But she looked wrong for an office. She hadn't got the right clothes and she couldn't get them. You couldn't get that kind of job unless you looked right and had done the right training, and you couldn't look right until you already had the job and the money that went with it. Don't waste your time thinking about office work, Eeva. There'll be a factory job for you in Helsinki somewhere.

He was still staring at her, as if he was trying to see inside her.

'Go and write your letter, Eeva, and I'll make sure it's posted,' he said.

'I'm making pea soup,' she objected. She wanted him to realize that he'd be banjaxed without her to make his soup. He didn't know where anything was, in the kitchen. Even Mrs Eriksson knew more about his kitchen than he did.

'Well, after you've made the soup.'

She was turning back to her work. He nearly said it then: *Eeva,*

Mrs Eriksson tells me that she is planning to teach you to read. Why did you tell her you couldn't read? I know that you can.

But the words stayed in his head. Her heavy calico apron was drawn tight around her waist. She stretched up, to reach a colander from the top shelf. That clumsy skirt was too short for her. Her ankles showed, and part of her calves in grey woollen stockings. She had thin ankles. The stockings were snagged and matted. Suddenly he thought of Johanna's stockings. She wore fine lisle, and silk in summer. Her stockings fitted exactly. Not that he saw much of them, he thought bitterly. And Minna's plump little calves, stuffed into warm woollen leggings. Johanna would pinch the sides of Minna's boots, gently, to make sure that the child's growing feet weren't cramped. If they were, there would be new boots at once. Soft leather boots with button fastenings. He left all that to Johanna. He was proud that she knew all the things the child needed, at each stage of her life.

Eeva's boots were heavy and they looked too big for her. Yes, that was why her feet clattered when she walked about. The boots slipped and her heel rose and then slid back into the boot. So she clumped and clattered across the kitchen. Oh God, he thought, she's slipshod. What Eeva's feet do, that's what the word means.

All the same her movements flowed like water. He could not stop watching her. She put the colander down on the table and tipped the peas into it. The surface of her forehead wrinkled in concentration as she picked over the peas and took out any that were shrivelled or black. He thought that her forehead was like a lake, quick to change as the wind blew on it. How quick her fingers were too. She was good with her hands, yes, anyone could see that there was a brain behind those fingers. Her forehead was round and high, her skin very pale after the winter. He must stop watching her. He must go.

I want to help you, Eeva. Up in her attic, she took her basin and jug off the little table and sat down. He had lent her a pen with a steel nib, and a white china inkwell full of black ink. She had four sheets of good paper, a sheet of blotting paper and an envelope.

But maybe he only wanted her to write a letter so he could read it. Her father had taught her about spies. Police spies, government spies: they were everywhere. They watched for years and years if need be, building up evidence and reporting back to their masters. Her father was on their lists for sure. Maybe she was on those lists too, because she was his daughter.

She remembered a meeting in their apartment, long ago. She hadn't seen this particular man before, but that didn't mean anything. People came and went, they gave her an apple and ruffled her hair, or showed her tricks with cards.

But she picked up the tension in the room. Her father spoke loudly and clearly, introducing the stranger who smiled readily and tried to give his hand to everyone. 'We have a friend from Petersburg with us tonight. He has a letter of introduction from comrades there.' She noticed something strange. Her father said 'a friend'. When people came, they were not usually called friend. They were called comrade.

The evening wore on. The man sat by the stove as if he would sit there for ever. Mika was there, and Lauri played twenty-one with Eeva. They played and played and no one told them it was time to sleep. Big Juha was there, and Eero. They sat one on either side of the stranger. Juha's broad hands were planted on his knees. Often she sat on Juha's knee, and he played at being a wild bear and she had to hold on tight so as not to be thrown to the floor. He had a thick beard and hair on the back of his hands and he looked a bit like a bear, so that there was terror in the excitement of the game.

But there was no playing that night. Lauri and Eeva kept giving each other quick little looks, checking if the other one knew what was going on. She'd have been scared, if Lauri hadn't been there. The men were talking, but not really saying anything. The new one was asking questions in a bright and friendly voice. The air was thick with tobacco smoke and they kept giving the strange man vodka even though he said, 'No, no, comrades, I've had enough.' They wouldn't let him refuse. He had to empty his glass but she saw that Eero and Big Juha weren't emptying theirs.

He said 'comrades', but they didn't. His questions grew longer and they didn't make sense. She knew from his voice that he was drunk. When men sounded as if their tongues were too thick for their mouths, then they were drunk.

It was late when the stranger got up to leave. He staggered and put out his hand to balance himself and she thought he was going to grab hold of her. She flinched towards Lauri, but Eero and Big Juha had already got hold of the stranger, one on each side. They said, 'Steady now, friend, you shouldn't try and walk alone, you need help.'

They helped him out of the apartment. Her father held the door, watching them go.

Much, much later, when she and Lauri were asleep in her bed in the corner of the room, there was a knock on the door. It was a very soft knock, but it woke her. Lauri was curled up so only the top of his head showed. But there was her father, getting up from his chair by the stove. Why, he hadn't gone to bed at all! He must have lit a fresh candle.

Her father's shadow stretched across the wall as he went to open the door. There were low voices on the landing outside, and then Big Juha came into the apartment. He looked bigger than ever in his thick coat, with his hat pulled down so that hardly any of his face showed. But it was him for sure. She knew his voice and shape and the shaggy rabbit-skin hat that she always liked to stroke. There was a pelt of snow on his shoulders.

'You've sorted it, then?' her father said quietly.

'That's right. He took a nasty fall on the ice, struck the back of his head. He's sleeping it off in a snowdrift. It's a bit of an out-of-the-way spot so it's not likely he'll be found before morning. Snow's coming down thick.'

'Keep it quiet, Juha. You'll wake the little ones.'

The bear shifted his feet and snow slid off his shoulders. 'I'll be off then,' he growled.

'No, you stay here. You don't want to be wandering about tonight. If you get picked up they might make the connection.'

80

'You're right. Should've thought of that. I'll doss down by the stove and be off first thing.'

'You can have my bed. I'm working tonight.'

'Well, if you're sure –'

Big Juha was going past her into the inner room. She felt his shadow, and squeezed her eyes shut. He halted by her bed and she heard his breathing come closer and closer as he bent down. She felt the cold that clung to him, and a drop of icy water fell on her chin. She didn't move. She kept her eyes shut tight, tight. Very gently, so gently that it didn't feel like Juha at all, a hand stroked her hair.

Why had she thought of all that now? She'd never even told Lauri about what happened in the middle of that night. In the morning Juha wasn't there, and her father was making porridge as usual.

She would write a letter to Lauri, but it would be a letter anyone could read. It would reveal nothing but where she was and that she was safe and well. Lauri would understand. The doctor would put her letter in the post for her, he said. She'd seen his letters waiting on the post table: letters waiting to go out, and letters that had come in. If she wrote this letter, if she dipped the pen into the ink and crowded the paper with words, then in a few weeks there might be a letter for her.

Would Lauri guess what she wanted to hear? They had never needed to write in the old days. Mika and Lauri were in their apartment most days, when her father was alive. Lauri stayed with them for weeks sometimes. And after her father's death she went to live with Mika and Lauri. Anything she and Lauri wanted to say, they just said it.

The paper was white and clear, like snow. She didn't want to make a mark on it. Snow's beautiful when it's white and intact but when it melts there's an ugly between-time, before the sun grows strong. You feel cold and wretched and mud soaks into your boots. Lauri was so far away. Probably he believed he'd never see her again. What would he think when he got a letter like a piece of snow with black footprints on it?

That's if nothing's happened, thought Eeva. If they're still there. Mika's apartment had been searched. They took away books and papers when they arrested him, and they took Eeva. 'They won't find anything,' Lauri had whispered. But they'd found her. Who was she, what was she doing there, what was her relationship with Mika and Lauri? Whose daughter was she?

Ah.

Mika had no right to stop them taking her. He wasn't related to her, was he? A friend of her father, that was all. You can't have a young girl living with an adult man and a boy who is rising sixteen. They're not children any more, to share a bed. Anyway, he was under arrest.

They said she was in moral danger. She was so stupid then, she didn't even know what the words meant. Only that her life was being taken away from her.

'I'll visit his grave every week, I promise,' Lauri said.

When she thought of Lauri, there he was as she'd last seen him. In the apartment with his hair sticking up where he'd pulled off his cap. His grey eyes were full of anger. He couldn't stop them from taking his father away, or Eeva. He couldn't do anything. Lauri had his cap in his hands and he was twisting it and crushing it. So the last look she had from him was a look of anger. She knew Lauri wasn't angry with her, but it was hard to blot out that memory of him, and remember him as he had been on ordinary days.

Her father didn't mind anger as she did. 'We should be angry, Eevi. If we aren't, then nothing will ever change. Why do you think the priests tell us to be patient and know our place in life, and wait for our reward in heaven? It's to keep us from demanding a better place now. Heaven's a very convenient place for the ruling class.' Her father had often said that.

She'd wanted so much to believe in heaven when he was dying. But she didn't dare believe in it for him, against his will. When Eeva was little, Mrs Peltonen in the next apartment had taught her to sing 'O brightest star'.

O brightest star, we praise Thy light.
Before we close our eyes each night
We sing our hymn, O brightest star,
Lead us to heaven where Thou art.

She had loved the tune, and thought the words beautiful. She'd sung it under her breath at home, half-wanting him to hear.

'What's that dirge you're singing, Eevi?'

'It's a hymn.'

'Go on, let's hear it properly. Strike up.'

She sang out loud, but the hymn didn't sound as sweet as it was inside her head. Her father grunted. 'Where did you get that one from?'

'Mrs Peltonen taught it to me.'

'She should know about seeing stars, the way her old man knocks her about.' He folded back his newspaper. 'It's superstition, Eevi. It's to make people feel better about their lives, without doing anything to change them.'

She'd felt crushed. She'd avoided Mrs Peltonen on the landing for weeks, even though she loved the way Mrs Peltonen smelled of bread and called her 'my little golden one'.

Eeva laid the paper straight in front of her, and dipped the pen in the inkwell. A heavy drop wobbled on the end of the nib. She tapped off the excess. She had forgotten how satisfying it was to have a pen that was just right, that sat in your hand and was full of words you hadn't even thought of yet.

She looked out through the attic window. There were the trees, marching eastward towards where Lauri was. Her city was still there and her words would reach it.

II

Dear Lauri

You will be surprised to hear from me after so long. I am in service
with a widowed doctor. I keep house for him. Do you ever visit the
place you said that you would visit? If you write to me at this address
I will get the letter. All the letters that come to the house are put on a
table in the hall, for the doctor.

I hope that you and all our friends are well and that you have not
forgotten me. Remember me to your father.
Your friend,
Eeva

Your friend, Eeva. Lauri was clever, he would understand that she
was being careful. They had both been brought up to watch what
they said outside the house. He'd know that she wasn't writing
freely. He'd understand what she meant by telling him about the
doctor's post table. He would write back just as guardedly, knowing
that his letter might be read by other eyes than hers.

But suddenly caution sickened her. She leaned back from the
table, distancing herself from the letter. And then what, she asked
herself. I send a letter which says nothing, and Lauri sends back a
letter which says nothing. Where does that get us? No, why be so
careful if it means that there's no meaning left?

She laid the letter to one side, and took another sheet of paper.
She'd write again, differently. She would ask the doctor for an
advance out of her wages, and pay her own postage. Matti would
post a letter for her. He'd think it was a love letter.

Dear Lauri

It's so long since I saw you. Sometimes I think I can't remember what
you look like, and when I do remember, your face is angry, just as it

84

was the last time. Do you remember? You wanted to fight them when they took me away. And I said inside myself, 'Don't fight, Lauri, don't give them any excuse to hurt you.'

I wonder where you're working? I'm in service, that's what we all go on to when we leave the House of Orphans. They train us up for it. The training seemed to last for ever, but when I look back it seems a short time.

There's just me here but the work isn't heavy. I don't do the charring and the laundry is sent out. I work for a doctor who is widowed and has one daughter who never comes to see him. He's a Swede. It's not a bad job but this place is stuck out in the forest and at night you can hear the trees rustling and the wind, and nothing else. There are no lights and no people.

I've already lived three lives. Our life in Helsinki that you know about, the House of Orphans, and here. I don't know how many lives you've lived. I'm the one who went away, and it's easy to believe that the ones who stayed behind are still the same, but I know it isn't true. Things have happened to you too, Lauri, and you won't be the same. Maybe you aren't even living at your apartment any more, and so you won't get this letter, unless the person who lives there now knows where you are. You could be anywhere. Didn't Mika used to talk about going to Petersburg again? Maybe that's where you are.

I must finish now. I've got cakes to bake for tomorrow. I nearly started to write about all the things we used to do, but I don't need to remind you about them. No, you'll understand that it wasn't that I didn't want to write to you before, it was that I couldn't. Maybe I could have found a way round it, but I didn't.

You remember how they were always telling us the world was changing? Here, it hasn't changed at all. It's like stepping back a hundred years. When I see you, maybe you won't be the Lauri I remember. You won't have your blue cap, and you won't be able to run faster than me and get to the corner just a bit ahead of me, and your hair will have fallen out. You'll be an old man and you'll say, 'Where have you been, Eeva? I gave up thinking of you long ago. I waited for a long while but I couldn't wait any more.' And then you'll show me your great-grandchildren.

85

But even if you can't answer this letter, Lauri, keep it. Keep it as a talisman.
Your friend,
Eeva

She sealed the letter, and wrote Lauri's address on the front. Then she sat for a while, gazing out of the window without seeing anything. At last, as if something had been decided, she took another sheet of paper and copied the first letter she'd written, changing Lauri's name. When she'd finished, she invented an address.

What do they do with a letter when the address on it doesn't exist? Eeva didn't know, but she thought that the letter would be put away somewhere in a corner of a post office, to gather dust. She would give it to the doctor. Even if he opened it, he'd find out nothing.

Thomas held the letter Eeva had given him to post. She'd already sealed it and written the direction. Strange, he couldn't recall a street of that name in Helsingfors. But she must know. Probably it was in one of the new workers' quarters that were springing up in the factory district.

He looked at the lines of the address. Her writing was good. An educated hand, almost an elegant one. How had she come by such handwriting? She'd written those words with the pen he had given her. It was his paper, his envelope. But these elements that belonged to him had become Eeva's letter, just as the food that belonged to him went into Eeva's body and became part of her.

He could own the food and the ink and the paper but he couldn't own her words or the mysterious change which transformed his food into the flesh that tormented him. Don't fool yourself, he thought. She was a servant and there were holes in her stockings, and yet she could write as well as Minna. Again he had the sense of another self inside her, inaccessible. What words had that private Eeva made?

He saw her as clearly as if he'd been in that attic room. He saw her dip her pen decisively in the pool of ink, and write on the

86

creamy surface of the paper he'd given her. He saw her catch her under lip with her teeth, and look up with her green eyes, then down, into her private self.

He had to know. He held the envelope she'd given him up to the light. There was just one folded sheet of paper, no more. Thomas could see the darker outline of the paper within the envelope. He could open it and reseal it and she would never know.

No. No, he wouldn't. What kind of a man would do that, in his own house?

He laid Eeva's letter down on the silver tray that held his letters. His house was around him, with all its habits. His hall with its smell of polished wood, the oak post table, the pair of high-backed chairs that no one ever sat on. All of these belonged to him and had shaped him. Before he was even born, he had walked in this hall inside his mother's body. Eeva was like the bird in the tale, that blew from one end of the hall to another, from dark night into dark night. She had no connection here. She was an orphan and a girl from nowhere, from generations of people who had owned nothing and left no mark on the earth.

She'll go away, he thought. She'll leave and I'll never find her.

I could pay her more. I could arrange lessons for her. No one ever plays Minna's piano. Eeva might like to learn.

As if Eeva had already learned, he seemed to hear the notes moving in the quiet hall. Her fingers would be sure on the keys. She would be one of those players who seem to listen their way into the music.

Something's happening to me, he thought. I'm going crazy. Lotta's right, I ought not to be living out here like this, with Johanna dead. Lotta wants me to move into town and shut this place up. Well, maybe I should consider it.

But he knew he would not. He felt a pulse of pleasure at the bare thought of everything Lotta didn't know and would never guess. Eeva, he thought. Eeva. In the kitchen, now at this moment, Eeva was. She would be stepping from sink to table, her heels clap-clapping. She would brush a piece of hair off her forehead with the back of her hand, because her hands were floury.

Eeva was under his roof. Let Lotta put that in her pipe and smoke it, he thought, his teeth bared in a grin Lotta had never seen.

Eeva gave her letter to Matti, with money for the stamp. She'd told the doctor that she needed an advance on her wages to buy personal things. As she'd reckoned, he asked no questions. Matti folded the letter away inside his jacket. His hands had a way of seeming careful of what they held, as if it were alive or might be. She trusted Matti: he would post her letter. Matti couldn't read, but he admired Eeva's handwriting. 'It's as good as the doctor's,' he said. 'Where did you learn that?'

'My father taught me.'

'Ah.'

Matti wasn't a man of words. He didn't read them or trust them much. 'Don't you worry about your letter, Eeva. I'll see it gets there safe, far as I can.'

He had that natural delicacy which stopped him asking who the letter was for, or what it was about. She stood in the kitchen doorway and the warm spring wind made her skirt billow, then blew it back against her body. She was wearing a clean white apron and the sun was so brilliant that they both shaded their eyes.

'Well, this won't get my carrots planted,' he said. 'Soil's just right, warmed up nicely. Anything you put in on a day like this's going to grow.'

'I'll come and look at the kitchen garden,' she said. She had a hunger for outdoors. At home she would have walked down to the wide, blowy harbour, to see the ships set out for Stockholm and Talinn and Bremen and Petersburg and all the far places. There were roads in the sea just as there were roads on the land, her father said. The emigrants went out from Hangö, and then they sailed to a place in England called Hull, then they took the big ships from Liverpool to America. That was the road they took.

She missed the smell and sight of the sea, and the feeling it gave that you could go anywhere and find new worlds if the old one wasn't good enough. Matti had never seen the sea.

'I'll come now,' she said, and untied her white apron so it wouldn't get dirty. They walked together around the house, down the path, through the hedge and into the kitchen garden. It faced south, and was set on sloping ground to trap every drop of sun. It had the dazed look of a garden in spring, with the earth turned and broken and smoothed again, the fruit bushes unwrapped from their winter wadding of straw, and the glass cloches glinting with reflected sun. The soil Matti had dug and raked that morning was still damp, and a darker brown than the bare surrounding soil. The breeze ran over it, drying it. Eeva stooped to crumble the earth between her fingers. It smelled good. Sun and rain had got into it and sweetened the sour smell of winter.

'I've never grown anything,' she said.

He stared at her.

'I haven't. Not a single flower.'

'You're a real city girl, you are, eating potatoes all your life without knowing where they come from.'

'They come out of sacks in the market, and if you've no money you can't have them, I know that.'

'Well, there's the difference. As long as I've got my patch of earth, I don't have to ask anyone for anything. All this here is grown for the house, but I keep my own garden.'

'What do you grow?'

'Same as I do here. Potatoes, cabbage, onions, carrots, beetroot, dill, cucumbers. I don't bother with all these fine salads the doctor likes. Raspberries I grow, and white currants. These here, Eeva, they're raspberry canes. The wild ones are the sweetest but for size you need the cultivars.'

He looked at home here, as if he owned the garden, Eeva thought.

'Have you been inside our glasshouse, Eeva?'

'No.'

'It's something to see. You want to take a look?'

'All right.'

It was the doctor's folly. He kept the glasshouse stoves burning through the winter, to keep out the frost. Pipes wriggled along the walls, filled with hot water. He'd had the system installed, on an

English pattern. There was a vine, and citrus trees in pots which had been brought back from Italy one summer years ago. Matti said the word 'citrus' with pride, and told her that it meant oranges, and lemons. She didn't say that she knew it already.

Matti opened the door. The air was dry and she snuffed the glasshouse smell of soil and earthenware and trapped sun. She could smell the lemon trees, too. They had fruit on them, green and yellow, and there were flowers opening on the trees at the same time. The leaves were dark and leathery, and the trees were as tall as Eeva, standing in their pots. She smelled the small waxen flowers, and their scent was so powerful that she closed her eyes.

'They take up more water than you'd think, for all they come from a hot country,' said Matti, bending to test the soil. 'In Italy they have systems to irrigate them, so the doctor says. He's been there a fair few times.'

'What does he do with the lemons? I've never seen them in the kitchen.'

'He uses them for medicine. Spring tonics and such.'

She put her hand under the ripest of the fruit, weighing it. How strange to hold a fruit when it was still alive and growing, instead of when it was rolled into a heap on a market stall. The lemon was perfect, like a model of itself.

'Should you like to taste it?' Matti asked. He took out his clasp-knife, opened the blade, and cut the stem of the lemon. The blade of his knife looked worn and thin, but the lemon fell plump into his hand. 'There you are, Eeva. It's for you.'

'Thank you, Matti.' He'd acted so swiftly she hadn't had time to stop him. Who'd have thought Matti would do that? She wouldn't have stopped him anyway. Imagine her having a lemon in her hand that had been cut from a living tree, while she watched.

'I wonder what it tastes like.'

'I'll cut it for you.'

He brushed some crumbs of soil from the board shelf by the glasshouse door, and laid the lemon on it. His clasp-knife sliced through skin and flesh, and the lemon fell into two pieces. Beads of juice sprang onto the cut surface, like beads of sweat. She picked up one half, and held it to her nose. The scent was quite different from the scent of shop lemons. It was fragrant and fruity, but not acid at all. She put out her tongue and licked off the beads of ripe juice.

'I like it,' she said.

'You should squeeze it out and make yourself a little drink. Lemon cleanses the blood.'

'Don't you want to taste it?'

'That's not my style, Eeva.'

And all the time, she thought, her letter was there in his jacket pocket, growing warm with the warmth of the glasshouse. She felt herself flushing with the heat. It was like being in the sauna, sweat prickling on her skin like a thousand bees. But in the sauna you are naked, your skin like that lemon with the juice on it.

'I come in here sometimes, in winter, just for a warm-up,' said Matti. 'But I keep the door locked, 'case someone gets in careless, and leaves the door open and we lose the trees and the vine.' The stubby ends of the vine had buds beginning to break.

'Is it a grape-vine? Do real grapes grow on it?'

She had seen grapes, but never tasted them. She had seen them pyramided in the windows of expensive shops.

'You'll see them in the autumn. Fine grapes we grow here. When Mrs Eklund was alive she'd have them in the centre of the table on a white dish, with the bloom still on them. She'd come down here and cut a bunch for the table, with a pair of silver scissors she had. I never cut a bunch the whole season.'

'But you do now.'

'That's right. 'Less you come down and cut them for me? It's a woman's place to do that, it seems to me. Mrs Eklund never washed the grapes 'fore they came to table, to keep the bloom on them. She kept a bowl of water on the table to wash the grapes.'

Eeva saw herself in this same glasshouse, when the bare vine was thick and heavy with fruit. She wasn't sure how grapes grew. Did they hang off the branches, like apples?

'Most likely the doctor's still got those silver scissors some-where.'

'What was she like?'

But he stared, blank, as if the question held no meaning for him, and she was embarrassed at having asked.

'I'd better get back,' she said, and saw that Matti was relieved. He wanted to be alone now, back with his glasshouse and his soft black earth waiting for the carrot seed. He'd wanted her here, and now he didn't.

You won't forget my letter? she wanted to ask, but she kept silent. That was the way she knew, keeping silent and waiting.

Clouds had blown over the sun. Good spring weather, sun and then rain. She was restless inside herself. It was spring fever, she knew that. You ate salads of young nettle shoots and dandelion leaves, to curb it. Or else you found a boy and went walking with him where no one else would find you. Her body shivered. She'd never done that, never gone courting as they called it. 'You'll be educated, Eevi,' her father had said. 'You'll make something of your life. Everything's changing and the more it changes the better the world will be.' But she'd ended up in the House of Orphans all the same. So what, she told herself. I'm out of that now. That was just a stage. A historical stage, she added, smiling, remembering the phrases that had droned in the background while she read and worked.

Her letter would go to Helsinki. She could trust Matti for that. But it was quite possible that Lauri wouldn't answer it.

She walked back to the house.

'You're on your own, my girl,' she muttered to herself in the rough voice she sometimes had to use against her own weakness. She stopped under one of the young birches Matti said the doctor had planted, to replace some that had been cut down. The leaves were unfolding, green and tender as they'd never be once the sun and wind had hardened them. She looked up at the colour of green against the blue sky that was half blotted with clouds. It was as true as she stood there. She felt the words coming true inside her. She was on her own and her life belonged to her, only to her.

12

Should she consult Karl? No, it would be useless. Karl never noticed what was going on. That was his forte, Lotta had realized it long ago. But perhaps it was her duty to talk to Karl. Thomas was such an old friend, such a dear friend, and now that he was on his own . . . (Already, she knew, she was phrasing her story as she would phrase it to Karl.) He had had such a difficult time. First Johanna's death and then Minna so cold and hard, not at all what a daughter should be. Minna hadn't visited her father for months, and he never spoke of going to see her in Åbo. (And a small part of Lotta was comforted, as it always was when other people's children failed them.)

Yes, she would go to Karl. She would talk it over openly and sensibly. It was no good getting too emotional about these things. Thomas was not himself. He seemed to be avoiding his oldest friends. But Lotta wasn't going to let herself be hurt. She had a duty to Thomas which was more important than the fact that he didn't seem to . . .

Better not to think of that. The sense of Thomas in her life, which had always been warm and consoling, was suddenly a bruise she didn't dare to press.

She would talk to Karl. She had reached this point, and it would be weak to turn back. Lotta squared her shoulders, drew in her stomach, and stepped down the gravel path towards Karl's workshop.

She rarely went there. The sight of Karl's long thin figure disappearing down the path – 'his' path – each morning was enough. He appeared to stroll casually, even to stray along as if he weren't quite sure where he was going, but she wasn't fooled. She knew Karl's iron determination to live as he wanted to live, and in no other way. Quietly, but with great force, he wore his world down until it did what he wanted.

She flung her head back, and tapped at the door. After an unsettling pause, Karl called, 'Come in.'

She pushed open the door, and the fragrance of wood wrapped around her. Everybody loved it. Visitors whom Karl invited into his workshop would stand and snuff up great nosefuls of it. 'Oh! How wonderful! Imagine working with this beautiful wood all day long. How I wish I had such a talent.' Karl would explain that every wood had its own scent, as well as its own density and grain. He would let the visitors smell apple wood, cedar, and a hard wood from South America which he said smelled of gooseberries. Lotta could never remember its name. They would sniff the South American wood, holding it close to their noses in rapture. 'Yes! You're right! It smells exactly like gooseberries.'

'My dear Lotta!' said Karl smoothly. 'This is a surprise.'

'I need to talk to you, Karl.'

'Well, here I am. Talk away,' he said, keeping a faint preoccupied smile on his face. What had he been doing before she knocked? He didn't seem to be busy. There were no curls of shaven wood on the floor. He hadn't even put on his working smock. He was just sitting in his basket chair, doing nothing. A pang of pain shot up her spine. She'd walked too fast down that path.

'I'm concerned about Thomas,' said Lotta. She was pleased with the calm seriousness of her voice, and the way she had chosen the word 'concerned' rather than 'worried'. Karl wouldn't be able to say she was being too emotional. *Surely you're overreacting, my dear Lotta. You're making too much of this.*

He sat there, silent, the preoccupied look on his face deepening.

'About Thomas?' he said at last.

'Yes. He isn't himself. He's unhappy.'

'How long is it since Johanna died?' asked Karl, as if he genuinely couldn't remember.

'This has nothing to do with Johanna,' rapped out Lotta, then she caught herself. Karl had done it again. He'd pushed her into saying more than she meant.

'A widower surely has a right to be unhappy. Almost, one might say, a duty,' murmured Karl. 'I should mourn you, my dear Lotta, if you were to die.'

She looked at him, but made no answer.

'Why are you so . . . *concerned*?' asked Karl. His tone was neutral. She couldn't tell if there were malice in the question, or not.

'Thomas is our oldest friend,' she said. 'Naturally I am concerned for him. He's living alone out there, and a man who spends too much time on his own gets strange ideas.'

'I thought he had a girl to look after him.'

'Yes.'

'So he's not alone.'

Lotta stared at her husband's bland face. He was sitting comfortably in his basket chair, his legs crossed, one hand clasping a slender ankle.

'Men get strange ideas, at Thomas's time of life. They are easily influenced,' she said at last.

'And who do you think is going to influence our dear friend Thomas?' he asked. How carefully he was watching her. Like a cat.

'You know exactly what I'm talking about, Karl. It's not suitable or sensible for Thomas to be alone in the house with a young girl who is . . . well, who is capable of exploiting his weaknesses.'

'Let me be sure that I've got this right, Lotta. Thomas is forty-five –'

'Forty-seven.'

'Forty-seven. I stand corrected. A professional man from a good family, well established, well connected. This girl, what is she?'

'He got her from the House of Orphans.'

'Precisely. She's a girl of no family, with nothing. What age is she? Sixteen, seventeen? And yet you say that *Thomas* is weak. So presumably you think the girl is strong?'

'That's not what I said.'

'Let us at least try to be logical, my dear Lotta. You are concerned about Thomas's weakness, not the girl's?'

'You don't understand, Karl. A girl like that can't be trusted.'

'I bow to your superior knowledge, Lotta. I have never laid eyes on the girl. But what I don't understand is why you are so troubled. Thomas is hardly going to marry her. In a year's time she will have moved on elsewhere and Thomas will feel that he has been a little foolish, and there will be the end of it.'

'I can't believe that you can be so cynical, Karl.'

He shrugged. 'It's not cynicism, Lotta. I'm a realist.'

He was waiting for her to go. She had exposed herself to him, and for nothing. Lotta pressed her lips together.

'I disagree,' she said. 'I can't allow Thomas to make a fool of himself. There are always consequences.'

'You must do as you think fit,' he said. 'After all, Thomas is your oldest friend,' and he half rose from his chair, as if she were a casual visitor who had overstayed her time.

We live together, she thought in horror, but we hate each other.

Quickly, she put the thought away where she would not be able to find it. She turned, and went out of the workshop into the bright sunshine. But although it was warm, it made her shiver all over.

She would go to Anna-Liisa. God has placed me here and I must do my duty, she thought. He has placed me here to take care of Thomas, and Erika, and Simon. And Karl. God gives us nothing to bear that we cannot bear. Yes, she would go now, immediately. She would think of the right words on the way.

Lotta put two pots of last year's lingonberry jam in her basket. Anna-Liisa loved sweet things. Lingonberry jam was always so much appreciated. I'll make more this summer, Lotta thought. She always supervised her own jam-making.

Already, summer dust was lying in the streets. Her skirts would need a good brushing when she got back. Yes, Anna-Liisa was a sensible woman. They would be able to reach an understanding. Anna-Liisa had sent the girl to Thomas, and it had been a mistake, but it could be put right.

Suddenly a child ran across Lotta's path. She'd nearly tripped over him, not looking where she was going. Had she actually tripped him? He'd fallen hard, but already he was scrambling to his feet. Like a little animal, she couldn't help thinking. Slowly, painfully, she began to bend towards him. He stared up at her, the tall column of her, and started to cry, squaring his mouth. His face was dirty. He was barefoot, in a shirt that was too big for him, and a pair of trousers that made him look like a little old man.

'Are you hurt?' she asked a little stiffly, bending further so that her shadow fell over him. She wasn't used to talking to this type of child. But he just yelled. Tears tracked down his dusty face, and he rubbed snot across his cheeks. A girl ran up, an older girl, maybe seven or eight. She was small and thin but she bent and hauled the little boy into her arms. She staggered under his weight but he clung to her like a monkey, wrapping his arms around her neck and his legs around her waist. The girl stood with her feet wide apart, to balance the child's weight, and stared up at Lotta.

'Has he hurt himself?' asked Lotta.

The girl shook her head. She hoisted the child higher. She looked so capable, so confident, though she didn't come any higher than Lotta's waist. But I'm a tall woman, and she's very small. Small for her age, perhaps. She's probably older than she looks.

'He always yells like this, 'cept when he's really hurt. He'll be all right with me. He gets scared, see.' And in a different voice, a real mother's voice, she said to the howling child, 'It's all right, give over now, Frossi's got you.'

Frossi? What an extraordinary name, thought Lotta. And she thinks the child's scared of me. Yes, very likely. She fumbled in her basket for a coin, and gave it to the girl. The girl stared, and then stuffed it away somewhere inside her skirt.

'Take him home to your mother,' advised Lotta.

'Mum's at work. I take care of the littl'uns, see.'

And the girl was off, disappearing round the corner into the warren of little wooden houses where Lotta never had occasion to go. She hadn't said thank you for the coin, Lotta realized. Well, never mind. Cast your bread upon the waters, she told herself.

Anna-Liisa was at home. She was just about to have coffee, she told Lotta, her eyes lightening at the sight of the jam. Lingonberry jam – her favourite! She liked her tea the Russian way, with a spoonful of jam. And sit down, please, Mrs Eriksson. Can I take your basket? No? Do you mind the sun, or shall I draw down the blind?

Lotta sat down carefully, slowly. The pain was bad today. She forced her spine straight. The coffee came, brought by a drab, nervous girl who didn't inspire confidence. But it was excellent coffee, fragrant and smoking hot, and there were little almond biscuits that Lotta couldn't have made better herself.

'If there's one thing they do all know by the time they leave me, it's how to make coffee,' said Anna-Liisa. Lotta couldn't help herself: a vision jumped into her mind of all the other things a girl might know by the time she left the House of Orphans. And now that she was sitting in Anna-Liisa's parlour, the subject of Eeva wasn't quite so easy to open. But then, blessedly, Anna-Liisa opened it herself.

'This is usually the doctor's day,' she said comfortably. 'But he's got an emergency. A maternity case.'

The two women caught each other's eye, then looked away. One of us unmarried, the other childless, thought Lotta. Why, Thomas knows more about birth than either of us. It was an odd thought.

'He's very good. We had a new girl with a really nasty throat last week – and he isolated her at once and came that same evening and then the next morning. It turned out all right, but you can't be too careful, what with the diphtheria that was in the paper.'

'No.'

'I don't know what we'd do without him.'

'Yes.' Lotta leaned forward. 'Anna-Liisa, I need to talk to you about a very delicate matter.'

'Delicate?' asked Anna-Liisa, as if the word were new to her.

'Yes. Delicate. You remember the girl who went to Dr Eklund as a servant?'

'Of course I do. But what do you mean, Mrs Eriksson, "went"? She's still there, isn't she? She's given satisfaction?'

'Oh yes, there's no difficulty of that sort,' soothed Lotta. 'It's not a question of her work. No. It's more the nature of her position.'

But Anna-Liisa clearly wasn't following. She looked baffled. 'The nature of her position?'

'That is, the girl – Eeva – is very young. She's used to a house full of people. And now she's on her own.'

'But she's not on her own. The doctor's there, living in the same house.'

Lotta let a silence fall, then lengthen. 'Exactly,' she said.

Anna-Liisa's healthy colour darkened. 'Well,' she said, 'well, if you mean . . . Well, if you're saying . . . No, I shan't believe such a thing of the doctor.'

'Of course not,' said Lotta quickly. 'It's not him I'm worried about. It's her. After all, with her background and the kind of inheritance these girls have, there's always a risk. All I'm saying is that I simply think it would be wiser if Eeva were found a family where there was a woman in the house, who could keep an eye on her.'

Anna-Liisa's flush deepened. But she wasn't embarrassed, Lotta realized. She was angry. 'I'll never believe that of the doctor,' she repeated, as if everything else Lotta had said meant nothing to her. 'He's a good man. Why, only last week he sat all night with the Makkonen boy, and you know as well as I do that none of those Makkonens have got a pot to piss in.' She caught herself. 'Pardon the expression, I'm that upset, I can't credit what you're saying.'

Her accent was lapsing, broadening. She was a working woman in the end, in spite of the coffee and the parlour. She was on one side of the fence, and Lotta was on the other, and Lotta realized that she'd been a fool to come to Anna-Liisa.

'I am not criticizing the doctor,' she said stiffly.

'I should think not,' said Anna-Liisa, as if Lotta were anybody. But Lotta kept her patience.

'I know it's difficult and unpleasant. Believe me, these are matters I'd far rather not discuss. But I would never forgive myself if things got out of hand.'

Anna-Liisa was silent. But she was thinking now, Lotta could tell. Thinking hard. Anna-Liisa filled both coffee cups, and munched another biscuit. The flush in her cheeks was still high, but when she spoke her voice was quieter.

'Of course,' she said consideringly, 'Eeva is growing up. I spoke to her after church on Sunday – I like to keep in touch with my girls – and I was quite struck how she's altered. She was almost . . .'

'Almost what?' urged Lotta.

'Well, how can I put it?' Anna-Liisa frowned, trying to recall what she'd thought. 'If I hadn't known it was our Eeva from the orphanage, I'd have said to myself, "What a beautiful girl."'

'Beautiful!'

'Yes.'

The two women looked at each other. Lotta felt as if Anna-Liisa had found her way to the bruise that lay deep inside Lotta, and pressed on it, hard. She took a deep breath.

'It can't go on. She has got to be taken away.'

'You'll have to speak to him then, for I'm not going to do it. I'm not going to insult the doctor, after all he's done for us.'

'You can leave it all to me. But I must ask you to keep this discussion to yourself.'

Lotta had risen. She towered over Anna-Liisa, bringing all the force of what she was to bear. The woman would keep her mouth shut. She wouldn't dare do otherwise, if she didn't want to find herself out of a job. In this town, what Mrs Eriksson said counted.

Beautiful! That thin, sly girl with her broken-down boots. It was only thanks to Lotta that she even had decent clothes to cover her body. And it was thanks to Anna-Liisa that the girl had insinuated herself into Thomas's house in the first place. No wonder she was trying to evade her responsibilities.

But you needn't think I'll let you, thought Lotta, looking down at the red, obstinate face. You can say goodbye to your parlour and your coffee and your lingonberry jam, if you won't do what's right.

It was later, much later, that she knew what to do. She hadn't gone to bed. Karl had raised his eyebrows, but said nothing. Lotta wrote a long letter to Erika, a long letter full of nothing, full of all the little details of daily life that Erika liked. The new preacher, the progress of the big spring wash, the plush monkey she had bought for Simon. A dozen precise, searching questions about health and clothes and development, to reassure Erika that nothing about her or Simon had been forgotten while she was away. But not too many questions about Frans . . . No, Frans rarely featured in their letters, and neither did Karl. It was the married state, not the man to whom she was married, that gave Erika pleasure.

We hear such alarming things in the newspaper, my dear Erika, about the political situation in St Petersburg. Be sure to keep away from crowds, especially when you are out with Simon. I don't have to tell you that the Russian temperament is very different from that of our own people. They are easy prey for agitators.

Lotta put down her pen. It was the same everywhere. People had forgotten that it was order that made civilization possible. Order, and the habit of duty, and acceptance of the situation in which God had placed you. Yes, she believed more firmly than ever as she grew older that the Almighty had a plan for everyone, no matter how lowly. To question God's order was the same as questioning His goodness. It could only lead to misery. Lives torn apart, society writhing in wretched turmoil, envy and hatred and the disappearance of all that made life good. And yet there were people who wanted this. More than that, there were people at this very moment who were plotting and planning to bring it about.

Lotta looked about her quickly, as if she might catch one of them in the act. But all was still. She let her gaze rest on the dear, familiar furniture of her little sitting room, her own room where Karl never sat. There was the oak chest that had come to her from her grandmother. It had been in the family since the sixteenth century, and was black with age. It held the family Bible, papers and letters. Her grandmother had left the chest to Lotta in her will, because, she said, 'My dear granddaughter Charlotta possesses an unequalled sense of family tradition, and will preserve our history as I mean it to be preserved.'

There'd been ructions, Lotta remembered, smiling faintly. Imagine leaving such a precious heritage to Lotta, not to the boys or her elder sister, Astrid! But the chest was hers.

Of course our good fortune is God's gift, not our own doing, she thought automatically, looking around her warm, comfortable room. But she didn't really believe it. Lotta knew that houses like hers were built up by generations of self-control, self-denial and public service. Her men had taken up their responsibilities. As soldiers they had defended and enlarged what was theirs. As men in public life they had fought longer battles, which called for guile as well as resolution.

Where would Finland be without such men? Who else could handle the Russians with such consummate skill? Lotta's men knew that they had to play a long game. There were extremes on both sides. Fennomania, Russification: both of them entirely wrong for our beloved country. Here was Governor-General Bobrikov, trying to turn Finland into Russia, with all that Slavophile nonsense about a Greater Russia that Lotta simply couldn't stand. On the other side there were hotheads who thought that they could take on the might of their Great Neighbour and win the battle. Well, Lotta had been as angry with the Tsar as anyone when the February Manifesto was issued. She'd seen the threat to the Finnish Constitution as clearly as anybody. But she was a realist. She had no time for extremism of any sort. The reality was that Russian power had to be managed, not defied.

And then, as if all this weren't enough, there were easily led, ignorant people, who grabbed at the idea that this was the right moment for strikes and civil disturbance. They hadn't the sense to realize that this would only give Russia the chance it wanted, to crack down harder than ever, and swallow up Finland into its greedy belly for good. Well, you couldn't expect an illiterate sawmill or shipyard worker to understand history, thought Lotta. All they cared about were their own interests.

But the unrest was spreading. Even in a small town like this there were agitators. Why, only last week Lotta had read in the local paper about pamphlets smuggled in from Helsingfors, denouncing the 'Swedish Elite' for its 'traitorous collaboration with the Tsarist Oppressor N. I. Bobrikov', and calling for all true Finns to 'rise up and throw off the Russian yoke'. In the pamphlet there was a phrase that chilled her: it called for 'the solution by blood'.

They believed that the problems of the world could be solved by blood, did they? But Lotta knew they could not. Most things could not be changed. She had fought long battles, praying for acceptance to replace the terrible anger that threatened to swallow up her life. In the end she'd won her battle. She'd come to believe in her deepest, inner fibre that it was God's plan that she should be childless, and married to a man who not only didn't love her but seemed sometimes to . . .

But God had not given her an empty life. He'd recognized her patience, and repaid it. He'd given her Erika, Astrid's little girl. He'd let a miracle happen. He'd ordered things so that Erika, the precious, astonishing baby who had caught at Lotta's heart from the first instant, had returned Lotta's love. She had always gone straight into her Aunt Lotta's arms, smiling as if they shared a secret no one else knew. As she grew older, Erika had come to Lotta with all her troubles. Astrid once said, 'Of course, when they get to a certain age, you can't expect their confidence.' Was there regret in her voice? Lotta said nothing. She hugged to herself the secret that Erika's heart was open to her, even though it might be closed to her cool, graceful mother. And now there was Simon, who looked so much like Frans, but was dearly and entirely Erika in character.

And all the time, Lotta had Thomas, her oldest friend. The way he liked to laugh at her! Nobody else laughed at Lotta like that, or told her that her new hat looked exactly like a fruit salad. And when he was tired or troubled, he could always confide in her. He used to talk over difficult cases with her. Nothing indiscreet, but she knew it eased his mind, and she was always there to listen.

How her back hurt. When she turned her neck, pain tightened

in her skull. She had walked too far. But it was God who had given her the pain, and He had done so for His own good reasons. The pain was there to cure her thoughts.

At that moment, she knew what she must do. Family, order, duty all demanded it. Thomas must be protected, even against himself. She must send for Minna.

13

Thomas opened the lid of the oak chest, and propped it against the wall. Every family has a chest like this, he thought, full of things you can't use and can't throw away. If your father and grandfather have kept your great-grandfather's sword, which has the blood of 1808 on its scabbard, then you'll keep it too.

'There's Russian blood on your great-grandfather's sword,' they'd told him solemnly, and he'd searched the metal until his eyes dazzled, but had never been able to find the stain.

If time has a smell, it must be like the smell from the inside of these chests, Thomas thought. Time rested there in layers, with the heavy steel sunk to the bottom. He lifted a fold of white cambric wrapping, and bright colour showed. Yes, there it was. The quilt made by his great-grandmother, perhaps at the same time that his great-grandfather was sticking his sword into Russian flesh during the Finnish War. She'd been a famous needlewoman, renowned for exquisite embroideries on christening caps and muslin collars. But with this quilt she'd broken the rules. No one had made anything like it; no one wanted to.

He lifted the quilt, and shook out its folds. It was too light to be warm. She'd made it for beauty, what she thought was beauty, out of silks culled from God knew how many long-gone dresses. Or maybe she'd bought these bright silks, just for her quilt. Such gypsy colours wouldn't be worn by the country gentlewoman she'd been.

'All that work, and it lay on the bed like a whisper. You couldn't feel it.'

He remembered someone saying that, not admiringly but critically.

He was going to give the quilt to Eeva, to cover her attic bed. He lifted it into the light. The colours hadn't dimmed in almost a hundred years. Maybe it had never been used, even in its own day. It was out of keeping with a Swedish home, as violent as a cry of pleasure in the middle of a church service.

What had his great-grandmother been thinking of, to put this luscious patch of orange next to crimson? He knew nothing about such things, but it disturbed him, as if there were a message trapped in the stitches.

Yes, he would give it to Eeva. The tail of the quilt slithered over the lip of the chest, onto the floor. He fingered the black oak and remembered when the chest had stood taller than him. He'd stretched up on tiptoe to rest his chin on the edge, one day when his mother had left the chest open. She'd pulled him away angrily. 'Don't you see, the lid could crash down? What do you think would happen to you then? Do you want your head to be cut off?'

In the depths of his mind, that lid remained ominous and potent. He always connected it with an engraving of the guillotine, from a childhood history book. There was the guillotine, with its sideways blade still dripping with blood, but ready to drop again. Even the King of France had been felled by that blade. Thomas's finger traced the engraving. The guillotine was an engine, pulsing with energy. Beneath it, women wielded their knitting needles or looked up to jeer. They were *Les Tricoteuses*. They had wanted the King and they had got him. It was the time of the Terror, when all order had dissolved.

The text of his history book clanged with anger and alarm, as if the King had only just died, and cartloads of brave, helpless men and women were still trundling towards the guillotine. The knitting women were still flashing their needles, while they watched the dreadful basket that held heads like coconuts. The individual features of the severed heads showed quite clearly on the engraving. Not all the eyes were closed. If a head could see its own body, would it faint with fright? But could a head faint, if it hadn't a body to fall down? And could it still think, and know that those things outside the basket were its own arms and legs and its own feet with the shoes it had tied that morning . . .

If the head wanted to, could it stick out its tongue?

These thoughts had teased Thomas when he was eight years old, as if they were live and present problems that he would one day have to solve.

Poor old chest. It was no good taking history so seriously. It was just a chest, full of things that now had no one but him. If he didn't care about them, who would? Certainly not Minna. I should give them to Lotta, he thought. She'd cherish them all right. Both of us are the end of a line. Lotta childless, Johanna dead, Minna gone. When I die they'll come and tip the whole lot out, silk and sword together. Minna might supervise the process, but I doubt it. She'll sell the house if she can, but I can't see who's going to live here, so far out of town. No one will buy the house, and it'll fall to pieces, quietly. People from the village will take banisters and tiles and floorboards for their own use. And good luck to them.

Yes, the poor old chest only had him to care about it, and he didn't care much. He wanted the quilt, because Eeva must have it. He wanted those violets and crimsons and flames to lap around her while she slept, and fill her dreams with colour. He'd seen those bare orphanage dormitories, and for all his fine thoughts and intentions the attic room he'd given her wasn't much better. He would change all that. Eeva must have boots that fitted, and decent clothes. They'd have to be plain and suitable for a servant, because anything more would set the tongues clacking, and Lotta would come to 'have a little word'.

In her room, though, in secret, things could be beautiful. First the quilt, then a rug for her floor, and why shouldn't she have pictures? The house was full of pictures that nobody looked at.

Would she be warm enough up there, when winter came? Those rooms beneath the eaves were stifling in summer. Kirstin and Jenny would always leave their windows open wide on July nights. Maybe they'd shivered in January, too. But surely Johanna would have seen to it? This was a house that had always kept its servants. Would they stay if they weren't content? But he remembered suddenly the smell from Kirstin's underarms, on hot days.

He would take the quilt upstairs now, and lay it on her bed

himself. He gathered up the silk. It was so light and slippery that it seemed ready to pour itself away from him, back into the chest. He would put it on Eeva's bed and when she came upstairs at night she would . . .

No. No. He must not do it. He mustn't go to her room. If that started, where would it end? He wouldn't be able to help himself. He would fall on his knees, and strip back the bedclothes to find the coarse sheets that covered Eeva's body, and smelled of her. He would bury his face in the hollows her body had left in the mattress. He would clench the sheets in his fists so tightly that nobody would be able to drag him away. And when Eeva finished her work she'd find him there.

His head hurt. He was clutching the quilt tight, pressing it to his heart. 'Eeva,' he said aloud. She was very near.

No, he said to himself. No, no, no. He folded the silk, closed the chest and laid the quilt down on its lid. His fingers trembled, as if he'd swum a long way in water that was much too cold. But he wasn't cold, he was sweating.

He walked down the corridor to his bathroom. The sunlight had swung away from its windows now, but the air was warm. The splendid bath he'd ordered from Stockholm all those years ago dug its claw feet proudly into the Turkish carpet. The screen Johanna had made stood folded beside it. There was no fire in the grate. He had installed that fireplace, to supplement the heat of the stove, because he had once visited London and stayed in a hotel where he took a bath by firelight.

The little green silk-upholstered sofa was pushed against the wall. Johanna sat there once, wrapped in a towel, her hair falling out of its pins. She was drying herself after her bath. There were two candles lit in the candlestick on the dresser, and firelight on her shoulders. She was drying her feet, bending down with an awkwardness which was so rare in Johanna that it touched him more deeply than her usual grace. She looked up when he opened the door and stared at him. She pulled her towel more tightly around her. But we're married, he thought. She is my wife. A frown gathered on her forehead as he continued to stand there.

'Close the door, Thomas,' she said at last. 'There's a draught.'

He stepped inside. 'Johanna,' he began. The firelight shone on her skin. The windows were quite black, but she hadn't drawn the blinds. What need was there? He saw their reflections in the glass. She'd gone still, watching him.

'Johanna,' he said again, and put his hand on her bare, pearly shoulder. She didn't shrink away, but her complete stillness unnerved him. His hand looked big and clumsy, as if it didn't belong anywhere near her. The sight of his nails and the little dark hairs on the back of his hand disgusted him. He lifted his hand, almost afraid that he'd leave a mark on her skin.

'I need to get ready,' she said. 'We're expected at the Aströms' by six o'clock.'

But it was daylight in the bathroom now. He glanced behind him to check that the door was locked. Quickly, he took off his clothes and put them on the sofa. The cheval glass was still there, its glass tilted up to the ceiling, and dusty. He never looked in it as a rule, but now he walked over and straightened the glass until it was looking at him.

He looked at himself long and close, until he began to seem strange to himself. His image swam through the dust. Good God, there was even grey in his pubic hair. But he was still strong. He was familiar with bodies and knew how old men dwindled, their legs skinny and their bellies turning to pots. That hadn't happened to him yet.

But it was impossible for him to tell if anyone would ever want him again. Johanna with her beautiful skin and hard grace had turned away from him. And Eeva . . . But the thought of Eeva overwhelmed him, as if she were in the mirror instead of his own naked flesh.

He looked away and glanced down. His penis stirred obediently, as if it knew he was thinking of it. Johanna had never touched him there. She had let him put 'it' inside her on occasion, as if she were humouring some childish caprice, and that was that. A prostitute would take you in her hands and caress you but the money that changed hands cancelled the touch; not at the time, he had to admit, but afterwards.

And there he was, his erection pointing hopefully at the glass.

'Ooh!' Sophie had squealed. 'It feels exactly like satin. But a bit suedey as well. It must be so strange, having one of those!' And she'd laughed, and then suddenly wriggled down the guest bed – good God, yes! That guest bed prepared for Sophie by Johanna – and pressed her face against his penis, as if it wasn't enough just to touch him with her hands. Her warm face, her round cheeks and beautiful open lips. Where had Sophie got her ideas from? How had a girl like Sophie emerged from the same type of home as Minna, and from exactly the same education? She was warm all through, Sophie, from her clusters of curls to her soft breasts and the dimples on her knees. She complained that she had fat feet, and let him put her toes in his mouth.

He shut his eyes, reaching for himself.

When he'd dressed again and left the bathroom, he felt quite calm. He passed the quilt lying on the old chest, and thought that he must put it away, to preserve the colours. Or perhaps he would get rid of it altogether. Inside his body there was a clean, empty feeling. He would find a counterpane for Eeva, of Swedish woven cloth. It would keep her warm, in the traditions of his house. If his madness stirred again he would tell himself over and over that she was his servant, living under his roof. He would never hurt her. She could sleep in peace, and he would never put one foot on the narrow staircase that led to the attic rooms.

A man's voice called from below. Matti. But Matti rarely came beyond the kitchen, unless there was a job of work to be done. Something must be wrong. He went to the head of the stairs and called down, 'What is it, Matti?'

'Telegram, Doctor. It's a telegram come from Åbo.'

14

'My daughter, Minna, is coming to stay,' Thomas said to Eeva. He still held the telegram in his hand, as if he needed to prove himself by showing it to her.

His first thought after he'd read it hadn't been pleasure at the prospect of seeing Minna. No, he'd thought: Now I can go and talk to Eeva. I need to tell her to prepare for Minna's visit. And he'd been flooded with warm pleasure at having a reason to go to the kitchen and talk to Eeva. He never rang the bell for her. Johanna had always rung the bell for Jenny or Kirstin, but now that there were only the two of them in the house the whole bell business seemed ridiculous. Odd how he had never felt that with Kirstin or Jenny. It had seemed entirely natural that they wiped their hands, slipped on a clean apron and ran to see what he wanted.

He had hastened to the kitchen. Eeva was chopping onions. She put down her knife when he opened the door, and pushed away that bit of hair which always slipped out of its knot and followed the curve of her cheek. But there must have been onion juice on her fingers. She turned away, rubbing her eyes with her knuckles.

'Don't rub your eyes. There'll be more onion juice on your hands,' he said sharply. 'Take this.'

He pulled a clean handkerchief from his pocket and gave it to her.

She scrubbed away her tears, rough with herself in a way that hurt him to see. He loved the perfect cut of her eyelids. Every day he noticed almost with fear some new aspect of her beauty, as her real face emerged from hunger and neglect. When she'd finished wiping her eyes she turned back to him, blinking, her eyelids reddened, the whites of her eyes bloodshot. It was hot in the kitchen and her face was shiny. Her hair needed washing and she'd bundled it into a knot without brushing it. She must have been in a hurry.

He listed all these flaws to himself. Did he want her to be less beautiful? Was that really what he wanted?

'My daughter, Minna, is coming to stay,' he said.

'When?'

'Tomorrow.'

There was something wrong with the way he and Eeva talked to each other, but he couldn't pin it down. It was intimate, but there was no warmth in it. They were like a couple of burglars swapping essential facts in undertones, while they passed each other the tools to jemmy open a window. They'd crossed some barrier that had kept them both safe, and now they couldn't go back to where they'd been before.

'Why's she coming?' asked Eeva, looking at the telegram. 'Is something wrong?'

'No. No, nothing's wrong. It's just a visit.'

'I'll get her room ready, shall I? I know how it should be. Agneta showed me everything.'

'Yes. Yes, you do that.'

He stared at the heap of cut onions. They were glistening, fresh from the knife. He knew he should go away but he kept standing there, thinking how sharp the knife was and that she must be careful, in case she cut herself. Eeva took up the knife and the piece of hair fell forward again. He watched the shallow curve of her cheek, her lowered eyes and the line of her lashes. What thoughts were in her?

'I posted your letter,' he said at last.

'I know.'

'Perhaps you'll have a reply soon.'

Her eyes flashed up at him, then down again. It was only the onion that made her look as if she'd been crying, he reminded himself.

She's coming now, thought Eeva angrily. The daughter who doesn't care tuppence for him, that's what Agneta says. But she still comes all the way up from Turku, while Lauri doesn't as much as write back to me. People like the doctor: they get everything.

I have nothing, she thought. Go on, rub my face in it. *My daughter is coming to stay. My dear friend, Mrs Eriksson, is coming to teach you to wash china.* Well, *he* didn't know that Matti had picked one of his precious lemons for Eeva. And Eeva was going to find those silver scissors, too, and cut the grapes when they were ripe. Yes, she'd cut off the biggest bunch she could find, and eat it where no one could see. She was going to cram those grapes into her mouth and stuff herself until the juice ran down her chin.

She'd share the grapes with Matti though, except that he wouldn't approve.

You're not going to have that, on top of everything else, she thought, glancing at the doctor again. Why had he made her write to Lauri? She'd been all right before, not thinking about Lauri too much, not hoping she'd ever be able to touch her former life again.

'I'll get the room ready,' she said aloud.

'Thank you, Eeva.'

'That fool of a girl didn't air the bed properly,' said Minna. She'd arrived at eight in the evening, and gone straight to bed after supper. She was tired, she said. Now, at breakfast, she looked exactly the same as she'd done on her arrival, as if instead of sleeping she'd spent the night sitting upright and immaculate in her bedroom chair, waiting for time to pass so that she could have the conversation she'd come for. He knew already she'd come with a purpose. She'd evaded his kiss, slipping easily past him. '*What* a journey! This place really is the back of the back of beyond.'

As if she hadn't been born and bred here herself. As if she'd never gone berry-picking or mushroom-gathering, or fallen asleep in her room with her nightlight burning safe. But she obviously didn't feel any nostalgia, or desire to go around touching the old familiar things, or smelling the scents of sherbet and resin that crept in from the forest. To Minna, this house was the past, and had no present meaning for her. She'd wiped off the years of her childhood like a teacher wiping a slate with incorrect sums on it. When her cool clear gaze brushed over him he felt like the past, too. She couldn't quite wipe him away, but she would try.

'The bed was damp,' Minna insisted.

'I'm sorry. It's been a while since your room was used –'

'All she had to do was light the stove, and take the mattress out into the sun to air. It's not that difficult.'

'I doubt if she could carry that mattress downstairs, my dear.'

'Oh, for heaven's sake, she could get Matti to do it. He's as strong as an ox. No, she just didn't bother.'

'She's an orphan, Minna. This is her first place.'

'I know that,' said Minna, and for the first time that morning she looked full at him. 'More coffee, Father?'

'No, thank you.'

'Are you sure? I'm having another cup. At least she can make coffee.'

'She was well trained at the orphanage. She works hard, Minna.'

'I'm sure she does,' said Minna in a voice so like Johanna's that he couldn't help saying, 'You sounded exactly like your mother just then.' But it was the wrong thing to say.

'Let's leave Mother out of this, please.' Minna snapped her coffee cup back onto its saucer with such force that the liquid shivered all over its surface. But being Minna, she didn't spill a drop.

'I had a letter,' said Minna. 'That's why I'm here. A letter from Lotta.'

'A letter from Lotta,' he repeated, tasting the absurdity of it.

'Yes. We've never been close, as you know, but she was very good to me when Mother was ill. And she was good to Mother.' She said it as if he hadn't even been there.

'I know.'

'No, you don't know. You don't know what it meant to me. Lotta's *your* friend, I've always known that. But there was nothing she didn't do for us.'

Us. That meant the two of them, Minna and Johanna.

She paused, as if expecting him to break in, but he said nothing.

They stared at each other, united against their will by the image of Johanna lying dead, her jaw slack. At the moment of death she'd looked not as if she'd gone away somewhere, but as if something had been gouged out of her. And then a little while later her look of shock vanished and she was peaceful, as the dead are meant to be.

'Lotta wrote because she knew it was her duty. She wrote to tell me,' went on Minna steadily, 'that you were making a fool of yourself over that girl. To warn me that if it didn't stop, soon everyone in the district would know about it. And she's a servant, an illiterate girl –'

'Minna! My God! You can't be saying this.'

'I can. I can and I will. There have been too many things I should have said, and I never said them. Not to you, not to Mother, not to anyone. But this time I'm going to say them and you've got to hear them.'

'My God, Minna,' he said again, but very quietly, as if he were standing in a house made of glass that had suddenly shattered. He didn't dare move in case a spear of glass pierced him through. Minna. Lotta. Eeva. Their three names struck in his head, louder and louder. Lotta had written to his daughter, saying that she'd seen everything Thomas had struggled with in secret. What he'd thought secret had been naked, obvious and shameful. She had ripped away the covers from him, and exposed him to his daughter. Lotta, he thought, Lotta, how could you do it? But he knew. There'd been a bargain between them, as there was a bargain in every relationship, and he'd broken it first. He'd pretended to himself that he hadn't. He'd pretended to himself that he didn't know what Lotta's feelings were. But she'd been more honest, and had put her anger and pain into a letter and sent it to Minna.

He sighed deeply. It wasn't Lotta who should be blamed. But now here was Minna, so firm and upright, so much in control of herself, even while she was consumed with anger.

'Minna,' he said, 'you're talking of things you know nothing about. Nothing has happened between me and – between me and the girl. Whatever Lotta may have written to you, she's mistaken.'

'Why should I believe you? I know you, Father. I know what you're like. Do you think I've forgotten Sophie?'

Ah, he thought. Now we have it. Now at last, we're coming to it.

He took another deep breath. 'I haven't forgotten Sophie,' he said. 'But you must explain to me what you mean.'

'I'll do that all right,' she said. 'We should have come to it a long time ago. Sophie was my friend. You didn't care about that, did you? She was under your roof, but that didn't make any difference to you. You couldn't control yourself. Mother told me men can't control themselves, and aren't to be blamed for what they are. But I don't believe that.'

Each of her words hit him, but he didn't yet feel the blows. There'd be time for that, he thought, staring at her dark, Medusa face. So firm and sculpted, even when she was spitting out her rage. She was like her mother.

'You don't know what you're talking about,' he said. He'd never imagined that it would be like this. He'd spent so long fleeing from the thought that Minna knew what had happened with Sophie, even though he knew what she'd seen. Not much, but enough. He'd thought that to hear Minna's silent condemnation put into words would finish him. But it wasn't like that. The words had been said now, they were out in the open and he could reply to them.

'You know nothing about what happened between me and Sophie.'

'I think I do!' she burst out. 'I think I do. There's not much to know, is there? She was my friend, she stayed in our house, and you – she – you took advantage of her.'

'I loved her.'

'You can't say that!'

'I can. It's the truth. It wasn't right or suitable, it should never have happened. I was a married man of forty, and Sophie was eighteen, like you. And I loved her. I won't say what her feelings were, because I can't be sure. But it wasn't as you put it. Sophie wasn't like that. You knew her, Minna, she was your friend. Did anyone ever get Sophie to do anything she didn't want? *Sophie wasn't like you, Minna*. You don't like it, and I don't expect you to like it. Your mother certainly didn't.'

'Don't talk about my mother.'

'We can't talk without talking, Minna.'

Minna sat as upright as Johanna. She had exactly the same carriage of the head. Everything was still and controlled except her fingers, which squeezed her bread to doughy pellets. She had always done that. Messed about with her food and then, when it had turned into something other than food in her mind, she'd been unable to swallow it.

'I do love you, Minna,' he said abruptly. 'I know you don't believe it, but I do.'

'You only love yourself,' she answered. Her voice was colourless.

'We all love ourselves, I suppose,' he said, thinking it over.

He saw them, the two girls in their linen summer dresses and identical straw hats with plaited brims. Sophie had liked Minna's hat so much she'd bought one the same, and Minna hadn't minded. Minna was never selfish in such ways. Tall, dark Minna, and Sophie with her brown hair and curling smile. She had been coming to the house forever, staying a week at a time, cutting out patterns with Minna, practising piano, learning German.

She came to him so quickly and eagerly, just glancing behind her at the door first to check that it was shut. There was no schoolgirlishness in her. She was ready for marriage, everyone had been saying that about Sophie for the past two years, and in fact she was now engaged. They'd held each other tight and then kissed again and again, a flow of long, warm, deep kisses that seemed to pull them down like gravity onto the bed. But no. Sophie had suddenly opened her eyes wide and laughed and said, 'Well!' like a woman twice her age. She'd have gone down on the bed with him that first time, he knew that. With Sophie it all felt so simple and natural and even funny. Her youth didn't seem like a responsibility, but a pleasure.

'You're so young,' he said. Cliché after cliché popped out of his mouth, and all of them were true – 'I love you, Sophie, I feel as if I've never touched a woman before', 'You make me so happy, I could do anything' – Sophie didn't reply to any of this, she just smiled happily to herself, as if everything that was happening was right and had to happen in exactly this way. She tidied her hair and shook out the crushed folds of her skirt, and then twirled in front of him. 'Is my hair all right at the back?'

'Perfect,' he said, tasting her neck, licking the downy hairs that were already salty and damp with sweat.

'I'm getting married in September,' Sophie said suddenly, on the next-to-last day of her visit.

'I know.'

'He's nice. I've known him for ever. I know we'll be happy, you can always tell.'

'Good.'

'I shan't say anything to Minna.'

'No, no, good God –'

'She wouldn't understand,' said Sophie thoughtfully. 'She'd get all serious and desperate about it, that's what Minna's like.'

'You're right, she is.'

'She gets so worked up about the two of you.'

'What do you mean?'

Sophie shrugged. 'Oh, you know. Because you aren't happy.'

The words just fell out of her mouth. *Because you aren't happy.* As if it were a simple fact, like the smell of creosote from the wooden verandah railings. *They aren't happy, everyone knows it.*

'Don't look so sad. It isn't your fault,' said Sophie. She smiled suddenly, took his right hand in her left as if they were two children in the playground, and swung it gently to and fro. 'You aren't happy. But you could be.'

'With you?'

'No, I'm getting married. You know that. And I'm going home tomorrow. That's the way it is.'

'But you'll come again?'

'No,' she said. 'I don't think that would be a good idea.'

'Have you got a better one?'

'Maybe. In a minute. Wait –'

It was then that Minna had walked along the verandah past the window, looked in, and seen them. He'd swung round to face Sophie and they were still holding hands, laughing, their lips close. He had lifted his free hand to touch a cluster of her hair. That was all. Both of them were fully dressed. Minna just stared, her eyes black, then she put out her hands as if to push something away, and suddenly she wasn't there.

'That's torn it,' said Sophie.

'I'm sorry,' he said to Minna now. 'I wish I hadn't ended your friendship with Sophie.'

'It's not my friendship you should be sorry about.'

'But you'd always known each other. And now she's married, and I think she has a child.'

'Two,' said Minna, quick as a flash. 'A girl, and then a boy.'

Minna doesn't see Sophie, but she doesn't miss anything that concerns her, he thought. Two children, a girl and then a boy.

'I hear she's quite fat these days,' Minna observed.

He touched his coffee cup with the back of his finger. It was cold. He'd like more coffee now, only it would mean ringing for Eeva.

'Well, there you are,' he said. He stood up. 'And so you've come all this way. I'm happy to see you, Minna, although you probably don't believe it.'

'I'm going into town later,' she said. 'I've already told Matti that I need the carriage.'

'That's good. That's good. The horses don't get enough exercise.'

'I'm going to Lotta's.'

He saw her departing, stiff, upright, angry. She would go to Lotta's and he wouldn't be able to follow her. 'But you'll come back?' he asked urgently. 'You won't stay there?'

She looked at him. 'Do you want me to come back, Father?'

'Minna, for God's sake! Of course I want you to. You're my daughter.'

'Yes. But I'm not going to change what I think is right, because of that.'

She was his daughter, but he'd always thought of her as Johanna's. No, that wasn't quite true. When she was little, but not a baby any more, he'd thought that she might be his, too. At three, she'd been an angry, passionate little girl. Lit by laughter and then by rage. Johanna didn't like it. She would withdraw, coldly, and remain unresponsive until Minna calmed herself and behaved as she should. Only then would her mother look at her and speak to her again. Johanna's method had worked, he supposed. But he'd liked Minna's fire. It hadn't troubled him when she threw herself face down in a puddle and thrashed her legs until the mud flew. He could see her now, her scarlet, furious face screwed up, her boots drumming on the ground. And Johanna walking away, leaving instructions that Kirstin and Jenny weren't to touch her until she was reduced to cold, shivering penitence.

He'd picked her up. He shouldn't have done it, but he had. She had been stiff and furious but he had lifted her close and walked away with her, through the trees. She'd kicked him, hard at first and then less and less convincingly. The forest would calm her.

The rain was over and the sun had come out. The forest was dense with resinous, simmering heat. He walked a long way with her, feeling her body relax in the rhythm of his walking. She was heavy: Minna was always a strong child. They came to a clearing and he spread out his jacket under a larch, for them to sit down. The jacket was ruined anyway, covered in dirt from her boots, and damp from her wet dress.

'Would you like to take off your wet dress?' he asked her, and she nodded. There were many fiddly buttons, but he managed them and she stepped out of the dress. Her petticoat was wet, too, but no matter. She wouldn't catch cold on an afternoon like this. She was already running about, chasing a white butterfly. She ran in and out of thick shafts of sunlight and he rested with his back to the tree, half watching her, half dreaming. When she's bigger, he thought, I'll take her fishing with me. She'll like that. And he knew all the best places for mushroom-picking. He would show them to Minna and she would come home proudly, with her pail full.

She was squatting down now, intent on something. A bee.

'No, Minna! Don't stroke a bee.'

She looked round at him, her hands braced on her knees, her face alive with pure, intelligent curiosity.

'Why not?'

'Because it can't help stinging you. Look.'

He went over to her, and showed her where the bee kept its sting.

'It wouldn't want to sting you, Minna, because when a bee stings it dies. But it wouldn't be able to help itself, if it was frightened, or angry.'

She nodded.

'You can look at bees as much as you like, but don't touch them.'

He went and sat down again. Now she was collecting sticks, pretending to make a fire and singing to herself. She seemed perfectly happy. It was a little cooler in the forest, although the air was still close. Probably it would thunder again that night, when she was in bed, and then in the morning the air would be fresh and sweet. But it was good for her to run around in her petticoat. That dress was too tight.

There she was, his little girl. It was as if he'd never realized it properly before. I have a little girl. I have a daughter, he thought. For the first time it seemed like a bag of riches that would be slowly undone, year by year. When they'd first told him he had a daughter he'd gone in and there she was, already swaddled in her cradle, neat and tidy, like Johanna's doll. He hadn't picked her up.

It was getting late. She'd be wanting something to eat.

'Shall we go home soon?' he called to Minna across the clearing.

'No,' she said.

'All right. We'll play a little longer.'

'I'm not playing, I'm cooking the dinner,' she said.

'Of course you are. I'm sorry, I didn't see. Can I have some when you've finished?'

She nodded, and bustled off to fetch more sticks for her fire. All the years to come, he'd thought with sudden happiness, leaning against the tree trunk.

But it hadn't happened like that, and here he was, and here she was.

'I'll get us some more coffee,' he said. 'Don't leave yet, Minna.'

'Lotta's very angry.'

'Yes, I can imagine.'

'But you don't care.'

'Yes, I do. Lotta's one of my oldest friends. What she thinks is important to me.'

'But not quite important enough,' said Minna. 'Not important enough to stop you doing what you want.'

'Haven't *you* done what you wanted?'

She shrugged. 'Out of all the things I could have done, you mean? Out of all the many possibilities that were open to me?'

'There were other things you could have done.'

'I'm married, Father. I have my own house. No one tells me what to do. If I choose to leave this house tonight or next week, that's my own decision.'

He could well believe it. She was stronger than Ulf and she would rule the marriage.

'But you'll have children, Minna. Everything changes then.'

'No,' she said. 'Not yet.'

He looked at her in surprise. 'But surely –'

'No. You have no idea what my life is like. You've never once visited us. You don't want to see my life. All you care about is your own.'

The injustice of it brought his anger up to the surface at last.

'So when did you invite me?'

'When did I invite you! You're my father. Strangers wait for invitations. No, you don't want to come because you'd rather stay here where you can control everything. This house, Lotta, all your patients who are so grateful to you, everyone who thinks it's so sad that Mother died and that all you've got left is a daughter who doesn't care about you, your damned trees that you keep planting everywhere so there's no light in this house, the memory of this and the memory of that – yes, you love it, don't you? And for heaven's sake don't ever take the risk of travelling a hundred miles and getting some perspective on it. And now, to make it all perfect, you've got this girl to moon after.'

'Minna!'

'Yes, it's shocking, isn't it? You would never have thought I could be so coarse. But I most certainly can be. *Mooning after*, that describes it exactly. And unlike me, she's stuck here. She can't get away from you. Have you ever thought about that? No, I know what you think: Poor old Minna, married to that dreary Ulf, no wonder she's so narrow-minded and can't understand my rich, complex life. Yes, I may be narrow-minded, but at least I've got a heart. I feel sorry for her, if you want to know. That girl. Just because she's poor and ignorant, she has to put up with you, and she can't get away.'

They glared at each other. Both had risen from their chairs. Both had their fists clenched, pressed against their thighs.

She was still there, he realized with a shock of recognition. That little girl, so angry and passionate; she hadn't died. She was still there, inside Minna. He'd got so used to the thought that she was Johanna's daughter, cool, critical and graceful like her mother, and he hadn't seen that there were other sides to her, equally powerful, but held in shadow. But now the hot light of her anger made them visible.

'Don't go yet, Minna,' he said again, but in quite a different tone. 'I want you to stay.'

She was listening, alert as a fox. 'You want me to stay?'

'Yes. You're my daughter. It's been far too long since I saw you. I didn't realize that you were waiting for me to visit. I was thoughtless, I see that now.'

'All right,' she said at last. 'I'll stay for a while.'

And then he went too far. As soon as the words were out he knew they should never have been said. 'I know it must seem like madness. I don't know why I feel like this about her, but –'

'*I don't want to hear about it*. If you talk like that any more, I'll leave at once.'

'We won't talk about it,' he promised her quickly. 'Sit down, Minna, I'll see about that coffee. And you must have something to eat. You've eaten nothing.'

He went out, closing the door. And there she was, as if she'd appeared out of his longing. Eeva, standing stock-still, with a letter in her hand. He hadn't even looked at the post that morning. He'd completely forgotten it.

She heard him and turned, stuffing the letter into the folds of her skirt as if she thought he'd snatch it from her. Her face was transformed, flushed with triumph and relief. Her eyes were wide, their pupils dilated as if she'd just emerged from a dark hiding place. He would never have thought Eeva could look like that. There she was, staring at him but not really seeing him, because he wasn't important, he didn't matter now. She was safe inside her own life. He'd thought of her as an orphan, and then as his servant, and then as Eeva, the object of . . .

No, she was never an object. She was everything. She seemed to have slipped into his innermost self and become it, crowding out every other thought. She *was* his thought. His dreams and all his longings walked about, cased in her flesh. But no, she was not his. She was a girl holding a letter which had nothing to do with him.

'So that's that, Eklund, you fool,' he told himself roughly, not believing it yet. It couldn't really be so. He couldn't feel so much, want so much, while she felt nothing for him and everything for someone else. Then the pain of it reached his mind and he clenched his teeth, shut his eyes, and blundered back, out of her sight.

15

We conclude that revolutionary violence is no more and no less than a necessary defence by which the oppressed classes defend themselves against the violent force of those institutions of state power which keep them in a state of subjection. For this reason such violence is not only to be considered as justifiable, but also as a morally correct course of action. Revolutionary violence, properly considered, represents a duty rather than a choice.

If only he could agree with the pamphlet without having to think about it. If he possessed that same hard, simple truth which didn't admit doubt, then how much easier his life would be. He'd be sure that the removal of one man, or ten – or ten hundred, maybe – would be a solution.

There was the Baltic, stretching out before him, with barely a wrinkle on it. Well, the sea wasn't going to argue with him. Lauri picked up a stone, weighed it in his hand, and hurled it as far as he could. It dropped into the water with a deep 'plock' and disappeared.

One man is removed – or ten, or maybe twenty, and there's a solution. Or at least, the beginning of a solution. There's no gain without pain, you can't make an omelette without breaking eggs, and how can social justice be achieved without destroying what stands in its way? Such deaths are a necessary part of a process which possesses its own victorious logic.

No, nothing was ever achieved without blood. There were deaths which were necessary, as a surgical operation was necessary to the curing of the body, no matter how dangerous and agonizing, no matter how bloody. It was Sasha who'd said that bit about a surgical operation. Sasha's eyes shone with conviction. He looked like a doctor explaining to a fearful patient that yes, there was still hope. Everything could be cured, if the patient would only put himself into Sasha's hands, and trust him completely.

But, thought Lauri later, it's only agonizing and dangerous for the patient. The surgeon doesn't feel it. That is, I suppose he feels the knife going in. Like cutting meat, it must be. Flesh doesn't want to be cut, it resists. And then the blade hits the bone.

When he was with Sasha, Lauri was sometimes sure with Sasha's sureness. Above all, when Sasha was there, Lauri could believe that to think like Sasha and be like Sasha was what he should aim for. Sasha was like that. He had a power in him. And he was Lauri's closest friend, ever since they'd first met in Petersburg nearly two years ago. And even though Lauri was back home in Helsinki now, he and Sasha were still together, sharing a room. Sasha came and went. He was always disappearing unexpectedly, staying away for a few nights, reappearing again. Sometimes he spoke at meetings, other times he sat for hours writing at the little card table in the corner of Lauri's room. He'd given up his clerical job, he told Lauri, to devote himself full-time to political activism. There were funds to support people like Sasha, Lauri guessed, people whose work was so valuable that it was a waste of time for them to keep on with their jobs.

Strange in a way to think he'd known Sasha for less than two years. He was like a brother. Lauri had gone to Petersburg when his father died, only three months after Eeva's father. Everything in Helsinki was falling apart. Lauri wanted to get out. An old work-mate of his father's took over the apartment.

He was glad he'd gone to Petersburg. It had all worked out so much better than he'd dared hope. He'd had a few contacts before he went, but essentially he'd been on his own. It was Sasha who'd found Lauri work at the bookbinder's. At first he'd been a dogs-body, but he'd shown some aptitude and he'd been taken on as a sort of apprentice. Nothing formal, but he got training. It was all thanks to Sasha – he had a contact with old Pavlov through an underground printing works.

If only Lauri could be as clear as Sasha, and share his certainties. After all, Lauri believed and wanted everything that the others believed and wanted. Before he'd met Sasha he'd tried to get a job in a textile factory. He'd heard a rumour they were taking on new hands at the Thornton Mills, and off he'd gone. But the conditions were far worse than anything he'd seen in Finland. It was bad enough for the men, but God alone knew how the women survived. They looked more like scarecrows than women as they streamed out of the factory into the Thornton hostel, with their shawls flung over their heads. He stood back as the machine-like rush of bodies went past him. Their faces frightened him. Hard, desperate faces of women who laboured all day and still couldn't feed and clothe themselves.

He'd told Sasha about that day, and Sasha said that it was an illustration of the effects of international capitalism. Didn't Lauri know that the Thornton Mills belonged to English plutocrats?

Then he'd tried a boot factory. The conditions were better there than in the mills, but fines were levied for everything. No matter how well you did your work, you couldn't stop your wages vanishing in fines. Every fiddling little thing that went wrong, every minute late, if you had to leave your machine to take a piss when you shouldn't – you got fined. It was a good racket for the bosses. They got the work out of you, and then they got half your wages back in fines. He stuck it for a couple of months and then he couldn't do it any more, couldn't go on with it. All those stoppages out of what he'd sweated for and desperately needed – no, it was too much. But you had to bear it because there was no choice. He was on the point of giving up and going back to Helsinki.

If he hadn't met Sasha at the Evening School for Adults, he'd have had no chance. He'd been wary that first evening, because he knew no one, but Sasha had been at the economics class. It was supposed to be a 'household management' course, but the teacher stretched the subject – he was 'one of us' – and Lauri and Sasha had got talking afterwards, along with Kiril Vasilievich, the teacher. It was clear that Sasha and the teacher were good friends, like equals, the way they talked. And they'd drawn Lauri in, asked him lots of questions about Helsinki and what was going on there.

They knew people Lauri knew. Kiril Vasilievich had met his father many times, and he'd known Eeva's father well, he said. He'd talked about them with a warmth that made Lauri feel for the first time that he wasn't a stranger in a foreign land. As he spoke, Lauri seemed to see Mika and Pekka, young men together, full of life and dreams, knowing nothing about their futures, or about him, or Eeva.

And now they were both dead, both their fathers. Life was so quick, you wouldn't believe it. One moment it embraced you and the next it let you go.

Sasha had not only got Lauri in at the bookbinder's, but he'd also made sure that Pavlov looked after him. With what Pavlov had taught him, Lauri had no problem getting a job when he came back to Helsinki.

Yes, Sasha had opened the doors of Petersburg for Lauri. He'd taken him along to meetings, and introduced him to comrades all over the city. Sasha knew everybody. He told Lauri which speakers were good and which weren't worth listening to. Sasha knew which of the Evening School teachers were 'one of us' and which were liberals, well-meaning but useless. You could always tell. There were little phrases and questions that showed where a teacher's sympathies lay. 'Our' teachers taught you far more than the others. They were dedicated to pushing you as far as you could go.

Kiril Vasilievich was typical of 'our' teachers. He taught maths, too, and took the class on to fractions and decimals, when they were supposed to stop at arithmetic. Political discussion took hold, and even though Sasha had warned Lauri that there would always be a spy from the Okhrana in every class, it seemed that almost anything could be said as long as the Tsar wasn't named, strikes weren't mentioned, and the Church wasn't attacked openly. There were ways round that: codes that everyone in the know understood, and explained privately to those who were politically inexperienced, as long as they showed signs of being 'one of us'.

It was like the talk in Eeva's apartment, years ago, when he'd still been a child. He and Eeva were always together those evenings, playing or reading or falling asleep. Eeva had studied at her little card table – just like Sasha, now he came to think of it – with that one candle to light her book and paper. She knew Russian and Swedish, as well as Finnish. She was supposed to be going on to English. She read Russian poetry and studied mathematics. He was lazy in those days, couldn't be bothered with education even though Eeva's dad tried to get him interested. He was half sorry for Eeva, having to work so hard, and half jealous because her father expected so much of her.

Well, Lauri spoke Russian now, and he'd learned mathematics and political theory. He and Sasha had shared a lodging in Petersburg. It wasn't much – a narrow room with damp running down the walls – but it grew to be like Eeva's apartment in the old days. People dropped in at all hours to drink tea and talk and argue, to discuss the last meeting and look forward to the next. Sometimes speakers would stay with them, rolled up in a blanket on the bed he and Sasha usually shared, while the pair of them slept on the floor.

It was when Sasha and he were talking quietly at home, after the others had left, that Lauri brought out the cold little doubts that he would never have raised in company. Maybe there were other ways of changing things, maybe everything didn't have to be swept away . . .

'You're talking like a liberal,' Sasha would say. '"Let's make things better bit by bit, hold a literacy class, improve hostel conditions, prepare a petition to shave half an hour off the working day for the poor things. Then maybe they'll put up with it all for a bit longer."

'But why should *you* be a liberal, Lauri? Liberals are people who've got something to lose. They've got a stake in the system and so they want it to last. That's why they work to make it just bearable enough so that the workers continue to put up with it. Liberals believe they're doing so much good with their Guild of Literacy, their Temperance Leagues, their campaigns for clean milk. The workers ought to be very grateful indeed.

'But they're papering over the cracks, that's all. No, it's even worse than that, Lauri. These liberals are trying to stick up wall-paper because they know that the walls are falling down. But why should *you* be fooled? You've got nothing to lose. You've got no stake in the present system. There are no thoughts you can't dare to think, Lauri.'

'What thoughts?'

'It's not going to happen peacefully. You know that. It's not poss-ible. They'll give us half an hour off the working day if they've got to. They'll give up a tiny fraction of their profits, if that means they can keep the rest. I would too, if I were in their shoes. It's logical. In fact the extraordinary thing is how blind they are, how they fail to grasp that if they gave just a little more now, they'd still be able to keep almost everything. But they don't realize it, and they will never realize it. Fortunately for us.'

'Fortunately?'

'Yes, fortunately. Because we are the ones who will see the whole thing swept away. We don't need to rely purely on our own strength. We can rely on their stupidity too. It's our greatest asset. It's like a lever, Lauri. You don't need an equal weight to shift a boulder. You don't even have to be all that strong. As long as you've got sufficient leverage, then you can use the boulder's weight against it, until you see it topple and roll away.'

Sasha laughed. He looked very young when he laughed, like a boy who'd got away with playing a fantastic trick against the adults. His face shone with life. When Sasha looked like that, everyone wanted to be on his side. Doctors cutting out cancers, levers moving boulders . . . Sasha had such a way of describing things.

'Have you ever killed a man?' Lauri asked abruptly.

Sasha's glow of life didn't fade, but his gaze sharpened.

'Have you?' he countered.

'No. But I think –'

'What?'

'I've been in a room when a death was planned. Long ago, when I was a child.'

'Where was that?' Sasha was always so quick. Too quick some-times.

130

'Doesn't matter. Maybe it never happened. I was just a kid, you know how kids are.'

'Was it in Helsinki?'

'Leave it, Sasha.'

Sasha leaned back in his chair. 'Sorry. I was just curious.'

'It's not the kind of thing you should be curious about. It's better not to know. You always wonder if you could have done anything – if you should have done anything. Or maybe just said something. And if you had, everything might have been different. You're better off not knowing.'

Sasha sat forward. A little smile still rested on his lips, and his eyes glistened.

'One day you'll have to know,' he said.

'Have to?'

'Yes. It's not going to happen like you're hoping, Lauri. Come on. Who's going to give up what they've got, and let us have it without a struggle? You can't keep your purity for ever. You're not politically naive, Lauri, you're part of the struggle. You've already made your choice.'

Somehow these conversations with Sasha failed to still his doubts. He felt uneasy when Sasha talked about 'political naivety' and 'failure to analyse the situation correctly'. There was no doubt that Sasha meant every word, in spite of the teasing warmth in his voice.

It was easier when they went to meetings. Sasha always knew where to go, when to set out, which courtyards to slip through and how to wait so that they could drift in at the door one by one, seemingly without purpose. At meetings, Lauri began to burn with the same fire as all the others. He drank in speeches and applauded until his watchful thoughts were swept away and he rose and fell on the wave that was lifting them all, ready to hurl them into the future. He wanted to topple, to overthrow, yes, to change every-thing utterly. He was sure with the same sureness. Yes, he knew all about the insults and injuries they described.

Years ago, he'd seen a man's arm drawn into a roller and crushed because the guard was off. The metal guard slowed production, and so it was always left off. The man was careless. It was his fault, but they paid for a doctor and gave him a job sweeping out the factory floor. They were good employers and he was glad of it. Grateful. They might easily have turned him off.

When a thing like that happens, you don't understand what it is at first. You hear shouting and turn and see a man in the wrong place, his face almost in the machine. And when they carry him out his face is grey-white but he isn't saying anything.

One day when he's sweeping the floor he shows you the shiny red skin over his stump. The skin looks tight to bursting point, as if another arm is waiting to push its way out. But of course it's not. The man says that he feels as if he still has an arm, a shadow arm. Lauri can't even remember his name now. He is just 'the man who lost his arm'.

He should be here, Lauri thought. He should be here, clapping with his one hand and shouting himself hoarse in agreement with the speaker. It's him we're working for, him and all of us. Yes, there was no room for doubt. And there was Sasha at the speaker's side – he'd had the honour of introducing him – his forehead damp with sweat, his eyes shining, looking out over the packed room in triumph.

But later, in the quiet, Lauri's watchful thoughts would return. He tried to crush them, as Sasha must have crushed his long ago. Sasha was whole, complete and untroubled by a double self.

Lauri tried to organize his mind, as Sasha did. He would analyse his own situation objectively, as Sasha urged. Yes, he was a worker and a nationalist, but the fact that he was a worker would always come first. He didn't hate 'the Tsar and his lackey Bobrikov, Governor-General of Finland' purely because they were Russian. No, how could that be, when so many of his comrades were Russian? He hated the Tsar and men like the Governor-General, who made themselves tools of his Empire, but it was not as men or as Russians. No. It was because of what they wanted to impose. The dead hand of a decaying autocracy, that's what it was. He'd read that exact phrase and every fibre of him tingled with agreement. Yes, they wanted to crush Finland, just as they wanted to crush the workers and peasants of Russia itself. They wanted to destroy the policies which for decades had allowed Finland to be part of the Russian Empire and yet separate from it.

This policy of Russification meant exactly what it said. Everything was now to be shaped to the mould of our Great Neighbour, the moribund pattern of Church and Tsar. It was Sasha who had said that: 'moribund pattern'. If something was moribund, then it was as good as dead already. How could it be a crime to kill what was already dying? That was Sasha's argument.

Nationalism was not enough. Lauri knew it. That knowledge was part of the hard, clear thinking he had to aspire to now. What use to him was an independent Finland with its class structures intact? There were mills in Finland, too, where men lost their arms and were turned off when trade was poor. There were children barefoot and hungry in the courtyards of Helsinki, TB running through entire families, people emigrating in their thousands because there was nothing for them at home. He had read and studied and listened, and he knew that nationalism could never ensure the rights of the workers. More was needed: the unification and common purpose of workers and peasants everywhere, beyond the barriers of language or nation. What would die would die, because its time was up.

He talked it all over with Sasha and was rewarded with the warmth of Sasha's smile. And from that moment he stopped discussing his doubts, even with Sasha. Sasha could trust him absolutely, and he could trust Sasha. They were like brothers, working for the same end.

Maybe, if he'd never lived in St Petersburg, he could have swallowed the nationalist package whole, and believed that everything would be fine as long as Finns were in charge. But now he knew it wasn't so. He'd had comrades in Petersburg whom he'd trust with the last drop of his blood. Who would give their lives for him without question, just as he would give his life for them.

Or so he said, and so they said. Could you really use those words until you'd been tested? Probably not. Maybe those pledges could never be spoken truthfully, except by the dead. Those dead who were taken away and mangled by the Okhrana, and then executed either in public or somewhere out of sight.

Death. Yes, that was it, that was the heart of the question. It was death that his mind grated on, like a boat on a sandbank. Why should he beach himself on the thought of death, when as far as he could see other comrades, Finnish or Russian – Sasha, Hannu, Eero, Fedya, Mitya – seemed to sail straight on, their keels skimming the water. Yeah, that's right, when you come to it we all die, and it's for ever. So? What's new about that?

Death. What does it really mean to die? We've all got to do it some day. How repulsive it is, Lauri thought. A prickle of dread ran over his skin. How can life really be arranged like this, so that it ends in death with no alteration and no appeal. And yet if life didn't end in death, what would life be?

Lauri looked down at his hands. They were clenched, and he made them relax. This was a good place. He'd come down to the sea to untangle his thoughts. There was space here, and the open horizon, the faint, sweet smell of water. He needed to think. Yes, there was death, always, like a friend you couldn't get rid of, grinning by your side wherever you went. When Eeva's father died she had crossed his hands on his breast while they were still warm. How did she know to do that? Where did such knowledge come from?

It was past ten o'clock now, and the sun was low, the light promising to fade but never fading. A clear, perfect evening, with a green tint in the sky. In the distance people were strolling, some alone, others arm in arm. Each of them looked absolutely distinct, as if God wanted to point out the importance of each of his creatures.

But Lauri didn't believe in God. God was there to keep people content with their lot. He knew that. He sat on the bollard with his knees apart, his fists resting on his knees, like any Finnish boy dreaming of emigration. The harbour water was calm. Everything was so vast, so peaceful. A couple of sparrows pecked the dust at his feet. How tiring it must be, to be a bird at midsummer, he thought suddenly. Of course they roost, but not for long. All the long day they peck and flutter and fill the bushes with cheeping.

But they seem happy, he thought, watching the dusty, slender sparrows as they bathed their wings in the dust. They're alive, that's all.

If I took three steps, Lauri thought, I'd be in that water. It's not so cold. Someone might hear the splash and look round, but if I waved back cheerfully, they'd walk on. And then, if I swam out as far as I could, I'd reach a point where I wouldn't be able to swim back. I might turn and look at the shore of Finland, but I'd know I couldn't reach it again. What does it feel like when you look at the shore and everywhere you've ever known and all the people you've ever known too, even though you can't see them, and you know for sure that you must say goodbye to them?

He shivered. Sometimes you frightened yourself with things that would never happen. If he drowned, he would sink through the calm water, his lungs waterlogged now and not buoyant with air. After a while he would swell up with his own gases. As his skin softened, crabs would move in on him, and fish would eat out his eyes. He would be thrown up on shore, and maybe a fisherman would find him and spit with disgust at the sight. Or maybe the sea would carry him where he'd sink so deep he'd never be found. Soon his flesh would be gone. His skeleton would emerge. How strange to have a skeleton all your life, and yet never to see it, Lauri thought. What would it look like, his own skeleton? Would it have any mark on it that would say *Lauri*, and make it different from any other jigging armful of bones? Probably not.

And then, after a long, long time, his bones would dissolve. How long that took Lauri didn't know. Hundreds of years maybe. But in the end even the bones would be gone.

Even that would only be the beginning of death. It would be less than a blink of an eye, for death. Death would have only just begun, and it would never end. Death would soon be tired of him, and he'd certainly be tired of death, but they'd be stuck with each other for ever.

But I'm still here, all of me, thought Lauri. My hands are on my knees. I have a cracked nail, and my shoulders hurt from lugging that stack of books yesterday. I'm here, all of me. But even if I live for a hundred years, death is soon, because that empty neverness is everything that my life is not, and it is all around me. Only three steps away now.

When we talk of taking away a man's life, it's not so simple. He has his life, as I have mine. He's walking about at this moment, just as I am. Maybe he's sitting at his table, swallowing some delicious little meat patties for supper after the theatre. If there's grease on his fingers, he'll lick them and taste his own skin as well as the meat juice. And he'll know how good it is to be alive.

Lauri raised his right arm. It was tanned, and muscled. As he raised his arm, and lowered it, his muscles moved beneath the skin. He'd always been interested in how his body worked. Maybe, in another life, he'd have been a doctor. He'd read a book about anatomy once. There were illustrations which showed how the muscles ran under the skin and were tied to the skeleton. Half of the body in one illustration was human, facing forward with one eye, half a mouth and half a nose. The other half was flayed, to show what lay beneath.

Lauri looked at his own arm. Yes, death was what lay beneath. Now his arm was strong and could lift and haul and handle machinery with fine, quick decisions that he didn't even need to think about. He had work because of it, and because of the knowledge that old Pavlov had put into his brain and his hands. Lauri smelled the familiar smell of his own skin. Yes, this was what it was like to be alive and warm, and able to smell your own smells and taste your food.

Maybe *he* was drinking at this moment. Raising a glass of beer to his lips. No, it would be wine, or more likely champagne. All Russians drank champagne whenever they could. He would see his own arm lifting the glass, just as Lauri did.

He would drink the whole glass, and then pour another so as to deepen the pleasure of alcohol going through his body and making it warm and excited and relaxed all at the same time. He'd be chatting to someone. A friend, perhaps, or a colleague. Or someone in his family.

No. Better not think about his family.

136

Who was *he*? Who was this man who had to be removed from the body of society so that it could flourish? Sasha wouldn't say. It wasn't yet time. 'A Russian in an important position. *Very* important. Almost, you might say, as senior as possible . . .' And Sasha had looked at him with a smile, making it clear that it wasn't necessary for Lauri to make guesses, not now, because he'd be told everything he needed to know, when the time was ripe. And Lauri had known that Sasha wasn't teasing or testing Lauri, or trying to make himself sound more in the know than he really was. He was serious.

A very important Russian official. No, Sasha hadn't said he was an official, but that he was 'in a very important position'. So who? Who was he, this man who was living but already had death's fingerprints all over him?

The fact is that he has to die. Not now, not immediately. But every time he raises that glass to his lips, he's raising it in the light of his death. He's going to die and he doesn't know when or how. He's just like the rest of us, then. But the difference is that we know more about his death than he does, even though I don't even know his name.

How strange and horrible it is that a man can fill his stomach and not know that an hour later he'll be emptied of his blood.

No, not an hour, Lauri promised the man. You'll have more than that. Days, weeks, months even. From the way Sasha spoke, it's not going to be yet. But you are going to die, even though you don't know it. Hardly anybody knows. Not Fedya, nor Mitya, not Hannu or Eero. They know nothing and will continue to know nothing. But Sasha knows.

16

But the next day everything changed, when his father's old work-mate brought Eeva's letter. She hadn't disappeared. She hadn't forgotten him.

He read it once, fast, grabbing at the words. The paper shook in his hands. When he'd finished he smoothed the letter carefully, spread it out on the card table where Sasha worked, and sat with his elbows on the table, to study it.

> . . . *Sometimes I think I can't remember what you look like, and when I do remember, your face is angry, just as it was the last time* . . .
> *I'm in service* . . .
> *You remember how they were always telling us the world was changing? Here, it hasn't changed at all* . . .
> *When I see you, maybe you won't be the Lauri I remember* . . . *You won't have your blue cap* . . . *and you'll say, 'Where have you been, Eeva? I gave up thinking of you long ago* . . .'

And she signed herself, *Your friend, Eeva.* The paper blurred. No, he wasn't going to cry. He hadn't cried when they took her away. He hadn't cried when his father died. He had knelt by the bed with his father's hand in his, until it grew slack. And then he rested his forehead on that hand which had given him life, and stayed there for a long time, even though the old woman who'd nursed his father said that it was time to lay him out.

Dad had never been the same since the Okhrana took him away. He walked with a limp and he was hurt inside, in his stomach or maybe his liver, Lauri didn't know and his father couldn't say. But he couldn't eat meat any more. Only porridge and crusts of bread soaked in hot water. He couldn't stomach vodka. The one time he tried, it doubled him over. They'd given him a kicking, on the floor of his cell. But he'd been lucky, he said: 'I was lucky. I know how to handle myself. Besides, I'm not a young man. I've had my life.'

Still, he had bad dreams, right up to his death. They'd planted something in him and he couldn't get it out.

'Animals,' he said once. 'Animals, that's what they are. And the Tsar's the zoo-keeper, don't ever forget it. He knows what's going on. Don't ever fall for that rubbish, boy, that the Tsar's up there above it all, with his arse smelling like angel breath.'

Dad, Pekka, Eeva. Dad and Pekka gone, and here was Eeva, who'd been as good as dead, writing to him. This was her handwriting, he knew it. She'd made these letters with her own living hands.

No, he hadn't wept then, and he wasn't going to now. It was the shock, that was it. He'd thought her gone, along with everything else. And now she writes that maybe he's given up thinking about her.

Has he? Did he ever give up thinking about her? No. No, surely that's not possible.

But he knew it was. You have to turn away from the dead or else you go down with them. He'd thought of her as one of the dead, like his father and hers. He'd hidden her in that corner of his mind where the dead have to go, so that the living can carry on with their lives. She'd been thinking of him all this time, but he hadn't been thinking of her.

'Eeva,' he said aloud, testing her name. How long was it since he'd said that name? *Eeva*. He'd grown up saying it twenty times a day.

He looked around the room. Thank God Sasha wasn't here. What would Sasha have thought, if he'd been there, with Lauri carrying on like that? He'd have thought Lauri was crazy.

'Eeva?' He wasn't calling for her. He was just saying her name, in exactly the way he used to when she was studying in the light of that one candle, her right arm curled around her paper, her left hand holding her pen. He'd even forgotten that Eeva was left-handed, until this moment. But she was. If they sat side by side to write, their elbows knocked together. He used to try to get her to write with her right hand, like him, but she wouldn't.

'It looks like spiders walking over the paper. Besides, *you* can't write with your left, can you? I like being left-handed.'

When she wrote this letter, she'd have curled her hand around the paper in exactly the same way. He was sure of it. Her writing hadn't changed a bit. She'd always been able to put exactly what she wanted onto the paper, like her father.

He knew where she was now. He could get on a train, and then find a cart that was going out that way and would give him a lift. If not, he'd walk the rest of the way. Never mind if it took a couple of days. He'd sleep in a barn. She was there, now, at this minute. He could go and find her. Yes, as soon as Sasha came in he'd tell him, show him the letter, and together they'd find a way for Eeva to come to Helsinki. She'd need somewhere to live. She'd need work. Sasha would know what was best to do.

Your friend, Eeva. He didn't think of her as his friend. She was too much part of him for that. And yet she wasn't his sister. If she'd been his sister they couldn't have taken her away.

Your friend. She'd written to him. She wanted his help. He would get her out of there, whatever it took. He saw her as clearly as if she was sitting there at the table with him, bending over one of her books.

'Eeva?'

She looked up. Her face lit with a flash of surprise and pleasure.

'I've been waiting ages! I thought you were never coming.'

Sasha came in very late, heavy-footed with tiredness. He'd been at a meeting, he said. He sat on the edge of the bed to pull off his boots, and it was clear that he was surprised and maybe not too pleased to find Lauri wasn't asleep yet. Dawn light was pushing strongly around the edge of the blinds. It must have been well past midnight, Lauri thought.

'I'm dead,' said Sasha. 'Move over, I've got to catch a couple of hours' sleep.'

'I've had a letter from a friend.'

'Who? A comrade?'

Lauri hesitated. It wasn't the way he thought of Eeva. She was just herself. 'She's one of us,' he said at last, 'she's Pekka Koskinen's daughter.'

Sasha grunted as the right boot came off. 'From what I've heard, Koskinen had liberal tendencies.'

'*Liberal tendencies?* Sasha, you don't know what you're talking about. You might as well say I've got liberal tendencies.'

'I sometimes wonder,' said Sasha. 'So, you mean, Eeva Koskinen?'

Of course, he must have mentioned Eeva to Sasha, even though he couldn't remember it.

'Yes. Eeva. She's written to me from where she's living now.'

'Where's that?'

Lauri discovered a sudden, surprising reluctance to tell Sasha exactly where Eeva was.

'It's about eighty miles north east of Turku, way out in the country.'

'Oh. Right. So why's she written?'

Sasha wasn't asking the questions he'd expected. But then what would be the right questions? It was hardly Sasha's fault. He couldn't be expected to understand how important it was that Eeva had written.

'She needs help,' Lauri said. 'They took her away to an orphan-age, and then she went into service. She was living with us, you see, after her father died. And then when my father was arrested, they searched the place and found Eeva – well, you know how it is, me and Eeva slept by the stove and my father had his own cubbyhole. And so they took her away. She was Pekka Koskinen's daughter, too. He was dead, but they could still punish him by putting Eeva in an orphanage.'

'I see,' said Sasha.

'We grew up together,' said Lauri, feeling a flush rise in his face. 'We were like –'

'Like brother and sister?' asked Sasha silkily.

'No,' said Lauri.

'It sounds like a fairy story. The orphans are about to be reunited after their long, sad parting. It's a happy ending, isn't it? At least, I hope it's a happy ending –'

'That's enough,' said Lauri.

Sasha turned round to look at him. He hadn't heard that tone from Lauri before. Lauri was sitting bolt upright, his face set, ready to shove back the bedclothes.

'That's enough, Sasha.'

Lauri knew Sasha in this mood. Goading his opponent in the heart of a meeting, barbing his words. When you took Sasha's words apart there was never an open accusation, nothing you could fight against. He was glad he'd put Eeva's letter away. He didn't want Sasha to see it.

But suddenly Sasha changed. He put out his hand, palm up.

'Don't mind me. I'm jealous, that's what it is. The only letters I ever get are about how I. M. Nicolaev will define our position on the rising price of essentials.' All at once his face was warm, alive with sympathy. 'I'm sorry, Lauri. I'm worn out and every-thing's gone wrong today – I'll tell you about it another time. I'm a clod and a clown and I deserve to be shot. Forgive me?'

Lauri smiled back. 'It was my fault. I should've waited . . .'

'No. This is important. She's to come to Helsinki, of course.'

'Here?'

'Yes. Well, no, obviously not here in this room. That's scarcely practical, is it? Unless you're going to marry her?'

Going to marry her? But Lauri said nothing aloud. Why had Sasha said that? Those things should never be said.

'But we'll find somewhere for her,' Sasha went on breezily. 'It won't be difficult. And then she must get work. She's in service, you said?'

'Eeva can do anything. You've no idea. She can write – you wouldn't believe how she writes. And she speaks Russian better than I do, even though she's never lived there, and Swedish. She knows pages of poetry off by heart, and she's read hundreds of books.'

'She'll be perfect in a dairy shop,' decided Sasha. 'As long as she's neat, and clean, and nice-looking. I expect she's nice-looking, isn't she? They're crying out for girls like that, with the dairy shops that are opening up all over the city. I've got contacts, I'll get to work on it.'

It was all being taken out of his hands. Sasha had the best intentions in the world, and this was just how he'd helped Lauri, finding him that job at Pavlov's. But Eeva was different. Somehow Sasha's fixing didn't feel right for her.

'When Eeva's settled here, she can decide,' Lauri said.

'She can't live in the street. I know a woman comrade who's looking for someone to share her room. You've met her: Magda, the German girl. But Eeva will have to get work straight away. There'll be her share of the rent, and then there's lighting and heat, and everything else, not to speak of food –'

'I can help her, to begin with. I've got some savings.'

Sasha looked at him quizzically, smiling. '*I* want to help, Lauri. That's all I'm trying to do. And yet you're angry with me.'

'I'm not angry. I know you want to help.'

'Has she the money for her fare?'

'I don't think so.'

'The trouble is, she's out in the back of beyond. You'd have to find out the nearest railway station. Or should we go there ourselves, to fetch her?'

But the thought of turning up to fetch Eeva with Sasha was a pair of boots that didn't fit. She might not even come.

'I'll write to her,' Lauri said. 'I'll send her the money for her fare, and she can decide for herself.'

Something in his tone silenced Sasha for a moment.

Long after Sasha was asleep, Lauri still lay thinking. He would be able to send her the fare. He had the money he was saving for next winter's boots, and that would do it. Of course Eeva would have to get work, but he hadn't liked the way Sasha talked about putting her into a dairy shop, as if Eeva wasn't Eeva, but just any girl fresh up from the country.

He turned over, very carefully so as not to disturb Sasha. It was no good trying to sleep now. It was full daylight outside, anyway, and on summer nights Lauri never slept long. He made up his sleep in the winter.

Eeva's letter made the last years seem like no time at all. He could shut his eyes and believe he was back sharing a bed with Eeva, in her father's apartment, when they were children.

That night – yes, the night he'd nearly told Sasha about once. But he'd stopped himself, and he'd been right to do so. Things like that shouldn't be talked about. What had he actually said to Sasha? Lauri frowned, trying to remember the exact words. *I've been in a room when a death was planned.* Yes, that was it. *Long ago, when I was a child.*

Long ago, when we were both children. When we snuggled up in the same bed, and Eeva's father laid his coat over us.

Eeva usually turned to the wall and humped out her backside. Lauri would push her into her own half of the bed. He can still remember exactly what that little backside felt like: bony, but somehow soft too.

He could always tell from her breathing whether she was really asleep or not. She didn't snore but she breathed more slowly. Eeva hadn't always been able to tell whether he was asleep or not. He was better at faking it than she was.

'Lauri?' she asked that night, in the thread of a whisper, and he didn't answer. He kept right down under the bedclothes, breathing away deeply and evenly. If she'd been able to see his face she'd have known at once that he wasn't asleep, but of course she couldn't.

'Lauri?'

He should have answered, but he lay dead still, listening.

'You've sorted it, then?' Eeva's father said that. And a deep voice – Juha – said that the man had fallen on the ice and hit the back of his head.

They meant the man who'd been at the meeting. Lauri knew something was wrong about him straight away. The way they talked to him and the way he asked so many questions. Lauri knew about police spies. He wondered if Eeva knew, too? They gave the man drink after drink and watched him to make sure he swallowed the vodka. His voice went sloppy and he kept saying he'd had enough, but they poured another glass as if they hadn't heard. And when everyone else had left, Eero and Big Juha took the man away. Lauri can't forget what he looked like. He had one arm over Eero's shoulder, and one over Big Juha's. In fact both men were bigger and broader than him and he dangled between them. He had a weak, blurred smile on his face. They said he shouldn't try to walk alone, and they'd take him where he was going.

He went out with them. From the back he looked like their prisoner. Had Lauri really thought that at the time, or did he only think of it later? The man was still asking a question as he went out of the door, but they didn't answer.

They'd killed him. Lauri knew that now and he'd known it then. Yes, children know things like that, even more clearly than adults, because they don't tell themselves that things are impossible and can't be happening. He'd known that they were going to kill the stranger, the man who might be a police spy. Did they know for sure that he was a police spy? Had they had a tip-off, or was it only that no one could vouch for him, and he asked too many questions?

Lauri had lain awake that night, cold and shivering. He'd thought that Eeva was awake too, but he didn't want her to know he wasn't asleep. He didn't want her to know how frightened he was. If Eero and Big Juha knew he'd been listening and he'd understood, maybe they'd take him out into the snow, too. Even Eeva's father might not be able to stop it.

No, Eeva's father would stop them, Lauri told himself. He wouldn't let it happen. But he hadn't stopped Eero and Big Juha, had he? Lauri lay shivering, with Eeva close but not touching him. That's how he knew she wasn't really asleep, because when they were really asleep and she was breathing slow, they always slid together somehow. But he didn't whisper her name. It might be dangerous. If she didn't know he was awake, maybe she'd think it was all a dream, and she'd forget it.

After a long, long time, he heard *them* come back.

'You've sorted it, then?' It was Eeva's father's voice.

'That's right. He took a nasty fall on the ice, struck the back of his head . . . it's not likely he'll be found before morning.'

Had Eeva still been awake then? He wasn't sure. And then one of *them* had creaked across the floor to where the children lay. He hadn't dared stir. He'd kept his eyes squeezed shut even though he knew his face was hidden. Something pressed down on the mattress. The bed creaked and the mattress moved. Maybe *they* knew. They knew Lauri had heard and were coming to silence him. And then, after a few seconds, the pressure lifted. Footsteps padded away, the door to the little inner room where Eeva's father slept clicked open, then shut again. The room breathed out.

Lauri didn't remember what had come next. One minute he'd been lying there rigid, the next it was morning. Maybe he'd fallen straight from terror into sleep. He'd never said anything to Eeva, nor she to him.

Yes, much better if Sasha didn't know any of it. To Sasha, it would be perfectly straightforward. A group of vigilant comrades had spotted a spy in their midst, and taken steps to eliminate him. That was Sasha's language. He was fond of expressions like 'in their midst' and 'taking steps'. And as for vigilance, it was one of Sasha's favourite themes . . .

But the question was, did Eeva remember that long-ago night, and know that it wasn't a dream? If she did, maybe one day they would talk about it. It was strange how important it seemed to know whether or not she'd really been asleep.

He would write back to her straight away. And he'd find a way to send her the money. She'd need her railway fare, and something to get as far as the station, and money for food on the journey. Maybe she could get a lift in a cart going to market, thought Lauri vaguely, if there was a market wherever the railway station was. He had never lived in the country, and had little idea of how people lived there, except that his political education had taught him that the peasants were just as badly off as the workers. And even easier to exploit, since they were tied to the land.

He couldn't imagine Eeva being tied to the land. She was much too quick and light. But even so, he felt a touch of panic at the thought of Eeva lost out there, in that foreign world of trees and crops and the smell of farm animals, as if she'd sunk to the bottom of the sea.

He turned over again, and shut his eyes. Soon he'd have to get up for work, and he'd not even slept.

In his mind he saw Eeva coming towards him over a sheet of green grass. She looked just as she had done before she left. He couldn't find a way to make her older, or different. She was looking at him across the wide stretch of grass that she still had to cross, and all at once he realized that of course it wasn't grass at all, but a broad green river, so deep that you couldn't see the bottom. The current was rushing along, and there was a wind that made Eeva's grey skirt blow out, and then in again, close to her body. Even though the water was flowing so fast, its surface didn't break and it remained coldly green. It looked like green snakes, he thought, as if hundreds of snakes were twisting just beneath the skin of the water. Eeva put a hand on her skirt to keep it from blowing up around her, and she stared at him across the water, as if to say, 'Are you going to come to me?'

'Sasha!' he called. 'Sasha, we need a boat!'

But there was no reply. He turned and there was no Sasha, only the echo of Sasha's voice saying, 'I've sorted it.'

Lauri slept. The mattress was old, and it sagged in the middle so that any two sleepers couldn't help meeting some time, in the course of the night. But whenever Sasha's body touched his, Lauri turned and moved away to the edge of the mattress, as if by instinct.

17

Yes, there she went! Scuttling away into those trees like a rabbit, but not quite fast enough to avoid Minna, who picked up her skirts and hurried after the girl. She'd have preferred to have this encounter in the kitchen. In the kitchen it was perfectly clear where they stood, and the strength of Minna's position was obvious.

Things weren't quite so clear in the open air, unfortunately. And having to run after her like this put Minna at a disadvantage. It was too hot to run. Her stays were tight and she couldn't get her breath. Where on earth was the wretched girl off to? She ought to be cooking, or cleaning something, not running about in the woods. Minna was panting now. This was completely ridiculous. Leaves brushed her face, dirty twigs snapped at her, roots caught her feet. She tripped, and nearly fell. And wearing her new skirt too – how annoying! Minna stopped, and shaded her eyes against the criss-crossing of light and shadow. That was the worst of trees. They took the light and broke it up and hid things in it.

Ah, there she was! Not doing anything, just standing there with a colander in her hands. A colander! Did she think she was in the kitchen garden? She'd seen Minna. Yes, she'd realized she wasn't going to get away from her. No doubt she knew exactly what it was that Minna wanted to say to her. Well might you run away from me, my lady, thought Minna. You've got something you hadn't bargained for now, haven't you? Yes, I've something to say to you and well you know it. Unless you're a fool, and you're certainly not that.

The girl's eyes were on her. Green eyes: what a colour. No, you're not a rabbit at all, you're a cunning little vixen. But not quite cunning enough. I'm on to you.

But, annoyingly, the girl didn't look worried. Her face was calm, even stern. Minna stopped, and let go of the skirts she'd been holding close to stop the branches tearing them. They were no distance from the house, but already they were in the forest. Its smell was in her nostrils. A sourish smell of earth that never got the sun, resin from the pines, a mushroomy smell of decay. Minna didn't like that smell, never had done.

'What are you doing here?' she asked sharply, to recover herself.

The girl showed the colander. There was green stuff in the bottom of it.

'I'm gathering nettles,' she said. But the girl's hands were bare; really, thought Minna with derision, it was so easy to catch her out.

'You'd be stung, if they were nettles,' Minna pointed out. 'Why aren't you wearing gloves?'

'I only need the tips,' said Eeva. 'If you pinch them off sharp, like this, see, they don't sting.'

Minna hadn't noticed the clump of nettles, just where the trees thinned and sun came through. They were growing strongly, into a thick, rank patch. She would like to roll the girl in them, she thought.

'See,' said Eeva, 'like this,' and she bent down, pinched the growing tip of a nettle hard between thumb and forefinger, and plucked it. 'If you do it like that, it won't sting you. Have a try.'

'I've no desire to pick nettles,' said Minna coldly. The performance reminded her of her father. He was always on at her to come mushroom-picking, or berry-picking, years after she'd grown out of it. 'And I can't imagine what you think you're doing here, when you ought to be at work.'

'I am at work,' said Eeva. 'The doctor asked me to pick nettle tips. It's for a tonic. He takes it to his patients.'

Wasn't that exactly typical of her father? Just the kind of thing he would ask the girl to do. Medicine wasn't enough for him, he always had to be asking a toothless old woman who couldn't even sign her own name about some remedy or other she'd been using since time immemorial. Imagine what people must think of him. *Here's the doctor, with his bottle of nettle tonic.* The doctor, subscribing to a pack of folk stories and superstitions. No wonder he'd never got on. No wonder he hadn't wanted to leave this place and move into town – not enough nettles there.

It used to infuriate her mother, and no wonder. He was determined to walk everywhere, while the horses ate their heads off in the stable. If a doctor makes himself look poor, people lose confidence in him. And even though he took the latest medical journals, and she knew for sure that he read them, how were his patients to guess it? He recommended that they drink cranberry juice for a chill on the kidneys, instead of giving them proper medicine. Birch sap, the first of a mare's milk after she'd given birth (Yes! How vividly Minna remembered that one!), poultices of mouldy bread, juniper beer, all kinds of concoctions and decoctions of herbs and berries, head massage, spinal massage, cupping . . .

As long as the remedy came from some wrinkled old peasant who looked exactly like a Karelian shaman, it was worth trying, first on himself and then on anybody else who was mug enough. Really, her father was maddening. Why refuse to go forward, into the modern world? Why bury yourself in the forest, when the future lay in the city? Why make yourself look like a failure?

Minna took a deep breath to steady herself. She must stop this: her mind was pulsing with years of anger. None of it mattered. What her father did in his profession couldn't hurt her now. She was free. She had her own life and he was no part of it. Her friends never saw him, and knew nothing about him.

It was the woods that were upsetting her. Too many memories. It would have been far better for this interview to take place in the kitchen, with the girl standing in front of her, her hands folded submissively against her apron. But never mind that. Nothing was going to stop Minna from saying what she'd travelled all the way from Åbo to say.

'Have you ever thought, Eeva, that you might be better off in another place?' she began. Eeva didn't reply at once. She waited, warily, but Minna wasn't having any of that. This girl wasn't going to force her hand with silence, or make Minna say more than she meant to. Minna was in charge.

'Well?'

'I've never been in another place. I came straight here from the orphanage.'

'I know you did.' Minna paused, softened her voice. 'And maybe that's the root of the trouble: your inexperience. You're very young. Dr Eklund is a generous man, he wanted to give you a chance, but he didn't realize quite how difficult it would be for you.'

'Why are you saying this to me?' said Eeva quietly.

This was too much. Minna felt her hair crisp with rage, and she took a step towards the girl.

'I am saying this to you because you are a servant in my father's house. I am saying this to you because you are not – because your work is not giving satisfaction.'

But it sounded limp, lame. It was not at all what she wanted to say. She wanted to slam words against the girl so that they knocked her into the patch of nettles. And then she'd find out whether nettles sting or not.

She wanted to spit out the most insulting words she could think of – words she'd never said aloud, words she hadn't even let herself know that she knew. Words her mother had never said in all those years.

'You needn't think I don't know what you're up to,' she said. 'You think I'm soft, and that you can make a fool of me, just as you've tried to make a fool of my father. But I'm not soft. Do you imagine that you're in the kitchen, up to your elbows in grease all day, because you know so much more than I do? You've got a lot to learn, my girl, and you can start by taking that look off your face when you talk to me.'

Colour had rushed into the girl's cheeks.

'It's only *you* that's saying this,' she said. '*He* hasn't said anything.'

'No, and you thought he wouldn't, didn't you? You counted on that. You thought nobody would stop your little game of making a fool out of a man who's alone, who's been widowed, who isn't quite himself. It's easy enough to make a fool out of any man from eighteen to eighty, God knows there's nothing clever about it.' *Where were these words coming from? What part of her?* 'You don't think he cares tuppence for you, do you? No, it's just because you're here. You're convenient. He loved my mother, and his life is over now that she's dead –'

Yes, that was it. The right words were tumbling out of her mouth now. It felt good, rich. She was panting with anger, not exertion. She had the power to say anything, do anything. If she had to drag this girl back to the house by her hair, she would do it. There was strength in her now, to move mountains.

'All you are, as far as he's concerned, is a little trollop who's handy and makes it clear she's available.'

Trollop, that was it. That was telling her.

The girl was pale now. She was clasping the colander against her stomach and staring at Minna.

It's no good pretending, my girl, thought Minna. You're no innocent. You've heard it all before. Do you think I don't know where you come from, and the way you've been dragged up?

The bare sight of the girl made her sick.

'You needn't worry,' said the girl. 'I'm not staying.'

'What do you mean?'

'That's it. I'm not staying. I'm going somewhere else.'

'You've got another place?'

'Yes. I've got another place.'

'You can't do that. You haven't given notice. Mrs Eriksson doesn't know you've got another place. Do they know at the orphanage?'

'You wanted me to go. I'm telling you that I'm going.'

She was sly, that's what she was. Calculating. She'd been thinking ahead, planning her next move, because she knew it would all come out sooner or later, what she'd been up to here.

'They will do,' added the girl.

'They will do what?'

'They'll know, at the orphanage. When I've gone. They always get told when someone leaves a place.'

For sheer brass neck she took some beating.

'So you've got yourself another place,' said Minna slowly, to give herself time, 'and without so much as telling anyone. What did you do, answer an advertisement? They'll want a reference, you know. Have you thought of that?'

'Why are you so angry? I thought you wanted me to leave.'

Minna couldn't help herself. She stepped forward, right up to the girl, and knocked the colander out of her hand. It thudded on the earth, and the green stuff scattered. Minna ground it with the heel of her boot, ground it until the green was mashed into earth and pine needles.

'You think you can do exactly as you like, don't you?' she hissed through her teeth. The girl was lucky. She didn't know how lucky she was. I don't often lose my temper, said Minna to herself, but when I do . . .

The girl crouched down to examine the mess of nettle and earth. Minna looked at the thin, pale nape of her neck. It had down on it, and tendrils which had crept out of the knot of hair. Minna had never had such thoughts before. Violent, cruel thoughts. If she'd had an axe she could have chopped that neck like a rotten branch. Get up, you fool, she thought, and, as if the girl had heard her, she stood up again with her empty colander, pushed back a stray lock of hair and faced Minna.

'There're plenty more nettles,' she said, 'I'll find a better clump. I know what you think. You think because I come from an orphange, my life belongs to Mrs Eriksson, and to the orphanage. But you're wrong. My life belongs to me.'

The two young women faced each other. Minna had never been so angry in her life, she told herself. Anger licked inside her, hot and almost lovable. She *wanted* to be angry. My God, she thought, I could kill her and grind her into the earth just like those leaves. Her hands had gone to her hips, her elbows were braced, she balanced on the balls of her feet, ready to spring.

And then they both heard whistling. Beautiful, melodious whistling. Not a bird, they knew that at once.

'It's Matti,' said Eeva. 'That's him whistling.'

Of course it was. How the sound took Minna back. She couldn't help it, she was five again, grubbing in the soil of the kitchen garden, digging up the radishes she'd planted to see how they were growing, while Matti worked in one of the beds near by, and whistled songs she knew well.

I'll tramp the roads as far as I wish
And I'll love the one I choose.

Yes, he would whistle a couple of lines, and then sing the song so beautifully that she would sit back on her heels in the dry dusty earth and do nothing but listen.

They were always Finnish songs. By rights she wouldn't have been able to understand a word of them, living as she did almost entirely in the Swedish-speaking world. But her father was determined that Minna should speak Finnish as well as Swedish, right from the start, so that the language would sit easily on her tongue. He had taught her himself, and encouraged her to talk in Finnish with Matti and with old Beata who came to do the washing in those days. Her mother had only Swedish-speaking servants in the house, and in those days the tongues of other mothers clicked when they heard Minna chattering in Finnish. But she didn't care, not then. Her father had explained his reasons to her.

Yes, in those days she'd been glad and proud to be taught by him. Quite puffed up with her own success, when she realized that she was more fluent than her mother. But her mother had soon pricked that bubble.

When you've learned a language as soon as you can talk, you can't get it out of your head, even if you want to. Matti had taught her all his Finnish songs, and she'd sung the verses after him, following him line by line. Funny how she'd nearly forgotten all that. But it came back: she could hear the words now.

But she didn't recognize the song Matti was whistling.

'What's he whistling?' she asked aloud, not even thinking that it was Eeva who would answer the question. Without realizing it, she dropped into Finnish. Eeva stared.

'What's he whistling? Do you know it?' repeated Minna.

Eeva listened. 'I don't know it,' she answered, speaking in Finnish too. Her own tongue. Who would have thought this stuck-up city bitch could have spoken like that? 'He'll sing the words in a moment,' Eeva went on. 'That's what he does, whistles a verse, then sings it.'

'I know.'

They stood there listening until Matti opened his mouth and sang the words:

> *And if you still refuse to love me*
> *I'll bathe myself in bitter memory,*
> *I'll go and feed on wild honey,*
> *I'll go and feed on golden berries.*

Yes, thought Minna. He whistles and then he sings the words. That's what he does. For a moment she was torn with longing. How had it all happened? She'd been that little girl squatting in the dust, not knowing anything about what lay ahead of her, and afraid of nothing. She could even remember the feeling of the love she'd had for Matti, as if she were rubbing her fingers on the fabric of a dress she'd worn long ago. Yes, she used to leave special little patterns of different-coloured stones around the garden, for him to find. It all seemed so close still that she could shut her eyes and feel the silkiness of dust between her fingers. And the bitter taste of those radishes that weren't ready to eat. But it was all gone. She could never go back there.

But she had her life. She was married, and she had her own tall house with new dove-grey paper in the morning room where she sat to write letters. The thought of that dove-grey paper was like a warm spot inside her. She'd barely looked at it yet, because the room had only just been finished when she'd had to come away. Soon she'd be sitting there again, writing letters beginning 'My dear father –' and signing them 'your affectionate daughter, Minna'.

No, it wasn't a tragedy that you couldn't go back. It was all very well listening to Matti whistle, but if she went to talk to him now it would just be embarrassing. She had nothing to say to him.

Life changes, and we change with it, thought Minna, and the words comforted her. Matti was still singing.

> *In the bitter smoke of memory*
> *You will be with me for ever.*

How feelingly he sang, even though he was an old man now. But it was all the greatest possible rubbish. People weren't like that. They soon forgot each other.

Her anger was cold now. All she felt was weariness; yes, weariness, that was what she felt, because she was always afraid now, she was hedged about with fear of this and fear of that. She did not dare even to think about having children. And the more afraid she felt, the more sure she had to seem. And there was no one she loved enough to leave little patterns of pebbles in the dust for them to find.

She would do her duty. She did not love her father. And this girl was nothing. She was in the way, that was all. She had to be got rid of, in a civilized way, so that Minna and her father could go back to being as they were, not loving each other or upsetting each other.

It wasn't possible that she, Minna, had thought of beating the girl to the earth.

No, she wasn't going to stand here 'bathing herself in bitter memory' like any hopeless peasant. That wasn't her way, any more than it had been her mother's way. Johanna had squared her shoulders and carried on. Bitter memory! Let *him* have that. It had been a mistake to come back here, but she had her duty. And fortunately, as it turned out, she didn't need to dismiss the girl. It had all been done for her. Minna was quite sensible enough to realize that the pleasure of telling the girl to go would be balanced by the inconvenience of telling her father that she had done so.

The girl would go of her own choice: good. She would not be missed. Even Lotta didn't need to know the detail. Let her think what she wanted to think. The girl would be gone, and that would be enough. And if she was lying and she didn't have a place to go to, then so much the worse for her. It wasn't Minna's responsibility. Yes, let her go as soon as possible, and let everything be calm again. Her father would be grateful. Not immediately, that was too much to hope for, but in time. Yes, in time, when he'd been able to reflect, and realized that Minna had done this for him. All

Minna wanted was to keep him from his own weakness, and in the end he would appreciate that her motives were good.

> And when the golden berries fall
> And the honeycomb is empty
> And we sleep in the heart of winter,
> I will still call for you.

The girl had turned away from Minna to listen, as if Minna were not there. Her lips were parted. Suddenly Minna's satisfaction was tinged with pity. Yes, she thought, that's what's going to happen to you. No more golden berries, no more honey. That's it for you, my girl, so listen while you can.

Very upright, drawing her skirts close, Minna made her way out of the wood.

18

There was something going on behind his back. He knew it from Minna's smooth face at dinner, and from the satisfied way she tapped her glass down on the table and announced that she'd be going home tomorrow. It always seemed to him that she took a special, hurtful pleasure in saying the word 'home' to him, when she did not mean the house where she was born and brought up, the home where her family had lived for generations . . .

But of course Åbo was her home now; Minna was a married woman with her own household to run, her own preoccupations and plans for the future.

All through dinner she'd been telling him about the redecoration of her morning room, and the English water-colours she'd bought at auction. She was like her mother in this love of things Anglo-Saxon. He could imagine her in a circle of young matrons like herself, each of them talking about her own drawing room or the improvements she'd made to the kitchen, and how her cook had said the new range had quite transformed her life. The young matrons would take turns, allowing one another just so much time, and turning their bright pleased faces from one speaker to the next.

'It all sounds most attractive, my dear,' he said at last. She looked at him severely.

'I don't believe you've heard a word I've said.'

'I've heard every word. First of all they brought a paper which wasn't in the least like the one you'd chosen. Couldn't they tell the difference between pearl grey and dove grey? But you insisted, and of course they had the right paper in stock all the time. They'd just made a muddle.'

'Yes.' But she was still suspicious.

'And so tomorrow you'll be back at home,' he said. 'Back with Ulf.'

Never, he thought, had a man suited his forename less. What could have possessed his parents? Surely, even in his cradle, Ulf must have been neat, even urbane. If his poor Minna had wanted a wolf, she certainly hadn't found one.

No children yet. Would there ever be children? When he asked Minna about it once, quite gently and tactfully, he'd thought, she'd flinched away.

She kept so much from him. What was she hiding now, he wondered. She was going back to Åbo satisfied, and yet as far as he knew she hadn't spoken to Eeva. Lotta's summons hadn't led to a confrontation. He'd surely have known if there'd been one. Eeva – yes, Eeva was the same as ever. The fire that had sprung up in her when the letter arrived had died down. Or perhaps it was still there, but hidden. My God, he thought, what am I, that they both hide things from me?

She was bringing in a dish of potatoes. She put it on the table, and began to collect the soup plates. No, she was absent. Her body was here, serving them, but her mind and spirit were withdrawn. Her hands moved quickly and deftly. Suddenly, seeing them against the plates, he saw how fine they were. Red and rough, yes, and there were burn marks across her knuckles. That would be from reaching for pots from the racks inside the oven. They were not deep burns, but everyday scorches across the tight skin of her knuckles. Kirstin and Jenny had always had such marks. On them it had seemed natural, but he flinched from the thought of Eeva's hands groping for an iron pot and brushing against the iron rack. She would pull out her hand, suck the burn and then carry on. She ought to run her hand under cold water for five minutes at least, but probably, like Kirstin and Jenny, she wouldn't listen to this advice and instead would rub the burn with a little piece of butter.

His daughter was playing with the stem of her glass, looking down at the cloth. She didn't want to look at Eeva. Her hands were smooth, but they were not as fine as Eeva's. No, he thought, that beauty of Eeva's, you can't do anything about it, and nor can I. There were Eeva's hands, balancing the soup plates and the

159

tureen. They hadn't eaten much soup. Eeva would eat it in the kitchen, after them. The same taste would be in her mouth as had been in his. It seemed a miracle that this could happen. He looked at her, and her beauty hurt him in the pit of his stomach, and made him helpless.

Helpless, and stupid. He dug the nails of one hand into the palm of the other. They mustn't see it in his eyes, neither of them must know. His daughter would be disgusted, and Eeva – Eeva would be frightened. It almost frightened him, what he felt for her. If she guessed it, she would leave.

There were cutlets on his plate in front of him. He'd have to do something with them. Cut them up, dip them in sauce, put them in his mouth, chew and swallow them. She'd made sauce because of Minna. His potatoes were almost cold. He put a piece of meat in his mouth, and his tongue quivered with revulsion.

'Why aren't you eating, Father?'

'I'm not hungry.'

'All the same, you must eat something.'

Minna was cutting her meat into the smallest possible pieces, dipping them in sauce and swallowing calmly.

And then, suddenly, she was there in front of him. Four-year-old Minna, sitting in her place in her blue and white ruffled pinafore, raging at the sight of the English custard which Johanna believed should be eaten by the child at least three times a week. Minna turned her face aside from the dish, her eyes tight shut, her nose screwed up to reject even the smell of it. Johanna sat beside her, chair drawn close to Minna's, spoon in hand, implacable. The custard must have gone cold, or at least lukewarm. Skin was forming on it. Suddenly Johanna seized hold of Minna's nose, gripped it firmly, waited until Minna had to open her mouth to breathe, and rammed in the spoonful of custard. He heard the spoon grate on Minna's teeth, and he flinched. She coughed, spluttered. She would not swallow it, she would not. Johanna held the spoon there, but suddenly Minna leaned forward and gagged with all her force, spitting out spoon and custard. Strings of saliva ran down from her mouth.

'Johanna! My God,' he protested. The next moment Johanna had stood up, shoving back her chair. She was behind Minna, looming over her. And then she did it. One hand plucked up the spoon which had fallen into the bowl, the other grasped the back of Minna's neck and pushed her face down into the custard. Yes, right down into the custard, so that it overflowed the bowl. And she held Minna there while the child flailed.

He leapt up, reached across the table, and seized Minna by the shoulders, tearing her from her mother's grip. He dragged her through china and cutlery, across the cloth, into his arms.

She was rigid, choking, her face a mess of slime. He cleaned out her mouth with his finger, wiped her nostrils, then her eyes, talking to her all the while, telling her that she was all right, he had got her. She was breathing. The custard was in her hair and running down inside her clothes. Suddenly she arched her back, went stiff in his arms, and let out a series of terrible, high-pitched shrieks without a breath between them, like the screaming of a child with meningitis. It was only for a few moments, and then she went soft again and he caught her close to him. She pressed her face into his shoulder and clung and sobbed until she was exhausted.

Johanna. What was Johanna doing? Her face rigid, she was cleaning the tablecloth with a napkin.

'Johanna,' he'd said. She'd looked at him, the custard-sodden napkin in her hand, her face pale. 'Never,' he said. 'Never do that again to her. Never.'

'She must learn.'

'Not like that. Never like that.'

He had carried Minna upstairs. She was limp and quiet now, and he thought she might have fallen asleep, quite suddenly, as children do after pain. But when he sat on her bed with her, and gently lifted her down onto his lap, he saw that her dark blue eyes were wide open. They were fixed on him, and there was a blankness in them that made him want to press her close to him again, so that he wouldn't have to see it. She wasn't crying any more, but she hiccuped suddenly, and he stood up with her in his arms, and poured her a drink of water from the covered jug beside her bed.

'I'll call Jenny in a minute,' he promised, 'and we'll bath you and make you comfortable. Look,' he went on, 'Papa's all dirty too. We'll get Minna clean and then we'll get Papa clean.'

She pulled at the neck of her pinafore. A wave of disgust and anguish crossed her face as she touched the slime of the custard.

'Never mind, Minna, those clothes can all be washed. Let's get you undressed. Look, I can untie your pinafore so that it won't even touch your face when I take it off.'

'I don't want Mama to come here,' she said. Tears rolled down her face again. It was no use pretending to her. She'd felt it, she'd known it. Johanna would have broken her, to make her obey.

'Mama was wrong,' he said quietly. Whatever happened, Minna was going to know that. 'It was naughty of Mama.'

Minna was watching him carefully. Her eyes were red and swollen in a puffed white face. 'I will tell Mama that she must never behave like that to you again,' he said. Minna nodded convulsively.

He said no more. He called Jenny to prepare the bath, and began to untie the strings of Minna's pinafore, taking care that the sodden material did not brush against her skin.

As far as he knew, nothing like that had happened again. Johanna would never admit it, but he thought she too had been frightened. Afraid of herself, the worst kind of fear.

Minna never mentioned it. Perhaps she had forgotten. It was the only time he had ever spoken to Johanna in criticism about her conduct with the child. He had left Minna to her mother more and more. Had he believed it was Johanna's right? Had he truly believed that Johanna's cool control was what his daughter needed to learn?

My daughter, he thought. Eeva had taken away the plates again. There was fruit to eat now: preserved gooseberries from last year. Before long, this season's would ripen. Minna ate steadily. If only we could see the marks that our lives leave on us, he thought, we'd be more tender with one another.

She'd be gone tomorrow. He longed to smoke. As soon as they'd had their coffee he'd go and walk in the garden. It was the best time. Evening light, the scent of tobacco, the pale moths starting to fly. Most especially, he loved the sweet, pure fragrance of tobacco when he first lit his cigarette. He would go and walk in the garden and think about Eeva, where no one could see him.

19

There she stood, by his desk. It was three o'clock in the morning. She had opened the shutters and the light was full, but unfamiliar, in the way of midsummer light. It searched out corners of the room that it would never touch in the later hours of the day. Every object looked strange, with its shadow leaning the wrong way.

He was still asleep, she was sure of that. His daughter was gone, and he'd walked about all evening, frowning and smoking. They certainly didn't make each other happy, those two. She thought of her own father and for a moment could have felt sorry for Minna. But she wasn't going to, no, she wasn't. Not for either of them.

The house felt empty and expectant. It knew something was going to happen. Just for this hour it belonged to her, and everything in it belonged to her. But it's true, she thought, that when you clean a place and look after it, you feel you know it better than the owner. In the House of Orphans Sirkka used to talk about 'my floors', or 'my tiles': 'I did have a job with my floors this morning, all scuffed up they were.' And then Sirkka would stare down the river of waxed, glowing wood with possessive pride.

Eeva smoothed her hand over the silky top of his desk. I could get like Sirkka if I stayed here too long. I must not get like her.

Go now, go now, ticked the tall clock in the corner. *Time to go, Eeva, or you'll find yourself down in the kitchen again making dough for his morning rolls.*

She shivered. But why be frightened? She was getting out of here. He was sleeping and would sleep for hours yet.

Even if he woke, he couldn't stop you. Nothing can stop you.

She glanced out. Morning light flickered over the tops of the trees. The birds were singing, full of themselves. So much green to fight her way through, before she reached the streets she knew.

It's myself I'm afraid of, she thought. It's so easy to stay. My floors, my tiles, my bed under the eaves. Food on the table three times a day. But it's not that; no, it's something else that keeps me.

I'm afraid of having my life again, that's it. I was never afraid before, not when I was little. I used to look forward and talk about when I grew up. It seemed natural that my life was my own. But in the House of Orphans they made us afraid.

They made us obedient on the outside, no matter what we felt like inside. We thought we were real rebels if we whispered in bed, me and Kirsti. Anna-Liisa was smarter than we thought. Yes, she knew how to get us ready for a lifetime of doing what we were told, and muttering under our breath where no one could hear us. We'd spit into her coffee to make ourselves feel big, or wipe her china she was so proud of with a cloth we'd used to clean the toilet. Dad was right. That's how it works and most people never realize it. You're trapped both ways. You do as you are told and you do things that you think will make you big, but all the time you're shrinking. In the end even if the door's left open you can't walk out of it. Maybe you work off your feelings by skimping the polish on the lock. So you look at Sirkka, or at old Agneta here. She's decent, she works hard. But she's living a life which has already been taken away from her.

If you were here, Dad, what would you do?

No, she would not think of him. She would not. Memories crowded into her head and they were always the wrong ones. How he lay there and told her that he'd wasted his life. No, Dad, no. It's not true. You can't have died thinking that.

"'My talisman, preserve me,'" she muttered. 'Make me strong. Make me strong. They've done something to me, I've changed. Maybe it was never really me that was strong in the first place.'

I've got to go now, she thought, there won't be a better chance. My life will be over if I stay. I'll go on living, I won't be able to help it, but it won't be my life. I'll grow pleased with how well I serve him. I'll start talking about 'my kitchen', just like Sirkka used to say. 'My floors aren't looking like they should.' And he'll follow me with that look in his eyes, and one day I'll give in, and that'll be the end. I'll be trapped.

He's asleep. He can't stop me. It's me that's stopping myself.

She hadn't slept. She'd lain on her bed for three hours. Her heart thudded as if she'd been running, and it wouldn't slow down. Better not to sleep, she told herself. She was resting her body, that was what mattered. It was a long walk to the station, but safer to walk than try to get a lift on a cart. Everyone knew the doctor. They'd want to know her business. Where have you come from, where are you going . . . Safer to follow quiet tracks and slip into the woods when she saw another traveller.

It would take most of the day. Twelve hours at least, Matti reckoned. Stopping to rest would make it longer. Once she got to the station, she could wait. Never mind how long it took till a train came. She was good at waiting. She had her bundle with black bread, hard cheese, a handful of dried cranberries. Even if she missed the only train of the day, it didn't matter. Another would come in the morning.

She'd never travelled anywhere, except when they brought her to the House of Orphans. She'd never even bought a train ticket. She would say as little as possible. She wouldn't ask questions, but watch what other people did, and copy them. She had money for her fare, and that would talk for her. No one would guess she'd run away.

She was a good walker, strong and steady. She knew the best way to the station. Matti had told her, and drawn a map for her in the soil, with the point of a stick. He asked no questions. Didn't ask why she wanted to know. Only remarked, 'Pity they never ran the railroad as far as our town.' He must have guessed that she had her reasons for leaving, but he never asked where she was going, or why, or whether she'd come back.

She could count on Matti's closed mouth. He'd say nothing to the doctor. She didn't know why she was sure of it, but she was sure.

'You don't even need to go through town, Eeva. You'll cut two, three hours off your journey if you follow the way I tell you. The high road's good for carts and carriages, but you go across country, that's the way. You take the Lindholm farm road as far as the first crossroads, and out east through Heimola forest. It's no more than a logging track, but you won't lose yourself. That'll bring you out close to the Black Lake. Turn north, keep clear of the bog, follow the shore until you reach the inn. There's a boatman there who'll row you across for fifty pennies. Once you're on the other side you'll see the track again, and that takes you through onto the high road. After that you've only an hour's walk north and you're there.'

Matti had paused and looked her full in the face. 'Five years ago I'd have walked you all the way myself,' he said. She looked down. There was something new in his face and voice. He was Matti, her friend. But she couldn't fool herself: she had called out feeling in him. Better not to let him see that she knew it.

'But my legs won't let me now,' Matti said. 'My time's past.' He said it as if she couldn't have noticed, hadn't ever seen the clench of his teeth as he bent painfully to the earth. 'You're a city girl, Eeva,' he went on, 'you don't know how to thrive out here, as we do. Keep to the track and don't wander off.'

'I won't.'

He was old. He sang and whistled like a young man but his life was almost over. Soon he would seize up and then he'd spend his last years sitting on his porch in summer, by his stove in winter. When he died he would be well spoken of at his funeral, and then forgotten, because he belonged to no one. Only the doctor would speak of him, and what use was that?

'Send a message if you find a way, Eeva,' Matti had said, taking up his hoe. 'So I know you got there safe.'

'I will,' she'd said, but she knew he could not read.

Go now, Eeva, said the clock. *Do you want to be like Matti? Life is quick, quick, quick . . .*

She had Lauri's money, but she didn't know if it was enough. Here was the doctor's desk, where he worked. She walked around it. There were drawers with brass handles and brass keyholes. She tried the top drawer, and it slid open easily.

It was full of papers, and letters tied with pink tape. No, she didn't want to read them. She slid a hand underneath to see if he had hidden anything there, but there was nothing. She opened the second drawer. Cigars in wooden boxes, cigarettes, and a tobacco pouch embroidered with pansies. She'd never seen him smoke a pipe. There was a narrow wooden box. Perhaps he kept his money in it. But when she opened it, there was only a lock of fine, silky hair. A child's hair, she thought. Probably his daughter's hair. Her heart was beating fast, fast, like a thief's.

There was the money. Not locked or hidden. Just left lying as if it didn't matter. A parchment envelope, open. Banknotes sliding out, carelessly, yes, just as if they were worthless. But she checked them, and they were good notes.

She counted them. She would take her wages, she decided. Only that. He'd given her money for clothes, money for what she needed, but he still owed her . . .

Why shouldn't she take more, for the months she'd worked for him? Good wages, hers were called, but they were nothing compared to this roll of notes. Nothing compared to what he had, and didn't even care about. He left it lying. Yes, he owed her all this. All of it, Eeva thought, taking the banknotes and shuffling them together as she counted them. Probably he didn't even know how much there was. Here was enough to pay the rent on their Helsinki apartment for a year. They'd gone without, to pay that rent. Maybe the landlord shoved the rent that they'd sweated for into envelopes like this, as if it meant nothing.

This money would have bought medicine for Dad. It would have bought a doctor to come every day. If she'd had this in her hands they'd never have dared take her to the House of Orphans. Destitute, they'd said she was. Destitute and in moral danger, living in the apartment of a political suspect, sharing the bed with Lauri whom she'd known all her life, who was like her brother.

She spread the notes out like a hand of cards. She would take this one, and this, and this.

I am a thief, Eeva thought.

I'm only taking what's due to me. I'm taking what's been taken from me.

But she would never put this money in with the money Lauri sent to her. He was bound to ask her about it. 'That money I sent you, Eeva, was it enough?'

That money of Lauri's was real money. An overcoat, a pair of boots. He would go without, because he'd given it to her. And she'd repay him every penny, but not with the doctor's money. It would be with proper money she'd earned and had a right to. And she wouldn't mix this money, a rich man's careless money, with what Lauri had given up for her.

Lauri. She seemed to feel him beside her, as he'd slept so many times. He had his own smell, like everyone. One night after they'd been swimming they licked each other's arms, to taste the salt on their skins. And then Lauri licked her stomach, and a most extraordinary feeling swelled inside her, like butterflies stretching their wings and trying to get out.

They were both bony little kids.

'You jabbed your elbow right into my ribs!'

'No, it was you, your knees are like razor blades.'

But more often they tumbled together in the centre of the bed. It was warm with Lauri there, and safe. The voices of the grown-ups sank away into a drone that didn't matter. Lauri would raise his eyebrows exactly like an adult: 'What are they on about *now*?' he'd whisper, and she'd giggle without making any noise. Or if there were visitors, important comrades from Petersburg or even from Berlin, Eeva would imitate the way their noses twitched as they pushed up their glasses, or the way they put four lumps of sugar into their coffee while pretending not to notice what they were doing. She would wrinkle up her face to look serious and important, while all the time her fingers were 'absent-mindedly' searching out the sugar. Plop, plop, plop, plop went the imaginary lumps, one by one into her imaginary cup. Lauri would be exploding with laughter, stuffing his face into the coat that covered them.

My God, she thought, I might see him tomorrow. It didn't seem possible. He was locked away in her mind, like a treasure she kept hidden.

Of course he'd have changed. He wouldn't be the Lauri she knew. People are different when they grow up.

Don't think of that now.

If she took the doctor's money, she'd still be tied to him. His money would come along with her. And he could send the police after her, and have her locked away. He could send a telegram to Helsinki, to tell the police there to look out for her. Her name might be enough for them. Eeva Koskinen? Don't we have a file on someone of that name?

Eeva put the banknotes back into the envelope, making sure that the money lapped out of the envelope just as sloppily as it had done before. She put the envelope into the drawer, slid it shut, and then she picked up her bundle and slung it over her shoulder. There was nothing in there which didn't belong to her. Her clothes, her three books. She had her food, and a bottle of buttermilk sealed with waxed paper. On her feet there were the new boots the doctor had given her. She'd never had boots like it: they fitted as if she'd had her foot measured for them. The leather was strong, and the soles thick. They didn't let in water. She certainly wasn't going to leave the boots behind.

And now it was time to go. She looked out of the window. *He* was always staring out of the window, as if there was something wonderful to be seen in the distance. But no, there were only trees. Trees as far as she could see, marching away to the horizon. Too many trees, they made her heart sink, they sapped her courage . . .

'Eeva,' said his voice from the doorway.

Fire ran up her body. She thought in a few seconds of a thousand things. He would get her taken away, put into prison, sent back to the orphanage. He'd seen her holding his money, and now he'd say that Lauri's money was his, and she had stolen it. He would seize her and not let her go. They'd all come – Mrs Eriksson, Anna-Liisa, his daughter . . .

Slowly, she drew in her breath. Slowly, she turned to face him.

'Eeva, where are you going?'

'You know where I'm going,' she answered.

'I don't know anything,' he said.

'I'm going away.'

'Away from me?'

As if her journey had anything to do with him. As if she wasn't living her own life.

'Just away,' she said. 'I can't stay here any more. I can't –' She heard her own voice squeak with misery, like a child's.

'If you'll only tell me, Eeva, how I can make it better. I know it's hard for you. I know how quiet it is here, and you haven't any friends, and I'm so much older –'

'It's not that,' she said. She braced herself. She was not a child, and he wasn't going to talk to her as if she was. Would his eyes follow her like that, day after day, if she was a child? No, she had her own power. She felt it flow into her fingers, and lifted her head.

It was still neither day nor night. It was a time that didn't belong anywhere. She could say what she wanted.

'I'm going home,' she said.

'You mean Helsingfors – Helsinki?'

'Of course.'

'But Eeva, my dear girl –'

He was shocked, she saw it, but already he was gathering himself, recovering. 'But what will you do there? You haven't any family. You haven't a job to go to, or anywhere to live.'

He said these things as if they were facts that couldn't change. She was homeless; she had no money or family. He had thrust the letter, and Eeva's radiance, out of his mind. He was not going to make them real between him and Eeva.

'I have a place to live,' she said quietly.

He stood there in his dressing gown. He felt old and crumpled beside her, lined with sleep. The stale air of sleep clung round him. He was afraid that she could smell him. He mustn't think of that, he must make an effort, make her see how things really were . . .

'So you were going to walk out of the house before I woke, and disappear,' he said. 'Was I even to have a letter?'

She shook her head. It was true. She hadn't even thought of it. She looked at him, pale and old with stubble pushing through his skin. His mouth was stiff with pain. She saw his Adam's apple move. He was swallowing something. He put his palms on the desktop, and leaned forward on them, heavily, with his head bowed. There was grey in his hair, and it was thinning, just there. She could see the colour of his scalp. She waited.

'I will give you money, Eeva,' he said at last. 'You can't go off like this, alone and with nothing.'

'You'll give me money?'

'I owe you your wages, at least. But you'll need more than that.'

'I don't want you to give me money.'

'What does it matter, Eeva!' he said impatiently, lifting his head. 'Money's not so very important. Take it.'

'You only think it's not important because you've always had it,' she said slowly. 'Because always having it has made you what you are.'

He flushed angrily. 'If money was important to me, I wouldn't do what I do. Why do you think I'm a doctor, and not a banker?'

'You don't understand. You've never known anything different, how can you? The life you have – this house – what you are – all of it – you've always had it and you're safe, you know you're safe.'

'You think I'm safe?'

She nodded, like a doctor confirming a diagnosis that the patient resists. 'Of course.'

They were silent. Light was spilling over her feet, onto the new boots. He was seized with a longing to lie down on the cool waxed floor. He would lay his head by her boots. He would ease her slender foot out of the leather and lay his cheek against it. Her fine bones, the articulation of them, the arch of her foot there, the planting of her toes on the floor. He would rest his cheek in the hollow of her foot.

He met her eyes. They were narrow, watching him carefully. She seemed to have light inside her eyes today, not colour. Was she afraid of him? No. Watchful, maybe, wary. But how could she not know that he would let her put her foot on his neck if only she'd stay and he could still watch her move around his house?

Suddenly she gave him an odd, nervous little smile. He must be calm. He was frightening her. He picked up a paperknife from the desktop, and drew it out of its leather sheath. A funny little paperknife, crude and gilded. Minna had bought it for him when she was six years old. How proud she'd been, how she'd watched him to make sure that he used it every time a letter came. He used it still.

'I chose this room for my study because it faces east and gets the morning light,' he said suddenly. 'When I don't sleep, I come in here and work.'

'East? Helsinki's east.'

'South east,' he corrected. 'No. East south east, probably.'

Her smile became more real. 'Anyone would know you're a doctor.'

'Why?'

Her fingers flickered a mime of things being put exactly in their place.

'You're so . . . careful.'

'You have to be careful, when you're responsible for patients. You can't play about with people's lives.'

'Do you think you're responsible for me?'

'I am responsible. You are living in my house. You're working for me.'

'But you're trying,' she said awkwardly, feeling her way into the words, 'you're trying to do what you said. To play with my life. You know it's not only as you say. Me living in your house, and working for you. You know there's more.'

'But Eeva –'

'What?'

'You don't understand. I'm not the man you think. What I feel for you –'

He was pressing forward, eager, his eyes bright.

'Don't tell me. I don't want you to tell me.'

'She's said something to you, hasn't she? My daughter.'

'No.' Eeva folded her arms.

'Eeva, that's not true.'

'Who are you,' she asked, 'to tell me what's true, and what's not true?'

'I don't know,' he said. His hands, which had stretched towards her, fell to his sides. He hadn't meant to say that. He *did* know what was true. He was himself, Thomas, Dr Eklund. Hundreds of people would testify for him. But this girl was digging pits under his feet. He was falling and he wanted to fall. He felt a moment of terrible pity for himself. He looked down and saw Thomas Eklund at his feet, lying in the gutter. Poor idiot, poor booby. You love her, do you? Well, look at yourself, this is where it gets you. You should have stopped before it was too late. You've not so much as touched her, and she's done for you. Finished you off.

'I won't stop you,' he said at last. 'If you want to go, go. But wait while I dress. You could have the carriage – Matti will be here soon, he can harness the horses –'

'The carriage!' She looked at him. 'I don't want the whole world to know.'

'Then I'll saddle up the mare and take you part-way at least.'

'No.'

'Why not?'

'I can walk. I know the way across country.'

The childish way she pushed out her bottom lip made him grow stronger.

'Eeva, my dear child, you no more know it than a baby knows how to light a fire. This isn't Helsinki, with a shop on every corner to ask the way if you get lost. You've got to go through the forest at Heimola, you'll need to get across the lake, and there's only one boatman and he's usually drunk –'

'You mean the Black Lake?'

He laughed, surprised. 'Yes, that's what they call it round here. Who told you?'

'I don't remember.'

'Eeva, please. Don't you understand that the reason I want to take you is that otherwise I'll never know whether or not you arrived safely? And how can I –'

He broke off. He'd been on the point of telling her that he

174

wouldn't be able to bear not knowing if she was lost or found, not knowing if the bog had swallowed her or the lake's water had closed over her head. She might hurt herself – fall – twist her ankle and crawl for hours without finding help . . .

She shrugged. Her shoulders were still thin. How fluid she was when she moved. So fluid that she was awkward sometimes, in the beautiful way a very young creature can be awkward. She shrugged, but this time it was different. She might look sullen but he knew she wasn't refusing him. She would let him. She would let him come with her.

'Wait,' he said joyfully, as if she might fly through the window. 'Are you sure you'll be warm enough? Yes, of course, it's summer –' *thank God, he'd made sure she had those boots* – 'and you'll need to eat before you go – I don't suppose you've eaten yet?'

'No.'

'We should have coffee before we go,' he said. 'Wait. I'll make coffee for us. And rolls. What about some of those little rolls? You must eat.'

He talked as if the rolls dropped down from heaven, Eeva thought. Didn't he know she made them fresh every morning?

'There aren't any rolls,' she said.

'Well, never mind, we can eat black bread. I've always preferred it anyway. Black bread with sour cream. You like that, don't you?'

She almost laughed with surprise. *You like that, don't you?* – just as if she was one of the family.

'I'll make the coffee,' she said. 'But don't get the horse. I can't ride a horse. I don't know how.'

Of course not, he should have thought of that. How on earth would she know how to ride? But they could get round that. He could put her up in front of him. No, it was too far. The mare couldn't take their combined weight for long. As long as Eeva could sit on the mare, he'd walk alongside, holding the bridle, making sure she didn't fall – but perhaps the long ride would be too much for her even so, if she'd never ridden before . . .

'We can walk,' she said.

'Yes.' He could not stop himself smiling. It was all so simple.

He felt as if a cool breeze had blown, at the end of an exhausted evening. To walk out with Eeva into the morning, to walk with Eeva and a knapsack and the whole summer day ahead of them – and when that day finished, another day, and a day again . . .

. . . to walk out of his life entirely.

'Yes,' he repeated. It was stupid, surely, to feel as happy as this. 'We can walk.'

20

I'll tramp the roads as far as I wish,
I will love the one I choose.

She couldn't get Matti's song out of her head. It was hot, so hot. Her feet hurt, in spite of the good boots. Flies buzzed around her head. She'd broken off a switch of fern but the more she fanned the flies away, the more they swarmed. Under her kerchief her hair was damp with sweat.

There wasn't a breath of air. The trees had trapped it and made it thick with heat. Those trees, everywhere. She couldn't see, she couldn't get beyond them. They marched for ever. He was walking at her side but they weren't talking any more. The track was narrow and overgrown. Brambles caught at her ankles. Birds flew away with screams of warning, and sometimes she heard the crash of a bigger animal moving off through the trees. A deer, maybe, or a fox. There were wolves in the forest, she knew that. Bears too, and elk. But they wouldn't hurt you, not in summer with their bellies full.

And now the trees were growing bigger. Huge pines, dwarfing her and pressing down on her.

She was tired, so tired.

They were close to the bogland. He could smell it: a touch of rankness, sweetish but mineral, too. When they came closer there would be the smell of water peppermint. And there'd be mosquitoes. Lucky he'd put a bottle of citronella oil in his knapsack.

He breathed deeply, drawing the smells of the forest deep inside him. Pine resin, and a tang of fermentation. He could smell his own sweat, fresh and sharp. How good it was to be here in the depth of the forest, part of its shaded, living quiet. He trod lightly over the pine needles. And there, just ahead, the sun was coming through. They'd been logging here. The ground was littered with stumps which were already half buried in the undergrowth that sprang up as soon as light touched the forest floor. Two young birches flourished, so close that their branches were tangled. And there was water near by – yes, just over here, where the moss was bright green and there was a thicket of wild raspberry canes.

'Listen!' he said. They stopped. Yes, there it was, the soft bubbling of water. He followed the sound to a spring that oozed out of the ground into a basin of stone. Flat stones, fitted together carefully so the water would pool before it leaked away. The loggers must have done that. He dipped his cupped hands into the little basin, scooped up water, and drank. It had a pure, cold, mineral taste. As soon as he swallowed, he knew how thirsty he was.

'We'll rest here,' he said, but when he turned from the water he saw that Eeva had already sunk onto a cushion of moss at the foot of the birches. How pale she was. Her legs were stuck straight out in front of her and her eyes were closed. He took his empty metal water bottle from his knapsack and took out the cork. Carefully, so as not to muddy the pool, he lowered it into the water, and filled it.

'Here you are, Eeva, drink this. You'll feel better.'

She took the bottle from him and tipped back her head to drink greedily, swallowing gulps of the fresh water. Some of it spilled out of the side of her mouth and ran down her jaw. When the bottle was empty he filled it for her again. This time she drank more steadily, and then she tipped the last of the water into her hands and splashed it over her face. The drops ran away, sparkling, into the moss. She was half in sun and half in shade. The greenish forest light wobbled over her and he smelled her skin. She reached to the nape of her neck and untied her kerchief.

'Is there enough water for me to pour it over my hair?'

'Of course.'

He hadn't drunk enough. He tasted his thirst as he filled the bottle again, from the basin that hadn't yet filled again. He had to lay the bottle sideways in the water. Slowly it bubbled itself full, and he gave it to Eeva. She closed her eyes and poured it in a long stream over her hair, her forehead, her neck. She was smiling.

'Wonderful,' she murmured. 'It feels wonderful.'

There were drops and rivulets of water all over her. Water was running into the lines of her smile. He caught his breath at the scent coming off her, as water touched her warm skin and the sweat in her tangled hair.

'You should try it, it's wonderful,' she said.

He had got to drink. He didn't bother with the bottle, but knelt by the stone basin and scooped up water, sucking it greedily into his mouth, swallowing, sucking again. And again, and again. How dry he was. He wouldn't have believed how dry he was. His skin was parched like a desert. He scooped up the water and tossed it into his face, over his hair, over his clothes. The touch of water made him shiver and want more. He would drink and drink until his thirst was gone.

'Is that better?' she called to him. She'd taken off her boots and was massaging her feet in their cotton stockings. The heels of her stockings were quite worn out, and her skin was raw. And there was still half a day's walking ahead of them.

'You should bathe your feet,' he said. 'You're blistered. I've a handkerchief, we can bandage your feet with it.'

'Turn your back while I take off my stockings,' she ordered him.

He turned his back. Even so he seemed to see her – or maybe it was her shadow falling over him as she balanced on one leg, and then the other, to strip off her stockings. No, of course he couldn't see her. It was only that he seemed to be aware of her all over. She wriggled her toes as she stepped across to the water.

'It feels so good to take off these boots. No, I'm sorry, I don't mean that they're not good boots –'

Looking at her he remembered what it was like to play by the stream, barefoot, plunging thigh-deep in the pool he'd dammed. The squelch of mud, so disgusting and so delicious, and then the mud sluicing off his feet, clouding the pool, and then drying between his toes with moss and wisps of grass – and the way his feet looked so white in the water, when they weren't white at all in the air.

She smiled back at him over her shoulder as she dipped her right foot in the shallow water. And then she bent, as he remembered bending, and spread her toes in the basin.

'It's so cold! It's freezing!'

'The water comes from deep in the earth.'

She wiped her foot dry on her skirt, and then washed the other. She looked absorbed and happy, as a child is absorbed and happy. Some of her hair was coming out of its knot. She glanced back at him over her shoulder with a flash of happiness that he knew was the first real smile he'd ever seen on her face.

They sat under the birches, eating bread and cheese. He thought that he'd never tasted anything better than the nuttiness of the black bread, the tang of the cheese. And he'd put in a slab of ginger-bread, Lotta's gingerbread, sticky-crusted and studded all over with almonds. Every time she made a batch she sent some over for him, in waxed paper. He broke the gingerbread, and gave Eeva the larger piece. They should have fruit, he thought, but he'd forgotten to bring any. But wait . . .

He got up and began to prowl around the clearing. It was too early for wild raspberries, but maybe, in this sunny clearing, there would be ripe strawberries.

Yes. There were the leaves, and the starry white flowers. Leaf, fruit and flower all together. He lifted the leaves. There they were, wild strawberries, flushed deep red. He pinched them softly. They were ripe. He would pick them all for her.

In the end there was less than a handful. When he'd picked them all, he laid them on a dock leaf, and carried them to her.

'Oh!' she said. 'Wild strawberries. Me and Lauri used to –' She stopped, and her old mask of caution dropped over her face. He pretended not to have heard.

'Yes, I didn't think there'd be any,' he said, talking soothingly for the sake of sound, not words, the way he would talk to the mare when she was nervous, 'but because the sun comes through just here, they're ripe. Look, they're quite big. Would you like them? Hold out your hands.'

She cupped her hands and he dropped the berries into them. She ate one of the strawberries, frowning. 'It's good. It's nearly ripe, but not quite. They'll get sweeter.'

'Maybe the others are better.'

She ate a few more, tasting them like an epicure. 'They want a few more days. But aren't you going to have any?'

'No.'

'Don't you like them?'

'Yes, I like them. But I'd rather you had them.'

She nodded. 'I know. I'm like that sometimes.'

With Lauri, he thought, tasting the name. You'd give him all the wild strawberries you picked.

'I used to pick berries for my father, the last summer when he was ill. One of the neighbour's boys, he was a delivery boy and so he had a bike, and he used to let me borrow it on Sundays so I could go berry-picking, as long as he got a pailful. My dad liked wild raspberries, but only when they were really ripe – you know how they go, dark purple and then they dissolve the moment you put them in your mouth. And of course it was hard to bring them back on the bike when they were as ripe as that. They'd get bounced about and they'd turn to mush. So you had to judge it just right and then he'd eat them.'

She swallowed the last of the strawberries, and licked the juice off her palms.

'We must go,' she said, but she didn't get up.

'Yes.'

The sun was growing hotter. He could hear bees, flies, a chaffinch, the rustle of the birch leaves as a breeze passed and then left them limp.

'We could sleep for a while,' he said, but he knew it was foolish. The heat would keep them sleeping until four o'clock or later. They would get there very late. But what did it matter? She was here, so close he could hear her breathing and watch the droop of her eyelids. He knew the forest well enough. There was no danger of getting lost. Just a few more hours, that was all he wanted.

'No,' she said. 'We must move on.'

I must remember every minute, he told himself. Everything that happens. It gave a strange extra consciousness to the journey, like one of those nights when the shadow of the waking world bulks against the brilliance of dreams.

There was the raw place on Eeva's heel, with its flap of rubbed skin, and his own fingers tearing and tying a bandage from his handkerchief. And then the smell of the citronella oil that they dabbed on their wrists, and behind their ears, to keep off the midges and mosquitoes.

White swans on the black water of the lake. Mute swans, sailing with their necks straight. The splash of the boatman's oars in the water and the smell of stale alcohol leaking out of his skin. Eeva's fingers trailing in the water, the jump of a fish. The soft knocking of the boat against the long wooden jetty on the other side of the lake, and the way the man grunted when he got his money, and bit into the coin, then spat on the water.

The weight of Eeva's bundle when finally she let him take it from her. Not really heavy, though, not really heavy when he remembered that in that bundle was all she possessed. Why, Minna brought many times that amount just for a few days' stay. Some people seem to dig themselves deep into the earth and stuff their burrows with goods, he thought, while others stray over the surface of it, empty-handed.

He would give her money. Whatever she said, he'd do that. He'd planned it, and he had the notes ready to slip into her bundle when she wasn't looking.

How the glare of the day dissolved into soft evening warmth and golden shadows. Their shadows marched with them along the high road. They were both covered in dust by now, so the differ- ence between them was less obvious than it had been when they set out. He no longer looked like the Doctor, and she could have been any peasant girl on her way to market. They walked like people who have no choice but to walk. Side by side they travelled on, stepping aside when a cart came by with its choking cloud of dust. Eeva called out, 'How far are we from the railway station?' and the carter called back that it wasn't more than an hour's walking, and that was when Thomas first felt a pang of fear. The journey would end. He would lose her.

The station looked as if it had been closed for a hundred years. The last train had gone. He wanted to give her money for lodging, but she wouldn't take it.

'There's no need,' she said. But he argued, told her she must wash and eat, that he would find somewhere decent where they'd look after her.

'They won't take a girl on her own,' said Eeva. 'They'll think I'm not respectable.'

The thought of sleeping in a room in that town frightened her. As long as she stayed out of doors she was still on her journey, and no one could break it. Anyway, it was going to be a warm night, she said. She'd go off into the woods and wrap her cloak around her. She wasn't frightened. This time of year, there was almost no night at all.

'It's better to keep out of people's way,' she said aloud, and he knew that nothing he said would change her mind.

They walked out of the town again. Eeva's head was bent and she moved slowly. Usually he liked to stride out, but her slowness didn't trouble him. He fell in beside her, and matched his step to hers.

She seemed lost in herself. The new boots were covered in dust, and she was limping, in spite of his handkerchief bandage. He would have given her his arm, but he didn't want to break the trance of thought that held her.

Perhaps she wasn't thinking at all. Perhaps she'd reached that stage of weariness when it was almost easier to walk than not to walk.

They passed the straggle of poor houses at the edge of town. Children stared after them. That meant nothing, but he could not shake off the long gaze from a woman beating her rag rug over wooden railings. Her face and body were gaunt as an old man's, but her belly bulged.

She was probably not more than thirty, although she looked sixty. He'd attended too many lined, worn creatures who looked more like the grandmothers than the mothers of the babies they bore. He did his best for them, but as they twisted in labour a look would come on their faces – hard, flat, antagonistic – as if he were to blame.

Eeva must never look like that. And yet common sense told him that she'd be lucky to escape it. He felt the woman's gaze on his back, as if he were being stalked.

He could never remember exactly how they found the place. They turned off the road, onto a track across the meadows. Now they were walking through long grass which was already damp with dew. He snuffed its sweetness and let the grass heads feather against his fingers.

And there was the little hut. It seemed to have been abandoned. The door hung open, its wood silvery and split at the knot-holes. Long grass rippled around it. Timothy, fescue, cocksfoot – they had all come into flower early this year, with the heat. The hay hadn't been mown. It should have been mown by now, he thought. As for the hut, surely nobody ever came there. The wooden walls and floor ran with spiderlings.

But the place was clean and dry enough. He pulled a bunch of grass and swept the floor for her, and once they'd sat down he dug what was left of the black bread out of his knapsack. He broke the bread, and gave her the larger piece. The bread tasted sweet, and he ate his share slowly, feeling that this was the first time he'd ever really tasted it. Morsel by morsel, the dense sour-sweet bread dissolved in his mouth. Strange, he thought, how often you eat when you're not really hungry, but when you are truly hungry eating becomes something serious, almost holy. He could feel nourishment flowing to every part of his body, like the warmth of a fire.

But Eeva wasn't eating. She kept her bread in her hand. He urged her, but she shook her head. 'It's too heavy,' she said.

Suddenly he remembered the chocolate he'd put in at the last minute. Weeks ago, it seemed, although it was only this morning. He rummaged and there it was, squashed at the bottom of the knapsack, misshapen but solid. It had melted and then hardened again, and the shine had gone off it. But it was still good chocolate.

He held it out to her.

'Go on, take it. You need strength for the journey.'

She took the chocolate and broke it as carefully as she could into two equal pieces, and then she put her own share to her mouth like a squirrel and nibbled at it, as if it were too rich for her to eat at once. Suddenly she shivered all over, reviving.

'It's good!' she said.

He sat, watching her eat. He would keep the rest for morning, and maybe she'd have forgotten that it was his share. He watched her face.

My poor Eeva, my dear little Eeva, he thought, but the thought seemed unreal and it fell away from him, into an enormous space. She wasn't poor or dear, and she was not his Eeva.

She'd taken off her boots. Tomorrow she'd set out again, but this time he wouldn't go with her. He would have nothing left of her. Only her name would stay with him. He'd be able to talk about her with Matti sometimes.

Do you remember when Eeva . . . Do you remember how Eeva . . .

Matti would think it odd, but he'd humour the doctor.

She lay down on the floor, and wrapped herself in her cloak. They didn't talk, nothing happened. She fell asleep. She wasn't afraid of him, he thought. She trusted him enough to fall asleep in his company. He watched her breathing for a while and then he propped himself against the wall, so that anyone coming into the hut would have to step over him before they reached Eeva. He would close his eyes and doze for a while, but he wouldn't sleep . . .

He fell instantly into a dream so delicious that it pinned his body down. After a while – less than an hour, probably – the stiffness of his neck woke him. The dream vanished like a perfume.

It was morning. Yes, the sun was already slanting across the grass. In the short space of his sleep a new day had arrived.

185

He never forgot the sight of the meadow through the open doorway. The grass was swaying in a light wind, as if a hand were gently stroking it. A swift darted into sight. It skimmed the flowering grass heads, and then was gone. They sleep on the wing, he thought. They fly from the moment they're fledged, until their death.

She was still sleeping. Her mouth was slightly open, and a little bubble of spit had collected at the corner. She breathed steadily and evenly, lost in sleep. There were the veins on her eyelids, delicately blue under the waxen skin. One of the spiderlings was exploring on her cheek. It twinkled down the line of her jaw, and then to the corner of her mouth. He stretched out, ready to sweep it away. If it got into her mouth or nose it would make her sneeze, and she'd wake.

But no. The minute yellow and brown spiderling felt at the moisture of Eeva's spit, and then it ran away into her hair. He smiled to think of it journeying through the tangles that had fallen out of the knot she wore on the nape of her neck. Eeva stirred and a smile flew over her face and vanished, just like someone trying to write in water. That was how babies smiled, he thought, and they frowned like that too. Fleeting processions of smiles and knitted brows that some people said were due to indigestion. But maybe they were signs of the baby's hidden life. He used to sit beside Minna's crib and think that her dreams were more passionate than her days, and wonder what she'd tell him, when she was able to speak.

The thing about a baby, he thought, is that anyone could end its life just by putting out a hand. But no one does, except a brute. So the baby has power, although it looks helpless. And Eeva had power, he realized, looking at her. He couldn't cross the tiny distance that separated him from her. He couldn't touch her. There was her face, still so new that her frown didn't have a line to hide in. It flowed over her skin like water, and disappeared. When she was thirty, thirty-five, how would she look? Would she be stripped of all her beauty, like that pregnant woman on the edge of town, carrying yet another ball of baby in the cage of her pelvis?

No, there was no sense thinking of it. He was old, and she was new. She didn't want what he had to offer, even though he could look ahead and see what it might save her from. For who wants to be saved? All Eeva saw was a hungry old man, itching to touch her. In a little while the light would grow so strong that she'd open her eyes. And that would be the end of it.

She opened her eyes. Before she even really saw him or knew who he was, she smiled.

He waited for the train with her. It was almost noon, and burning hot. The heat took the place of speech. What a summer: as hot as Italy. But in Italy it would have seemed more natural. Italians had planted their gardens for shade, put in pools and fountains, and tiled their floors with cool stone. But here, we don't know what to do about such heat, he thought. Every time it comes, it surprises us. We lie panting like dogs.

They sat side by side on the bench. A silence that was almost like boredom had fallen between them. He was so intensely aware of her body that he could not think what to say to her. At last he said, 'You've got the food safe?' and she nodded. He'd bought more food than she could carry, as soon as the shops opened. White rolls, black bread, ham, raisins, cheese, fresh milk, more chocolate, almond cake, some cans of sardines . . . Poor girl, she could barely lug it along, and as for the cans of sardines, they were digging into her back.

Suddenly a zizzing noise came from the rails. It's just a vibration, he told himself. The heat. But no, a bell rang twice, a long harsh ring and then a shorter one. The half-dozen other passengers waiting for the local train began to gather up their bundles and baskets. A woman who had taken out her chicken for a breath of air stuffed it into its carrier, squawking.

The bell rang again. The rails were trembling. Yes, it was really coming. The train whistle shrieked, and Eeva started violently.

'It's all right. It's only whistling to warn people off the track,' he said. And then the train was in sight.

'You remember where you've to change?'

She nodded.

'Ask if you're not sure. And you've got your ticket safe?'

My God, he sounded exactly like her father. When she unpacked, she'd discover the money he'd tucked into the bottom of her bundle. He had thrust it down between some books. She had let him buy her ticket in the end.

'You didn't choose to leave Helsinki. Why should you have to pay to go back there?' he'd argued, when she told him she had enough money for the fare.

The train let off steam. Suddenly everything fell into stillness around him. Eeva was up there at the window, looking at him or perhaps even beyond him. Midday heat simmered with the smell of coal. Maybe the train would stay there for ever, breathing like a horse, and Eeva would continue to stand and he'd stand too, looking up at her and finding no words. They stood there awkwardly, their wait lengthening into embarrassment. And then the train jerked, the whistle shrieked and the engine began to pull. Slowly at first, as if it didn't really mean to leave. And then the deep, wide-spaced chuffs of the engine grew more rapid and began to join together. For a few more seconds he could keep pace with the train, but suddenly he seemed to be walking backwards. The train was passing him without effort. He lengthened his step, but it still wasn't fast enough. The train's wheels beat faster and faster like a hammer in a dream which is really the rush of blood in your own head. He began to run and the train shrieked again, warning him off, and then it gathered itself and cantered past him, blowing down a plume of smoke and steam. And there he was at a standstill, on the cinders beyond the end of the shallow platform, watching the end of the train sway off down the rails.

She was gone. No matter how far he looked he wouldn't find her. Only a grey cat twisting its belly in the sun as it rolled in a bed of nasturtiums. Slowly his hands crisped.

'Fool,' he said aloud. 'You fool. Why didn't you stop her?'

But that wasn't what he meant. If only he could go back, that was it, that was what he meant. If he could go back to sitting in the hay hut, against the wall, while Eeva slept. If he could smell the sweetness of the grass. And this time he'd put out his hand, and touch her, and she'd open her eyes.

He'd missed his chance.

He doubled over, hands on his knees, gasping with pain. It was running in the heat that had done it. After a night without sleep, it had been too much for him. His heart beat thickly, and he tasted metal in his mouth. All your fine dreams, my friend, this is where they end up, he told himself. On the end of the end of the platform, in a little town in the middle of nowhere.

Those nasturtiums seemed to be pulsing, red and orange. He smelled their hot peppery scent where the cat had crushed them. He would never see her move about his house again. Give me a minute, just a minute, and I'll be myself again, he thought. It's the heat, it's too much for us. We don't understand it. We know how to shelter from the cold but when it comes to the sun we can't defend ourselves.

But the cat rubbed her flanks into the flowers and yowled softly with pleasure.

21

'But if you want to kill someone, first you have to get close to him,' said Sasha. He swallowed more beer, wiped his mouth, and smiled.

'In what way close?' asked Lauri.

'Physically close, that goes without saying. Unless you're close enough to see the whites of his eyes, you'll screw it up. You're a bag of nerves on a mission like that, all keyed up so a touch'll set you off. The bullet ends up going through some gormless official, and your man gets away. That's if you're using a pistol. If you've a rifle and some nice lead-alloy bullets, then naturally your range improves ex-pon-en-tially. But whatever happens you don't want to be up so close that there isn't a hope in hell of getting away afterwards.

'We're not talking martyrdom here, Lauri. We've had enough martyrs. Shooting your man at point-blank range and then turning the gun on yourself, leaving a note behind to explain your noble actions: no, that's out. We're too valuable, my son. We can't afford to throw ourselves away.'

'I've never fired a gun.'

'No,' answered Sasha easily, as if this was exactly what he'd hoped Lauri would say. 'Why would you? Where would you get a gun? And besides, would it be your role in this situation, to fire a gun? Probably not.'

'Who decides?'

'Us. We decide. This business is ours. *Nash.*'

'If it's ours,' retorted Lauri, 'we've got to know what we're talking about. You're talking about assassination, Sasha, but neither of us can shoot. All I know about bomb-making is what I've seen on the back of an Anarchist pamphlet, and I wouldn't trust that cack-handed lot to get it right.'

'Fair point. You'd be more likely to blow your own foot off.'

Sasha was smiling again. He's having a laugh, Lauri thought. We've been working away to create the correct conditions for Sasha's 'in-ev-it-able' revolution, and now all of a sudden we're switching to blowing people's feet off.

'Ass-ass-in-ation,' drawled Sasha. 'Scaa-aary word, isn't it? I often think that if there was a better word, people would be able to cope with the idea, move forward, understand what's going on. But *pol-it-ic-al ass-ass-in-ation* . . . No, as soon as you say it, off they canter on the old moral high horse. Out it all pours for the thousandth time. Is it *wrong* to kill, is it *right* to kill, what does *God* say, what does my *conscience* say, is it a *sin*, does the end justify the means?' Sasha's voice took on a narcissistic whinge. '*"Will I ever be able to live with myself afterwards?"* Forgive me, Lauri,' he interrupted himself with quick warmth, leaning forward, 'I'm not putting *you* into that category. You're different. You're one of us. You've got your head screwed on. But it's what they say. They can't get it that all this conscience stuff is completely beside the point. It's not even part of the argument.'

'So what is the point?'

'Method. It all comes down to method. Nothing else matters. Get the method right, and everything else falls into place. That's what you've got to focus on, and then other questions don't arise.' He spread out his open, weaponless hands. 'Right. Method One. Ambush your man in the middle of the night, coming back from a party somewhere, preferably drunk, probably careless. Knock him over the head, and then run away. That doesn't sound too hard, does it?'

'No,' said Lauri. Voices crowded into his head. Big Juha, Eero. The shape of the stranger who was a police spy. *He struck the back of his head . . . not likely he'll be found before morning.*

'But Method One, admirable as it is, won't do in this case. We're not talking about a nobody here. Your man will have protection all the time. So, on to Method Two. Poison. Get someone into his household, trusted servant, whatever, arsenic in the caviar or what-ever else it is that he can't resist. It sounds all right, but it won't work. We're not living in Italy in the fifteenth century, and it's too chancy. These are modern times. Everybody loves caviar, and someone else will get at it first, even if it's got a great big label stuck on the jar saying "Personal – Exclusive – Governor-General's Caviar". Besides which, that way they can easily cover it up, say he had a stroke or something. And your man's dead, but you haven't made your point.

'So, on to Method Three. Bombs. Plenty of good points here, as long as you don't follow the instructions on the back of Anarchist pamphlets. They work, they're not hard to make, they don't cost much, they can be lobbed out of a crowd or planted beforehand, and they create terror as well as achieving their end. Two for the price of one, in fact. But then there's the *innocent bystander* question –' and here Sasha's voice whinged again – 'not that it's possible to make an omelette, as we all know, without breaking eggs – but all the same, if you keep breaking eggs all over the place and it turns out your man's changed his route and you've blown up a crocodile of schoolchildren instead . . . People don't like it. Not that I'm saying bombs can't be exactly what's called for, in the right time and the right place.

'And then there are the exotics. Mostly they're far too ingenious, and so they go wrong. Garrotting, smothering with pillows, drowning in the bath, defenestration, poisoned umbrellas . . . plus points to all of them, I grant you, but plenty of minuses, too. Really, there are no limits to the ways a man can die, if you put your mind to it. As a rule of thumb, the more imaginative the method, the less chance it has of succeeding. And so we're back where we started, with guns.'

'You're having a laugh, Sasha.'

'Why?'

'A crocodile of schoolchildren? You're not serious.'

'I am perfectly serious. What we're all working for won't happen, unless we have method. I'm being straight with you, that's all. Telling you straight. Maybe you don't like it. Maybe you rather like the status quo, in your heart of hearts. There are plenty of so-called revolutionaries who are wedded to the present and can't see beyond it. Keep on holding meetings, advancing our political education and everybody else's, defining our targets and our objectives, running around the country until we're burned out. But that's not political activism. It's masturbation. Another word for it is liberalism.'

Lauri flushed angrily. 'I'm no liberal, you know that.'

Sasha threw his arm around Lauri's shoulder. 'Of course you're not, I know that. We're in this together, bro. But don't get trapped by thinking of one man, one single life, when there are so many lives.' His tone darkened. His eyes blazed with a passion that Lauri had seldom seen. 'Don't get trapped by pity for one man who's had everything the world's got to offer, while there are workers with their arms crushed and cut off after factory accidents which need never have happened. While there are women who can't feed their kids or get a doctor to them, families rotting in tenements with damp running down the walls, old people who haven't got a coin to bury themselves with even though they've found kopecks for the priest all their lives, while you can work all your life long and still have to beg.

'These are our people, Lauri. Not *him*. He's had his turn. They need us and they're relying on us, even though they've never heard of us and they probably never will. They're our people. What does a man like Bobrikov count beside them? What's conscience worth when all it's capable of is keeping things the way they are? And yes, all right, let's look at the innocent bystander question. Let's not duck it. Suppose one child dies, so that a hundred children can live?'

But slowly, Lauri shook his head. 'No. No. No, Sasha. I mean, I agree with you up to a point, but not with a child, not a real child.'

'All right. That was just an illustration. We're not using bombs this time, so nothing like that's going to happen.'

'You sure of that?'

'I swear to you, Lauri,' said Sasha. Again, his eyes shone with that fervour which can't be faked, it has to come from the heart. 'You believe me, don't you? The operation with Bobrikov, it'll be like – well, think of it like a surgeon cutting into a body to get rid of a diseased organ. I mean, it's not safe, there's blood and mess and danger, but if he didn't do that operation, then the patient would die. The whole body would die for the sake of that one part that's a cancer to it. In-ev-it-ably. All this is about life, Lauri, not death, even though we have to talk about death. Like a road, you understand? You have to go through death to get to life.'

Lauri took a deep breath. His own heart was pounding with an emotion he couldn't name. When Sasha was like this, you felt you could refuse him nothing.

'Only Bobrikov? Just him?'

'Just him.' Sasha's eyes were fixed on Lauri. 'I've told you this much because I trust you. I've been watching you a long time, don't you know that? Don't go soft on me now, Lauri.'

'Who're you calling soft?'

'Hey, no need to get angry. But what's the point of political activism if all we do is preserve this rotten status quo? We know where we stand. Unless we're prepared to take the next step we might as well all pack up, go home and take up fishing. I won't do that, Lauri. I'm not going to betray everything I believe in.' His dark eyes glowed, pupils dilated. Yes, Lauri had heard something like this a hundred times, but not from Sasha, not direct like this. it wasn't theory Sasha was talking about, it was reality. It sounded fresh, new, like snow nobody else had ever trodden on.

Sasha's face was naked in its intensity. For once, Lauri saw, he'd thrown off his mask of control to reveal the raw passion underneath. And he'd named his man. Bobrikov. The Governor-General, the Tsar's man. You couldn't aim any higher, not without . . .

Now it was said, Lauri couldn't help a chill of fear. The name was too big. Was it possible that they could think of killing Bobrikov, a man as much part of the Tsar as his right arm?

'But he's so high up,' he said, and as soon as he'd said it he felt as stupid as a ox, balking on his way to the slaughterhouse. The weight of Sasha's arm was heavy around his shoulders. He smelled Sasha's sweat.

'All the better to fall,' said Sasha. His mouth was so close to Lauri's ear that the warm moisture of his breath curled into it. There was a long silence. Lauri began to wish that Sasha would take his arm away, but it didn't seem comradely to move. After a while, however, he shifted position, trying to make it seem natural, as if his leg was cramped.

'All this, but I still can't fire a gun,' he said, trying to make light of it. They seemed to have moved beyond the point of agreement, before Lauri realized that they had reached it.

'There'll be someone else for that. You'll meet him when it's time. He's a Swede, a student, from a good family.'

The way he said it made Lauri curious. 'Sasha, you never talk about *your* family. What are they like?'

'They're not like anything,' said Sasha, his face closed. 'I don't have anything to do with them.'

'Oh. I see.'

'I doubt if you do. To put it simply, *he's* an animal. *She's* very religious. My mother. Everything she thinks and does, she has to hide it from him, because if he found out he'd smash it. He's as stupid as shit, but he's cunning. He can get into everything. Even your feelings, your thoughts. He smashes everything. So everything's got to be hidden away. You've even got to hide the fact that you breathe. It's the only way to survive, until you can get out. I got out, but she never will. My mother.'

'You could help her.'

Sasha shrugged. 'She's weak. You can't help weak people. I've learned that.'

'So what about this Swede of good family, then?' asked Lauri.

'You don't need to know his name yet. He's perfect. He can get as close as you like to Bobrikov, and they'll never think of suspecting him, because he's close in all the other ways that matter, too. He's part of them, born to be one of those high-ups you were talking about, the ones who keep the system running. Our precious "administrator class". They have all kinds of high ideals about service and social responsibility and preserving Finland's autonomy through cooperation with Russia. But all it means is that they do the Tsar's dirty work for him, until the work gets so dirty that even they can't help noticing it. And then they retire to their country estates and tug their moustaches and enjoy their moral virtue.

'But our student, for some reason, is different. He doesn't want to administer Finland for the Tsar, because he's a real old-fashioned patriot, and for once it's not all talk. He's ready to put his money where his mouth is. Or, in this case, his gun. He's nobly agreed to shoot Bobrikov in order to "free Finland from the yoke of Russian oppression".'

Yes, there it was again. Sasha, mocking the ideals he was about to make use of. Lauri thought again that he wouldn't like to be on the wrong side of Sasha.

'Shoot Bobrikov,' Sasha continued, 'and then the Tsar will *immediately* see sense – the Romanovs are well known for seeing sense – and we can get back to the old comfortable state of affairs where the Tsar will let the Swedes run the country for him, and we'll all call it Finnish autonomy.

'So you see, the goals of our student and his friends aren't quite the same as our goals. In fact they are completely different. We know that the Tsar won't see sense, no matter how many Governors-General are shot. It's not remotely possible for a Romanov. In fact the Tsar will probably oblige us by bringing in a crackdown which will make the present situation seem like heaven on earth. A crackdown's exactly what we want. Then, my friend, we'll start to see some friction. And after the friction comes the action. It's precisely – *pre-cise-ly* – such extreme situations that will create the correct conditions for revolution. They draw together all the elements that should be drawn together: workers, peasants, students, even, God help us, the intelligentsia.

'So never mind what our Swede thinks is happening. It doesn't matter. He can shoot, that's the only thing about him that matters. We took him out to a birch wood and set up a target and I can tell you he was impressive. Right into the heart of it without a blink. And he can get close to Bobrikov. He's got no previous form at all, the Okhrana have never even heard of him, and he doesn't look like one of the comrades.' Sasha laughed appreciatively. 'He's so nice. Brushed hair, good clothes, smells of Cuir de Russie, beautiful manners. Above all, he's got that milk-fed innocent look those Swedish high-ups always have. They've got this knack of finding themselves at the top of the pile without so much as soiling their gloves,' said Sasha. 'Yes, our Swede is perfect. You could take him anywhere, and that's exactly what we're going to do.'

'All right, so he's firing the gun. So what do you want – what's my role?' asked Lauri, feeling pleasure at using the correct word.

'You'll be a diversion,' said Sasha, looking Lauri full in the face.

'A diversion?'

'I know. Not very flattering, is it? But absolutely essential.'

'What do I do?'

'You'll create a disturbance. You'll shout slogans, wave a stick, try to hurl yourself in Bobrikov's direction. You'll attract police attention. They'll be taken up with trying to arrest you. But they won't arrest you, because there'll be our people round you making sure you get away. Most of Bobrikov's protection won't even try to go after you, they're a bit too professional for that. They'll be looking after their man. But it'll scatter them. And it'll distract them. If everything goes right, they'll believe that there's been a minor threat and they've got Bobrikov away to safety. And so they'll relax. They're only human. They'll drop their guard.

'I'm not going to lie to you, Lauri. You won't be the only one. There'll be others along Bobrikov's route that day, doing the same job, creating diversions, rattling them, getting them on the back foot. It'll work at the time, and it'll work afterwards when they conduct their post-mortems. They'll look back and they'll know it wasn't just one crazy Swede, it wasn't something they can explain away like that. They'll have to believe that our Swede was the tip of the iceberg, and that's exactly what we want them to believe.

'It's a small role, and maybe it's not what you were hoping for. But believe me, it's vital.'

'I understand,' said Lauri. The words resounded inside his head, as solemn as gongs.

'So will you do it? Are you with us?'

Lauri shrugged impatiently. 'Don't you see, I've already agreed.'

'Good,' said Sasha. 'Goo-ood,' drawing out the word not with mockery now, but with a satisfaction that drew Lauri in, welded them together. 'He's ours,' he said. 'He belongs to us.'

'Who?'

'Bobrikov. He's ours. His life belongs to us, because we have already decided to end it.'

His life belongs to us, because . . .

But the man's not dead yet, Lauri thought. Maybe at this very moment he's sitting with his legs apart, sighing with relief as a turd eases its way out of him.

Why think of that, for God's sake? They give condemned men what they want to eat, don't they? So even when they're about to die they're still putting food into their bodies and chewing it and letting it go down. It'll never be digested. But they know they're going to die, at least they know that. They don't have to eat if they don't want to. Bobrikov doesn't know. This whole business is ours. He's ours. *Nash.*

He's standing up. He's done his business. He's got the same look on his face as everybody has then.

No. Don't think about him any more.

Sasha put his hand on Lauri's shoulder and gave it a friendly shake, as if to wake both of them from a dream.

'Where's our Eeva?' he asked.

'She went mushroom-picking with Magda. You remember.'

'Oh yes,' said Sasha, without much interest. 'They went off early, didn't they?'

'Yes, early.'

Lauri had wanted to go with them, biking out of the city into woods which were just beginning to smell of autumn. He'd have been able to borrow a bike from somewhere. But Magda hadn't wanted him along. It was Eeva's company she wanted. You wouldn't think the girls had only known each other a few weeks.

Magda acted as if she was Eeva's sister. There they were together in Magda's apartment, chatting and laughing all hours of the day and night. But Magda wasn't really a girl. She was a woman. She must be thirty, Lauri thought, and her age and air of experience made him feel that he had done nothing and gone nowhere. She talked like a man. She was serious, direct, handling ideas as confidently as a skilled man handles his tools. She could make Eeva laugh, too. When he knocked at the door and waited for one of them to open it, he always believed that he could hear them laughing.

Eeva didn't make him wait. She came straight to the door. But not Magda; no, he even had the feeling sometimes that Magda liked keeping him waiting, liked it that she and Eeva shared a life he couldn't enter unless she let him. Magda would give him a long, cool stare at the door, as if he had to prove himself to her.

Eeva's return to Helsinki wasn't working out as he'd imagined. He couldn't remember exactly how he'd thought things would be, but certainly Magda hadn't been part of the picture. She seemed to be there all the time, between him and Eeva, worse than a mother. She'd even found Eeva a job in a bookshop.

Sasha had raised the idea of Eeva working in a dairy shop, but Magda wasn't having any of it. She was sharp with Sasha about it. 'Put Eeva into a dairy? Why? What's the point of that? She's educated. She already speaks three languages.'

Lauri felt that Magda was taking Eeva away into a different world. For all her dedication to the workers, Magda didn't live in the factory quarter. She wouldn't have dreamed of getting a room in Kallio, where tenements were springing up to house all the factory workers who'd streamed in from the countryside. Helsinki was swelling, sucking in lives from farms and forests. Some of them would find work and stay, but plenty of others were only passing through the city on their way to the new world, just as timber and paper passed through the city to the harbour and out in the new steamships to the new world. The same railroads carried them all from the back country, to the lip of their new lives.

There was a part of Lauri that envied the emigrants, with their bundles containing everything they'd got. They looked dazed, some of them, as if the decision they'd made was too big for them. A string of children would traipse in the wake of parents and grandparents, each carrying a bundle suited to the child's size.

Who knew where they'd be in two or three years' time? On their own land, building up their own farms. It was what most of them longed for, but there was more than that to America. Eeva's father used to tell him about it, years ago. Pekka Koskinen could recite the opening of the American Constitution:

We the People of the United States, in Order to form a more perfect Union, establish Justice, ensure domestic Tranquillity, provide for the common defence, promote the general Welfare, and secure the Blessings of Liberty to ourselves and our Posterity, do ordain and establish this Constitution for the United States of America.

'People say it sounds even better in the English,' he would always add at the end of the recitation.

Pekka was no wide-eyed idealist, not him. America wasn't going to be perfect, no place was, he told Lauri. But the ideas they started with were better than ours.

He should have listened more to Eeva's father. He should have sat down to those lessons Eeva had to learn. But he didn't want to, that was the truth of it. He preferred to play in the street. And, to be honest, he still didn't want to. The sight of a page of print made him bored, restless.

Magda was educated. She came from a bourgeois family in Berlin, Sasha had told him that. Her father was a university professor who had written several books about Schiller. Sasha had not gone on to say who Schiller was. Magda might live in a shabby old apartment building, but it wasn't far from the city centre. Magda needed to go to concerts, lectures and exhibitions. She didn't even think about it: it all came naturally to her.

Sasha and Magda were two of a kind in one way, he thought, even though they were so different in others. Both of them were good with words. They loved arguing and reached for the words they needed with absolute confidence that they'd know how to use them.

Magda was passionate about the rights of women. Sasha accused her of 'bourgeois feminism', but Magda wasn't having that. What use was a revolution which left women exactly where they were, slaves in the workplace on half a man's wages, and slaves at home? And as for maternity provision! Why didn't Sasha open his eyes and see the number of women whose bodies were wrecked by childbearing? Why should she fight for a revolution that didn't concern itself with women's lives? Perhaps he'd like to tell her? No, if Sasha thought Magda should fight alongside him, he was going to have to accept that it worked both ways, and women wanted equal rights. 'And if you won't accept that, then don't you see that your revolution becomes irrelevant to me?' Magda's face sparkled with challenge. You knew that she would go ahead and do what she wanted anyway.

The world had always belonged to her, really. Lauri understood that. It was in the way she talked to him, not even realizing the tone in her voice. Sasha sometimes said she was a patronizing bitch. But she wasn't patronizing, not really. Just sure, born sure. Magda realized immediately that Lauri not only wasn't educated, but knew nothing about the books and theatres and composers that meant so much to her. He wasn't cultured, and probably he never would be. But Eeva, Eeva . . . a cold wind whispered to him that it wouldn't be long before Eeva spoke Magda's language fluently. Eeva had been reading novels and poetry since she was seven. Already she was going to the same concerts and lectures that Magda attended.

Maybe it's easier for women, Lauri thought. They adapt more easily, they fit in more. And Eeva was so finely made, with her long fingers and her delicate neck. She could go anywhere. But working in the bookshop hadn't tamed Eeva's tongue, Lauri thought with a sudden, inward smile. She was still as sharp as a knife when she wanted to be, she wouldn't put up with any crap from anyone.

As far as Lauri knew, Sasha had never mentioned the subject of 'pol-it-ic-al ass-ass-in-ation' to Magda. He was certain Eeva knew nothing about it. And that was right, he decided.

Fair enough, you couldn't fault Magda for arguing about women's rights. He'd never thought of things that way himself, but when you added it up it didn't come out fair. But the thought of Eeva with a gun in her hand – let alone a poisoned umbrella – made him feel sick.

Eeva didn't argue much. She listened. It was clear that she liked Magda, respected her. She pondered Magda's beliefs, testing them against her own experiences. The two of them would talk, breaking into each other's sentences, not to argue, but to take the thought farther.

'Yes, I see –'

'But what if –'

'I know what you mean, it's exactly the same for me –'

It was equally clear that Eeva didn't have much time for Sasha, even though the four of them sometimes went about together. What she had against Sasha, he didn't know. She never argued with him, or criticized him.

Here she was, his Eeva, in the same city as him. He could see her every day if he wanted. But she'd seemed closer when she was far away. Then, she was really his Eeva. Now, she belonged to herself.

Maybe if they had more time alone together, without the others, it would be better. But she and Magda shared a room, and he and Sasha shared a room. Lauri worked long hours, and so did Eeva. Even when they were free, how could Eeva say no if Magda wanted to go mushroom-picking, and how could Lauri not go to a meeting with Sasha?

Eeva had a new dress. Magda had given it to her. It was deep, rich green. Forest green, it was called. It had belonged to Magda's sister, and it was the right kind of dress for Eeva to wear in the bookshop.

Eeva had nothing like it. She'd never had a dress like it, but it suited her as if it'd been made for her. It fitted her body, and made her look quite different, like a woman he barely knew at all. There was even a little lace collar. Magda said that the lace came from Holland.

Eeva had come up from the country covered in dust, the same Eeva as ever with her cloak and bundle and stout boots. She'd looked older, of course. Taller. Her face had filled out and changed. But she wasn't a stranger.

Maybe if he'd gone to the railway station to meet her, it would have worked out differently. But he hadn't even known she was coming that day. She found her way to the room he shared with Sasha, and as ill-luck would have it, Lauri wasn't at home. So it was Sasha she saw first, not him. It was more than an hour before Lauri got back, and somehow the freshness and newness of Eeva's arrival had already worn off. Maybe if Sasha hadn't been there . . .

But he was. Eeva was sitting on a wooden chair in the middle of the room, drinking coffee. She looked very stiff. Her bundle was at her side, and as she started up when Lauri came in, her coffee slopped onto her skirt and she almost tripped over her bundle. She recovered herself, but the moment was gone. And for some reason he just stood there like an idiot. He could have helped her wipe the coffee from her skirt. He could have done or said so many things. But he didn't, he just stood there. Probably it was only a few seconds, but it was a few seconds too many. He ought to have – well, he didn't know what he ought to have done. He was shy of her, that was the problem. All the thoughts he'd been thinking about her since he last saw her seemed to crowd between them. And so what did he say, with Sasha standing there watching? 'Hello, Eeva.'

Hello, Eeva. What a fool, what a cretinous idiot. After all those months, adding up to years, she comes back, and all you can say is *Hello, Eeva.* He just stood there with his arms hanging down by his sides. She licked her lips as if they were dry, and said in a funny little voice, not her real voice at all, 'Hello, Lauri.' And that was their meeting.

And then Sasha had suggested they go over to Magda's right away. Magda had folded herself around Eeva somehow, talking to her quietly and saying just the right things; he could tell that from the way Eeva relaxed and let go of her bundle and even smiled. She'd gone off to the sauna with Magda, and when they'd all met later that evening, Eeva was quite different. Her skin glowed, her hair was clean, shiny, and smoothly drawn back into a knot. She wore the green dress and she carried herself differently. Instead of heavy boots, she wore a pair of Magda's shoes. Their feet were exactly the same size, Magda said, as if this was a wonderful sign of their friendship.

There was time to talk then, in the café that evening, but Magda and Sasha were there. And he was buggered if he was going to say *Hello, Eeva*, again, so he didn't say much, and it was Magda who talked. But even so, it was getting easier, things were warming up. And then suddenly he had to go and tell her, right out in the middle of everything, that he expected she'd like to go and see her father's grave. A shiver went all over her face, but she struggled and nothing happened. She didn't cry. He ought to have leaned forward across the table then, and taken her hands. If he had, she'd have cried – he knows she would – and then it would have been right again. The others would have melted away. He and Eeva would have talked until they'd told each other everything about what their lives had been since the day they took her away. It would have been just like when they used to hide under the bedclothes and tell each other everything. They'd have talked to each other about her father and his, and what was left of those days. He could have comforted her. But no. He didn't lean forward across the table. Magda and Sasha stayed, and Eeva didn't cry.

There were two hollows at the base of Eeva's neck. He'd never noticed them before. The dress clasped her waist where it was drawn in by the narrow leather belt which Magda had also given her. He wanted to put his hands there.

He wanted to touch those hollows at the base of her neck. But not with his fingers, with his lips. He'd put his lips there, he'd close his eyes, he'd taste her.

How he wished that he'd been the one to give Eeva that dress.

22

Autumn was on its way. You could smell it, even though the sun still shone and the leaves on the birches hadn't yet changed colour. But they were stiff and dry. They rattled when the wind blew through them, and the early mornings were chill. Mushrooms flourished, growing fat on the ripeness of summer.

Magda's basket and her own were full of chanterelles, Eeva's favourites: even ceps didn't taste quite as good. Eeva was going to show Magda her way of drying them. She'd pickle some too, and make mushroom liquor with any that were damaged. Magda said she usually gorged on fresh mushrooms, eating everything she'd picked straight away. She did not know how to preserve them. She went to a particular stall in the railway marketplace for dried mushrooms: the market-woman knew her well.

Hard to believe that anyone could be so wasteful, in the face of the long winter. Why, even close to Helsinki the woods were full of mushrooms and berries for the picking, enough for everyone to fill a store cupboard for the months ahead. But Magda laughed, and said that she couldn't be bothered with all those housewifely arts. She was careless, Eeva thought. Probably she had never had to look at an empty shelf.

'It's wrong,' said Eeva seriously. 'My father would've said you were spitting in the face of nature.'

'Do you believe that?'

Eeva considered it. 'Yes,' she said at last, not wanting to offend Magda, but not wanting to lie to her, either. 'I don't like waste. We used to go out into the forest every chance we had, and we'd pick everything in season. Lingonberries, rowanberries, wild strawberries, raspberries. Cranberries later on, when they'd had a touch of frost on them. He knew where they all grew. He knew all the mushrooms, too; we never had to go to the chemist to identify anything.'

'Who knew all the mushrooms?'

'My father. It was him I was talking about. I didn't like it when I was stuck out in the forest all the time – where I was before – but there's nothing better than a day out to pick mushrooms and berries.'

'Maybe I am wasteful,' said Magda, frowning slightly as she did when she addressed a political question.

'You are because you can be,' said Eeva.

'I'm on a tight budget, you know, Eeva.'

'Maybe. But it's not –' She broke off, because she didn't want to offend Magda. Maybe, although it was possible to talk to Magda about everything from childbirth to women's suffrage, it wasn't possible to discuss the difference between what Magda called 'being hard-up' and being poor. 'Being hard-up' meant that although you lived in a modest room in a modest apartment building, and made your clothes last, you always had just enough for concert tickets or for a quiet hour in a café, talking, talking . . .

What had poverty to do with being hard-up like that? No one who was poor looked out at the world as Magda did. It wasn't just having the money to buy concert tickets, it was having the confidence to believe that concert tickets rightly belonged to you. But Magda was kind. Maybe that was more important than anything.

'Winter's long enough,' said Eeva at last. 'You need everything you can get hold of, to keep you stocked up until spring.'

And now they'd picked all they could carry, eaten their bread and cheese, and were lying on their backs on a piece of mackintosh with their faces up to the sun. Its light was yellow. Beautiful warm, soft light. Make the most of it, squeeze every drop of light and warmth out of these days before winter comes, because once it comes, it stays so long. Eeva sighed, and closed her eyes. There was a rosy fuzz inside her eyelids. Her calf muscles ached, pleasantly, from cycling. Not only had Magda got a bike of her own, but she'd borrowed another from a friend, for Eeva. They'd skimmed the dusty roads, calling and laughing, then bumped along the forest track until it got too rough and they had to dismount and push their bikes.

'Tired?' Magda asked.

'No. Not a bit.'

She still couldn't believe that it was going to go on like this. That she was allowed to get up, wash and dress leisurely (she didn't have to be at the shop until just before eight), drink her coffee, take the tram, do work that wasn't tiring at all, compared to what she was used to – that was, in fact, quite pleasant. And then she could go to the park in her lunchtime and eat the sandwich she'd made that morning, even buy herself a cup of coffee or a newspaper from a kiosk if she felt like it. There wasn't much money, but for the first time in her life there was a little more than she needed for the raw business of living.

Her share of the rent was small. Magda said she'd been paying the rent for the room anyway, so whatever Eeva could contribute was all bonus. Magda was a bit embarrassed, hurrying over her words, but you could tell she meant them. And it didn't cost any more to heat a stove for one person than for two. In return, Eeva kept the room clean, and bargained hard in the market. Magda was so soft that all the stall-keepers took advantage of her.

'It's best if I do the shopping,' she said to Magda, without offering an explanation.

Occasionally she met Magda at lunchtime, but more often she didn't and would sit quietly, watching a sparrow bathe in the dust or a child learning to push a wooden truck. She liked to be alone. It was enough to sit there, while the sky glowed with light and the leaves shook in the breeze.

Sometimes she would be consumed with happiness. Not only was she back in Helsinki, but she had a life here, an adult life which belonged to her. Everything had turned out so much better than she'd dared imagine. Somewhere to live, somewhere to work, enough to eat, the green dress, and, if she saved hard, a proper winter coat this year rather than a cloak like a country girl. She didn't want ever to look like a country girl again, scurrying the city streets as if she didn't belong in them. She belonged here.

But the happiness was like sunshine in days of gathering cloud. More often, doubt swept over her, shadowing her. She felt as if she were acting in a play of her own life, dressed in someone else's clothes. One minute she was in the doctor's kitchen, the next she was in Helsinki, part of the expanding city, at the centre of a snaking web of new roads and railways that grew more complex every year.

Although she'd been away less than three years, plenty had changed. Helsinki was growing so fast. They were tearing down old wooden houses and putting up stone buildings, they were sweeping away people's little vegetable gardens, straightening roads, putting in gas lamps, enlarging the cemeteries. Lauri said there were twice as many people living here now as there had been when he was born. More ships in the harbour, more trains arriving and departing, more people streaming along the streets, new shops, new laundries and saunas and dairies, a new theatre – new everything.

They were straightening the roads into the city, too, widening them to carry the weight of traffic. It was all happening so fast it made him feel like an old man, Lauri said jokingly one day. His past was being swept away around him. Places he used to go and play now had factories growing on them instead of trees. He found himself talking about what Helsinki was like when he was a kid, as if that was fifty years ago.

Eeva was finding her way along different streets these days, in different quarters. Magda and she walked around the university, climbed the cathedral steps and looked out as if they owned everything. Or at least, as if Magda owned everything. Eeva's eyes ached from the magnificence. She ought to have been proud of it: it was her city. But even Magda, who was German, seemed more at home than Eeva. She knew her way around, she was nonchalant and possessive as she explained the architecture to Eeva.

'This part of town always reminds me of Petersburg,' said Magda. 'But I prefer the work that Engel did here. The architecture knits together so beautifully, doesn't it? A perfect ensemble. It's full of the loftiness of human ideals, but the scale isn't designed to crush the individual.'

'My father used to say that you felt like an ant crossing a desert, when you walked across one of those Petersburg squares.'

'Did he? Engel was from Berlin, you know.'

Magda spoke as if she owned Engel, and Berlin, and Helsinki, too. Eeva remembered how her father always added, with grim humour, 'First make people feel like ants, then stamp on them. That's the way of the Tsars.'

'We'll go there together one day,' said Magda. 'To Petersburg.'

'My father lived in Petersburg for years. Lauri, too.'

'You would like it,' said Magda. 'You would appreciate it.'

'But would I be able to find a job?' asked Eeva drily.

And then back they went, to stroll where women with parasols picked their way across the cobbles, along the quay. Men walked very upright, breathing deeply and swinging their canes. They too were at home. Only Eeva was not at home. Not yet, not now, if she ever would be. Helsinki wasn't the city she remembered, the one she'd belonged to without ever needing to think about it. Maybe it was only the difference between leaving as a child and coming back as a woman. But the changes were real too, as Lauri said. Life ran so much faster. People and goods whirled about everywhere. The wheels of carts and wagons and carriages rumbled until the ground shook under them. Trams clanged, horses plunged forward and sometimes there was a terrible scream and a horse would be down in its traces, its hooves smashing the air.

She would hurry on, always with the feeling there was somewhere she had to get to, but she couldn't quite remember where it was. Men glanced at her face as she passed, and then ran their eyes slyly down her body. Shops glowed with goods that she was sure she had never seen before. She both wanted them and didn't want them. A pineapple sitting on top of a heap of oranges! Surely it must be made of wax?

But she also saw the same faces as she'd seen in her childhood. The hollow faces of kids who had TB, or whose parents had TB. The pinched, stretched look of the skin over shallow cheeks. The long stare that expected nothing. Magda said that in spite of the increase in population, people were still emigrating faster than ever.

Magda was kind, there was no question of that. She wanted to know all about Eeva's life. She listened intently when Eeva told her things she'd never thought she'd tell anyone. She told Magda what life was like in the House of Orphans, things that she'd thought she'd have to keep sealed inside her for ever. When bad things happen to you, they shame you, as if somehow you must have done something to deserve it. You want to squirm with the humiliation of it, as if you're naked in a public place and trying to hide yourself.

She told Magda about the way rags were counted out to the big girls when they had their periods, and how they had to wash out the blood in front of everyone. As if they had no feelings. And they'd be told off if there were too many rags, too much blood, as if they were dirty.

How they were always hungry, and how they snatched food from one another. Hunger doesn't make you good, she told Magda, for Magda could be sentimental about things she had never experienced. Not having things doesn't make you generous. You should have seen the way the stronger girls would barge the weaker ones away from the soup pot.

How they were all watched for signs of 'immorality'. Little girls who didn't know what the word meant, standing dazed with sleep, weeping because they'd been caught snuggled up in bed together to try to keep warm. They had to learn better. But they were like puppies or kittens, Eeva thought, they only wanted to roll up together. The rooms were big and bare and the little ones were scared of the dark. Pity we weren't kittens or puppies. But then, if we hadn't been human they'd have drowned us in a bucket.

Chilblains and whitlows and warts and impetigo, blisters and boils and weeping sores. Yes, the doctor treated them, when he came. But he didn't know what went on between his visits.

One little girl had a piece of rag, this big, with a hem on it that she would rub against her lips until she slept. She hid it day after day in different places. And someone got hold of it and handed the rag over to one of the big girls. It got put in the stove. The cry she gave, you would think it was her own flesh burning. The little girl started wetting the bed and then you'd see her toiling over big wet sheets she could hardly lift, out in the yard, her hands blue, Sirkka watching her with that stupid smile.

How they went to church in a long line, and the preacher looked at them with special meaning whenever sin was mentioned. How they went out into service on remote farms where they'd be worked like dogs, beaten, or raped by the farmer when his wife was pregnant. And a place in service was the sum of all success. Anna-Liisa's duty was done and they were settled in life. No more could be hoped for.

But the worst thing was the way their families were made worthless. They had to be grateful for everything, after their mothers and fathers had failed them by dying, or being too poor to keep them. They came from bad homes. They had to be watched, or they'd take bad ways.

Magda listened. Her eyes were wide, drinking in what Eeva said as if in a way this was what she had wanted to hear, because it confirmed all her beliefs. Eeva felt a pang of doubt. Had she said too much, and betrayed herself? But at same time it was a relief to talk. Like telling someone the symptoms of an illness that you've kept to yourself, not daring to admit them, hoping that one morning you'll wake up and find the illness has dissolved.

Magda said, 'So they took you to church twice each Sunday?'
'Yes.'

Magda's smile was somehow a little too knowing. 'It's curious, how much they talk about prostitution in the Bible.'

'Why?'

'I don't know.' She shrugged and her smile grew deeper. 'But it fascinates them, you can see that. Those holy old men can't get away from the subject. Why, you must have been meat and drink to them, all you little orphans.'

Eeva frowned. Suddenly it felt as if she had given her past to Magda, for Magda to make use of it.

'Some of us were not so little,' she said, rather coldly.

Magda was different from any woman Eeva had known. She didn't care what people thought of her. Being foreign, of course, gave her an advantage, because people didn't know quite what to expect. She'd lived in Helsinki for eight years. You could hear the German in her voice, but she was one of the rare foreigners who had mastered not only Swedish but also Finnish.

She was thirty but she looked much younger. It was something about her eyes; they had a way of opening wide which usually belongs only to children or very young women. Magda had given up working in the bookshop a few months ago, and now earned her living as a journalist, writing pieces mainly for German newspapers. It wasn't a good living, she said, but it was adequate. She showed Eeva pieces she had written, carefully cut out and pasted into scrapbooks.

She must have been doing all right, Eeva thought. Magda bought her clothes new, her stockings were always without holes, and she went to cafés with friends quite regularly. Most of her articles were published in the German press, but she wrote on the Finnish Question, too, and she knew Alexandra Kollontai. Not well, but she knew her. When she first told Eeva that, Eeva hadn't a clue who Alexandra Kollontai was, but she knew enough to look impressed. She remembered all that business from her father's house: certain names were spoken in low, significant voices, and you showed your understanding by an answering, equally significant nod.

Magda had the physical self-confidence of a cat. She pulled off her clothes at night and stood naked in the middle of the room, yawning. She had one of those strong, dark, smooth bodies that somehow look clothed in themselves. On hot nights she didn't bother with a nightdress. She manicured her nails perfectly, brushed her dark hair until it crackled, and would not dream of wearing a corset.

'Why should I? I want to breathe.'

Magda's underwear was very plain. But when I have enough money saved, Eeva thought, I'll buy a camisole trimmed with lace. When I have money I'll never again wear anything against my skin that someone else has worn before.

Eeva rolled over and propped herself up on one elbow. Magda was half smiling, perhaps asleep. But she must have felt Eeva stir.

'Ready to go back to town?' she asked, without opening her eyes.

'Not yet.'

'Nor me. It's nice here.'

Magda pillowed her head on her arms, and appeared to sink

back into a dream. But suddenly she asked, 'What do you think of Sasha?'

Eeva considered. She didn't really know what she thought of Sasha, but she was sure life would be better if he was not there.

'There's something strange about him,' Magda went on in her cool, confident voice. 'I can't work him out.'

'Maybe . . .' said Eeva, thinking, but she didn't go on.

'Oh Eeva, you don't need to be so cagey, not with me.'

'I'm not being cagey.'

Magda opened her eyes. They were beautiful eyes, so wide that a little rim of white showed all around the iris. 'I'm sorry, Eeva. You've every right to be cautious, if you want. I mean, after what you've gone through –'

And again Eeva felt uneasy, that Magda should talk about her life like that, in the same way as she walked around Helsinki – as if she knew it, almost as if she possessed it.

'No,' continued Magda, 'everything about Sasha sounds right and looks right, but it doesn't feel right.'

'I don't like him,' said Eeva, discovering that this was the case.

'Nor do I. I shouldn't think many people do, would you?'

'Lauri does.'

'Yes,' said Magda, with a slight, dismissive gesture. 'But I'm not just talking about personal feelings. It's the way Sasha is – don't you agree?'

'He's Lauri's friend.' He certainly was, so much so that he might have been performing in a play where he had been given the part of Lauri's friend. You could never forget about him, or his friendship with Lauri. He doesn't want you to forget him. And all the time he's really waiting for you to leave, so he can be alone with Lauri.

'Yes, he's that all right,' Magda said. 'I don't know why Lauri likes him so much, when they're so completely different.'

'In what way different?'

'Oh well, you know. Sasha's not exactly an intellectual but he's in the vanguard of political theory all the same.'

'And Lauri isn't?'

'He doesn't need to be, does he?' said Magda lightly. 'After all, he's the real thing.'

'What do you mean?'

'Well – Lauri's one of the workers, isn't he?' Magda sounded embarrassed, as if this was so obvious it shouldn't need to be said.

So Lauri is one of the workers, and I'm a little orphan, and that takes care of both of us, thought Eeva, but she said nothing.

'We shouldn't stay here too long,' said Magda. 'It's a long ride back.'

But they still didn't move. There wouldn't be many more days like this, and they knew it in their bones. They were fine-tuned to the coming cold. Already summer was closing down, and the touch of chill in the air would grow stronger every day. The frost would come and the last mushrooms would vanish into the earth. The sun would slip down onto the horizon and stay there, red and weak, giving no heat and little light.

But at least she'd be in Helsinki this winter, Eeva thought, not out there in country silence, watching branches bow down under their load of snow, and split, and break with no one to see them. The pavements would be swept, the shop windows would be bright. There'd be braziers flaming on street corners, trams charging down polished rails, smells of roasting coffee beans and morning bread curling out of shop doorways . . .

Yes, she'd escaped.

'Maybe it's something to do with him being Russian,' she offered, going back to the subject of Sasha.

'No, it's not that.' Suddenly Magda sat up, and began to brush bits of dry leaf off her shoulders. 'But be careful, Eeva. That one might do anything.'

'What do you mean?'

'That's it, that's exactly what it is with Sasha,' said Magda excitedly, punching her left fist into the palm of her right hand. 'I couldn't put my finger on it before. With most people, after a while you know more or less what they are capable of. The things that they won't do – those are even more important than the things that they will do. Of course you can't predict exactly what anybody might do – or be forced to do – in an extreme situation. But I'm not talking about that with Sasha. It's that he might do more or less anything, simply because he felt like it.'

'But Magda, why do you say that?'

'He steals, did you know that? And yet he has money. He always has plenty of money. That's something else which troubles me.'

'Steals? Where from?'

'There was one particular time that he came into the bookshop when I was working there. Sasha often comes in to buy books. But this time he put two books under his coat. Expensive books, on natural history. He saw that I'd seen him do it. He just looked at me and smiled. He didn't try to hide it from me: in fact I am sure he wanted me to see.'

'What did you do?'

'I said to him, "Sasha, two books have slipped under your coat. Put them back on the shelves before you leave."'

'That was good. And did he?'

'Yes. I waited by the door. He knew I meant it. He shrugged and said, "All property is theft," and he dropped the books on a table where they didn't belong. I said to him, "Sasha, you're not an Anarchist. You're not even a very good book thief." He was quite angry.'

'Why do you think he did it?'

'God knows. But later on it occurred to me that maybe it was to make me lose my job. At the time I needed that job because I hadn't built up enough journalism. If I hadn't said anything, then he'd have come in again, and again, and stolen books each time. I'd have been responsible for the lost stock.'

'Do you think he'll try it again, with me?'

'I shouldn't think so. But watch out for him. It'll be something different, that you're not expecting. He's very inventive, you must have noticed that.'

'Yes. Magda . . . do you think he'd ever do something like that to Lauri?'

'Oh Eeva, how should I know?' said Magda impatiently. 'Lauri's chosen his friendship, and he must take the consequences.'

'Lauri trusts him. Lauri's known him a long time.'
'Has he?'
'I think so. He met Sasha in Petersburg.'
'And how many years ago was that? Two?'
'Something like that.'
'Not so long, then.'
'No.'

Eeva scrambled to her feet. It hadn't been a good idea to lie so long on the ground like that. She was stiff, and her right foot had gone to sleep. She stood on one leg, shaking her other foot until it fizzed with life again. And she was cold. Yes, autumn was coming fast. Thin white cloud filmed the sun that had been warm an hour ago. But there in the basket was their mushroom harvest, rich gold, frilled and scented.

Lauri once said that chanterelles looked like the waves of the sea. She'd always remembered it, because he didn't usually say things like that. His closest thoughts never went into words. No, it was no use trying to join the present to the past with words. She and Lauri needed to be together, side by side, eating and sleeping and playing cards, telling fortunes in candle wax, dragging heavy bags of potatoes home from market, keeping out of the adults' way when they had hangovers, doing all the things that just naturally fell into place when there were two of you, almost all the time . . . the way they used to be.

But you can't go back to that, Eeva told herself. My father is dead, and Lauri's. We are the adults now. We have to find a different way. But she knew, she was sure of it, that the fabric of Eeva-and-Lauri could weave together and grow strong, if only it had a chance. Was it her fault, or his, that each time the eagerness of seeing each other faded to disappointment?

Or maybe, worse than that, he wasn't even disappointed. Perhaps he was quite satisfied and hoped for no more, wanted no more, had never expected more. He had been glad to see her for old times' sake, but childhood was over, they were grown up now, and naturally they had grown apart.

23

One day she would set a stone for him, Eeva thought. She didn't even know how much it might cost. There'd been some discussion after her father died. Mika had talked of a gravestone, but at the time it wasn't a practical possibility. Paying for the grave was as much as they could do, and there was a wooden marker that gave the dates of her father's birth and death.

She would set a granite stone, close to the earth. Her father would like that. He would not want a metal cross or any of the fancy designs. A piece of Finnish rock, set deep into the earth of his own country, because in the end he had never left it.

The wooden marker already looked worn with age. The earth had closed up again over his body. He was there beneath her, actually beneath her. Her father, who had carried her so often on his shoulders.

She explained to him why it had been so long since her last visit, and told him everything that had happened to her while she had been away. There was a stiff, chill breeze coming off the water, and the birches and larches rustled. Leaves were falling now. Soon it would be time to go indoors, close the double windows, light the stove and keep it lit until spring. Not many people would come here in winter, except to light their candles on All Souls' Day. But he was used to that.

'You didn't waste your life,' she whispered into the earth.

He used to bring her to the beach not far from here. He taught her to swim at Hietesaari, in the shallow Sunday water. Before he was ill he was a fine, strong man. She loved to see him wade into the water without hesitation, dip his head so that he was wet all over, and then set off straight out from shore with a steady trudgen stroke that he could keep going for hours.

They went fishing too. What he liked best was fishing on

evenings in midsummer, when the water was smooth and the little wooden jetty where they sat was warm with the day's sun. He knew all the best places to fish. How he'd have loved to have a little boat and row himself out . . . but although they often talked about it, it never happened. Sometimes they rowed to Hietasaari in a friend's boat – she couldn't remember whose boat it was. Only the feeling of sitting crouched in the bottom of the boat along with the friend's picnic and coffee pot wrapped in a cloth . . .

Those were good days, before he got ill. She remembered those summer evenings so clearly. Maybe there hadn't been all that many of them, but they had cut deep into her memory, like diamonds cutting into glass. They were clearer than a thousand ordinary days. He brought bread and cheese and a bottle of sour milk. Sometimes they built a fire.

She remembered one day, very late in the summer, or even early in the autumn. The beach was quiet. Her father was reading, and she was bored. She pointed at a rowing boat anchored some way out, and told him that she could swim to it.

'Go on, then,' he said.

She knew she could not really swim that far, but she was too proud to back down. She waded into the sea, looked back at him, and then plunged forward, dipping her head briefly under the water. The surface was completely calm, like silk. At first she thought it was going to be easy. Her heart rose with delight. She was cutting through the water, and the boat didn't look so far away. She would be able to reach it for sure.

She swam on. The water was colder than she'd thought at first, or maybe it was because she was getting tired. The sun was in her eyes. She pushed her arms through the water and tried to kick firmly, as she'd been taught. The black outline of the boat wavered in front of her. How far had she got to go? Surely it was almost as far away as it had been to begin with?

Her strokes were becoming more jerky. Could he see where she was? Was he standing on the edge of the water, to track her progress? But she wasn't going to look round. She was only going to look at the boat. She was going to keep on swimming . . .

But suddenly she knew she wasn't going to make it. She was too cold. Her arms and legs had no power left when she tried to move them. Water slopped into her mouth and she coughed, choked, then spat it out. She wasn't really swimming any more. Just treading water, trying to keep her head above it. That was the first thing her father had taught her. *As long as you can tread water, you'll be all right.* She couldn't even see the boat. She kept her eyes on two big chimneys, far away, but even they seemed to drift away from her. Another wave washed over her mouth, but this time she knew what to do, and she kept her lips pressed tight together.

He came up behind her. Before she knew it, he had his right arm around her chest, under her arms, bringing her up.

'Hold on, my girl,' he said, and with a powerful sidestroke he began to tow her back through the water. 'Don't wriggle.'

It only seemed to take a few minutes for them to reach the shore. She could barely stand. He picked her up in his arms, carried her up the sand and wrapped her in his jacket.

She thought he would scold her, tell her she shouldn't boast of being able to do things unless she could really do them, but instead he said, 'That boat's farther away than it looks. It's a trick of the light.'

'I didn't know you were swimming after me.'

'No. You never looked back, did you? Just kept on going.'

She smiled, nestling into the jacket that smelled of him. By next summer it was a game to swim out beyond all the anchored rowing boats, into clear water.

'You didn't waste your life,' she whispered into the grass that covered him. 'It wasn't so good at the end, but that's all over and done with now.'

He wasn't an old sick man any more. He wasn't even the father she'd known. He could slip about through time like a fish, doing what he wanted. He could be a boy or a baby or a proud twelve-year-old wearing a cap that was too big for him, off to his first day's work. He could be the father Eeva didn't remember, the one who'd taken her out of her mother's arms and scrutinized her, before accepting her as his.

24

Eat it, you fool, eat it! Thomas looked at the slice of almond cake he was holding. *For God's sake, just put it in your mouth and take a bite.*

Anna-Liisa's smile was becoming stretched. This was her best almond cake, rich and crumbly, moist with butter and scented with lemon peel. She'd cut him the first slice, apologizing as she did so. It was so fresh, she said, it might not cut well yet . . .

But of course it did. And she put it on his plate and gave him a little silver fork – how he detested little silver forks! – and then she waited, expectant, triumphant.

But what the hell was he going to do with it? The longer he held it, the more impossible it seemed that the cake could be eaten. It might as well have been a pad of lint. No, he could not, he simply could not swallow it.

'I'm very sorry, Anna-Liisa. I've got to confess, my stomach's not too good today. Even your delicious cake –'

And she leapt into sympathy. No, no, of course he mustn't, she knew what it was like, with a bad stomach even your favourite foods made you feel as if you'd swallowed a rat, pardon the expression. He mustn't think of trying to eat. She'd ring the bell at once and send for some fennel tea. Nothing better to calm the stomach than fennel tea.

But he put out his hand blindly, to stop her. For now he really was beginning to feel ill. Nausea churned in his stomach. He felt sweat on his forehead, and a taste of metal in his mouth that told him he had to get out now, into the cold air.

She was close behind him as he blundered out of the room, down the long hallway. The door, there it was. A smell of carbolic and washing, and another smell behind it, the smell of the children. Yes, that was what it was. They smelled, because they weren't loved.

And maybe he smelled that way, too, no matter how much he washed. He ripped open the door and stepped into the air, the good cold air that smelled of nothing. He closed his eyes, leaning against the wall and breathing deeply. His heart pounded and his body was cold with sweat.

'Are you all right, Doctor? You're so pale. I could fetch someone.'

He opened his eyes. She fussed about in front of him, spots of red flaring in her cheeks.

'I'm not ill,' he said. 'All I need is some fresh air.'

'I'll get you a glass of water – and my salts. Or brandy? Would you rather have brandy?'

'No. Just water.'

If only she would go. He needed to sit down on the ground. He let himself slide down the wall and there he was, safe on the cold, packed earth. He put out a hand to steady himself. Not so dizzy now. Deep breaths. He'd feel better in a minute.

He looked up. Good God, he was being watched. The front gate had opened and a little train of children had wound its way in and stopped, staring at him. The big girl in charge of them stared, too. They were babies, really. Their pinched, elderly little faces watched him without surprise.

'It's the doctor.'

'The doctor.'

'Look, he's fallen down.'

'He's drunk,' piped up one of the little ones.

They couldn't get enough of staring at him. Little grey figures in their grey cloaks, their skin colourless, their eyes sharp. He thought that if they came close they would have the musty smell of baby birds that have fallen out of the nest. And suddenly he was afraid of them, for no reason, afraid of these little ones he'd always done his best to help, as if each of them might pick up a stone and throw it at him. And then another stone, and then another. Each stone quite light and small – they would not be able to throw it otherwise – but each one sharp enough to cut.

'What are you standing there gaping for? Get inside, this minute! Soila, you'll come to my room before supper.'

Anna-Liisa with the glass of water. She held it to his lips. No, he could manage it. The glass shook. He had never heard her talk like that to the children.

'They weren't doing any harm,' he said. 'They were surprised to see me like this, that's all it was.'

'It's not their business to be surprised. Who does that girl think she is? I've had my eye on her, oh yes, she doesn't know it but I've been watching her –'

'They're only children,' he said.

'Children!'

'What else are they?'

'They're orphans. And you can take it from me, orphans want watching.'

Perhaps it was because he was down on the ground, looking up at the bulk of her, that he suddenly saw Anna-Liisa quite differently. The underside of her chin jutted and her eyes were like currants in dough, without kindness or warmth. He would not like to be in her power, he thought. Quickly, his thought rushed to bury itself. She was a good woman. She did her best in difficult circumstances. What more could be expected?

But the thought would not be buried. Her harsh voice rang in his head. What would she say to that girl Soila, when she came to the little sitting room before supper? How would Anna-Liisa punish her?

'Don't be too hard on her,' he said.

Instantly he knew he'd made things worse, as Anna-Liisa's face contracted with anger. 'Allow me to know what's best,' she said. She was stronger, more powerful than he'd thought. He did not ever want to sit in a room with her again.

But next week he would be there was usual, he knew that. These children needed a doctor more than he needed not to eat cake with Anna-Liisa. He was trying to persuade her to give the children cranberry juice each morning in winter. Anna-Liisa was doubtful. Surely porridge was enough? No doubt he'd set back the cause of cranberry juice by years, in one day. He must smooth her down, make her believe that he liked and respected her, as he

223

used to believe he really did like and respect her. Otherwise, she'd find a reason to keep him out of the House of Orphans. She wouldn't be able to help herself. She wouldn't even know why she didn't want him there.

It was always going to be a matter of compromise, he thought, in a small place like this. You can't choose your neighbours, you have to get on with whoever is there, and make the best of it. That's reality. Everything else is just the most ridiculous of dreams.

An immense weariness filled him at the thought of all the getting on and making the best of it that lay ahead of him, before . . .

Before what?

Before it was over, of course.

Thank God it's Friday and this evening Matti will be heating the sauna. In the sauna some of this at least will wash away.

He was up on his feet again, no longer dizzy, his heart beating in its normal rhythm. If he weren't a doctor he'd have been scared he was having a heart attack, but he knew it wasn't that. No, it was just a moment of weakness.

He wouldn't go straight home. Home was empty, even though Lotta had found him a big strong raw-boned girl who scrubbed as if the devil were after her, and couldn't cook to save her life. He'd go over to Lotta and ask her to give him supper. She'd be glad to do it, and it would help to heal the breach between them. Indeed, it was already healing over. Threads of scab were feeling their way across the raw surface. Soon the scab would be solid, then it would itch, and at last it would drop off. For a while the new skin would be bright pink and shiny, but in time it would grow dull, and fade in colour, and look more or less like the original.

You couldn't keep a quarrel going in the country, he thought, especially with winter coming. You needed each other too much.

'But where is Karl?' asked Thomas.

'He's gone to Stockholm. There's an exhibition of lathes. He's staying for a couple of weeks.'

'I see.'

'It's nice to have the house to myself,' said Lotta crisply. He looked up.

'Why pretend?' Lotta continued, her voice firm. 'Karl's in Stockholm, and I'm glad of it. It's all gone too far: I'm really beginning to wonder if he's quite all there. Come with me,' she said, as if she'd reached a decision. 'There's something I want you to see.'

He got up from the table, dropped his napkin, and followed her. She picked up a shawl she'd thrown over a chair, and wrapped herself in it.

'You'll need your coat, Thomas. Wait here, I'll fetch it, and I need to get a lantern.'

The temperature outside had risen slightly. After nights of hard frost, it was getting ready to snow, he thought. There were no stars, and the air was still. All day the sky had been a heavy iron-grey, tinged with yellow. A sky loaded with snow, wanting only a touch to make it fall.

'This way,' said Lotta. Light spilled on the path from her lantern, and the shadow of her cloak swung wildly one way and then another. Her face was set.

'But Lotta,' he said, as they reached Karl's workshop, 'do you think we should go in here, when he's away?' A man's workplace was private. He would have hated anyone to go into his surgery, and move his things about, and read his books.

'I told you, I've something to show you,' she said, producing a key and unlocking the door. She found a switch, and light flooded the workshop.

'Yes,' she said, 'he's got everything here. He had a generator for the workshop before we had electricity in the house. And his bed, his stove, his books and pictures. Everything he loves is here. Wait.'

She was fumbling behind a green velvet curtain. There was no window behind it, he knew that, only an alcove.

'Yes,' she said, her voice muffled by the curtain. 'It's still here. I thought for a moment he might have taken it with him. But even Karl's not crazy enough for that. Not yet.'

'But what is it?'

'Look for yourself.'

The brass rings rattled as she drew back the curtain. There it was. A sculpture. Its lines were elongated, slender, delicate. For a moment he couldn't identify it, and then he saw it was a sculpture of a girl, half life-size. Or perhaps it was a boy? It possessed the extraordinary grace that some boys have at sixteen or seventeen, before their muscle thickens. But the figure was not life-like. It wasn't like a real body at all, but the idea of a body that had been unlocked from a man's mind and turned to wood. The figure lay on its back, head turned to one side as if lost in sleep. The wood ran like water, dark and silky with touch. The sculptor had not marked the sexual organs, and the shallow curves of breast and hip might have been either female or male. But somehow that only made it more intensely erotic. He couldn't help himself, he put his hand out to the wood, then he caught the flash of Lotta's anger, and drew back.

'That's what he does. All the time. He thinks I don't know. He thinks he's so clever.'

'I didn't realize that Karl could carve anything as good as this.'

'When he wants, he can do anything,' she said bitterly. 'But Thomas, I think he's ill. I really think he is mad. He sits here for hours, stroking, touching – that thing. It's more real to him than any of us. It's all he wants.'

'But he didn't take it to Stockholm,' said Thomas, trying for humour.

'He thinks it's safe here,' said Lotta.

The tone of her voice troubled him. 'Lotta, you wouldn't –'

'Why wouldn't I? Why shouldn't I? Can you imagine what it's like, to live with a man who only wants a piece of wood?'

'Then you shouldn't live with him,' said Thomas suddenly. 'You're right. Why should you live like this? You deserve better, Lotta.'

She looked at him, and a small, very sweet smile touched her face.

That smile has been there in Lotta all the time I've known her, he thought. I must have seen it before, but I can't remember.

'No, Thomas,' she said. 'I can't leave him. It's my duty to stay

226

with Karl. This is where God has placed me. And besides, I haven't the courage. What could I do, away from here, away from all my friends?'

'You could live with Erika. You know how fond Erika is of you.'

'No, no, that wouldn't work. Erika is fond of me precisely because we've never lived together. You have to be realistic, Thomas, at our age.'

'At our age,' he repeated gloomily. 'Really, Lotta, you talk as if we're already dead. Pull the curtain over, let's not look at that thing any more.'

But Lotta didn't do so. Instead she just stood there, staring at the carved figure as if it were a puzzle she couldn't solve. 'The absurd thing is,' she said at last, in a low voice, 'that in a way I'm jealous of Karl. He's got something that means so much to him, and nobody can take it away from him. If I destroyed this sculpture, he'd only make another. Karl's got what he wants.'

'And you haven't?'

'You know that, Thomas,' she said, even more quietly. 'You know that. And there's nothing to be done about it, not by you, not by me, not by anyone. Why does God place us on this earth? To test us. To try us. To see what we can endure, and still be faithful.'

'Do you really believe that?'

'Yes. To see how much we can endure.'

'I'm sorry, Lotta.'

'Good heavens, Thomas, it isn't your fault. Your friendship – You know that our friendship means a very great deal to me.'

'And to me.'

Lotta pulled her shawl around her, and straightened her shoulders. Briskly, she caught hold of the edge of the curtain and drew it across the alcove. The brass rings rattled vigorously.

'There. That's enough of Karl's nonsense. I can't think why I wanted to show you. Well, we all have our moments of weakness.'

'We most certainly do. Lotta dear, you're shivering. This place is as cold as a tomb. It can't be good for you. Let's get back to the house.'

*

Already, big soft flakes of snow were falling. They stuck to the cold ground, prepared by nights of frost.

'Lift the lantern, Lotta.'

She lifted it, and they looked up as they'd used to look up when they were children, into the whirling spirals of the first snow of winter, coming faster and faster, falling onto their eyelids, their lips, their cheeks. The flakes seemed to be drawn to the lantern light like moths. Yes, when they were children they would run about with their boots ringing on the hard earth, scraping up hand-fuls of the first snow and throwing them at each other. It was the metal tips of their boots that made the ringing sound.

In the morning everything will be covered, he thought. Everything will be smooth and mysterious and full of light. That morning after the first snowfall! How he used to wake up to strong white light on the ceiling, and he'd jump out of bed in ecstasy and stare at the white garden without a single footprint in it. It wasn't happiness, it was ecstasy so strong that his living body couldn't contain it, but must run and rush and leap and punch the air until he fell headlong into the snow like an angel with his wings open.

And he was still here, with the same house around him, the same garden and birch-groves and stream, the same forest. But all the people who had made his life then were gone. Imagine if someone had told him when he was that little boy: *One day they'll all be dead, your mother and father and old Katariina, and even the wife you're going to marry, who's still a little girl . . . one day they'll all be dead, and you'll still be alive.*

If you put it like that, it sounded incredible. But it all happened slowly, and so it was bearable. Indeed it was absolutely normal, and what life did to everyone. You mourned people, you missed them, and as they faded from your life others replaced them. Only sometimes – now – the dead seemed so close, so real, more real than anything he could touch. As if they'd been secretly present all the time, just waiting until the snow began to fall and they could reveal themselves. He could almost hear the excited screams and shouts, the ringing of the boots.

Lotta was part of those lost times, and she would always carry

228

them into the present for him, so that wherever Lotta was, those times would be close. Lotta would never let the present break away from the past, any more than she would smash a piece of family china. That was her gift. If Karl didn't understand it yet, he would when she was gone. He would mourn Lotta's gifts, when she was no longer beside him.

'Dear Lotta,' he said, 'if you won't leave him, you must at the very least go on a long visit to Erika, and make Karl realize what his life would be like if you weren't here.'

She laughed. 'No doubt he thinks it would be a great deal easier.'

'Then he's deceiving himself. He may not know it, but he depends on you, believe me. Without you here, Karl would be lost. He'd sit in that shed until he froze to death.'

'You were urging me to leave him a minute ago.'

'That was for your sake, not for his. Now, let's go in.'

25

Sasha had vanished. It was Sunday now, and he'd been gone since Thursday morning. Or at least, Thursday was the last time Lauri had seen him.

When Lauri left for work that morning Sasha was still asleep. Sasha had said nothing to indicate that he was going away, but that evening he didn't come home. At first Lauri thought maybe there was a meeting that Sasha had forgotten to tell him about, and it had gone on so late that Sasha had slept on some comrade's floor. There was always a meeting. But there was still no sign of Sasha on Friday after work. They were due to go to the sauna together: they always did, and then relaxed with a few beers afterwards. He asked around in a few bars, but nobody had seen Sasha.

Sasha was a grown man, well capable of taking care of himself. But late on Friday night Lauri suddenly got worried that he might have been picked up by the police. He knocked on the neighbours' doors, giving nothing away, but no one had seen or heard anything. But that's the way of neighbours, thought Lauri. When there's trouble they make sure they don't know anything.

Lauri saw Hannu next morning, smoking on a corner, watching a gang of kids scream along the street in a game of tag. Hannu looked as if he'd like to join in. He had one of those boyish faces which stay the same until well into the late twenties. Lauri leaned against the lamp-post, watching as a kid tripped in a pothole, pitched forward and lay there bawling until he got hauled up by one of the others. And then off they went together, arms over shoulders, to sit on a step.

'Seen anything of Sasha this last day or two?' asked Lauri casually.

'No. Where's he been?' For Sasha was always off somewhere.

'No idea. I haven't seen him since first thing Thursday morning. He didn't say he was going off anywhere, did he?'

'Not to me.'

'Nor to anyone else either, as far as I can make out.'

'*You'd* know, if anyone would,' said Hannu. Suddenly his tone became more serious. 'You look worried. You thinking he might of been picked up?'

'What do you think?'

'Could be, but I don't think so. Not our Sasha. He's too –' Hannu made a quick little movement with his hand, weaving it in and out. 'Listen, Lauri, I'd get on to Fedya if I were you.'

'Right. I'll get over there.'

They talked in quarter voices, like professionals. One of the first things you learned was not to whisper. Hannu even threw back his head and laughed loudly, as if Lauri had come over to tell him a joke. Maybe Hannu took the whole thing a bit far, Lauri thought. As far as he could remember, his father and Pekka and all the rest of them didn't use to carry on like this, as if they were on stage.

Fedya didn't know where Sasha was. Didn't even know he was missing, but he was sure there was nothing wrong.

'If he'd been picked up, we'd know. There's a system.'

'A system?'

Fedya frowned with a touch of self-importance that Lauri didn't like. All right then, he thought, so you know something I don't. Keep it to yourself, then.

'See you,' he said, and left.

'Lauri!'

'What?'

'Don't worry. You know our Sasha. If anyone can look after himself . . .'

Lauri walked fast down the cold streets. Somehow those two encounters had irritated him more than he'd have thought good comrades like Hannu and Fedya could irritate him. As if the pair of them were playing a game, and enjoying it.

It was only fair to say that Sasha played games, too. Sometimes he behaved as if the act of pretending to be what you weren't

– or pretending not to be what you were – was the most important part of the 'political education' he was always on about.

Lauri walked faster. His irritation suddenly switched to anger, but he wasn't angry with Sasha now, or Fedya or Hannu or any of them. No, the person who deserved his anger was himself. What kind of a friend was he, thinking such things just at the time when Sasha might be on important Party business, taking risks Lauri didn't even know about? Some friend. Some comrade, he thought, almost taking pleasure in the indignation that swelled against himself and seemed to resolve all his doubts. Loyalty, that was the thing. Even if you didn't understand why something had to happen, you were loyal.

By Sunday morning, Sasha still wasn't back. Lauri woke as usual, into the Sunday quiet and winter darkness. He'd slept late, worn out after a heavy week and some beers the night before. There were his boots on the floor, where he'd kicked them away. If Sasha had been there, he'd have put Lauri's boots neatly alongside his own. Sasha didn't like mess and untidiness.

How quiet life was without him. Sasha talked like a Russian, not like a Finn. Every thought that went through his mind was worth turning into words. Fair enough, since he *was* Russian. Sasha talked, and Lauri listened. He would never have missed Sasha saying he was going away for a few days. He hadn't said anything, and that was what was so strange. And where could he have gone? Nobody knew.

Sasha knew everyone Lauri knew, although Lauri had realized some time ago that he certainly didn't know everyone Sasha knew. But that was fine. They didn't live in each other's pockets. Who'd want that anyway? They were men, not boys.

All the same, Sasha was by far the closest friend Lauri had ever had. But even as he said that to himself, it struck false. For there was Eeva, shining in his imagination with her own steady, mysterious light. She hadn't seemed mysterious at all in the days when they'd curled up in bed together. She'd felt like part of himself, no more special than his arm or his leg. He'd taken her for granted, but surely that wasn't wrong? It was like taking your own arm or leg for granted. It didn't mean that you didn't value being able to spoon soup into your mouth, or walk.

She'd been ordinary, but during the years he hadn't seen her she'd grown mysterious. He watched and watched her now, but he still couldn't make out what she was going to do next, or what she was thinking about. And yet the Eeva who was closer to him than he was to himself was still there somewhere, within this girl in the green dress. He had to believe it. There were moments when he was sure of it.

It was these two things together that made a barrier: her mystery, and the dearness that lay behind it. He could have dealt with either of them separately, but together they made Lauri stiff and silent. He was always thinking of what he should have said to her, immediately after she and Magda had gone off together. When the past came up, as it couldn't help doing sometimes, he'd go and say something clumsy that he didn't mean, and feel her withdraw from him. And there was no one who could help him. Magda wasn't inclined to do so, you could see that straight away.

He caught sight of Eeva across the street one evening, getting off the tram, looking at the ground to make sure she wouldn't slip. She was frowning slightly, holding her skirt to keep it out of the dust. The sight of her seemed to rush into every corner of his mind and stop his thoughts. She didn't even see him.

Best not to think about any of it. Sasha would be back soon. And in one way – a way that Lauri wasn't too proud of – it was a relief to have a breathing space. The more he thought about that conversation with Sasha – 'talking about Bobrikov' was how he phrased it in his own mind – the more fantastic it seemed. 'Talking about Bobrikov' drew a veil over that fantastic, dreamlike conversation about bombs and bullets and poisoned umbrellas. It seemed unreal now. Like a dream, or something he'd invented. He almost wanted to bring up the whole 'talking about Bobrikov' subject again, just so that Sasha could laugh and say, 'You didn't really swallow all that crap, did you? Lauri, Lauri, when are you going to stop being so politically naive? That's not the way things are done.'

To kill a man, Lauri thought. He could imagine doing it in

anger. Yes, if he saw a man knock down a child, and seize the lump of bread in her hand, he could do it. Or if someone tried to hurt Eeva. He wasn't going to pretend that he didn't have that anger in him.

He got up and began to walk quickly around the room. He felt hot, restless. But what Sasha was always saying was that you had to act on the basis of what you knew. It wasn't right to base your actions on your emotions. You must analyse the situation objectively, until you found the correct response to it. In fact it was not up to one individual to carry out such an analysis. It was a collective responsibility. Lauri couldn't help smiling as he remembered the relish with which Sasha rolled out words like 'objective analysis of the situation' and 'collective responsibility'. Somehow, Lauri could never use those words himself. They didn't belong to him, and he felt like a fraud using them, no matter how much Sasha nodded approval.

But if someone was trying to hurt Eeva . . .

Instantly the picture jumped into his mind. It was Eeva, backing against the wall with her bundle. They'd come to take her away. It was for her own good. A new life, a better life.

She was very pale. He wanted to fight the man with brass buttons down his front, but Eeva whispered, 'Don't, Lauri, or they'll take you away as well.' Lauri's father was already in prison, and Big Juha was standing there scowling at Eeva as if he hated her. Lauri knew he scowled because he couldn't do anything, and had to let them take away the daughter of his dearest friend. But did Eeva know that?

My God, he thought, she never saw Big Juha again. He'd died not long after. That would have been her last sight of him, scowling, refusing to say a word. Did she understand? And then Lauri's father died too, and most of the others were scattered.

He was hot. It was the anger that had never gone away, burning in him. They'd taken Eeva, and he hadn't been able to stop them.

He would have to imagine that it was Bobrikov behind those brass buttons. That would make it easier. You can't kill a man without thinking of him as your enemy. When it comes to blood, political education isn't enough. But there was no question of blood, of course there wasn't. That was not Lauri's role, Sasha had said so. Besides, maybe Sasha hadn't meant any of it. The whole conversation was some elaborate kind of test. But why wasn't Sasha here?

Suddenly the solution came to him. He would go and ask Magda if she'd seen him. Yes, that was the answer. Joyfully, he pulled on his boots and his heavy coat. It was quite likely that Magda knew something he didn't. On a Sunday morning, the two women would be at home together.

While he'd been thinking and walking around the room, the sun had come up. What a morning it was – he couldn't remember when he'd seen one more beautiful. Lauri pulled down the flaps of his rabbit-skin hat, and strode along the street in the centre of the moving white plumes of his own breath. The midwinter sun was low, clinging to the horizon like a child to its mother. It wouldn't leave it today; no, not for weeks yet. Lauri smiled at his own thought. Yes, one day the sun would grow strong and brave and throw itself right up into the summer sky, leaving the horizon behind.

But he'd always loved the days of midwinter. You were free to love winter when you were young and strong and your blood kept you warm. The taste of frost in the air made his blood rise to meet it, beating hard.

The sun threw rich blue shadows where cleared snow was heaped at the street corners. There'd been another heavy fall in the night, and then it had frozen again. The dirty old heaps of snow were covered in glistening white. Just by looking at those heaps he could tell how thick the crust of ice was on that fresh snow. Nothing would melt today. The sun was too weak, the frost too strong.

But all the same, the snow had to be cleared. In front of one of the old wooden houses that they hadn't managed to pull down yet, an old man was scratching at his steps with a twig broom. But he was so old, so feeble, that the broom barely dented the frozen crust of the snow.

Lauri stopped.

'Here, give us that, Grandad, I'll do it for you.'

The old man looked at Lauri. His eyes were faded and milky. Lauri wondered if he could see out of them at all.

'I'll sweep those steps for you,' Lauri repeated more loudly.

Probably the old man was deaf as well as half blind. Suddenly he caught on, tottered down the steps, thrust the broom handle into Lauri's hands, and crawled painfully back up to the top step, where he stood watching.

'You go in and keep warm,' Lauri shouted, beginning to sweep, but the old man shook his head. He thinks I'm going to make off with his broom, Lauri thought. Really, these old guys. I hope I never get like that. If he had a metal shovel, now, I could get these steps clear in a minute. But I don't suppose the old man could even lift a metal shovel.

Energy surged through him. He'd soon show the old feller. Even with this miserable broom that looked as if half its bristles had dropped out.

Sparkling powder flew up from the snow and whirled around Lauri as he knocked the steps clear. He dashed the twig broom from side to side, giving the old wooden steps such a clear as they'd never had in their lives. There wouldn't be a trace of snow left by the time he was finished.

'You got some ashes, Grandad?' he shouted.

The old face furrowed with suspicion.

'Ashes! Ashes to put on the steps so you don't slip!'

The old man's face cleared. He wagged his head triumphantly.

'Ah!' he said in a voice that scratched exactly like his broom. 'Ye're after something! Ye're after something! Soon as I saw ye, I knowed ye were after something.'

Lauri gave up. All right, fall down your steps if you want to, he thought. But he couldn't get angry. The day was so beautiful and the old man was so absurd, waving his broom in triumph now that he had it back, as if he'd got the better of Lauri.

'I know ye! I know ye!' he chanted.

He, Lauri, was never going to get like that. No, he swore to God, if he ever felt himself going that way, he would take himself off and jump straight into the harbour with his boots on.

'All right, all right, you've got your precious broom back. Go and lock it up safe.'

He still couldn't help laughing. And suddenly the old man started to laugh too, even though the suspicious look was still on him.

'Ye're all right!' he cackled. 'Ye're all right, I know ye!'

When Lauri got to the corner he turned and there was the old feller, still standing at the top of his steps, gripping the broom and jabbing it towards Lauri. But an old woman had come out too, a tiny old woman bundled in shawls, who didn't even come up to the old man's shoulder. She had her hand on his arm and she was looking up into his face, saying something to him. And he stopped waving the broom at Lauri, and looked down into the little face like a nut that didn't come any higher than a child's.

Well, the old man had someone to look after him, at least. He was luckier than he looked. For some reason Lauri felt his spirits soaring even higher. Even that old man, scrawny and miserable as he was, had someone to take care of him. But of course Lauri would never get like that. It was impossible to believe that the shrivelled little old woman, wrapped in her shawls, had ever been young and fresh like Eeva, or had ever stepped off a tram so easily and so carefully, into her own life.

He could brush a hundred flights of steps if he wanted. He could run from one end of Helsinki to the other if he had to. The frost was making his blood sparkle like that snow powder. Just think of having to creep along the cold streets like a crab, steadying yourself in case you tumble and break your bones. Or having to huddle over a stick and peer at everything before you can even make out what it is. No, it was impossible. It couldn't happen to him, and it wasn't going to happen. On a day like this you knew you'd live for ever. Or if not live, then die. Suddenly, without any pain and without ever growing old.

'Eeva?'

'Lauri!'

'Is Magda at home?'

'Magda?'

'Yes. I mean, I only wanted – I wanted to ask her if she'd seen Sasha anywhere.'

'Why, what's happened to Sasha?'

'I don't know. Nobody seems to know. I haven't see him since Thursday morning.'

'Did he say where he was going?'

'He didn't say he was going anywhere.'

'Well, Magda's not here either. She won't be back until tomorrow.'

'Oh. It's only you at home, then?'

'I stayed in because I've got mending to do. I'm sorry you're disappointed.'

'Don't be like that, Eeva! I only wanted to talk to Magda, because of Sasha.'

'And now you only want to talk to me because you only wanted to talk to Magda, but only because of Sasha –'

She was smiling. Her face glowed with life as if she, too, had that sparkle of snow in her veins. Her eyes shone. He took a deep breath. She was too powerful. She was like the sun in summer, leaping far above him. But at the same time, surely . . .

'Eevi!' he said. The name her father called her.

She was silent, stilled.

'You know I don't come here because of Magda,' he said.

'No, I don't know that,' she answered very quietly. 'You'll have to tell me.'

Suddenly he knew it was all nonsense. She wasn't the sun leaping in the sky. She wasn't anything strange. She was mysterious, but she was also closer to him than she'd ever been, even in those days when they'd slept together like puppies in the same bed.

'I'm not sure I understand,' she went on. 'Tell me, Lauri, if you don't come here because of Magda, then why do you come?'

She looked at him as if she were searching for something inside him. She was wearing an old grey dress, and she'd thrown a shawl of Magda's around her shoulders. It was a Russian shawl, made of dark woollen stuff with crimson roses embroidered on it. The roses glowed and Eeva's eyes shone green. Was she teasing him?

'So, you don't even know why you come here?' she demanded,

as he didn't answer. She'd never talked to him like this before. Not as if he was her friend, not as if he was her brother or her comrade. Not as if he was Lauri at all, but as if he was a man.

But that was what he was. A man who'd come to her door, pretending to look for something else but really searching for her. She knew it now, yes, she did, she was sure of it. Her blood beat fast with it. He was looking for her, not for Magda or Sasha. But did he know it yet?

She took a quick, shallow breath. Her fingers were prickling. She couldn't go on meeting Lauri almost every day but never going any further. *Hello, Eeva.* And then what? Then what, she thought, looking in his face and then away, quickly, as if the sight of him stung her. Is that all you can say? Is that all there's going to be between us now? But it's not right, not for us, we deserve more than that. If you make me close the door on you now I swear I'll never open it again. You'll have had your chance.

'I know why I've come here,' said Lauri.

'You do?'

'Yes.'

'Then tell me.'

'No. No, Eevi.' He shook his head. 'It's not something you tell. You just . . .' He put out his hand. He touched one of the crimson roses that blossomed on her shawl, and traced the outline of the petals with his fingers. He came to the stalk of the rose and the raised roughness of it travelled through his finger-ends and made him shiver. Her eyes held his and he saw the black pupils dilate until there was only a rim of green.

'Magda's away,' she said softly, barely moving her lips.

'Maybe she's gone with Sasha,' he answered at random, touching another rose just where its embroidered petals brushed Eeva's neck.

She shook her head. 'No. Why should those two be together? They don't even like each other. They're not – they don't –'

'They don't love each other as we do,' he said, astonishing himself.

'No,' Eeva repeated, 'they don't love each other, as we do.' She smiled, parting her lips so he saw the soft inside of her mouth.

'Anyway, they aren't here.'

'Only you?'

'Yes, only me.'

'Can I come in?'

'Yes, you can come in.'

The day had sunk into its winter gloom. He could barely see her any more. But he didn't want more light. Her soft warm body was rucked round with the clothes they'd pushed away. He thought she was asleep.

'Eeva?'

But she didn't answer. Yes, she was deeply asleep. She trusted him. He'd never do anything to hurt her.

'What if I have a baby?' she'd asked.

'You won't – you won't –' he'd groaned. He'd die if she made him wait another second.

'I could.'

'You won't – I'll look after you –'

She was the last barrier, and then he was in her. He'd groaned again, because he didn't know what he was doing, didn't know where he was any more.

'You hurt me,' said her voice, very quietly. So she wasn't asleep.

'I didn't mean to.'

'No. It's not important.' She sighed, rolled over. 'I feel as if we aren't anywhere, don't you? As if all the walls have gone.'

'You don't want to worry about having a baby,' he said. He felt rather than heard her spurt of laughter.

'That's a good one! What've we just done? Don't you know how babies are made?'

'Well,' he said, thinking aloud, arguing with himself and her, 'if a baby *is* made, that's not the worst thing, is it? We've got no one else belonging to us. I'd look after you.'

'What about Sasha?'

'Sasha!' he said in surprise. 'What's Sasha got to do with it?'

'Try asking him,' said Eeva, but her sharpness was engulfed in a yawn. 'I'm so sleepy,' she said, 'I can barely feel my legs. I feel as if I'd lost myself. What day do you think it is?'

'No, you didn't lose yourself.' She could hear him smiling in the dark. 'Your self was just misplaced.'

She was surprised, almost shocked that Lauri would use such a word and so accurately.

'So where was it *misplaced*?'

'Wherever mine is.'

How had he learned to talk like that? In the past, she was the one who had the words, not him. As if he sensed her thoughts he said, 'I've had a life since you went away, Eevi, you must know that. I'm not the same as I was –'

'I don't want to know everything,' she said quickly, afraid he was going to start telling her about other girls.

'All right then,' he said, after a pause. 'Maybe it's best not.'

At once she was seized with curiosity for what he'd been going to tell her. But he was right. Best leave it now.

'I wonder what became of Sasha?' she went on dreamily. He didn't like it. He didn't want Sasha in bed with them.

'Eevi,' he said. 'Eee-vi.' She was coming closer to him. Her warm body was pressed against him, lightly and then more surely. He turned and caught hold of her. She had a way of seeming about to vanish, even when she was in his arms. So warm and fluid and soft, as if she could slip away. But she was solid enough. He could smell her skin and her hair. He kissed her neck.

'Is it all right to do it again so quickly?' she asked.

'I don't know,' he muttered.

'Nobody tells you about things like that, do they?'

'Eevi!' he said again. Her name filled his throat and there was no room for any more.

They could do anything. They only had themselves to think of. The day stretched itself into the night. A cold night, very cold. Even with the stove you could feel it. He heaped everything he could find on top of her, and brought her tea while he drank vodka.

They were lying quietly, side by side. One candle burned. Sometimes the flame dipped and shadow flew across the walls, then it straightened again. The curve of her cheek was as clear as a seashell, he thought. Those shells he picked up in autumn, after the first storms, when sky and water were the same iron grey. His mind kept jumping back to their childhood. The things they did, where they went. Things weren't easy then, but he and Eeva were free. The world of talking and politics and action was above their heads. They knew about it and in a way they were part of it. They were the future their fathers worked for, but they were free of it.

That world which once felt so solid was gone. Eeva's father, his father, the men who came and went, Big Juha, all of them dead or elsewhere.

Death came so quickly, and everything that you thought would last dissolved, just like that. Nothing lasted. Eeva was right, the walls had disappeared.

He wanted to run away with her and make a life where they would be together, safe. He would build a house in the forest for her, and work for her. At night they'd close the door. The thought of it was like an old song coming alive inside him, full of longing.

> I build a house for my love
> In the dark forest,
> The deer come to our door
> And the snow is our blanket.

But Sasha's voice was in his head, too. *Typical Finnish song, full of death and fatalism. I wouldn't have expected it from you, Lauri. You're a city boy, one of the workers, for fuck's sake.*

Don't you realize that's exactly how the system works? They hold up a dream in front of you. Wife and the little ones and a roof over your head, your newspaper and your glass of vodka, as long as you're a good boy, do as you're told and accept what fate brings. Fate! That's a good one.

But you only get the dream for as long as it suits them. And then they'll kick you out of it. No job, no roof, and you're on the street, in the snow you sing those lovely songs about. You're nothing to them. You know that. A pair of hands with some skill in them. Part of the means of production. The dream's there to keep you quiet until you're not needed any more.

'What's the matter?' asked Eeva.

'Nothing.'

'You were like this.' She clenched her body to show him.

'It's nothing. I was thinking about the future. Listen, Eevi. You know Sasha?'

'I should think so,' she said drily.

'There are things you don't know. Things he does.'

'Nothing Sasha did would surprise me. If you told me he was an axe-murderer, I'd believe it.'

From his sudden stillness she knew she'd guessed right.

'He's a murderer.'

'No! I mean –'

'He's killed someone.'

'Not yet.'

'*Not yet?*'

'Listen, Eeva. It's not what you think. There's a reason for it.'

'An informer?'

Did she remember? Had she been awake that night, when Eero and Big Juha took the man away?

'No, it's more serious.' He found he was whispering, and cleared his throat. 'It's someone high up. Very high up. They're planning a –' He wanted to use the words Sasha had used. *Political assassination.* But somehow those two words wouldn't come out of his mouth. 'They're planning to kill him,' he said.

She didn't say anything for a while. Then, 'Why?'

'Once he's dead, things will be better.'

'Why will they be better? What sort of man is he?'

'The Tsar's man.'

'But then if he's killed, it'll only lead to worse things.'

'No, that's true in the short term, but in the long term, people will organize against oppression, they'll rise up. Killing a man like that isn't an end, it's a means to an end.'

'You mean, he isn't being killed because of what he's like.'

'In a way he is. But it's more than that.'

'I don't see how it can be more than that. What people are like, that's what matters, isn't it?'

'But Eeva, it's not the only thing. You're being – you're being naive.'

She was sitting up in the bed now.

'So it's Sasha who's doing it, on his own? He's not getting you to do his dirty work?'

'We're all in this together.'

'I'll tell you something, Lauri, you say I'm naive, but I wouldn't be soft enough for that. Let Sasha kill if he wants. It's in his nature, anyone can see it. But it's not in yours.'

What were they doing, arguing? She slipped across him, out of the bed, as quick as a fish. She scooped up her dress from the floor and wrapped it around her. 'He's dangerous, Lauri. He's the sort that leads you across a swamp and says you'll be all right if you follow his footsteps. And then suddenly he skips away so light that you can't see where he's put his feet, and you're sinking, but he's gone. He's safe and you're sinking, with your throat full of mud.'

He wondered if anything like that had happened to her, in the years he didn't know about. One day he would know about those years.

'Let him get on with it, Lauri,' she urged. 'It's all right for someone like Sasha, because he's the sort who won't go crazy afterwards, when he realizes what he's done. He's not like you.'

'Let's not talk about it any more.'

'No, you don't want to,' said Eeva. Her hands clutched the stuff of her dress close to her. But he'd seen her body, touched her, been inside her. So why was she hiding from him?

'What I'm saying,' Eeva went on, 'I'm not saying it to make you angry. That man you're talking about, he's living his life, now. This minute, he's doing all the things we do. Maybe he's even got a girl with him. He doesn't know you're going to kill him. Don't you see that it's terrible, that he doesn't know?'

'He won't have a girl with him, he's too old.'

'You're doing it for Sasha. And Sasha's pulling you in so that afterwards you'll be the kind of person he wants you to be. You'll be like him.'

26

Sasha came home two days later. He was there, sitting on the bed, head bowed, when Lauri returned from work. Lauri's first thought was that he'd been beaten up. There was that battered look about him. But there wasn't a mark on his face.

'So there you are,' Sasha said. There was a note of accusation in his voice, as if Lauri had been the one who'd disappeared.

'But where were you? What happened? We thought you'd been picked up.'

'Nothing happened,' said Sasha. His voice was flat. He might have been reading out someone else's words. 'Nothing happened, and nothing's going to happen. It's all off.'

'What is?' But he knew, of course, instantly. Bobrikov was off. No more 'talking about Bobrikov'. He was going to live.

'That fucking Swede's pulled out,' Sasha went on in a monotone. He examined his nails closely, and began to push back the cuticles. Sasha had very well-kept nails.

'Why?'

'Christ knows. Of course he's trotted out his reasons. His father's dying, so he's got to take care of his old mother. What would she do without him? And the estate, of course, it's his now. An inheritance like that tends to change your point of view. He's got his life mapped out for him now. The old mother, hunting, fishing, selling timber . . . and then he'll get married to some old friend of the family and the cycle will begin all over again. Give him a few years and he'll be talking fondly about the wild days of his youth.'

'I suppose, if you have all that handed to you on a plate –'

'Pre-cise-ly. But would our Swede have come up to scratch, even without the convenient death of papa? The fact is, when it came to the crunch he didn't like the look of Bobrikov's blood. He'd rather shoot capercaillie.'

Bobrikov's blood. There it went again. Sasha spoke of the blood as if it had already been spilled. It didn't belong to Bobrikov, but to Sasha, or Lauri, or anyone else who had an interest in it. Bobrikov wasn't his own man now. He was 'about-to-be-shot Bobrikov'. If he was shot his blood would spread out, naked and public, for anybody to gawp at. That was what Sasha wanted and intended.

'A crisis of conscience, you could call it,' added Sasha, his voice touching the word 'conscience' with a flick of contempt. 'Don't look so worried, Lauri. We'll find someone else.'

'It's not finding someone else that worries me. He – the Swede, I mean –' for Lauri still stumbled over this business of people having no names – 'he knows everything, doesn't he? What if he –'

'He won't. We've made sure of that. No, we'll find someone else,' went on Sasha. 'But it'll be tricky. You should have seen the way he shot the heart out of that target. A beautiful bit of shooting. I don't know when I've seen anything as good. But I was wrong about him, wasn't I?' His voice became even more inward, meditative. 'That's the trouble with idealists. They have ideals. They get a massive hard-on talking about them but when it comes to bedtime they just can't . . . get it up. The reality is never quite beautiful enough.'

'Don't take it so hard, Sash.' He would have done anything for Sasha at that moment. Promised anything. The relief was so huge, like being given back your life. He wanted to throw his arms around Sasha, hug him and dance him around the room.

'I'm a failure,' said Sasha, his voice leaking with sudden self-pity. 'Everything I touch goes wrong.'

'That's shit and you know it. Take your boots off and have a lie-down. You're dead tired, that's all it is. I'll go out for some vodka.'

'No, don't go. Don't leave me. You're my friend, aren't you, Lauri? You believe in me, don't you?'

No need to rush for that vodka, Sasha must have had plenty already. Suddenly he sounded quite drunk, which cast a different light on everything he'd been saying. Was there even a real Swede? The whole thing could have been one of Sasha's elaborate games, thought Lauri suddenly. No, the thought was so disloyal that he pushed it away. But Sasha was looking as if he expected something. He hadn't answered Sasha's question, that's what it was.

'Course I do,' said Lauri.

'We're mates, aren't we? Comrades?'

'That's right.'

But 'mates' always sounded wrong, coming from Sasha. It wasn't his language. Sasha had studied at a gymnasium, he'd told Lauri that. He knew Latin.

'Never give up,' said Sasha, and laughed loudly. His eyes glistened. 'There's always a second chance. Just because this has turned into a prize fuck-up doesn't mean we can't try again.'

'No,' said Lauri. Probably Sasha wasn't fooled by his show of disappointment. *It wasn't going to happen.* Bobrikov was never going to know a thing about *pol-it-ic-al ass-ass-in-ation.* Whatever Bobrikov was up to at this moment, he could carry on with it, whether it was wiping his arse or wiping the brow of his widowed mother. If he had a mother. Probably not, he was too old. And Lauri didn't have to wake in the night with his thoughts grinding like stones, wearing him away. The Swede had pulled out.

He wanted to get drunk – or no, not *get* drunk, *be* drunk, now, this minute. 'I'll get that vodka,' he said.

It took Sasha less than a day to find out about Eeva and Lauri. Maybe he talked to Magda, or Lauri let something drop, but Eeva didn't think so. Magda didn't trust Sasha, and she certainly wouldn't confide in him. And surely Lauri would want the same as Eeva did. Not to have other people's sticky paws all over what they did, before they even knew what they were doing.

Sasha dropped into the bookshop the morning after he came back. He picked up a volume of Runeberg, flicked through it as if to find something he liked, and then settled himself to read, absorbed, lounging against a bookshelf. But he couldn't be very absorbed – he barely spoke Swedish.

Why did he annoy her so much? There was no reason he shouldn't stand there and read. Students who had no money came in day after day to finish a book. Shabby students with eyes that swallowed books like food. She never minded their hours of browsing. They'd buy later on, when they had the means.

Some of them would never have any money, you could tell that already. They were born to study and be poor. They would talk to her, once they'd got over their fear that she'd make them buy something.

'If you'll permit me, I'd like to show you a poem I've written . . .'

Sasha was pretending to be like those students, but the poems he held in his hand meant nothing to him, and not only because he wasn't fluent in Swedish. There he stood, like an actor who had been directed to look absorbed in his book. He could convince an audience, maybe, but not her.

He waited until she'd served half a dozen customers, and there was a lull, and then he came over.

'So . . . how are you?' he asked with a kind of intimate pity, as if she had an illness people didn't usually talk about.

'I'm fine.'

'Good. That's excellent news. Your health is equal to the involvements of your life.'

'I'm certainly busy,' she said briskly. 'These books have to be shelved, and we're stocktaking.'

'I know you've *been* busy,' he said silkily. 'You and Lauri. I came in to offer my congratulations.'

He was a devil. Why Lauri couldn't spot it, she didn't know. She'd given Sasha the benefit of the doubt at first, wanting to like Lauri's friend. But she soon realized that Sasha didn't even want her to like him. He wanted her to have to pretend to like him, to have to put up with him because she had no choice. But Sasha was on her territory now.

'You've got a good imagination, Sasha. No wonder you like books so much. Why don't you put your hand in your pocket and pay for that one?'

'Lauri's in seventh heaven. He told me he couldn't believe how – *willing* – you were.'

'Get out.'

248

'You're a lucky girl. He really appreciates you. He was making me quite jealous with his descriptions.'

Eeva put down the pile of books she was holding.

'You've got it wrong,' she said.

'What do you mean? Lauri was quite specific.'

'You've got it wrong, because you think you can talk to me how you like. You're mistaken. No one is ever going to do that to me again. You can show me some respect.'

There was a fire inside her and she was only just keeping it from leaping out of her mouth and scorching the pile of books. She was back there. She was sweeping the floor of the House of Orphans, knocking her broom against the beds where rows of sick children lay. She was watching Anna-Liisa fold the hands of a dying child so it would look tidy. She was in the kitchen of the doctor's house, and Mrs Eriksson was washing the china with her hat on, showing Eeva how it was done but not trusting her to do it. She was marching to church in a crocodile, two by two, glanced at by the people of the town. *There go the orphans.* Luckier children, who were not orphans, would prink in their Sunday clothes, and stare boldly from the shelter of their parents.

'You've got it wrong,' she said to Sasha. 'All your plotting and planning and you know nothing. You come in here and steal books, not because you're hungry and you want to sell them, not because you're desperate to read and you can't afford to buy books, but because it feels exciting. That's all. That's the only reason you want to do anything. You want a thrill. You get your excitement, and you dress up what you do in words to make yourself sound good. *Comrade.* That's a laugh. Who are you a comrade of? Where do you come from? You're not fit to put the word in your mouth. You leave me alone and you leave him alone.'

She faced him, kept her eyes fixed on him. She had spoken low, so no one else would hear. She would keep her job, and she would get rid of Sasha. She wouldn't turn her back on him. Very slowly, he put the book of poems down on the desk.

'I thought we were friends, Eeva,' he said. She saw that his eyes were ripe with tears which he could shed at any moment. He could

249

make himself feel anything he wanted, she thought, any time he needed to. Already he was flooding with pity for himself. He was so good at it, so real. He was a snake with a thousand skins.

'You've never given me a chance, have you?' he said, as if appealing to a larger audience that was to be the judge between them.

'Nobody gives anybody any chances,' she said. 'You have to make them.'

He showed his teeth. 'Hold on a minute, Miss Bookshop Educator. I don't happen to need your valuable lessons. You've got nothing to teach me about making chances.' The self-pity dropped away. Suddenly he was full of himself again, cocky with secrets, Sasha the initiator. 'I'm a man of action, not words,' he bragged.

A man of action. His meaning hit her like a blow. She glanced round to check that no one was listening.

'I know what you're talking about,' she said, still quietly. 'You think I don't, but I do. You disgust me with your *action*. You want to drag Lauri into it, so he'll finish up the same as you. But Lauri's not your type and he never will be.'

'He's been talking to you.'

'Yes.'

'That was extremely stupid.'

They were speaking under their breath now. Close, too close. She shouldn't have put the books down. Sasha was pressing up to her, so close she could smell him.

Suddenly she became aware of a student who came in most days. He wasn't reading, he was watching them. He was one of the students who showed her poems. He liked her. He was watching Sasha, sizing up the situation, not happy. He was a thin, mild young man, but he was bracing himself. Any minute now he'd come over and ask if she was all right.

'You'd better go now,' she murmured. 'People are watching you.'

She'd done it. She'd got him out of the shop. After the heat of her anger and his, she was cold and shaky. He'd frightened her more than she'd thought he could. Yes, he was a snake. But he would leave her alone now, she was almost sure of it. He wouldn't dare do anything to her face, and she would never turn her back on him. She'd scorch him with words he didn't expect, the way she had scorched him just now, until he backed off. But why did Lauri choose a man like that for a friend? What was the attraction? Surely it wouldn't last. Lauri would soon see Sasha for what he was.

'There's a meeting tonight,' said Sasha, falling into step beside Lauri. Lauri was on his way back from work, and hadn't expected to see Sasha.

'Why didn't you tell me before? I'm meeting Eeva.'

'She'll understand. Something's come up.'

Something's come up. How well Lauri knew that sentence, after two years with Sasha. *Something's come up.* A switch of meeting place, a bundle of leaflets under a coat, a roll of banknotes, a new location for a clandestine printing press, a stranger sleeping on their floor and vanishing at first light, a change of tactic, a policy agreed at the highest level . . .

Each of these things introduced in the same way. Laconic, businesslike, toughly conspiratorial. That was the style Sasha preferred.

'Something's come up. It's essential that you're at the meeting. It's about that business of the Swede.'

'I thought you said it was all off.'

'For now. Not for ever. There are people who need to meet you.' Lauri couldn't help feeling flattered. He had progressed, then, if people needed to meet him.

'Where's the meeting?'

'I'm going to take you, but we need to hurry.' Sasha glanced at his watch. 'We've got exactly twenty-five minutes. We'll do it. There are comrades from Petersburg who're waiting for us. They've got to leave later tonight.'

'But Eeva's expecting me –'

'For God's sake, Lauri! She understands. She's one of us.' Sasha was terse tonight, a man of actions not words.

'How long will it last?'

'Not more than an hour. I've filled them in about you, but that's not enough. They need to see you in the flesh.'

Eeva would be waiting for him. She was making beef and barley soup with dumplings, and after supper Magda was going out.

Once Magda was gone, the apartment would be their own. His body ached. He wanted a stove, food, warm water to wash off the day's work. He wanted to sit at the table, stupefied by heat and the smell of food, watching Eeva, his elbows propped on the wood. She would stir the soup with her back to him. He would watch the nape of Eeva's neck, her shoulder blades, her thin, supple waist. She'd be flushed with steam and a bit preoccupied until the supper came out perfect.

A thin wind was working its way down the street like a blade of ice. These side streets were almost empty at this time. Everyone home from work, boots off, as close to the stove as they could get.

'All right, then, let's go,' said Lauri. The image of Eeva by the stove shrank inside his mind, but it was still as bright as a lamp. A child darted across the frozen street ahead of them, carrying an armful of kindling, and hammered on a door. It opened, a slice of warm light spread onto the snow, then vanished as the door slammed shut again. Lauri turned up his collar, pulled his earflaps down and lengthened his stride. They were walking into the wind. It stung until his eyes watered, and he lowered his head to protect them. For a moment the streets were blurred so he could hardly see them, but Sasha was at his side.

'You're a good cook,' said Magda, watching as Eeva sliced carrots. Her little knife flickered and made fine, even slices.

'I should be.'

'Look, I got these.' Magda opened her bag and showed Eeva four tangerines.

'Weren't they expensive?'

'Not for what they are.'

'Not for what they are? How much were they?'

'I can't remember. I bought them with some other things.'

'What other things?'

'Really, Eeva, what does it matter? I bought some walnuts.'

'Walnuts!'

'Look, aren't they beauties?'

'Magda, how are we ever going to keep to our budget if you carry on like this?'

'I sold another article,' said Magda, stripping off her gloves.

'Yes, but all the same, we must keep to the budget. Otherwise –'

'Don't look so serious, Eeva. We're not going to end up in the workhouse.' Magda flushed suddenly. It was obvious that she had remembered the House of Orphans. She remembers, but then she forgets, thought Eeva. But that's fair enough, it didn't happen to her.

'If you spend money on things I can't afford, then I'm not paying my way,' she said.

'Oh, for heaven's sake, Eeva, they are just a few little treats. It doesn't mean you aren't *paying your way*.'

The carrots were all sliced. Eeva gathered them together on the board. 'If I'd seen those tangerines I'd only have thought of all the potatoes I could get for the same money.'

'Yes, but potatoes don't bring the same joy as tangerines.'

'No, you're right, they don't, joy is not what potatoes bring. All the same, it's lucky I do most of the marketing. There, those are done. Give the soup a stir, Magda. The barley sticks to the bottom of the pot.'

Magda took the lid off the pot and rich, savoury steam gushed into the room. It was good beef soup which Eeva had made with marrowbone stock, onions, a handful of dried mushrooms, and paprika. When Lauri arrived, she would add the parsley dumplings that lay waiting on a white plate, and the sliced carrot. And then, when the dumplings were plump and feathery and had risen to the surface of the soup, they'd eat.

'Lauri's late, isn't he?'

'He'll be here by seven.' Her words were calm but a nervous pang went through her.

'It's past that already.'

Eeva mended her stockings while Magda read through the rough draft of an article she was writing. Magda wrote well, everyone said so. Eeva wished that she could read the German, but even in Magda's translation, the words were clear and sure as bells. Both of them sat at the table. The lamp hung on its chain above them, giving good light, although the rest of the room swam in shadows. It was a big room, much bigger than anything Eeva would have been able to afford on her own. Magda was paying the larger share of the rent. She made nothing of it, barely referred to it. They were equals, she insisted.

Magda seemed lost in thought tonight, looking up from her scribbled pages into nothing, with her pencil in her hand. Occasionally she made a strong, quick mark in the margin. She'd been working all day on that draft, and being Magda she probably hadn't stopped to eat. It was getting really late now. Eeva's nervousness had settled into a steady, burning sensation in her stomach. They couldn't wait for Lauri any longer.

'I'll put in your dumplings,' she said, getting to her feet.

'I don't mind waiting.'

'If you don't eat now, you won't have time before you go out.'

She tipped in the sliced carrot, then carefully lowered the dumplings on a slotted spoon. They disappeared into the soup. Normally cooking made her calm, but tonight her spoon clattered on the metal. Where was Lauri? She counted out the minutes under her breath, timing Magda's dumplings. Lauri's share and hers remained on the plate. She would cook them fresh when he came.

'Here you are, Magda.'

'Oh! Is it ready?'

'Just push your papers aside.'

'Aren't you eating, Eeva?'

'I'm not hungry yet. I'll wait.'

'Did Sasha give any explanation to Lauri, about his mysterious absence?' asked Magda.

'I don't think so.'

'I don't suppose it was anything much. Sasha enjoys speculation, especially when it's about him.'

Could she tell Magda what Sasha was planning? Should she tell her now? Magda's face was dark with thought. She hadn't really emerged from her article. She spooned up her soup, but Eeva could tell she wasn't tasting it. Cooking good food for Magda was a waste of time. Lauri, though . . .

'Yes, he's an odd fish,' said Magda at last.

'Who?'

'Sasha, of course.'

Odd fish! But Sasha was much worse than that, and Magda knew it. She'd made it clear that day in the forest that she knew it. So why pretend that it was 'just Sasha', a problem that no one needed to solve? Maybe she should talk to Magda – tell her what had happened in the bookshop . . .

'D'you want me to stay?' Magda asked suddenly. 'I'm only going to a concert. I don't mind missing it.'

'No, Magda, you go. I'm fine. Lauri will come soon.'

'Of course he will.' Magda smiled affectionately. 'It's wonderful soup, Eeva. I don't know what you put in it. When I make it, soup never tastes as good.'

'Be quick, or you'll miss the opening piece.'

In spite of the tangerines and walnuts, how she relished talking to Magda like this. Here was Magda, off to a concert, to sit there upright and alert before the music. She had no hesitation. She believed that the music was played for her, as much as for anyone. Being in the cheapest seats didn't matter. Besides, she had friends among the musicians and critics, and would often exchange her seat for a better one.

The first time Eeva went to a concert with Magda she was nervous, but there was no need. No one looked at them as if they shouldn't be there. No uniformed official came up to her, pretending to be deferential so as not to disturb the rest of the audience. 'Excuse me, miss, would you mind moving? This is someone's seat.' Eeva sat at Magda's side as if she were the equal of all those calm, serious, professional-looking listeners. This was her life now, her own life that she had earned. These walls, the heat of the stove, the soup she'd made, the books she handled all day and the concert Magda was about to go to: these were all Eeva's life. Sometimes she still couldn't believe it. She caught herself listening for angry voices. *Eeva, Eeva, where've you got to? Why hasn't this floor been swept?*

As soon as the door shut on Magda, Eeva's fear grew. She couldn't settle to mending again. She washed up, dried the plates carefully, and swept the floor. She polished her boots for tomorrow, taking care to rub polish into every inch of the leather, and buff until it shone. One boot would need re-soling soon. She calculated quickly: yes, she'd be able to afford it next week. But soles wore out so quickly. Wouldn't you think that by now they'd have discovered a method of soling shoes that made them last longer? All those boots and all those holes. Rows and rows of them in the orphanage, clumsy boots that cut into soft flesh. Their metal heels and toe-caps struck sparks off the pavement.

Now her boots shone. She couldn't polish them any more. She looked around the room, but there was nothing left to do except her mending.

Or no, there was something. Magda had bought a length of brown velvet, second-hand. It was worn in parts, but the worst parts could be cut out. Their plan was to make curtains, to screen Eeva's bed and give her some privacy. Magda's bed was in an alcove, almost like a separate tiny room, and she had long ago made curtains to screen it. Or rather, Magda had had the curtains made, since she could not sew. Eeva had thought this must be an exaggeration, at first. Surely no girl could have grown up without learning to sew? But Magda had said her mother didn't sew, either. She was a fervent believer in the education of women. She'd wanted Magda to learn Greek and Hebrew as well as Latin, although in fact Magda had preferred philosophy. Besides, they had a maid for the sewing, one of those Bavarian girls who do the most wonderful embroidery.

'Yes, I'll make a start on those curtains,' said Eeva aloud, as if to convince herself that it was a normal evening. But she didn't move. She stood in the middle of the room, her hands at her sides, waiting. It was very quiet. Where was Lauri? Sasha's face swung into her imagination, smiling at her. She heard him say, 'I'm a man of action,' and she saw again the glee and malice that played beneath his skin. His face seemed to ripple with that malice, like the skin of a dead rabbit that was busy inside with flies and maggots. Maybe there was more going on. Perhaps Lauri hadn't told her the full story. Sasha would love it, if he hadn't told her. *I know something you don't know, you don't know, you don't know . . .*

It was nine o'clock now, and Lauri still hadn't come.

27

The room was icy. They sat around the table in their coats and hats, while their breath smoked around them. It was a bare, heavy pine table with dints and knife marks, ingrained with dirt. There was no light apart from a tallow candle on the table. The room smelled of melting tallow. Everywhere was sour and dirty, as if the house had been empty for years.

He and Sasha had come a long way to this bare room. It had taken more than twenty-five minutes, that was for sure. Even quite recently, this area would have been a village with its own life, separate from the city. Probably, when Lauri was a kid, it had been one of those places you strolled out to on summer evenings. He'd probably scuffled barefoot through the warm dust in the lane that ran between the houses. He couldn't remember. But the expansion of Helsinki had already opened its mouth to swallow up these wooden houses. Soon there wouldn't be a trace left.

A few candles burned in windows, but most were empty and black. No doubt the land had already been bought by developers, and the houses were waiting to be torn down and replaced by stone apartment buildings. It was lucky that there was a moon, because there were no street lamps out here. The moonlight lay blue on the snowy ground. He and Sasha picked their way across disused vegetable plots. They ducked under lines where washing once hung. A piece of cloth had been left on one – just a rag – and it hung stiff with ice. The ground was frozen hard, and no one had swept the snow from the lanes and paths.

The house was at the far end of the village. It was a good house, with a small verandah. No light showed in the windows, but Sasha seemed sure it was the right place. An old sign still hung, to show that the house had belonged to a leather-worker. Why hadn't he taken his sign with him? Perhaps he had died, Lauri thought.

The front door was open, but they walked into darkness. The air had a cold, close, musty smell.

'Are you sure this is right, Sasha?'

'They'll be upstairs.'

They felt their way along the wall towards the staircase. Suddenly a door above opened, and light appeared on the landing. It wasn't much, but compared to the blank darkness it was enough. There was the staircase. The rail had been taken away, and Lauri tested each stair before putting his weight on it, in case the wood was rotten. Sasha followed, stepping confidently. No doubt he'd been here before.

And now they were in the upstairs room. Why was the stove not lit? It was a good stove, with logs stacked beside it. Lauri noticed that the edges of the logs were freshly cut. They must have been brought here recently, perhaps even tonight. So why not burn them? Maybe these people didn't want smoke rising from the chimney. They didn't want anyone to feel the stove and know from its warmth that people had been there recently. But why come all the way out here anyway? There were plenty of comrades' rooms where they could hold a meeting and be welcome, and warm too.

It didn't feel right. None of it felt right. He didn't know any of these men. Three of them were Russians, the 'comrades from Petersburg' that Sasha was on about, presumably. There was a Swede, pale, with a nose so thin it looked as if someone had ironed it. He nodded at Sasha and Lauri, examined them for a moment, then walked out of the room and did not return. Lauri listened to his tread going down the wooden stairs, but couldn't tell if the front door opened or not. Maybe there was another room down-stairs, with people sitting round another table, waiting. He didn't like the thought of that.

One of the Russians stood aloof by the cold stove, swinging his arms, chapping them against his body as if to warm it.

Sasha and Lauri sat down in the places left for them. Sasha seemed to have separated himself from Lauri somehow. He didn't introduce him. He seemed to slide into the group of Russians, and to belong to them. As if he'd simply brought Lauri along, and now had no further connection with him. Well, why shouldn't he be with the Russians, Lauri reasoned with himself. They were Sasha's people.

These chairs were uncomfortable. Too low for the table, that was it. No, the problem was that the chairs were of different heights, and Lauri found himself sitting low down. The chairs didn't belong to the table, and must have been brought here, like the logs. So perhaps this place was often used for meetings, then? No, probably not. There must still be a few old people clinging on in their houses until the building work began in the spring. Old people noticed everything, just as kids did.

His thoughts seemed to be flying everywhere, unable to settle. Get a grip, he told himself. What does it matter who lives here or who used to live here? But he could not shake off an uneasy awareness of the empty houses, the vegetable plots where nothing would be grown again, the fruit trees that were waiting to be chopped down.

One of the men around the table took out a cigarette furtively, as if afraid that others would want one if they saw the packet. He smoked through his gloved fist, not letting the cigarette touch his mouth. Rich blue smoke trickled through his glove and into the room.

'This is the man I told you about,' said Sasha in Russian at last, indicating Lauri. One by one, faces turned to him, but he couldn't see them clearly. The candle was guttering, and their eyes were in the shadow of their hats. Their mouths were hidden by drawn-up collars. It irritated him not to know their names, but he wasn't going to ask. It seemed to him that people should tell one another their names.

'Isn't there another candle?'

Silently, one of the men rose, felt in his coat pocket and brought out several wax candles. He lit one from the dying candle, and crushed its hard wax stub into the puddle of tallow.

But why not light good candles in the first place, if you'd got them? It was all crazy, perverse. Wood that didn't warm you, candles that didn't light you.

That man with the candles: his coat was magnificent. You could see it fully when he stood. Fine thick wool, the sort that keeps out damp as well as cold. Fur cuffs and collar. Fox fur, like the hat he was wearing.

'Aleksandr Kirillovich, as we were saying,' said the smallest of the Russians in a sharp, irritable voice, 'this man is not known to us.'

'His credentials are impeccable,' answered Sasha smoothly, 'im-pecc-able. I've already told him about Bobrikov.'

'What about Bobrikov?' asked the man in the fox-fur hat. Quality fur, expensive, Lauri could tell that right away. The fur glistened in the candlelight. The man looked as if he belonged in a different world. By nature he would never be found in a house like this.

'That the Swede's pulled out,' said Sasha. 'He knows all about it, don't you, Lauri?'

Lauri nodded. He felt like a bull Sasha had brought to market for them to look over before they decided to buy it. But he wasn't going to lumber up and down at their bidding. All this was going too fast for him. Everything was was pushing him back towards Bobrikov. Bobrikov, Bobrikov, Bobrikov. *About-to-die Bobrikov. Allowed-to-live-a-little-longer Bobrikov.* There was no getting away from him.

'We'll find another Swede,' said the man in the fox-fur hat. 'There's always another Swede.'

There was a grunt of laughter. Lauri knew that laughter. It defined things, said who you were and who you weren't, made you part of the group. But this time, Lauri didn't laugh. Whatever these men were part of, he did not belong to it.

What was he thinking of? He was always too quick to judge people. Sasha was his friend.

'And is your friend still willing, when we find the next Swede?'

Suddenly Lauri was sick of it. He spoke Russian, didn't he? Maybe not so well, maybe he sounded like what he was, but he could make himself understood.

'I might be willing,' he said, 'if I knew what "willing" meant.' His fists were on the table, and they were all looking at him. If only their eyes weren't in shadow. Eyes and mouths tell you what you need to know.

'Willing to do what's necessary,' said the man in the fox-fur hat.

'Necessary,' Lauri repeated. Every word struck him suddenly not as a thing made out of air, but as something that might be a weapon. 'But who says what's necessary?'

'The decision has already been taken.'

'Yes, but you see, I don't know about that.'

'The decision has been taken in the proper manner and after due discussion,' said the man in the fox-fur hat, a shade of the master in his voice. 'It's time to move on.'

'Move on . . .' Lauri repeated slowly. His fists were tense. He was angry, yes, that was it. But he mustn't show it. He might tell himself he was among friends, but his body knew the truth. It was wary, watching, waiting, ready to defend itself. His body knew more than he'd let himself know in his head, he thought, looking at his bunched fists. He had got to look out for himself here. There was Sasha, looking away, detached, as if Lauri was none of his business.

'But don't you agree?' said the small Russian, leaning into the candlelight. To Lauri's surprise he had switched to Finnish. Good, fluent Finnish, better even than Sasha's. 'Don't you agree,' he went on in his quick, emphatic voice, 'about the necessity? Surely we've established the value of removing this one individual?'

'Just the one, is it?' said Lauri. 'Just the one and that'll do it?'

The small man threw off a smile.

'No one man is as important as that, not even Bobrikov,' he said, caressing the name with his tongue. 'Let's not deceive ourselves. There is plenty of work to be done.'

'So there'll be others, after Bobrikov. Is that what you're saying?'

The man in the fox-fur hat clicked his tongue impatiently. The small Russian put out his hand calmingly. 'Let's not deceive ourselves,' he repeated, fixing his gaze on Lauri. There was a tone in his voice that Lauri hadn't noticed before. 'To remove an individual is one thing. To use terror correctly is quite another, and requires the gift of timing as well as that of acting decisively. Terror must contain an element of the random if it is to be effective; that is, it must not be predictable. But terror must also be educational.'

'How do you mean, educational?'

'The successful political application of terror teaches those in power that they are not secure. It teaches those without power that the system which oppresses them is not invulnerable. Most importantly, it teaches that *we* are not like *them*. We do not apply their rules to our own behaviour. The less we apply those rules, the greater our strength becomes. So, ideally, we would choose to kill Bobrikov naked in his bath. But in his case there are operational reasons for doing otherwise.'

Naked in his bath. Lauri could not prevent himself from seeing Bobrikov sitting in the sauna, his skin glistening with sweat, his haunches spread on the slatted shelves. But the sauna was a place where a man should never be disturbed.

'Why in his bath? Why not in the street?'

'You'd prefer that? Maybe you'd allow him a weapon of his choice, to make it fair?' chided the small Russian. 'No. No, no, no, no, no. That's not how it happens any more. The world has changed, my friend. We have moved on from all that. Listen. Imagine that our man – let's not call him Bobrikov, let's call him by another name, just for the sake of argument. Aleksandr, that'll do.

'Aleksandr's riding along a forest path. He's been hunting, he's got his companions along with him, his not-very-effective bodyguard, all the usual suspects. The horses have had a long day and they're trotting slowly, in single file because the path is narrow just here. Suddenly a young woman appears at the side of the path. She calls out to him, "Your honour! Excellency! Little Father!" and she's holding a baby in her arms. A fine, fat future citizen. And she's a beautiful young woman so the whole picture is enchanting and even our friend – Aleksandr – can't resist it. He slows right down, and as he does so the beautiful young woman pulls out a pistol from the baby's long clothes and shoots him in the head.'

'A woman with a baby wouldn't do that.'

'But don't you see, that's exactly the point? She *wouldn't* do it, but she *does* do it. Or maybe she throws a bomb, at close range, so that she and the baby are caught in the blast and killed. But our friend Aleksandr is killed, too, and his useless bodyguards along with him.'

Slowly, Lauri shook his head. 'Such things don't happen.'

As he spoke he saw the young mother as the Russian had described her. But she had Eeva's face, and the baby locked in her arms, hidden in the folds of a shawl, was his own flesh and blood.

'No mother would agree to such a thing.'

'Aha! *Aha!* You still don't see. That's precisely why terror is effective, because it's composed of things that don't happen and can't possibly happen. And that is why the most effective acts of terror can never be foreseen.'

There was a long silence. The small Russian leaned back in his chair again. He put his hands together in a steeple, and rested his chin on them while he looked at Lauri from under his brows. They were all looking at him now. They wanted their answer, that's what he was here for. They wanted to know if he'd be part of it. But why did it all matter so much? He was unimportant. All they wanted him for was to create a diversion in the street. Shout and wave a stick about, that's what Sasha had said. Or was there more? Yes, surely that was it. They wanted more of him. They would never have brought him here, and let him listen to so much, unless there was more.

Sasha leaned forward. His face at last was visible. He looked relaxed, although there was sweat on his forehead. But the room was cold, icy cold. If Lauri once let himself shiver he would shake all over and he wouldn't be able to stop. However, he was not going to give way.

'All right, Lauri?' Sasha asked softly, as if they were alone. Lauri made no response. How had he got here, to this room? He knew Helsinki like the back of his hand but he had taken one turning too many this time. The woman with the baby? No, it was impossible. Sasha would have to see that it was impossible. They'd kill Bobrikov, but it wouldn't finish there. Bobrikov would only be the first step. If terror was as the small Russian had said – *educational* – then where did the lesson stop?

Yes, he was cold. Not only from the chill of the room but from fear. *Don't ever waste time asking yourself why you feel fear,* his father had taught him long ago, *act on it. Fear's there for a purpose, except if you're a coward, which I know you're not.*

Fear was there all right. They were watching him, all of them. They had formed a solid group, with Sasha a part of it. What chance had he of getting out of this room, if he made a break for it? What chance of walking back across those vegetable plots, unless they felt sure of him now? Just as he'd thought, the man in the fox-fur hat had risen, and was drifting towards the door, right hand in his pocket.

'I'm willing,' said Lauri. 'If there's no other way.'

'If there's no other way,' repeated the small Russian. *'If there's no other way.* What can you mean by that?'

'Only what I say.' Lauri held his ground. Best not to seem too pliable all of a sudden. They wouldn't credit it.

The fox-fur hat whistled under his breath and looked at Sasha. 'Oh dear, oh dear, oh dear,' he said. But the small Russian jumped up, and slammed the table with the flat of his gloved hand. Even as he did it Lauri thought it looked wrong, somehow. Stagey, as if he didn't believe in what he was doing.

'This is impossible!' he said rapidly, stammering a little. The calm had gone from his voice. He was speaking Russian now. 'It is absolutely impossible and out of the question that we can be talking like this. Bobrikov is to be disposed of and that is already decided without further argument. We have already moved on from that. Is it not the case? Eh? Is it not the case?'

'It is the case,' said Sasha.

'Then why are we wasting our time in discussion?'

Wasting our time. But was he really angry? No, thought Lauri, he's working himself up to be angry. It's the same thing as saying 'terror is educational'. None of it is real.

But Lauri recognized that even if the man was not really angry, he would still do everything that an angry man would do. Lauri took a deep breath. His body tingled with the life it wanted to keep, the life that was his and no one else's. He would get out of this dead room, out of this dying village. He would get back to Eeva. He would make them trust him, and believe he was one of them, and then he would get out.

'I see,' said Lauri slowly. A phrase that he'd heard at some meeting fell into his mouth. 'It's what history demands of us. And it's our – our role –' he went on, finding just the right words again, as if an angel were sitting on his tongue. 'Yes, I recognize that we must each play our part – in providing the answers that history demands.'

The small Russian nodded eagerly, like a good teacher whose pupil had finally come up with the right answer. 'Exactly. *Ex-act-ly*. But at the correct time, and under the correct conditions. We can't afford any more amateurs.' His voice rapped like a knuckle on wood.

'I'm no amateur,' said Lauri. 'I'm the real thing. Ask Sasha,' and he nodded and grinned towards Sasha in a way that felt as false as everything else that had been said and done in that room.

But the small Russian took it for real. His face relaxed, and, as if he'd given a signal, the tension in the room fell away. Sasha leaned towards Lauri, claiming him again, and clapped him on the back. Lauri smelled the used-up alcohol seeping through Sasha's skin.

'He's the real thing, all right,' said Sasha. Then he pointed his first two fingers, pulled an imaginary trigger and puffed out his lips. 'Bang!' said Sasha. 'Bang, bang, they're dead.'

The man in the fox-fur hat shook his head impatiently. 'Really, Aleksandr Kirillovich.'

'But that's what it's all about.' Sasha's face was brilliant with glee. He pulled off his glove, put out a finger and whipped it through the candle flame. A smudge of carbon bloomed on the skin. Sasha examined it closely, lifting his finger to his nose and sniffing the singed hairs. Then he moved his finger back into the flame, slowly, slowly, drawing it to the left and then to the right. A small noise came from deep in his throat.

'Sasha, for God's sake!'

'One small bang and it's all done,' said Sasha. 'Everybody happy?'

He put the glove back on his hand, and stood up. The stench of burned skin hit Lauri's nostrils. Sasha swayed a little, because of the burn or because of the drink still working in him. He steadied himself, holding the chair back. 'Goodnight, gentlemen,' he went on, 'until we meet again. Come on, Lauri, time to go.'

'I'll find my own way,' Lauri said. He didn't want to say Eeva's name in this company. 'I've got to meet someone.'

'I brought you here, remember. You'd never have found it otherwise.'

'Try me,' said Lauri.

'All right, then. Do without me. See where it gets you,' and without waiting for Lauri he flung out of the room. The Russians looked at one another, weighing what had happened. Their shadow heads nodded on the walls. How small they looked, hunkering under their shadows, Lauri thought. But in spite of its coldness the room was oppressive, full of dead air and sweat and fear. He had got to get out, before he took another breath.

28

She thought it was Magda come back, but it was him at last. She sprang to the door and opened it. Lauri shambled into the room, head down, blank, exhausted.

'What happened? Where've you been? What's wrong?'

''Mall right. Cold, that's all.'

His face was sallow purple. She touched his cheek. 'Give me your hands. But Lauri, you're freezing! No, don't sit by the stove, that's not good when you're so cold. Come over here, onto the bed.'

He sat down heavily on the side of her bed. She knelt and began to undo his boots.

'I thought you'd be here hours ago.'

'I couldn't find my way.'

'You couldn't find your way,' she repeated, trying to make sense of it. It wasn't possible that Lauri could lose himself in his own city, on a clear night. He wasn't even drunk. But he looked starved with cold, as if he'd been wandering the streets for hours.

She eased off his boots and woollen socks, and began to rub his bare feet. He had holes in his socks, too. 'You'll be lucky if you've not got frostbite. What were you thinking of?'

'I was at a meeting,' he said heavily. 'One of those meetings, you know, when you don't know where it's to be held until they take you there.'

She nodded. She knew about those meetings, all right, and she was beginning to have a feeling towards them which wasn't distrust or dislike but more like an immense weariness, as if she'd been waiting all her life for something that never quite happened. She held Lauri's right foot between her hands. He had big feet, and was always having trouble with his boots. She remembered how Mika had despaired as Lauri's toes burst through yet another pair of boots, when they were children. But it had been good for her. She'd had a line-up of Lauri's old boots, waiting for her.

More gently now, she rubbed his toes.

'Then after I left the meeting I seemed to go off walking into nowhere,' Lauri went on. She couldn't see his face. 'Like I'd never seen the streets before. By the time I came to myself I was miles away.'

'Were you with him? Sasha?'

'He was at the meeting.'

His voice sounded thick, as if his tongue was too big for his mouth.

'I knew it. That Sasha,' she said, under her breath. She rubbed his feet more vigorously. 'So he was the one who took you there.'

'So cold,' he mumbled. 'It's got right into me.'

'Open your coat and let the warmth in.'

But he fumbled with the buttons and she had to help him undo them and then pull the heavy coat open.

'That's better. How do your feet feel now?' she asked, chafing them again. 'I could go down and get some snow to rub them with.'

'It's not that bad. They're not frostbitten.' His hands were on his thighs, his weight pushed down on them. 'I'm starting to feel something now.'

Burning and prickling, sensation crawled back into his flesh. He shifted one foot, then the other.

'How are they now?'

'On fire.'

'That's good. That's the blood coming back into them. What about your hands?'

'They're all right. Give me a minute, Eevi, don't rub any more.'

The warmth of the room pulsed over him in waves. It felt good, like getting drunk, but his feet fizzed and burned until he had to get up and stamp the pain out of them. There, that was better. He sank back on the bed. She hadn't moved. She was still kneeling there, her head bowed as if she was mourning. He saw the pale line of the parting in her hair. She looked up at him and smiled.

'Better?' she asked.

'Yes, better.'

Her smile was so young and warm and full of life. It was crazy that a few moments ago he'd thought she might be crying.

'You could get into the bed,' she said, 'only Magda'll be back any minute now.'

He sighed deeply. There was nothing he wanted more. To lie beside Eeva, both of them warm with each other's warmth. Drowsing – sleeping – waking – touching . . . He hadn't the energy even to touch her now, but in the middle of the night he would wake and be strong again and full of hunger for her.

'I wish we had somewhere to be,' he said.

'I know.'

'A room where nobody else comes.'

'Yes.'

'Where we can lock the door,' he went on, thinking so intently that he could almost see his own key, and how it would fit into the lock of the room he shared with Eeva alone. How powerfully he did not want to go back to the room he shared with Sasha. He did not want to smell Sasha beside him in the bed. He did not want to feel Sasha's weight pressing down into the hollow of the shared mattress.

'I need to get a place of my own,' he said.

'Can you afford it?'

He smiled faintly, and shook his head. But together we could. Together it would be possible, with both our wages, he thought. But it was too early to say anything like that. Eeva believed he was tied to Sasha, and maybe that was true. And Magda was her friend . . . Magda had done a lot for Eeva. But why did that thought make him feel a pang of resentment, rather than gratitude? It was all too much to think of now. All he wanted was to lie down, to sleep . . .

'I made a meal for us,' she said, getting up. 'I can heat the stew now, and cook the dumplings. It won't have spoiled.'

'No, wait.' He took her hand and drew her down to sit beside him. 'Stay here. This is nice.'

Nice. She smelled clean. She had washed her hair, and little tendrils were slipping out of the knot, tickling his neck. A shiver ran down his body. Maybe he was not so exhausted after all.

'You haven't even taken your coat off properly,' she pointed out.

'I told you before, I'm not very cultured,' he said.

'Take it off, though. It smells funny. As if you've been sitting in a graveyard.'

He stood up, and let his coat fall on the floor. 'This meeting was in an empty building,' he said. 'There wasn't any heating, and it smelled as if something was rotting somewhere, but very slowly, because of the cold. Maybe a cat had got trapped in one of the rooms.'

'Who was there?'

'They were mostly from Petersburg. There was a Swede as well, but he didn't stay. I'm not sure what he was there for. What a face. He could have chopped wood with his nose.'

She listened to the trouble in his voice. 'Was the meeting about what you were telling me before?'

He saw that she didn't want to name Bobrikov directly. He sat down on the bed again, and put his arm around her shoulders.

'That's right.'

'You didn't agree?'

'I said what I had to say, because there were five of them and one of me.'

'So you told them you were going to take part?'

'Not in so many words.' He shifted his feet again, stamping them gently on the floor, first the right and then the left.

She had tensed in the circle of his arm. 'They won't let you pull out now. If you try they'll find a way of stopping you.'

'You don't need to tell me that. I've seen them. I know how they *operate*,' he added, putting one of Sasha's favourite words into his own mouth.

'But what'll they do?'

'I don't know. I've got to think. But the truth is, Eevi, I didn't agree. Not when it came to it.'

'You don't know what they might do,' she said quietly.

He had a sudden, vivid picture of a hole in the Baltic ice. Two

271

men dragging a body, bumping it over the rough surface. A third chipping away at the film of fresh ice that had grown over the hole. So far out from shore that they'd be dots to anyone who could be bothered to look seawards. They'd look like a group of men going ice-fishing. Slide a man under the ice and he won't be seen until spring.

'Anyway it's all my own fault,' he said, as if to himself. 'All of it. I got myself into it. But I still don't understand how we got here, to this point. I mean, I agreed with everything we were doing. You've got to educate, you've got to organize, you won't get anywhere without solidarity. And you've got to take risks. It's not a picnic on a summer day,' he said, and then remembered that was one of Sasha's expressions. He wouldn't use any more of Sasha's expressions. Even if his own words weren't as good, they were better, somehow. 'Yes, you do have to take risks,' he went on. 'Lose your job, be blacklisted, maybe imprisoned, get beaten up by the police . . . That's all part of it. We know all that. It's what we grew up with.

'But everything's changed so fast. You go from *here*,' he stabbed a finger on one thigh, 'to *here*,' he stabbed the other, 'and you might as well have flown through the air for all you know about how you made the journey. They were talking about killing him in his bath. Naked. How that would be better. And about women blowing up their own babies. And I thought, how did we get here? Surely I never agreed to this? But I suppose Sasha would say that was political naivety.'

'No, he would say it was pol-it-ic-al nai-eev-tay,' said Eeva tartly. 'I wish you'd never met Sasha.'

He didn't reply.

'So you've decided? You're not going to be part of it?'

'I've decided . . . but *can* I decide, Eevi? That's the thing. Is there still room for me to decide? Sasha – and the others – they think I'm committed.'

'Do you want to be?'

He thought of the house that had formerly belonged to the leather-worker. It would have been full of tools and the smell of leather, and people coming and going, wanting bits of harness mended, or a new stitching on a saddle. A man like that would serve the whole village, and farms for miles around. But the leatherworker was gone and his house was empty. Those men – Sasha's friends – they met in it like ghosts.

I know everything about what they want to destroy, Lauri thought. But I don't know much about what they will put in its place.

'So they still think you're in on it?' asked Eeva.

He shrugged. 'I suppose so. I don't know any of the details. Nothing was said. Only that he's going to be . . . got rid of. The Swede who was going to fire the gun, he backed out, but they'll find another. Maybe they've already found another.'

'At least they're not thinking of teaching you to shoot,' she said. A bubble of laughter broke from them both.

'They'd be waiting a long time,' he said. 'But they've got more in mind for me than they had before, I'm sure of that. A more important *role*,' he added, emphasizing the word that was Sasha's.

'Does Sasha know, do you think?'

He shrugged again. 'It's beyond me. I can't make it out. I'm not even sure that they –'

'That they what?'

'Trust Sasha.' He wouldn't tell her about Sasha burning his own skin, and the smell of it in the room, or the way the man in the fox-fur hat had wrinkled his nose fastidiously, as if Sasha had farted in the middle of a handsome dinner.

She sat there thinking. At last she said, 'The trouble is that you've already heard too much. And you've seen them all? Their faces and everything?'

'Yes.'

'And they're not people we know?'

'None of them. The only one of them I knew was Sasha.'

'Did you hear their names?'

'No one gave any names.' It was so. He'd noticed it at the time and he hadn't liked it. The Russians hadn't even addressed each other by name and patronymic. The man in the fox-fur hat and the small Russian had called Sasha 'Aleksandr Kirillovich'. But of course Lauri had known Sasha's name already. The Swede had gone out without a word.

'They were high-ups, then.' She pondered for a while. 'Isn't it strange,' she observed,' how everything comes out like that? Every organization has its own high-ups, its own order, even if it starts out without one. I suppose you can't get away from it –'

'They rise to the top like cream,' said Lauri, thinking of the Russian in his fine wool coat with its fox-fur cuffs and collar. 'One lot of cream replaces another.'

'No,' she said with a passion that startled him. 'That's not true. Cream rises, because it's in its nature to do that. But people don't just rise like that. They claw their way up, and then they trample on those who are beneath them. There are some who'd claw their way to the top over a pile of corpses.'

They were both silent for a while. At last he said, 'I suppose you're right. But the thing is that I still feel I'm letting them down.'

'Who?'

'Oh, not *them*. Not that lot at the meeting. But all my mates. People like Hannu and Eero and Fedya, and everybody else. The ones who come to political education, and give out leaflets in the factories even though they'll lose their jobs if they get caught. And they'll put their hands in their pockets for a man who's sick or out of work. They think together, they don't always think separately, about themselves. And that's what we've got to do, isn't it? *They're* the ones I'm thinking of.'

'I'm not sure, Eevi, and that's the truth. Am I letting them down? Because in the end maybe that little Russian is right and I'm wrong. I don't like what he said, but maybe there's no other way. You have to –' his teeth clenched into what looked like an angry smile – 'you have to *break eggs*. Because if you don't, it all goes on for ever in the same way. Suffering. Injustices. That same as what happened to you, Eeva. The way they carted you off. Haven't we got to fight them? What would your father think of us, or mine? We can't shut the door and live behind it. Not even if we had a room, and our own door.'

She frowned, concentrating. The look on her face made him remember how she would read and study by candlelight, all those years ago. She'd set up her little card table and work away, and everyone respected it. There was force in Eeva, there always had been. Men who visited her father would stop behind her chair and maybe touch her shoulder. 'That's right, you keep at it. That's the way. She's a proper scholar, your Eeva, isn't she?' they'd remark to Pekka.

'That's true,' said Eeva. 'You can't shut the door, not if it means pretending that things aren't what they are. You don't have to . . . to abandon the struggle,' she went on, consciously using one of the phrases that always made her feel as if she had cloth in her mouth. 'I'm not asking you to do that. But you have to preserve yourself, too.'

'You mean, save my own skin. Put myself and my blessed conscience first,' he said bitterly.

'No, I don't mean that. *Preserve yourself* – I mean, keep yourself what you are. Because if you're no longer yourself, you're not Lauri any more, then what use can you be to anyone? What's the point of the new world you've made? Look at Sasha. He's not right, is he? *Nothing's* real with him. Deep down he's watching and laughing at everything. Don't you feel it?'

'Maybe,' he answered reluctantly.

'You don't have to agree with me. I know he's your friend.'

'Yes.'

He sat brooding.

'Maybe our lives aren't the important ones,' he said at last. 'We sink down into the mud. We betray ourselves until there's only our bones left. But maybe it all happens for a reason. We sink down into the mud, so that those who are to come can build on us. We're like a – like a foundation.'

'You can't think that,' she said. She came in close to him and the smell of her hair and skin filled his senses. 'You can't think that we don't matter, when this is our only life.'

'Yes.'

'And when you're everything . . .'

'What?'

He turned to face her, looked hungrily into her dark, light-filled eyes.

'You're everything, to me.'

'Eevi –'

'It's true.'

His eyes prickled, burning just as his feet had burned while the blood came back into them. Her words echoed in his head. *Our only life. Our only life.* Yes, that was what it was. He was here, with Eevi, living his only life.

He leaned towards her, and touched her lips with his. They barely moved, barely kissed. How soft her lips were, full and a little dry with winter. She'd closed her eyes.

Neither of them moved. They seemed to have grown together, as if their lips joined and spoke for their whole bodies. How much time passed then he never knew, and never could guess.

She stirred and moved away from him, smoothing down her hair with both hands.

'Sasha,' she said. 'I've worked out what it is about him. You know when you were talking about our fathers? They were working to an end, like you said. Educating people, getting them to organize, improve working conditions, living conditions – all that was what we grew up with.'

'They were doing a bit more than that. It wasn't all roses.'

'I know. But what I'm saying is that for them, political activism was a means to an end. For Sasha it's an end in itself. He wants things to be overthrown, to dissolve. That's what he likes – no, it's what he *needs*. Everything falling apart.'

'But don't things have to fall apart, so that they can be put together differently?'

'Maybe. Maybe. I don't know. I'm not explaining myself properly. What I mean is that for Sasha the falling apart is *the whole point of it*. It's what he wants, what he longs for. The putting together bit doesn't really interest him at all, although he has to pretend it does.'

'You're making him sound like an Anarchist, but he's not.'

'He's not anything, don't you see? He just wants chaos. That's why he steals. He's got no call to steal. Why don't *you* steal? Why don't I steal? God knows we've needed things badly enough, and haven't had them. And wanted them.'

'Because we don't want to get caught.'

'It isn't only that. I can't see you coming into our bookshop and slipping a book under your coat and walking out with it. I just can't picture it.'

'I couldn't be bothered with all that.'

'No. But what I'm afraid of is that for Sasha, killing could be the same as stealing. There'll always be a reason for it, a very important reason. He's so convincing. He'll almost make himself believe that whoever gets murdered, it's done because it has to be done.

'You must have heard him going on about surgeons cutting a cancer out of a body. But the truth is that any killing Sasha's involved in won't have anything to do with cancer or surgeons. It'll be done *because he wants to do it*. And that's what he wants to drag you into.'

'Let's not talk about it any more now, Eevi.'

She got up, picked his coat off the floor, and brushed it with her hand.

'I wish you had a better coat. Look at this.'

'It's all right.'

'I'm going to sew more padding into it. Look how thin it is here – and here – all worn away –'

'You've enough to do, leave it.'

'I'd like to do it.'

She smiled, holding the coat to her. 'I've always liked sewing. In the House of Orphans, I used to make pinafores for the little ones. The thing was, when you were sewing you were sitting down, and close to the stove as well, because your fingers have to be warm to sew quickly. Otherwise you get stiff fingers, you see, and you don't go so fast. Anna-Liisa knew that. She was very practical in those ways. One of the girls told me when I arrived: "Say you can sew."'

'But Lauri, you haven't had anything to eat. I'll heat the stew.'

'Have you eaten?'

'Not yet.'

She opened out the little table that she and Magda used for coffee. It looked exactly the same as the card table she used to study at, years ago.

'Did this come from your father?'

She looked surprised. 'No, I've nothing of his except some books. All this stuff is Magda's. She even gave me a set of sheets.'

'You get on well with her, don't you?' he said rather gloomily.

'Sometimes I don't like her all that much. But it doesn't matter. She's the sort of person you love rather than like.'

He was silent, shocked. Surely he'd never even heard Eeva say she loved her own father.

'Look at her tonight,' went on Eeva. 'It's way past the time she should be back from the concert. She'll have gone off to stay with a friend somewhere, because she knows you're coming here. And she's quite jealous of you in a funny way. I don't know why.'

'Like Sasha.'

'No, not like Sasha. Exactly not like Sasha, and that's the point. Magda's a bit jealous, and we both know it, but tomorrow she'll pretend she bumped into an old friend she hadn't seen for a long time, and they couldn't stop talking so they went back to drink coffee or whatever. She'll even say she hopes I wasn't worried. All that, just so that I won't feel she's made a sacrifice for me.'

'Not such a great sacrifice, spending a night at a friend's.'

'No, maybe not. And Magda's friends are well-off, some of them, they have spare rooms and everything. I'm not saying she's perfect. But she's kind, Lauri, she really is kind. It's the same with all this stuff. This furniture and everything. You wouldn't guess it was Magda's. She really believes that sheets and tables and cups belong to those who need to use them. No, that's not it – what it is: she doesn't even think about believing it or not believing it.'

'That's nice,' said Lauri. Eeva laughed.

'I know, now *you're* jealous.'

'I'm not jealous! What should I be jealous of?'

'I'm not saying you've got anything to be jealous about, only that you are. I'll get the stew for you. Those dumplings should be ready by now.'

The beef stew had grown thicker, richer, stickier. The vegetables were almost dissolved into it. But she'd cooked the dumplings fresh, and they were the best he'd ever tasted, he told her. So light.

'I put a lot of parsley in them.'

Yes, now he could taste it. A sharp green scent. He sopped the last of his dumpling in gravy and swallowed it. Immediately she was on her feet to bring more.

'Don't you need to keep some for tomorrow?'

'No.' She scraped the pot onto his plate. 'Magda ate before she went out, so I don't need to leave any for her.'

'But what about for yourself?'

'I'm eating well. Look at me.'

'It's true. You look well.'

'We cook every day. We sit down together and talk and eat. The food seems to do you good that way. I had as much as I wanted at the doctor's house, but I always ate on my own. You don't have the appetite for it when you're alone.'

'I like to eat with you,' he said.

She blushed a little, and said quickly, 'We can't always rise to beef stew and dumplings.'

'You know I didn't mean that. I meant, to be with you. To eat with you sitting at the other side of the table.'

She dropped her gaze. Now they were shy with each other as if they'd never lain naked in bed together. He'd thought that with a girl when you moved forward, you stayed there, but it seemed that this was different. Sometimes you found yourself back where you'd been before, wanting to touch but not feeling you had the right. He bent over his plate, finished the last of the stew, and wiped the plate with bread.

'It's very late,' she said in a neutral voice.

'Yes, it must be.'

Did she understand that he could not bear to go out there again? To leave the circle of warmth and light and put on his socks, his boots, all the layers that tried to keep the cold out. But no matter how hard you tried it crept in and froze you. He could not bear to walk away from her house, down the late, quiet streets, to the room he shared with Sasha.

'Magda won't come back now. It's too late,' she said.

He reached towards her left hand, which was lying on the table. The sleeve of her dress was rolled back, because she'd been cooking. Gently, he turned her hand over. The skin of her wrist was beautiful.

'If I met you after twenty years and I only saw this much of your hand,' he said, putting his fingers an inch apart, 'I'd know it was you.'

She shivered. 'Don't say that.'

'Why not? It's true. I would know you.'

'I don't like thinking about it.'

He stroked her skin where the blue came up near the surface.

'I couldn't do without you,' he said very quietly, so she hardly heard him. But soft though the words were, she was sure of them.

She saw it all lying in front of them. It was like walking out of the forest onto the shore of a huge lake. There they were, blinking in sudden light, with all their days ahead of them.

'Yes,' she said, and took his hand, raised it to her face and gently bit his knuckles. Suddenly she thought of the doctor, walking alone with his head down, lost in thought, his shoulders a little bowed. But when he caught sight of her, his face would open into a smile that made her feel older than him. A smile that had something naked and timid in it, and changed his face completely. He hadn't been the master then.

Her forehead contracted. She screwed her eyes shut. No, she wasn't going to think of the doctor. He had had his life.

'What is it?'

'Nothing. Lauri, don't tell Sasha.'

'Don't tell him what?'

'What you told me. That you aren't going to go on with it.'

'He's got to know sometime.'

'Not yet. There's no telling what he might do. Those others mustn't know.'

They both sat silent, thinking of it. For some reason all Lauri could call to mind was Sasha laughing. His eyes shining like toffee, his lips moist, the points of his teeth gleaming.

'Hush!' said Eeva sharply. 'Did you hear something?'

He listened. From the landing there came a faint scuffle.

'There!'

'Is it Magda coming back?'

'I don't know.'

She was standing, one hand on the back of the chair, listening.

'Aren't you going to open the door?'

'Magda's got her key.' She was whispering. 'She wouldn't stand outside the door like that. Lauri, I don't think it's her.'

'Who else could it be at this time?'

'I don't know.'

'All right. I'm going to look.'

'Don't! Don't! Please don't, Lauri. They'll know you're here.'

The back of his neck hackled. 'I'm opening it. If there's anybody there, he'll get more than he bargained for.'

'No.' She seized his arm, holding him back. 'You don't know who it might be. Wait. Listen.'

There was no further sound. Absolute stillness, as if whoever was outside the door was waiting and listening too. And then Lauri was sure that he heard the faintest padding, like the footsteps of someone who has taken off his boots, going away from the door, across the landing, down the stairs.

'Lauri! Don't!'

But he had crossed the room, and wrenched the door open. The landing was dark, empty. The stairs ran away into the shadows of the stairwell. Below, he heard the muffled thud of the apartment building's outer door. He turned back into the room.

'You were right,' he said calmly, 'there was somebody there, but he's gone now. Don't worry. It was nothing.'

She didn't answer. Her hands were like claws, ready to gouge the air. It had happened to her before, and he remembered every instant of it, when they had arrested his father, and taken Eeva away.

'It was nothing,' he repeated. 'Come on, let's go to bed.'

'If they came for me again,' she said, 'I wouldn't let them take me, no matter what. I should have fought. I used to lie in bed in the House of Orphans and think about it. *I should have fought.*'

'Then I should have fought too. But we weren't strong enough.'

'I didn't even try. I should have used my teeth, my nails. I wasn't that weak. But I couldn't do it. I was frozen. I just let them take me away.'

'For God's sake, Eeva, it wasn't your fault.'

'We let things be done to us. But never again,' said Eeva. 'No matter what happens. Never, never, never again.'

29

Dear Dr Eklund
I am writing to you in the hope that you can help me. I know there is
no reason why you should want to do this, but I have to ask, because
you are the only person of importance whom I know.

He'd recognized her handwriting as soon as he'd taken up the
envelope. Her confident, educated hand, so much stronger than
Minna's.

I have a good job now, and a place to live. Please don't think that I am
asking you for money. I am approaching you on behalf of my friend,
who has been arrested.
He has done nothing wrong. You can be sure of that. He has not
committed any crime. But the way things are these days, it is possible
to be arrested for less than nothing. You'll understand that I don't want
to write too much about it.
Is it possible for you to come to Helsinki, so that I can explain every-
thing to you face to face? Believe me, I know that I have no right to ask
this. I have nothing to offer you in return.

She had signed her name. And then, in smaller writing, she'd
scribbled:

I must ask you not to tell anyone, not even your close friends.

She meant Lotta, of course. Who else would he talk to?
Underneath the postscript, she'd added her address. This disorder
was the only clue to her state of mind. The body of the letter
sounded as contained as she'd always been. *I have nothing to offer*
you in return. What kind of a man did she think he was?

He read the address again, but didn't recognize the street. Probably she lived in a part of Helsingfors he wasn't familiar with, but he would find it easily enough. He didn't know Helsingfors all that well – he was the typical country bumpkin who just about knew his way around Kruununhaka but got lost anywhere else – but she was right, he did know a few people in the capital. But whether they were the type of people she needed, those professors and doctors with blossoming private practices who were the friends of his youth – that he very much doubted.

But one person could lead you to another. Old Magnus Bergström, for instance, who'd given up medical practice years ago in favour of some sublime form of civil service – he was forever quietly making it clear that he knew everybody who was anybody, everybody who 'mattered', even in the highest circles – it would be worth looking up old Magnus as soon as he arrived.

For he knew instantly that he would go. Nothing could stop him. Here was her handwriting. The link to her lay in his hand. He'd been sure he would never see her or speak to her again, but here she was. Quick as a breath, it all rose up in him: her way of moving around the house, her silence as she put a bowl of soup before him, the click of her heels. The curve of her cheek and the way she looped back a stray piece of hair behind her ear. The sight of her standing at the stove.

Strangely, those thoughts of her in his kitchen were more real than the journey they'd taken together. Yes, the real Eeva remained here, in this house, with him.

But could it ever be? Was it possible that he could make it so again? She'd sat down and written to him. To that extent, he was in her mind. To ask someone for help is an intimate thing, he told himself.

He wouldn't waste time writing back. No. By the time a letter got to her, he could be there in the flesh. He ran through his patients rapidly in his mind. There was no case so desperate that he couldn't be spared for two or three days. He would set off at once, just as soon as he could send word to old Anders Holmberg to keep an eye on his patients until he returned. Anders would grumble, but he'd be glad enough to have something to do. Retirement didn't suit him. And then I'll throw a few things into a bag, he thought. I'll call Matti to get the horses ready. It's a long drive to the station, and it'll be dark before we get there. I must remind him to check the lanterns – and we'll have to put up in town overnight.

In the middle of his tumult, his thoughts halted. He touched the paper that Eeva had touched. She had laid her hand on it, like this, to steady it while she wrote. She had written a line or two and then looked up, thinking what to write. He knew exactly how her eyes would have looked. Wide, unfocused and full of light. He walked over to the window and stared out at the woods, where they lay shrouded in snow and ice. It was a windless day and the trees were perfectly still. The forest appeared to be deep in its winter sleep, and yet he knew that it was full of hidden life. The bare snow under his window was patterned by birds' claws, which had sunk into the fresh new fall. A fox had come near, and then swerved away.

How beautiful it was, and already the days were growing longer. February, and yet another winter passing away. It seemed to him that a lifetime wasn't long enough to look out of the window and see those claw marks and paw prints sunk into snow and then frozen there, bluish and glazed in their hollows.

Why was he so happy? There was no reason for this happiness. It swelled in him and wouldn't be quieted, as if it were not his own emotion, but a dear guest. She might not come here ever again. Almost certainly she would never come. But for some reason those paw prints reminded him so forcibly of Eeva's presence that he almost heard her footsteps.

Without realizing it, he had crushed the letter between his hands. He unfolded it carefully out of its creases, and smoothed the paper. There were Eeva's words again, but the ink was a little blurred now, from the sweat on his hands.

Eeva could not keep still. At work, she had to be on the move. In and out of the stockroom, checking orders, stacking books, back

285

in the shop asking customers if she could help them with what they were looking for. She did not sit down, even to drink her coffee. She had walked to work instead of taking the tram. Only constant movement kept down the thoughts that were swelling in her head. Her mouth was dry. She had to keep licking her lips, and now the skin at the corner of her mouth was cracked.

He was in prison at this moment. *Now, while I lift my hand like this. Now, while I eat this bun.* Now. As she drank her coffee, he might be lying on the floor, thirsty. At this moment they might be questioning him. She knew their methods. They asked the same questions over and over, looking for holes in the story. They claimed to have information from other prisoners.

'There's no point trying to keep anything from us. We know all about you already. Your chums have been singing like canaries.'

Everybody knew how the Okhrana worked. They wanted admissions, confessions, evidence. They wanted the outline of a crime down in black and white, and they worked fast. A man could be arrested, interrogated, convicted and hanged in the space of a few weeks. A woman just the same. Look what happened to Perovskaya after the assassination of Alexander II: she was arrested and hanged within five weeks.

They weren't strangers who died like that. They were people you knew. Eeva's father had met Perovskaya once, long ago in Russia, when they were all young. Someone took him along to the apartment she shared with Zhelyabov. He didn't agree with everything she stood for, but she was a woman you had to respect. A lovely smile, she had. He told Eeva that. They hanged her outside on a gibbet, along with Zhelyabov and the others.

But no one has died this time, she told herself. There hasn't been an assassination. It's all just words. What's to link Lauri with anything? But the reassurance rang false in her ears. Plotting was enough. Gathering and talking would do it. Nothing had to happen to create a conspiracy, and only a fool would pretend otherwise.

Even the degree of involvement didn't matter much. It didn't matter what you said. Once an arrest was made, what happened next had very little to do with what had happened up to then. You might think you were innocent when you went in, but there was no place in jail for innocence. One man pulled the next down, as if they were chained together and drowning.

Why should the truth interest the Okhrana? It wasn't their job. It was not the point. Getting a confession out of someone was the point, and if that confession implicated others, and if those others implicated others, then so much the better. The job was going along nicely. The bigger the sweep, the more likely they were to pull in someone who really did know something juicy. But the others were useful too, the ones who begged and swore and protested their innocence, and couldn't give any information because they had none to give.

She knew all these things. They'd been learned so early that they were in her blood rather than her thoughts. They were the reality that lay behind every meeting, every pamphlet, every speech where an agent of the Okhrana might well be present.

It had been like that in Russia for generations, her father had taught her that, and these days the Tsar and his Governor-General had taken off the gloves as far as Finland was concerned. The Empire must kneel. Finland was part of the Empire, and Finland must be brought to her knees too.

All they needed was a confession. Perhaps Lauri was hungry, thirsty. Or they had beaten him up and left him lying on the floor without a blanket. People went crazy from being left alone in the dark, or drinking salt water because they were left with that or the rage of their thirst. Their families were told that they'd had mental troubles all along.

The Okhrana could do all these things and any others they thought of. In the case of terrorism everything was justified. When the security of the State, the Tsar and the Empire was at stake, the end most certainly justified the means. The Okhrana were in the front line of defence. They answered to the Tsar. That was their job, and it drew a certain kind of person like honey. Those were the people who had hold of Lauri now.

They'd plucked him out of his life. Not a word was left behind. Such vanishings were all part of their method. She had no clue as to what he was accused of, if there was even a charge yet. 'Taken in for questioning.'

He'd been lifted at four in the morning. An Okhrana job, for sure. He was probably at the Okhrana House now.

Sasha hadn't been sleeping at home that night. He was away for a couple of days, at a meeting in Turku. When he'd come back, one of the neighbours had crept out to tell him what had happened. Three men, in plain clothes. Police.

All this had come to Eeva second-hand. She hadn't even spoken to Sasha yet. She would have to talk to him, but he was avoiding her and she was avoiding him. When she wasn't working, she was running around the city trying to get help, advice, information, anything.

Magda said, 'Keep calm. Wait. Don't draw attention to yourself. It's hard, but it's the only way you'll get through this. The most likely thing is that he'll be released in a few days.'

She must see Sasha. It was weakness in her not to see him, but she shrank from it. She was afraid. Her fear wasn't because of what Sasha might do to her, or even what he might tell her. It was like the fear you have when you lift the cover from a dish of meat that has been standing too long in summer, in a warm place. The stink of it and the crawling of flies.

But what would Lauri think, if he knew that she'd already written to the doctor for help, but hadn't even seen Sasha?

She must offer to leave Magda's apartment. It might be risky for Magda to have Eeva here, with her link to Lauri.

Even the thought of leaving the apartment frightened Eeva. It was like the beginning of the end of her life. Her new life in Helsinki had sometimes felt too good to be true, and now it seemed that it was. What if the Okhrana took her in too?

I would go mad, Eeva thought. As soon as the door was locked, I would begin to go mad. They wouldn't have to do anything to me. But perhaps everybody thinks that, and then they find strength. She'd heard of a comrade who asked to be shut in a cupboard which was too small for him to sit down, so that he would be able to practise and overcome his fear.

If she was arrested, she would lose her job. Eeva couldn't believe that the bookshop would keep her on after that. It would be hard to find work. No job, no apartment. No Magda.

If only we had a place of our own.

Yes. She and Lauri, far away and together. It wasn't escapist romantic rubbish, but the only thing that might save them. People who talk about the revolutionist having no private interests, no affairs, sentiments or ties: they are the escapists. 'He has severed every link with the social order and with the entire civilized world.' Those are words that sway a crowd and make its blood leap. Yes, but then what? It's impossible to do those things, to 'sever every link' and be a 'merciless enemy' and all the rest of it. In a private room it sounds hollow. Nobody can live like that and nobody does, thought Eeva, unless it's death that interests you and not life. And even then, death gets its own way.

'You don't die in a group,' her father said once. 'Even if they string you up in a line, you die alone. It's a private thing.'

He knew that. He prepared for it. But in spite of everything, when the time came to die, he struggled. She moistened his lips and washed him and sat up with him, but she could not lay her head on his pillow, or die in his place.

A place of our own, far away.

Lauri's a marked man, now, even if they let him out. He'll be watched.

Why did she send that letter? Probably the doctor won't come. Why should he want to get mixed up with all this?

30

Thomas stood in the middle of the room. A fair-sized room, not badly furnished. A bed in one corner. What gave life to the place were the colours. A splash of red from the rug on the floor, blue and white tiles on the corner stove. There was a vase of dried beech leaves on the table, and a plate of apples. Framed drawings hung on the walls. A good room.

So this was where Eeva lived. She had only the one room, he supposed. He stood in the middle of it, looking around because he was afraid to look at her.

'I'll take your coat.'

He unbuttoned his overcoat with clumsy fingers. Before he could take it off, she was there, helping him, sliding the sleeves off his arms. She folded the coat very carefully, as if it were precious, and laid it on the bed by the far wall.

'Sit down, please,' she said. 'I'll make coffee.' He dared to look at her as she lifted the pot from its shelf and began to prepare the coffee. He glanced quickly and then away, as if the sight of her burned him. She was wearing a close-fitting woollen dress and she looked older, different.

No. Be honest, he told himself. The difference is that she is not your servant any more. This is her place, not yours. You don't know where her clothes came from, or how she bought them. It changes everything.

She looked like a young student teacher. Poor, but that didn't matter, because everyone in her milieu would be poor. For them, money wasn't the important thing. They were young, they had their lives stretching out vividly ahead of them, like clouds at sunrise. They had sacrificed everything else for the chance of education. Their heads were full of books and ideas and dreams. A pang of envy went through him as he pictured her life, and the friends of her own age who would crowd into her room and drink coffee and eat buns and laugh about things that no outsider could possibly find funny. There'd be no barriers between them, no awkwardness. They belonged together.

It made him think back to his own student days; although, of course, he had never been poor. Only a little foolish sometimes, wasting money he didn't have.

'You found the house, then,' she said, still busy with making coffee, her back to him.

'Oh yes, very easily. But what a lot of building's been going on everywhere. It must be five years since I was last in Helsinki, and there are new buildings shooting up wherever you look. The place is like a building site.'

'Yes, there's even going to be a new railway station.'

'I suppose that's progress.'

Why were they talking such a stream of inanities? He had no interest in the new railway station.

'Please, have a piece of coffee-bread,' she offered.

'What?'

'There, on the table. Please take some.'

He hadn't even noticed it. A plaited loaf of cardamom bread, its surface sticky with crushed loaf-sugar. She had already cut it into slices.

'Thank you. It looks delicious.'

'I didn't make it, if that's what you mean. It's from the bakery.'

Yes, he thought, of course, everything has changed. You've better things to do than bake coffee-bread for me, and you want me to know it. Yes, that's exactly what a young student teacher would do: she'd dash out to the corner bakery and then back again with the warm, greasy paper bag.

'This is a very pleasant room,' he observed. She came to the table, poured the coffee, looking down, and then suddenly looked up and smiled. But he dropped his eyes.

'I've been very lucky,' she said. 'I have a friend called Magda, and I share this apartment with her. You'll meet Magda, I think, if you're staying in Helsinki for a while.'

So there were two of them in this one room. You wouldn't think it was big enough. There weren't even two beds. In his house Eeva had had her own room. Didn't she miss the privacy?

'That's Magda's bed, behind the curtain. It's such a big room that you hardly notice the beds. All our friends are envious – and the rent's quite reasonable –'

'You deserve good fortune,' he said in a low voice.

It was the first personal thing he had said, and he felt her stiffen like a cat.

'I was glad to get your letter,' he went on. 'I'd be happy to help you in any way I can –'

'But?'

'Please, Eeva. All I mean is that I need to know what help you need. You say that your friend has been arrested. Do you know why?'

She put down her coffee cup. She'd gone very pale, and he noticed that the skin around her mouth was chapped. Her eyes were red with tiredness, and there was a spot at the side of her nose. Her hair was scraped back, lustreless. He took in these things, one by one, but they refused to make her less beautiful in his eyes.

'For no reason,' she said. 'It's never for any reason.'

He leaned forward. 'Listen, Eeva. Don't you believe that you can trust me? If I'm to help you, I've got to know more than this.'

Her fingers, which were lying flat on the table, quivered.

'I have some schnapps,' he said. He rose and fetched the little flask he carried in the breast pocket of his coat. 'Have you a glass? No, please don't get up. Just tell me where it is.'

'In the cupboard, to the left of the stove,' she murmured. She was paler than ever, and her forehead was sweaty. He poured a shot of schnapps into the glass and gave it to her.

'Drink it. You'll feel better.'

She screwed up her eyes, and gulped the stuff down. A few seconds later, colour flooded into her cheeks.

'Does that feel better?'

She nodded.

'When did you last eat?'

'I don't know, I –'

'Try a little of this coffee-bread.'

She chewed a little of the sweet bread. Her throat moved, and she swallowed.

'Just a little more,' he urged.

Soon she had eaten the whole slice. She looked at him, surprised. 'I do feel better. I kept getting a noise in my head, but it's gone now.'

'Yes. That's from weakness. You mustn't let yourself get so weak, Eeva. You have a duty to yourself as well as to – well, to anybody else.'

'They took him away. I don't know where he is.'

'Haven't you any friends who can find out for you?' he asked, supposing somehow that there would be a network of the young hotheads, who all believed that they could bring about Finnish independence by the middle of next week, no doubt.

'Don't you have any –' what was the word? – 'contacts?'

'Yes. I suppose so. I know people.' She paused, sighed. 'The Okhrana have arrested him.'

'That's what I thought when I received your letter.' For he'd known immediately that Eeva wouldn't be mixed up with common criminals. And it all fitted together: the way Eeva was, her education, her reading, things she'd said . . .

'So it's political,' he said.

'Everything's political, to them. Even being alive is political.'

'But they must have had a reason. Or a pretext, at least. People don't get arrested for nothing.'

She looked back across the table at him. 'You think so.'

'Well, in spite of everything, there are laws to protect the innocent.'

But as soon as the words were out of his mouth, he doubted them. Here in Helsinki, in Eeva's room, he felt fusty and out of touch, like a man who had been buried in the forest for much too long. Life was moving on fast, but he hadn't moved with it. All those new buildings, all those new people.

'For you, maybe, there is protection. For a man in your position.

But that's because you don't rock the boat, and so they leave you alone.'

'But your friend has rocked the boat?'

'They think he has.'

'Is there any truth in what they think? Is he an . . . an activist?'

She almost smiled at the way he brought out the word. 'He's done nothing wrong,' she said at last.

'Would you like a little more schnapps?'

'No, I feel better.'

'Eeva, don't be afraid. If your friend has done nothing wrong then they'll release him. Not immediately, perhaps. But if there's no evidence – no proof against him – then all this will come right eventually.'

'They make people tell them things,' she said after a long pause, almost in a whisper. 'Who they know and where they meet.'

A pang of fear shot through him. He'd thought of all this as a danger at one remove. But now he realized suddenly that it was a danger that might touch Eeva herself.

'You think he might talk about you? Incriminate you?'

'Oh no,' she said at once. 'No. Not Lauri. I'm not worried about that. Besides, if they've got a file on him, they probably know about me already.'

'But you can't stay here, if that's the case.'

She shrugged. 'Why not?'

'My dear child, don't you realize that you could be arrested yourself?'

'Moving to another apartment wouldn't prevent that. Anyway, I can't afford to move.'

'But listen. Listen, Eeva. That's not the only alternative. No, please, you must listen to me. This is too serious for us to play about. Don't you understand that you could be arrested and taken away, and then it would be impossible for me to help you?'

He saw her flinch at the words, although she tried to hide it. Eeva would be very afraid of being taken away. This was the right line to take with her. He must go ahead, he must be ruthless in using her fear to protect her from herself.

'You can come home with me. Listen. They won't follow you there. Who cares about an old doctor living in the forest? It's only if you're here in Helsinki, putting yourself in their way, that they'll even think of taking action against you. People do it all the time, don't they – they go off to the country and wait until everybody's forgotten about them.'

Her face was mute, stubborn, but there was something there that convinced him she was listening. He took a deep breath to calm himself. It wouldn't do to plead with her, she wouldn't respect that.

'Just for the time being, Eeva, until things calm down. I'm not going to ask you what group it is that your friend's involved with. I don't know what kind of people he associates with, and I don't need to know.

'But they're mistaken, to my mind. Terribly, criminally mistaken, even if it's with the best will in the world. You can't turn the world upside down without unleashing forces that you can't control. When you're young, you think that if you change the world, then people will change, too. But they won't. They can't. Things have to happen slowly. It's like the healing of a wound, you can't rush it. Little by little, with time and medicine and care, it begins to get better . . . if you're lucky, and depending of course on the seriousness of the wound. That's what our country is like too; our whole society. We're wounded, of course we are. But you don't heal a wound by driving a knife into it, or shooting a bullet into it. You don't and you can't.'

An image sprang to his mind. A young man, working at the Nordström mill, years ago, in old Nordström's time. He'd slipped, and his thigh had been laid open almost to the bone.

What a job that had been. For a long time he'd privately suspected that it might come to an amputation. But he'd said nothing and allowed no one to mention the word. He'd put the fear of God into old Nordström, and made sure the boy had clean bedding, a clean mattress, good hot broth, and as much pure water as he could drink. It was slow, so slow. The wound closed, then opened again. How that boy used to stare up at him, his eyes leached with pain. He didn't have any family.

But they got him through it. Emil, that was the boy's name. Young Emil. He remembered so well the desperate patience in that boy's eyes.

'Don't you understand, Eeva, that it's not weakness to go slowly?'

'We go so slowly that we're almost standing still.'

'Almost. Almost. But not quite, Eeva. I know it's easy for me to talk, because life has been good to me. But look at how your own life has changed. You cannot want to throw it all away now. You must let me help you. I'm not asking you to go backwards, and return as a servant. Everything would be quite different.'

He stopped. The thought of how it might be, with Eeva in his house, constricted his chest. Eeva, sitting in a chair by the fire in a dress like the one she had on now, reading, studying, and looking up as he came in. They might talk about his patients. With her intelligence and insight, she would see straight to the heart of a difficult case. Perhaps she would like to learn to play the piano.

She would play well, he was sure of it. There were certain Mozart piano sonatas that he could almost hear, blossoming under Eeva's fingers. The heavy curtains would be drawn, but before they went upstairs he would open both curtains and shutters to gaze out at the trees in the moonlight. That cold winter moonlight that smelled of snow and drew the wolves from the north east. She would stand at his side, breathing lightly. Before they went upstairs . . .

'You could change the rooms. Re-paper them if you liked. Everything would be as you wished.'

She stared at him in astonishment.

'You see, I'm asking you to marry me.'

She got up from her chair, pushed it in under the table and stood behind it. Her fists were clenched at her sides.

'To marry you?'

'Yes.'

'Then you love me.'

Her voice pealed out. She looked pale and frightened, but he believed he saw a flash of triumph in her face. She hadn't believed in him before. She'd thought he only wanted to make use of her.

'Yes,' he said. 'I love you.'

But as the words left his mouth he knew it was already too late. She was shifting away from him. It was like nightfall: one moment you can look into the forest and see each separate trunk and branch, the next they've vanished into the thickness of dusk. She was with him, connected to him, and then she was not. She was gone from him. He heard an intake of breath, but she didn't speak. She was measuring her words, thinking how to answer him.

'But I have to think of Lauri now,' she said carefully, at last, as if she were showing a child how to share a toy.

He poured more schnapps into the glass she had emptied, looked at its quivering, slightly oily surface absently for a moment, then drank it down. There, that was better.

Everything was over. Don't think of that now. Strangely, he felt quite light, and free. He took a little more schnapps. There was Eeva's face, hollow with worry and weariness. Now she was worrying about him, as well as about the boy.

'It's all right, my dear Eeva,' he said. His tongue moved thickly in his mouth. 'We'll forget about it. We'll be as if those words had never been spoken.

'Now, we must think of what I can do to help your friend. I haven't a large acquaintance in Helsingfors, but I'll do what I can. I have an old friend who always tells me that he has the ear of the ear of the Tsar.'

'The ear of the ear of the Tsar?'

'He knows Bobrikov. Not that it's any recommendation, as far as I'm concerned.'

'Bobrikov!'

'Yes. Our Governor-General, you know. The great emissary of our Great Neighbour.'

'I know who Bobrikov is.'

'I don't doubt that, Eeva. I'm not boasting of this second-hand acquaintance, I can assure you. And I can't promise anything. Probably my old friend will turn out to be the smallest of small herrings, making himself sound big to a know-nothing provincial doctor. But he's the only possibility I can think of. At least, I can try to find out what's going on. You'll tell me all you can? You'll trust me?'

'Yes.'

'At any rate,' he said, moving on quickly, 'I doubt that they'll think of arresting me. An old country doctor with mud on his boots,' he joked, trying to lighten her expression.

'It's very good of you,' she said, and although her voice was colourless he believed that she meant what she said. It was good of him, and goodness was all he had left.

He would go to the hotel, and straight up to his room. He would fall onto the bed and make himself sleep at once. He would not eat or bathe or undress. He could feel the dark waiting for him, just behind his eyelids. If it was impossible to sleep then he would lie there quietly, without moving or crying out, until morning came. Time would pass, that was what time always did, not being able to help itself. Whatever happened, morning would come in the end. He would shave and bathe and put on clean linen and go downstairs. Tomorrow would have the great virtue of not being today.

He must talk to Eeva about the boy. He would take down all the details quite calmly, as if they were symptoms that might lead him to a diagnosis. And then tomorrow, and the next day, and for however many days it took, he'd try to find out what was really going on. He would do everything he could to help Eeva, and his conscience would be clear.

'Eeva,' he said, looking straight into her eyes for the first time.

They were as wide and light-filled as he had imagined them, but they were not unfocused. She was looking at him, and her eyes were full of tears.

31

Eeva knocked on Sasha's door, but there was no answer. Now what could she do? Everything had been leading up to this moment.

'You're really going?' Magda had asked.

'Yes.'

'Apparently he's been holed up in his room since he got back from Turku, not seeing anyone. Hannu went round and couldn't get an answer. But he was sure Sasha was at home.'

'Why?'

'Just a feeling.'

'Did he try the door?'

'He didn't say.'

A sudden crazy thought leapt in Eeva's head. Lauri hadn't been taken away at all. It was all a lie. He was there, in that room. Sasha had done something to him. *Holed up.* A shudder of horror went through her body.

But no, it couldn't be true. A comrade with contacts in the Okhrana administrative offices had confirmed Lauri's arrest. She must not let her thoughts go crazy like this. She must keep in control, whatever happened, or she would lose sight of what was real and what was not.

'Listen, Eeva, I'll come with you.'

'There's no need for that.'

'I really don't think you should go on your own.'

'What's going to happen to me? Besides –'

'What?'

'He might talk more – more freely, if there's only me.'

Magda frowned. She wanted very much to come with Eeva. It was because she wanted to protect Eeva, she told herself. Eeva was vulnerable. But there was another factor that Magda barely even

299

voiced to herself. She did not like couples, and however much she disguised this fact from herself by being generous, or by keeping out of the way so that 'Eeva and Lauri have time to develop their friendship', as she put it to herself, there was a bright, buzzing sense of excitement in her now that Lauri had been taken off the scene.

But if there was an inner betrayal, then there must also be a chivalrous readiness to do whatever Eeva needed Magda to do.

'If you're gone more than an hour, I'm coming straight over,' said Magda firmly.

'I won't be that long.'

Magda pushed her papers together.

'Eeva, you know what Sasha is. Or rather you don't know, none of us knows. That man is a mass of possibilities.'

'I wish Lauri had never met him.'

'Yes, but it happened. Sasha did like Lauri, that was genuine. They'd never have become so close otherwise, because Lauri was no fool.'

'Magda, don't, please don't talk about Lauri in that way, as if everything's finished –'

'Oh Eeva, I'm so sorry, I've made you cry.'

Magda jumped up, knocking her papers to the floor, ran to Eeva and took her in her arms. Eeva stood awkwardly, unyielding.

'There now, I'm so sorry. Listen, it's going to be all right.'

It was what Magda didn't say that counted. Magda never lied. She didn't say that it would be all right because Lauri would come back.

'It'll be jamfedora, pet, you'll see,' said Magda, rocking Eeva's stiff body in her arms.

'Jamfedora?'

'Don't worry, it's nonsense, something my mother used to say to cheer us up when we were sad. It's not even German. Just nonsense, a family thing.'

'It's nice.'

'I used to think that when I had children, all the things my mother used to say would come back to life again. That's the way it goes, isn't it?'

'Magda, would you like children?'

'Oh no,' said Magda instantly. 'Not now.'

'Why not?'

'For me, this isn't the right world for children.' She released Eeva, and stepped back. As always she stood very upright. 'But I'll be glad if you think otherwise, for yourself. I think you'd have very nice children.' She smiled quickly, and Eeva thought how smiles didn't change. Magda would have greeted her best friend with just such a smile when they were little girls in pigtails, meeting on the corner to walk to school together. It was much easier to imagine Magda as a little girl than to imagine her with children of her own.

'To me,' Magda continued, 'at this stage of history, we are passing through time rather than inhabiting it, if you understand what I mean. We think not about what's here, but about the changes that will come. We put our lives second to that. Things will be better, but perhaps not for us.'

'But – it's a big thing, not to have children –'

Magda frowned, then smiled even more brightly. 'Perhaps. But anyway, I'm not so young any more. See.' She bowed her head, so Eeva could see the parting of her hair. 'Can't you see the grey hairs? I keep pulling them out, but they come back.'

It was true. There were a few grey hairs, like wires, in the mass of Magda's hair. You couldn't see them from a distance.

'But you're still young.'

'Not so young, not really young at all,' said Magda. For once there was no animation in her face, and Eeva saw that Magda was right. She was growing older. 'It passes away quite quickly. *You're* young, Eeva, look at you. No, not with that face. You're not allowed to feel sorry for me. I'm much happier than most of the people I know. I love my work, my friends, the theatre, music. But children, no.'

'Magda, you know when you're having a bad dream, just for a while in the middle of it things seem normal, as if you'd got back into daylight. But there's a part of you that always knows it is still the nightmare, and wants to cry out and warn the other part. But you can't even whisper.'

'Yes.'

'This is like that. When I go to work – and someone comes in to complain about an order that hasn't been delivered in time . . . and I look very carefully at the ledger and apologize and explain what's happened . . . and all the time there's this noise in my ears, like a black wind, so loud that I can hardly hear what the customer's saying.'

'You must eat. You won't sleep if you don't eat.'

'I can't. My throat closes up.' She thought of the doctor, and how he'd urged her to eat the coffee-bread. It was true that she had felt better. The schnapps was good, too. Perhaps even now he was talking to one of his friends. People of influence all knew one another in just the same way as her father knew everybody, it didn't matter if it was Petersburg or Helsinki, or Berlin. They were comrades, that was all that mattered.

He had opened his black notebook with an elastic strap around it, to write down what she told him about Lauri. She had to tell him that it was crazy to write things down.

That was the notebook he used when he was visiting patients. Later, he wrote up the cases at his desk. She recognized it at once. He was a good doctor, everybody said so. It made her feel safer, to think of being written into that notebook. But of course, once she'd said that it was risky, he hadn't written a word . . .

'We'll try some soup tonight,' said Magda. 'Carrot soup with dill is good for the stomach. I'll put it through a sieve so it's easy to swallow.'

Eeva couldn't help smiling. Magda made soup with great lumps of potato and turnip, which bobbed about in boiling water for hours without imparting much flavour to it.

'Magda, I don't know what I'd do if you weren't here. I'd go crazy.'

'No, you wouldn't. You're not the type. Things will be better soon. If they're going to charge Lauri, we'll find out what the charge is. But I don't think they'll charge him,' went on Magda, glowing with self-sacrifice. She was giving Lauri back to Eeva. 'They'll question him for a few days and it won't be pleasant, but then they'll release him. Forgive me, Eeva, but Lauri simply isn't of sufficient importance to them. Sometimes people get arrested, not because of what they are or what they've done, but as part of a game we don't even know about.'

Eeva said nothing. She couldn't accept Magda's comfort, or explain why Lauri might be of importance.

'We just have to wait,' Magda said, as if this was a cause for comfort.

'How did you come to be so sure, Magda? You're like a house which has a roof on it that doesn't leak, and windows that fit, and the stove's always burning.'

'Well,' Magda began briskly, 'I don't know about that.' But her colour deepened. 'When I said that about passing through life, I didn't mean that it makes what we do any less important. What is life for, if we don't look out for each other? I can't count the activists I've known who were selfish or even cruel in their private lives. We make excuses for them. But I don't want to be like them. In fact I refuse to accept that private life is something separate, with rules to which our political understanding doesn't apply. It's all of a piece. What we do is what we do. What we do is what we have to answer for, not what we intend to do.'

'You mean Sasha?'

'Not especially. But I don't trust him any farther than I could throw him. You peel off one Sasha and there's another underneath, and another, each of them with a different face.'

'I know what you mean. But isn't everybody like that?' She thought of Anna-Liisa's face, wreathed in pleasure when the doctor visited. She even had a special voice for when the doctor was there. But her eyes flashed warning, and all the orphans knew it. 'One step out of line and you'll answer for it later.'

'Maybe,' said Magda. Her voice was constricted. 'My God, Eeva, we'd theorize at the gates of death. You must go.'

Again, she lifted her hand. She rapped on the blank wood until her knuckles hurt. Surely there was a stir behind the door. She paused to listen. Yes, she was sure he was in there.

'Sasha,' she said, 'open the door.'

A second later, without warning, the door opened and she almost fell into the room. Already Sasha had turned his back to her and was walking back to bed. He sat down heavily, then lay back, closing his eyes.

'Sasha!'

'Close the door.'

She closed it, and came over to the bed. The light was grey and cold. She had forgotten that the room was so dark in daylight, because it overlooked a courtyard wall. The bed was a mess, and it smelled of sleep and sickness. The thought of Lauri sleeping here made her shudder.

An enamel pail stood by the bed, with a sponge at the bottom of it. Beside the pail was an open bottle of vodka. There was no glass. He must have been drinking straight from the bottle, and there were only a couple of fingers left.

She looked around the room. Clothes and books lay scattered over the floor. On the table there was an upturned box, and papers tipped out into a plate of porridge. The bronze mirror on the wall had been knocked sideways. Its glass was shattered. The whole room looked as if it had been slapped across the face. But by the wall there was a rack with four pairs of boots placed immaculately on it, all of them freshly polished. None of the boots was Lauri's.

'Wake up, Sasha, open your eyes. I need to talk to you.'

Sasha lay sunk into the stew of the bed. If she hadn't seen him open the door, it would be easy to believe that he'd been lying there, unmoving, for days.

'Don't come near me,' he said. 'I've got grippe.'

'You've been drinking,' she said.

At last his eyes opened and looked at her. No light came into his face.

'Don't stand so close,' he said. 'You wouldn't want to catch what I've got.'

His face was the colour of candle fat. His features seemed to have spread, as if there was nothing to hold them in place.

'I'm not leaving,' she said. 'I want to talk to you about Lauri.'

'Lauri,' he said, turning his head on the pillow. 'You've come to talk about Lauri.'

'What else would I have come for?'

'Maybe to see if there is anything I need?'

His eyes were small and dull. He looked at her resentfully. Perhaps he really was ill, and had wanted to be left alone with his sickness. His face looked very strange with the life gone out of it. She had the uneasy feeling that this Sasha was a complete stranger, and that it would be hard labour to get to know him.

'Lauri,' he said again, rolling the r in the Finnish way, as if imitating someone, 'Lau . . . ri.'

Suddenly, with a terrible cat-like movement, he sprang up into a crouching position on the bed. He swayed on hands and knees, thrusting his yellow face at her.

'Don't you come here talking to me about *Lauri*, as if he belongs in your handbag,' he said. His voice shook with rage.

She would not flinch. She would hold him back from her. He was not going to rise off that bed or come a finger closer to her. She would beat him down, as she'd beaten him down in the bookshop.

'What had you to do with his arrest?' she asked.

'I?' he exclaimed theatrically. 'I? Why, nothing. Nothing, nothing, nothing, nothing, nothing. Why are you looking at me like that? Don't you believe me?'

'It's not a question of my believing or not believing. What I think doesn't matter. All I want is to know what happened.'

'Lauri's my friend.' His voice thickened. He was letting himself be drunk now, sliding into it. Drink's a good refuge, she thought. You can hide whatever you want in drink. 'Good friend. Comrade. Women don't know bout that. My comrade. Do anything for him.'

'You're right,' she said coldly. 'I don't know about it. I want you to tell me.'

It was very warm in the room. She was sweating inside her coat. He was falling apart, she could see it happening second by second. Whatever had held him together was slowly giving way. He must

305

have been drinking for days. Or else he was letting himself come to pieces.

'You think you're so high and mighty,' he jeered suddenly. 'I bet you look in the mirror a hundred and twenty times a day, don't you? *Oh, it's me, it's me. How lovely, it's me.* That's what you think.'

'Why do you say that?' she asked.

'No reason. No, no reason. It just popped into my head.'

He seemed to be playing with the words in his mouth, as if he were a child sucking toys.

'Can't you get up? You say Lauri's your friend, but here you are lying in bed drinking, when he's been arrested. What good's that to Lauri? Don't you want to help him?'

'Makes no difference,' Sasha muttered.

'What?'

'It makes no difference what I do or what you do,' he said. His voice was suddenly clear, challenging. 'Do you think it'll help if you go sniffing round the Okhrana, you stupid girl? Do you think that I'm a miracle worker? The only thing that affects the outcome is what they happen to need at this par-tic-ular his-tor-ical moment.' He reeled off the possibilities in a mocking sing-song: 'In-terr-og-ation, con-fess-ion, charge, arrest, trial, sentence . . . or maybe none of those at all, what do you think? *Throw-the-young-hothead-into-the-cells-and-let-him-cool-his-heels-there-for-a-few-days.* And all the rest of it, de dah de dah de dah. What matters is what they need. No, that's still not right. Not what they need: what they want. And de dah de dah de dah.'

'Why do you talk like that? This isn't a game. It's *Lauri* we're talking about. Your friend.'

'*I'm* talking about Lauri. But you aren't listening, because your head is full of crap that doesn't apply any more. You think that everything happens *for a reason.* Isn't that it? A leads to b and b leads to c and de dah de dah de dah.'

'Why don't you stop saying that? They haven't arrested him for nothing, have they?'

'Bobrikov's alive. Nothing's happened to Bobrikov *whatsoever.* You know about good old Bobrikov. Not only is he alive but he's also in robust health, busily signing decrees and proclamations and Russifying Finland as fast as he can. Get rid of the silly little Finnish army, get rid of silly little Finnish postage stamps with lions on them, and, for heaven's sake, get rid of all the trouble-makers. Russian manufacture is so much more reliable, don't you find? It's business as usual for Bobrikov, and the Tsar's happy as a clam.'

'So why have they arrested Lauri?'

'Maybe he stepped out of line.'

'*Stepped out of line.* What's that supposed to mean?'

'You tell me,' said Sasha. He flopped back onto the bed and lay there grossly, all his handsomeness gone. She glanced around the room again. There was another bottle of vodka on the washstand, half full. She picked it up, went over to Sasha, and slowly, delib-erately, began to pour out the vodka onto the floor.

'What are you doing, you bitch? That's my vodka.'

'Not any more.'

He lunged across the bed but the move made him dizzy and he fell back on the pillow.

'Got more bottles anyway,' he mumbled.

'I'll set a match to this vodka and every other bottle in the place if you don't get up. Someone should set a match to *you*, Sasha. Then you'd jump. You're going to get up, wash yourself, get dressed and go out and you're not going to come back until you've talked to everyone you know and found out everything *they* know. All your wonderful *contacts* that you're always boasting about. They can make themselves useful for once.'

'What would you know about it?' said Sasha, as if to himself. 'You think it's all so simple. In your little porridge life with Magda, you're safe. Friends stick together, true love lasts for ever, com-rades are loyal, enemies have horns on their heads and hard work brings its own reward. But everything has its double, don't you know that? If you love someone, you also hate them. If some-thing's true, then it's also a lie. So why not be honest about it . . .' He was mumbling now, deep in the labyrinth of his own thoughts. 'Why pretend? Cowards – hypocrites – that's what they are. *Love.*

They should be made to swallow poison to wash away their lies. Everything's been betrayed already, don't you understand that?'

'Everything?'

He looked at her suddenly, sharply. 'I'm your friend, Eeva, that's why I'm telling you all this. I'm not going to lie to you. But I could kill you now, and no one would be any the wiser. They would think you'd been arrested, just like Lauri, and by the time they found out that you hadn't, you'd be far away.'

A taste of iron filled her mouth. She gripped the vodka bottle tightly. This had all happened before. The man who was vanished out of her father's house. They got him drunk and took him away and that was the end of him. An informer, working for the Okhrana, probably. No one ever saw him again. He had never even been to the apartment, they could all swear to that. They had all worked together, like parts of a machine, to remove him. But Sasha was careless. He could never work like that.

'No,' she said. 'You're not going to kill me. You're not going to touch me.'

His eyes measured her. She knew how fast he could move, but she would be faster. She would crack the bottle down on his head. But the bottle wasn't enough. He must fear her.

'Don't be silly, Eeva,' he said at last. 'Put that bottle down, for heaven's sake. It was purely a the-or-et-ical remark.'

'Magda knows I'm here. I told her I wanted to talk to you about Lauri. She's coming over if I'm not back when I said I would be. She doesn't trust you. So you see, no one will believe that I've been arrested.'

She saw his body relax. He wouldn't try anything now, she was sure of it. He was relaxing. He didn't have the hardness in him to do it. All the same, she kept her grip on the bottle.

'How you girls do stick together,' he said lightly.

'Was it you?' she asked. It was all coming together in her head. That man pretending to be a comrade. Laughing and drinking with her father and the others, while they watched him. He was no good. His acting wasn't up to standard, and he asked too many questions. But Sasha was a wonderful actor.

'Tell me, Sasha.'

'What do you mean?'

'Was it you, Sasha? Was it you? Is that what you meant when you said everything has its double? You said that everything's been betrayed already. So tell me, who's done the betraying? You were Lauri's friend, but at the same time –' She swallowed.

His hand brushed the air in irritation.

'That's just silly, Eeva. Sometimes things simply happen . . . and you don't know why,' he said.

'Nothing *simply happens*, Sasha. *Someone makes it happen.*'

His eyes held hers. His expression changed. Pure, childlike surprise lit his face, as if a six-year-old Sasha had come back to find himself trapped inside the flesh of this man who smelled of vodka, piss and sweat. He had been so clever for so long. He had got the better of them all. It should have gone on for ever and now it was stopping.

Maybe he's not acting any more, thought Eeva. Maybe this is it, and there are no more Sashas left to show themselves.

'They'll release Lauri,' she told Sasha. 'I'm sure of it. Whatever you did, or why, I don't want to know any more. It doesn't matter. Lauri will come back, and it won't have anything to do with you. He won't have anything to do with you any more.'

But Sasha was still gazing at her with clownish, childlike surprise.

'He had to do it,' said a different Sasha-voice, through the doorway that the vodka and God knows what else had made in him. The voice was very young, not more than six years old. The pupils were dilated, as if they had swallowed the man. The face stared up at Eeva.

'Why?'

But there was no answer.

She was back in the House of Orphans. They were whispering after dark, out of their nightmares, while she sat by the bed of a sick child. She had a spoon in her hand, and a cup of water with salt and sugar mixed into it. The doctor had told Anna-Liisa to let Eeva stay up and feed the child. Sometimes she almost slept. She couldn't help it. Her head dropped, her eyes swam, and then she jerked back to herself. A mutter of pain rose from the bed, and the little girl gabbled out words, too quickly for anyone to follow.

'It's all right, drink this.' She must have said those words a hundred times before morning came.

Sasha's fist crept to his face. He crammed his knuckles deep into his mouth, as if to silence himself. Nothing moved.

You had to stand in line, in the House of Orphans. When they were walked to church, the line had to be perfect. The little ones stumbled out of line sometimes, because they were cold or tired, but they learned not to.

And then it was over. Sasha's face jumped into shape, bright and mocking. 'You believed me, didn't you?' he jeered. 'You were fooled, weren't you? You girls are too soft to live. My father knew all about that. He used to say that the way my mother brought me up, I would be too soft to live. My father did me good, don't you understand? He made a man of me. But even that wasn't enough for him. He was like all fathers, he had ambition. I was his only son, and he had big ideas for me.

'He didn't stop at making one man out of me. He made two, Eeva my darling, he made two. Two men for the price of one. Isn't that one of God's most holy miracles, as my mother used to say? But she was weak, she was no good.'

'I don't know what you mean,' she said stonily. But she did know. He thought he was dangling something just out of her reach. Teasing her with knowledge that he was going to twitch away before she could seize it. But she knew more than he realized. He thought he was acting, but he was telling the truth, and now she knew what all the Sashas added up to. She wouldn't stay for this. She would go home.

'No, you don't know anything, do you?' he went on, cocky again, full of swagger. 'Poor little Sasha, is that what you were thinking? You went all soft, didn't you? I saw you!'

She watched him in silence. Magda was right. One face pulled off to show another underneath, and then another face pulled off, but you never got down to the flesh. And why even try, when it was always going to be for nothing.

'Aren't you going to say anything, Eeva?'

She could turn her back on him now. She moved towards the door.

32

Bobrikov

Very slowly, he swung his feet over the edge of the bed, and shuffled them into his slippers. A moment's pause, to gather himself. There was no shame in that. The body stiffens in sleep and has to come back to life slowly. It was important to follow doctor's orders. *You must take your time, sir. Give your circulation time to get going, or that leg might buckle under you again. We don't want to risk another fall.*

Doctors talked like that, as if your body belonged to them. He was a young whippersnapper, but all the same he'd known what he was about. He wasn't a butcher, like most of them.

But it was nonsense to talk of caution and taking things slowly. A man couldn't start being soft with himself at this late stage. He was a soldier and proud of it, with a body he'd used as hard as if it were a block of varnished wood, or a metal trunk taken on campaign. It's this damned prostate trouble that's woken him again. How many times has it dragged him out of the warmth of bed to pee interminably, a thin dribble forced past a stone.

How he used to piss when he was a young man! Up against the wall, or into a bush on an icy morning. A jet of urine that steamed proudly as it fell into the snow. That was him. Even his urine had had his signature on it. *Bob-rik-ov.*

But now he was stiff, and slow. He had an old man's shanks, mottled skin and pot belly. Knots of varicose veins on his legs. All right, you had to expect it. His body had done the work it had been made to do. The old horse was willing, but he couldn't push it much farther. If he wasn't careful it would stop altogether, head down, hooves planted apart, flanks heaving with exhaustion. And then it would be time for the knacker's yard . . .

But not yet. Not at this time of threat to all that we hold most dear, Bobrikov told himself. Not when there is vital work to be done.

There were ways of helping the old horse. A walking stick, a little more wax on the ends of his moustache, so the hair didn't droop and draggle, a military overcoat that pulled his shoulders back and braced his spine. Put on a pair of pince-nez and he can see again, well enough to read papers and weigh up the man sitting opposite him. He'd always been an excellent judge of character.

Ugh, it's taking so long. An old man's pee is a miserable thing.

But all the same, the young don't know everything, thought Bobrikov. It's something to have used up your life in the service of the Tsar. To labour, and not to look for any reward . . . no, not even the chestful of medals, important though they are. They are not what really counts, in the end. Duty to God and to the Tsar, that's what counts. The Tsar's confidence. His faith that I will do whatever is required. Unquestioningly, unswervingly. With gladness.

The path is hard, but that's only how it should be. Dissidents, activists and mischief-makers are everywhere, but even though it's necessary to handle them with the utmost firmness, it's also necessary to remember that they are like children. They do not and cannot understand the quality of the Tsar's vigilance over his people. They throw up their petty leaders without realizing that leadership has nothing to do with giving the people what they think they want.

Petitions! People's addresses! The will of the people! Yes, they are like children in the nursery, thought Bobrikov, shaking the last drops from his flaccid penis. Dangerous children. And as such they must be dealt with harshly, for their own good, and so that one bad apple does not corrupt the barrel. Elements that threaten Russia's imperial unity must be extirpated. In Manchuria, in Central Asia, in Persia, here in the Grand Duchy of Finland, the dangers are exactly the same, although they take different forms. And the solution is exactly the same. Like children, they must learn that defiance only breeds punishment. Like a good father, the Tsar must chastise.

Those who deny the will of God's anointed, thought Bobrikov, letting the folds of his nightshirt fall over his shanks, they deny the will of God Himself.

And now back to bed. Maybe not to sleep any longer, but to lie in the warmth of the bed and review the day to come. That's another thing they don't know, these young ones who believe that a shuffling pace, inflamed joints, grey hair, milky eyes and an ear-trumpet will never come their way. They never guess that it's just as good to be alive *now*, as *then*. Inside yourself, you don't change. A dish of roast partridge tastes just as good – no, better – and love is stronger. Because love is a principle, not an emotion. And love is not a soft thing that can be blown away, but is as hard as iron. They don't know that yet.

He groped towards the bed. He knew his way in the dark, always had. It was an old soldier's trick. You had to know where you were, even when you were asleep, and be able to orientate yourself instantly on waking.

He lay back, grunting with pain as he straightened his legs. And now that damned cramp was beginning in his thigh. Always the same. He set his teeth and hissed through them as if he were quieting a recalcitrant horse. The cramp rose to a peak and slowly faded, as he'd known it would.

February. Not too long now before winter ends. Even though the years rush by so fast, the winters somehow seem longer. Spring, that's the ticket. A stroll in the June sunlight across Senate Square, taking a few minutes' break from the long day's duty that begins at six in the morning and won't end until dusk. A glance up into the perfect sky, a glance at your watch and it's time to get back to work. You're expected in the Economic Division.

A last deep breath of the delicious late-morning air, knowing that you deserve it, you've done your duty, you haven't closed your eyes.

314

Thomas held his fingers to Ida Runeberg's pulse.

'I don't know why you're doing that,' she interrupted. 'I'm not ill.'

'If you'll allow me.'

He'd known Ida since she was a baby herself, although he hadn't delivered her. He wasn't qualified then. She was always a strong child, racing about with the older brother who'd died of meningitis when he was twelve. He'd almost forgotten his name: Bo, that was it. And yet they'd all felt it so much at the time. 'A terrible tragedy for the family,' Johanna had said, pulling Minna to her and hugging the child close until she wriggled and protested, 'Mama! You're squashing me, I want to get down.'

He could see them now, as clear as clear. Johanna, Minna. Even now, the air echoed with Minna's impatience.

'You're doing very well, Ida,' he said, 'but it's my job to be vigilant.' He smiled. 'Even if it's rather annoying.'

She almost smiled back, then something caught her and her face darkened. She placed her hands on her belly and rolled sideways in the bed, drawing up her knees. Then, with a convulsive movement, she scrambled up until she was kneeling, knees apart, hands braced on her thighs. She breathed shallowly and rapidly, then gave a groan. It was over.

'The pains are getting worse,' she said accusingly.

'It's normal. It's natural. You're doing well.'

Her husband, Nils, had asked Thomas to attend Ida's labour almost as soon as he'd known she was pregnant.

'You see . . . she's delicate.'

Thomas didn't agree. Ida was as tough as a pony, and would have done perfectly well with a midwife alone. But it would do Ida no good to have a husband who was beside himself with anxiety for nine months.

'Perhaps you should lie down,' he suggested now, gently. 'Nils will come in and sit with you.'

'I can't lie down, it feels terrible,' she said. 'Everything presses on my spine.'

'Where? Show me.'

'Just here.'

He examined her carefully. As before, the foetus was in a normal longitudinal lie. The head was engaged. He took out his stethoscope and timed the heartbeat. Yes, all was well.

'I need to stand up!' said Ida fiercely. Another pain was coming. Clumsily she began to clamber off the bed.

'My dear child! You'll fall, you'll hurt yourself –'

'*Don't touch me.*'

She bent over, clutching the bedpost and panting. Her long white nightdress clung to her sweating body. Suddenly he thought of his mother, walking in the birch grove, waiting to give birth. She hadn't let anyone come near her but old Katariina.

And when the time came you just slipped out like a fish.

'Get Nils,' hissed Ida. 'I want him, fetch him here.'

Thomas crossed to the door. As he'd thought, Nils stood behind it, his face pale.

'Why didn't you come in, man?'

'Is she . . . Is it very bad?'

The worst thing is your wife's temper, thought Thomas, but he said, 'It's a completely normal labour. Ida's making excellent progress.'

Nils glanced timidly towards his wife, and saw her sweating, contorted features. His own face froze.

'But she's in agony! You must help her! Do something for her!'

'Nils! Don't be . . . such a baby!' gasped Ida. The contraction was easing. She straightened, and wiped her face.

'How long will she go on like this?' whispered Nils, horrified.

'It's hard to say,' answered Thomas. 'Maybe three hours, maybe four. Her pains are quite regular and frequent now. With a first baby, everything takes longer. But Ida, don't you want to lie down?'

'No.'

Ida reached to her bedside table and sipped from the glass of water that stood there. Her lips hurt. They were cracking. She took another sip of water. The two men were both staring at her.

Useless, her face told them. Neither of you can help me. It would be more comfortable for you if I were lying down and covered up so that what I'm suffering is hidden from you. But I'm not going to lie down.

'Let me help you to put on your wrapper,' suggested Nils.

'It's too hot.'

'All the same,' said Nils, advancing towards her with the blue silk wrapper in his hands. He wanted to hide his wife from himself, but did not realize it.

'No,' she said, putting out her hands to ward him off, and then seizing hold of the round ball at the top of the bedpost. 'Don't touch me, don't touch me, it's coming again,' she muttered, as if to herself. Her stomach was tightening, lifting. She put her hands on the hard flesh and felt it rise as pain came over her.

As soon as the contraction finished, Ida pushed herself away from the bed and walked to the window. She rested there, leaning against the heavy velvet, and then with an effort she hauled aside both inner and outer curtains, to reveal the black space of night.

But it wasn't true night any more. Not long now until dawn, Thomas thought, glancing at his watch.

'It's still snowing,' said Ida. Now that she spoke, they could see the thick hurrying snow which came at the window and then retreated.

'Wind's in the east,' said Thomas.

Nils moved towards his wife. Now they were standing side by side, looking out of the window. She leaned against him, resting, and his arm came around her. Her breathing seemed to fill the room.

At the next contraction Ida turned from the window.

'It hurts me,' she said thickly, fighting with the folds of her night-dress. 'Take this off, it's too heavy.'

Even the fine lawn was a weight on her. She couldn't bear the constriction of the cloth. Thomas heard the fabric tear, and Nils's protest, 'Ida! Ida, don't do that.'

Her was afraid of her nakedness. But it was her nakedness that had made this baby, Thomas thought. How strange people were.

How strangely they lived. Ida stopped struggling with the nightdress. She and Nils were face to face now, like lovers. He was holding her up, taking her weight as she fought her way through the pain.

The bulk of the child between them made him hold her clumsily, but all the same the sight of them stung Thomas's eyes and made him turn away. By morning they'll be a family, God help them, he thought. Another family, and it would all begin again.

She rested, her arms around Nils's neck. He had his feet planted firmly apart now, braced to take her weight. He was beginning to look like a man, Nils, instead of the boy who had fallen in love with strong-willed Ida because he had no choice: she wanted him, and that was that.

Again, Ida broke free and began to pace up and down the room, turning at the same spot each time, as if there were a line there that no one else recognized.

He had been wrong to want Ida to lie down. Her pain seemed less than it had when she was writhing on the bed, although her labour was now further advanced. He must remember this.

He had only one concern with Ida. He always took a careful family history, and it had emerged that Ida's mother had bled heavily between the delivery of the child and the afterbirth. She'd survived, but had taken more than a year to recover her health. There had been no more children. Ida knew all about it; he supposed that mothers and daughters often talked about such things, though he couldn't imagine that Minna and Johanna had ever done so. But then, if Minna had become pregnant while her mother was alive, things might have been different. Minna, pregnant. Perhaps it would happen one day. For the first time, recently, she had said, 'If I should ever have children – not that it's very likely –'

He hadn't dared answer; had hardly dared let her know that he'd heard what she'd said. But his face must have given him away. She'd coloured, and looked down. 'A child, Minna!' he had said, but not aloud. 'Is it really possible?'

Haemorrhage was the thing he feared most. It became a battlefield, sleeves rolled up, the bed a swamp of blood. He had ordered ice packs to be made ready, without specifying their use. Ida was a strong girl, but she had an imagination, and he knew from experience that fear was the enemy of a successful delivery. But very probably nothing would go wrong. Physically, Ida resembled her father's family rather than her mother's. She was very like her aunt Birgit, in fact, who'd had her six children with only her old nurse as midwife. Like his mother. How close the dead seem some days, as if their planet is swinging close to the earth.

He had done his duty. He had done everything possible. He could meet his mother's gaze, if the dead have eyes to see with and hands to reach out to those they once loved. He very much doubted it. He had done what he could for Eeva, about that boy. He had stood old Magnus Bergström a handsome dinner, listened patiently to hours of self-satisfied pratings from 'the ear of the ear', as he now always thought of him. Old Magnus had drawn his brows sharply into a frown when Thomas at last 'brought up the subject'. Instantly, Magnus had changed and become alert but distant. Really, he could say almost nothing.

'Discretion, you understand, my dear Thomas – although of course in your neck of the woods, in your enviable state of bucolic peace and quiet, it's hard for you to understand the pressure of affairs under which we labour here in Helsingfors – discretion must be our watchword. But I can without the slightest indiscretion inform you that there have been a number of arrests – call them pre-emptive – call them speculative – which are highly unlikely to result in significant convictions. Small fry, my dear Thomas, small fry. And you know from your fishing days what we do with small fry. We simply assess its maturity and then throw it back into the lake.

'It is all purely and simply a question of whetting the knife. And once the knife is whetted, it can be put back in the drawer.'

'Small fry? Whetting the knife?'

'I ask you to use your imagination a little, my dear Thomas. Obviously the knife is . . . ah – a figure of speech.'

And old Magnus sat there, looking so quietly and solemnly

satisfied with his mixed metaphors that Thomas wanted to flick a pellet of bread in his eye.

But he had done what he could. He had been true to his word to Eeva. He hadn't seen her again; he hadn't been able to face it. He had written a short, practical letter, as discreet as her own, and come away from Helsingfors as fast as he could. Fortunately this baby of Ida's had insisted on arriving almost straight away.

My God, he thought, if I live, if I'm still capable of doctoring, it's just possible that one day I'll deliver Ida's grandchild.

We'll know a little more by then, he continued, as Ida cried out with the strength of a new contraction. Surely, by the time this baby of Ida's is full-grown, we'll have learned to do things just a little better?

Lauri

In Helsinki the snow had stopped hours ago, and there was a thick crust of ice on the new fall. Light was seeping into the sky, although sunrise was still half an hour away. But it was mid-February, and the worst of the dark was over. The sun would struggle up to the horizon soon after eight, but with this thick, low cloud it probably wouldn't be seen all day. People hurried to work, heads down, muffled, clinging on to the warmth of home. Trams clanged, and far away a railway whistle cut through the still air.

Everything was as normal. Schoolchildren hurried to school, shops opened, the smell of roasting coffee made the streets fragrant, and a baker's window glowed yellow.

Lauri slowed down. He would stop for a moment to get his breath. Even if you had no money, you could look in the baker's window. A girl with floury arms was putting loaves onto a wooden tray. Fresh loaves of sweet, sticky black bread. His mouth filled with saliva.

He must walk on. He must get to Eeva. But the yellow light in the baker's window danced and dazzled. He knew what to do about that. Put your head down, take a deep breath. Get a grip of your-self. But the dizziness increased. His heart was banging. Weakness, that's all it was. Get hold of yourself.

'Are you all right?'

The baker's girl had come out. He could barely see her now. She was dancing and dazzling too, going in and out of blackness. Her voice rang like a bell: *Are you all right . . . all right . . . all right?*

'He's going off,' said another voice. Someone took his right arm, someone else his left. He was being steered indoors. He leaned on them, he could not help it although he wanted to spare them his weight. His legs were buckling under him.

'Here, sit on this stool a minute. Put your head down.'

There were two voices, one young and one old. A hand held out a cup of water, and he tried to sip but couldn't. He was shiv-ering all over, he couldn't help it.

'He's cold.'

'Go on in the back, warm him up a drop of milk and put some sugar in it,' said the older voice.

He couldn't get out of the darkness. He was trying to get some-where, he knew that.

'Put one of those flour sacks around his shoulders.'

A blue cup appeared, close to his mouth.

'Drink it up, you'll feel better.'

The milk was sweet and warm. He took a sip, and his throat closed up.

'Slowly now.'

Another sip. Another. The taste of it flowed over his tongue, the warmth of it spread into him, strengthening him. He sipped again and suddenly there he was, drinking a cup of milk just the same as he'd always done. He put out his hand and gripped the cup. His mouth hurt, but he could get the milk down. He could see blue and white checks in front of him. The girl who held the cup to his lips was wearing a blue and white apron.

'Thank you,' he said.

'What's he saying?'

Lauri cleared his throat. His voice wasn't right. His neck was bruised where they'd had him in an arm lock, and he'd lost his top teeth. He tried to smile at the girl, but this didn't have the effect that his smile had always had before. She stared at him in consternation, taking in his bruised, swollen face with clots of dried blood at the corners of his mouth.

'You have been in the wars, haven't you?' said the old woman. 'Put a bit of that black bread into the milk, Kirsti; he'll be able to mamble it down.'

No doubt she thought he'd got into a fight when drunk, and someone had beaten him up.

'I haven't been drinking,' said Lauri. 'You can't smell drink on me.'

'I know that,' said the old woman. 'You think I'd have had you in here if you were a drunk? Don't use up your strength talking. Swallow that bread and milk now it's nice and soft and then you can be on your way. You've got somewhere to go?'

'Yes,' said Lauri. 'I've got my girl to go to.'

'You're lucky, then. But she's going to get a shock when she sees you. You're no oil painting this morning, I can tell you.'

'She won't mind about that.'

The old woman's face cracked into a smile.

'You're lucky twice, then.'

Why they had let him out he could not guess. Everything happened at random. You were beaten up or yelled at or locked in the dark or given a bowl of soup or interviewed by a soft-voiced man who seemed to have got into the police by mistake. You could make no connections. One minute they didn't seem to know anything, or have any reason for arresting you. The next they put their mouths to your ear and screamed that you were a conspirator against the Tsar, an assassin with links to international terrorism. But no one mentioned Bobrikov. All the time, Lauri had the feeling that they were whipping themselves up to it, that the frenzy wasn't real and they didn't really believe in it. It was all a strange sort of play-acting. And yet the kicks were real. His teeth lying in the straw were real. The ringing in his ears was real.

Maybe they were playing cat-and-mouse. He was part of a huge game and he didn't know the rules. They'd released him so they could watch where he would take them, and find out what was going to happen next.

There would be no next, he knew that now. Not for him. Whatever it took to make a people's martyr, he hadn't got it. They had shown him photographs of a row of dangling men. But when he looked closer there were women as well. They had their skirts tied at the ankles, for decency.

He would go away, with Eeva. They did not have to stay here. He had never thought he would really leave his country for ever, but then he'd never felt like this before. It seemed to him that the sun had stopped shining on his life here. He was living in an eclipse. If he stayed, nothing lay ahead of him but weariness and risk and a long blunder through darkness towards a goal that he wasn't even sure he wanted to reach.

Thousands and thousands had gone already, on the emigrant ships, making new lives from which threads of marvellous news reached back to home. *We have built our own house now. Olli bought six fine milkers at last month's market.*

It wouldn't be paradise, he knew that. The ones who didn't write home had their own tales of hardship and disappointment to tell, no doubt. But whatever happened, they were out of all this. There was no Tsar in America, and even the Okhrana's long arm didn't stretch across the Atlantic. There, he'd be just a man like any other.

Why wait, why try to play this game when other people had made the rules long before you were born? He had never chosen to play it. If they hung him up on a gibbet he would be the fool who didn't really know what he was dying for. His card was marked here, for sure. Maybe they'd try to stop him leaving, but he'd find a way, through Sweden, or down through Germany. As long as Eeva would come with him, nothing else mattered.

And if she wouldn't, then there was no more to be done, and nothing to fight for anyway. He'd stay here and take what came.

But surely she would come with him. Surely there would be

somewhere in the world they could go, where they could make a life that belonged to them.

He swallowed the last of the black bread soaked in milk. He could feel it giving him strength. The girl was busy again, piling up loaves behind the counter while customers went in and out. Some of them glanced curiously at him.

He handed the empty cup back to the old woman.

'Here a minute,' she said. One dry, work-worn old hand tipped up his chin. In the other hand she held a soft, clean rag, dampened with water. With firm, sure movements she cleaned the dried blood from his face.

'There,' she said. 'You look more respectable now. Get on home quick. You don't want to get into any more trouble than what you've already been in.'

She knew. He could tell from her face that she knew.

'The way things are these days,' she went on very quietly, 'you can get arrested only for looking too cheerful when they think you ought to be looking sad. You get along quick to that girl of yours.'

He put his hand over hers. 'Thank you,' he said. He got up from the stool, and crossed to the shop door. He looked right and left up the street. Nothing but ordinary people, thinking of their own business. He stepped out, and melted into the crowd.

Sasha

Sasha had remembered to put on his overcoat, but not his sheepskin boots. Instead, he wore the light polished shoes he kept for special occasions. 'Sasha's dancing shoes', Lauri called them.

The problem was that the smooth leather soles didn't grip on snow and ice. He had scored a criss-cross pattern on them with a knife, months ago, one night when he really was going dancing. But on these icy paths he might as well have been wearing slippers made of glass.

He had thought of going to the railway. He'd heard the sound of a train's whistle, and for a while he'd walked in that direction, thinking to find the track. But he veered off-course somehow, away from streets and houses, and now he was in among frozen trees and sheets of snow.

He wasn't even sure where he was any more. Everywhere he peered, there were black tree trunks, branches, snow-covered boulders. Perhaps he was in a park. One of the pleasure parks where people sprawled on the grass in summer. Or perhaps he'd walked farther than he knew and he was right out of Helsinki altogether, in the forest. Or he'd walked over the sea and now he was on a little island in the middle of the Baltic . . . But he knew that wasn't really possible. How could he have walked so far in these shoes? If he was sober, he'd know where he was.

It was getting light. Nobody anywhere. He was going so slowly, barely moving at all. He'd had some idea of finding the railway track and making a pillow out of it for his head. But it wouldn't work like that. The rails would be icy cold and they would hurt him. It might take a very long time before a train came.

How he'd ended up here he could not begin to imagine, but it seemed that there wasn't a way back. There were a lot of things he could not afford to think about. They lay in his mind, jumpy as shadows, but he wasn't going to let them rise.

He would keep them down. He would recite a poem; that would do it. He had many poems by heart. He hadn't had much use for them lately – no, not for years.

> When I am locked alone in foreign lands,
> When my only nurse is tedium,
>
> Blessed deceit, star of the sea,
> Preserve me.

No, that wasn't it. His memory was shot, like everything else. But he remembered the ending:

> No memory, no, no memory to salt the wounds
> That have cut my heart.

Was that right?

Farewell, hope . . .

Sasha laughed. *Farewell, hope.* If only it was so easy. That was the trouble with human beings, they never stopped hoping for better things. What idiots they were.

Farewell, hope, sleep, desire . . .

That bit was all right. He knew what he was talking about there. Not to sleep, that was the worst of all. You had a drink, and then another drink, and it sent you off, but you woke up half an hour later with the whole black night in front of you, and your head teeming.

The wounds . . .

What wounds? Why make such a fuss? Everybody has them. Strip the cover off any man and you'll find the scars. Don't think about them. Don't let those wounds open their lips and talk to you again.

Suddenly he knew where he was. He'd come all the way down to Kaivopuisto. No wonder everything was so quiet. Trees and boulders and trees and boulders. It was dead as a dog in the depth of winter. There was the frozen water. There were the frozen islands, sticking out lumpily from the frozen sea. He must have crossed Puistokatu without realizing it. Time kept jumping. You shouldn't be in one place and then in another, without knowing how you got there. He had to keep a hold of time. If he had a drink he'd feel better.

But of course he did know how he'd got here. He knew every step of the way. There they were, all his footprints, going in one direction and then another, doubling back on themselves. He had planted his feet in just those places.

He should never have come to this cursed city. It was a pissy little village compared to Petersburg. He should have stayed in Petersburg. Now there wasn't anything for him here, and there wasn't anything for him there. He'd been too clever by half, that's what they would say. So clever that he wasn't any good to anyone any longer. And when you're no more use to anyone, then what's the next thing that happens to you? You get got rid of, that's what.

You get got rid of, and nobody misses you. But waiting for that to happen is not so pleasant.

'Do you want to know a joke about agents?' Sasha asked a tree. 'All right, then. First agent says to second agent: "Are you a secret agent?" Second agent says to first agent, "No, I'm a double agent. Are you?" "No," says the first agent. "In fact I'm a double double agent." "A double double agent? Very good. But I have to inform you that in fact I'm a double double double agent," says the second agent. "Well then, since we're exchanging confidences like this, I'm a double double double double agent," says the first agent. "But I've never heard of a double double double double agent." "Exactly!" says the first agent. "Our cover is so deep that no one knows we exist at all." "Aha!" says the second agent. "But as you know, a true agent never discusses his status with anyone."'

The tree laughed. Sasha laughed.

It was getting much too light. He didn't like the look of it at all. Fortunately these bushes had their branches so weighed down with frozen snow that they had made themselves into a little tent. He crawled inside. Not so light there. Quite comfortable, in fact. The twigs and branches made a criss-cross pattern when he looked out through them.

He sat down and began to pull off his dancing shoes, and then the black silk socks that went with them. His feet were a very strange colour. He put them in the snow and they were exactly the shade of beef sausages.

If only he had found the railway line. It would have taken him with it, carrying him along like a silver snake. In eight hours it would have taken him back to Petersburg. But of course he didn't want to go there. Anyway trains made a noise he didn't like. And de dah de dah de dah de dah.

Sasha took off his overcoat and folded it carefully. It would make an excellent pillow. Vodka is the best overcoat, and overcoats are the best pillows. Fancy discovering such useful things so late in life, and having no one to tell them to.

Now to lie down. He had thought of taking off all his clothes, but when it came to it he couldn't be bothered. Yes, the coat was warm. There were spiky little bird marks in the snow.

It wasn't really cold at all. His feet had gone to sleep. Little house, little cosy house all around him. The new day's light was making the snow pink. In the distance he could hear the large confused noises of the city, like blood moving.

A brief historical context to
House of Orphans

House of Orphans is set in what was then the Grand Duchy of Finland, and the main action of the novel takes place between the late winter of 1902 and the late winter of 1904. Finland had been part of the Russian Empire since 1809, but had enjoyed a relatively significant level of autonomy. Finland kept its own currency, police force and border controls, for example. However, during the period in which this novel is set a policy called 'Russification' had been instigated, wth the aim of forcing Finland into closer integration with Russia. The 'February Manifesto' of 1899 was a key statement of Tsar Nicholas II's intent to extend Russian autocracy into Finland, and to violate the Finnish Constitution. It aroused fierce anger and resistance. Within a month, half a million Finns had signed a petition to the Tsar asking him to uphold the Finnish Constitution. The Tsar would not do so.

The Governor-General of Finland at this time was General Nikolai Bobrikov, a former soldier and politician, and a much-hated figure in Finland. He drove the policy of Russification, and was assassinated on 17 June 1904 in the Council of State building in Helsinki, by a twenty-eight-year-old Swedish Finn, Eugen Schauman. Eugen Schauman then turned his gun on himself.

Eugen Schauman is said to have acted alone. *House of Orphans* deals with the forces that propelled young people to commit what were variously described either as terrorist acts or as heroic acts of martyrdom and patriotism. It also concerns the activity of revolutionary groups in both Finland and Russia, and the efforts of the Tsarist secret police, the Okhrana, to penetrate these groups using double agents.

In the year following the assassination of Bobrikov, political unrest and the disastrous outcome of the Russo–Japanese War led to a wave of strikes throughout the Russian Empire, and took

Russia close to complete revolution. As a result of this turmoil, and the Finnish National Strike in autumn 1905, the Tsar was forced to make huge concessions in Finland. These included the establishment of a unicameral parliament, and universal suffrage.

However, Finland had still to endure a bitter and bloody civil war between Red and White forces in 1918, following the Russian Revolution in 1917. About 30,000 Finns, or approximately one per cent of the population, died as a result of battle, execution or imprisonment in camps.

The impact on Finland of its 'Great Neighbour' cannot be overestimated. The most remarkable feature of Finland's history is not that it suffered so much oppression, but that it won so much liberty.